I0590160

The
Moscow
Circuit

A SEMYA NOVEL

M. D. Hansen

EVERYTHEN

PRESS

everythen.com

EVERYTHEN

PRESS

Published in the United States by Everythen Press
12 High Street East
Glassboro, NJ. 08028

Everythen Press Website: www.everythen.com

Author Website: www.mdhansenbooks.com

Paperback (Amazon/KDP): 979-8-9936297-0-4

eBook Edition: 979-8-9936297-1-1

Trade Paperback (Ingram): 979-8-9936297-2-8

Think The Little Drummer Girl with the investigative tension of A Spy Among Friends, the cold-burn intelligence of Tinker, Tailor, Soldier, Spy, and the psychological edge of The Girl with the Dragon Tattoo.

Two families, torn apart by a terrorist attack, find their lives intertwined in a web of espionage, manipulation, and betrayal. This remarkable thriller will leave you breathless until the last page—where you will discover the cost of love—and the price of salvation.

Tormented by a betrayal, **a woman** finds the chance to exact retribution and achieve redemption. Her choices will ultimately alienate everyone she loves, leaving her isolated, risking that she will destroy herself—and everything she has fought to accomplish.

Searching to understand his past, **a young man** investigates his father's inexplicable death. Unexpected allies emerge, allegiances shift, and unseen enemies lurk in the shadows—each revelation pulling him closer to a devastating truth.

Haunted by a profound act of disloyalty, **a man** makes for himself the case for courage. Recruited into a role that would last a lifetime, he must now decide what he is willing to sacrifice—to quiet the ghosts of his past and restore his broken spirit.

Swept into a global conspiracy, set in motion before she was even born, **a young woman** is thrust into a dangerous world of secrets and deception. She must navigate a treacherous path to reclaim her identity—and decide her own future.

From small hamlets to big cities, from remote military bases to dangerous urban streets, they will all face their own demons as they race to expose a plot that could change the course of history.

Tabel of Contents

For all the people,

who have been patient with me,

through all my years.

I remember you all.

One 'tis 'en omen, something lost,

Two 'tis sorrow, count d'cost.

Three da spark, fire's light,

Four runs wild, free ta fight.

Five d'chance, toss 'em bones,

Six a mark, cut 'en stone.

Seven ta flee, ne'er turnin' back,

Eight a choice, ye heart turns black.

Nine 'tis tha answer, secret kept—

Never told, nor e'er wept.

PART I

"Nothing great is created suddenly, any more than a bunch of grapes or a fig. If you tell me that you desire a fig, I answer you that there must be time. Let it first blossom, then bear fruit, then ripen."

- Epictetus

CHAPTER ONE

AS HE WALKED, HIS FOOTSTEPS echoed down the long hallway. Chest forward, shoulders back, he carried himself with a posture that made him feel larger, more important—steadying whatever uncertainty still lingered. At just twenty-eight, he was young, beginning his career, and embarking on his first overseas assignment. Tall and lean, he projected the easy confidence of a man not yet touched by the weight of the world.

The CIA's clandestine analysis arm had sent Donald Chestnut to meet with a politician—a man who knew things, could anticipate outcomes, and help them plan for the future. His supervisor's instruction had been simple: "Pick his brain before he is gone."

Don wasn't sure what that meant, but he knew his assignment and was eager to accomplish the task. He was being trusted. Dutifully, he flew from the Berlin Station down to Salzburg to interview the man—a man who would be dead within a few months.

The meeting room had been set aside for a private conversation—plain, windowless, and safe from prying eyes. As Don stepped inside, he wondered how many others had come to ask this man similar questions. The man rose, and they shook hands.

Don asked, "How should I address you?"

"Call me Gurgen. Titles mean nothing to me now." He waved his hand. "Please, sit."

As Don settled into his chair, he took a moment to observe. The man across from him had clearly seen the world—and it showed. His hair was receding, streaked with ash. His eyes were dark, yet still sharp, still penetrating. Authorities had jailed him many times. A former president in exile, he now drifted from international conferences to global symposiums, winding down his days. Such a life—once a rebellious Georgian dissident, then the leader of his nation, and now, simply, a man called Gurgen.

With a thin smile, Gurgen asked, "Why are you here?"

"To talk," Don replied, unsure how much to share. Keep it simple.

"About what?" Gurgen suddenly demanded. His initial relaxed posture shifted in an instant.

Don fidgeted in his chair, trying to regain his footing. "I'm writing a report, collecting insights."

Annoyed, Gurgen pressed, "About what?"

Don was losing control of the conversation. He needed to distill it simply. "What will happen now that the USSR has dissolved?"

"You work for a government?" Gurgen pressed again.

"Who sent you?"

"No... just a firm putting together an analysis," Don lied. His cover story was thin, but the mavens at the agency had assured him it was enough.

Gurgen stared at Don for a long time before saying, "I don't believe you."

Ignoring the rebuke, Don pressed on. He needed momentum. He had an assignment to complete. "You have a complicated past, but you may be able to predict the future. Will you answer some questions?"

"I am not a Gypsy fortune-teller. I have been wrong about many things..."

"Every great man makes mistakes," Don said, playing to his ego. "But you have a unique understanding. What will happen?"

Gurgen smirked. "There are celebrations. Everyone is happy. Read the papers. It is good."

"Uh-huh, yes, I read the news. But maybe you feel something else?" Don asked again, softening his voice. "What does your experience tell you? What will happen?"

Gurgen shifted in his seat and shook his head. "They move too fast. The people will suffer," he said flatly.

Don was surprised. "Isn't that what you always wanted? A free republic? Georgia declared independence last year... free from Soviet control."

"Culture matters. We needed time to become what we will be," Gurgen replied.

Confused, Don probed. "What does that mean?"

"We needed a gradual transition—from a socialist

command economy to a capitalist market economy."

Don glanced at his notes. "You proposed labor freedom, guarantees of social rights, respect for private property and social utility, free entrepreneurship, honest competition..."

"Yes, yes," Gurgen interrupted, flicking his hand in annoyance. "But I also advocated for a transition period—wage indexation, consumer protection, safety nets for vulnerable groups, and price controls on basic goods. It will take time—which means it won't happen. The world is impatient. It moves too fast."

"That is Georgia. What about Russia?"

"The Russian people will suffer as well. Underground markets will flourish, organized crime will run rampant, expected freedoms will not materialize. People will long for the past."

"That's the near-term. Change takes time."

"Yes," said Gurgen, "but it will also be true in the long term."

"And the Russian elite—what will they do?"

"The smart ones will capitalize now—buying state assets, forging alliances with the West. There will be many rich and powerful people in the new Russian Federation. Some will survive. Many won't."

Don jotted a note in his notebook, deliberately slowing to pace the conversation. Then he looked up and asked, "And the others—the remnants of the KGB?"

"Some will plan—holding onto the hope of a quick rebirth. They will cling to what they know, following the old playbook."

"How will that work?" Don was finding a rhythm. Ask

simple questions. Keep him talking.

"I'm sure it's already working. They will be active, setting the stage. They will use Maskirovka—military and political deception. They will use Kompromat—blackmail and manipulation. Active measures—noisy, propagandistic. These efforts will fail."

"Then what will succeed?"

"There will be a smaller group. More strategic. Quieter. These thoughtful men will look to The Doctrine of Patience."

Feeling that he was finally uncovering something new, Don looked up sharply—his eyes urging the man to continue.

"They will make long bets. Deep cover. Reflexive Control."

"Reflexive Control?" Don asked.

"A strategic psychological method. Sometimes you place assets. Sometimes you guide your adversary into making decisions that benefit you... while they believe they are acting alone."

"And they'll be able to do all that?"

"It will take time. Decades."

"That is a long time to orchestrate a deception."

"It is not just deception. It is an engineered belief—strategic misdirection at the cognitive level. Very Russian. They will do all these things and more: long-game manipulation with cold precision."

"And the people—the masses—what becomes of them?"

"They will hope for the best. It is called Avos'. They will ignore their problems and suppose no consequences."

"That doesn't sound like democracy." Don kept his comments and questions short.

Again, Gurgen's emotions surged. His voice rose. "They don't know democracy! Or capitalism!"

The outburst startled Don, but he watched as Gurgen slowly regained his composure, breathing evenly.

When he continued, his voice was softer. "The Russian cultural mindset will always blend nationalism, resignation, and invention—with the certainty that, somehow, it will all work out."

"And you? What do you believe?" Don asked.

Gurgen leaned back slightly, his gaze turning inward. His voice dropped further, to almost a whisper—wistful and worn.

"I have my faith. All problems stem from the destruction of belief. This is what the church teaches me. There was a time... a time when I believed we could do it differently. A gentle revolution—not with tanks and guns, but with ideas... with faith."

He paused, eyes fixed somewhere beyond the walls, as if watching a memory drift just out of reach.

"We thought we could take the old system apart piece by piece—preserve the soul, discard the rot."

Silence followed. Long enough to feel like absence. Then he returned.

"I have learned... you do not get to ease a country into freedom. You rip it loose—and then pretend it's what the people wanted all along."

Don wasn't sure how to respond. He felt a sense of something deeper, beyond his understanding. Quietly, he asked, "Are you also playing a long game?"

Gurgen turned toward him with a faint smile—resigned,

unafraid.

"Maybe my game is the longest. They will almost certainly kill me... that is the way of the Caucasus, and of the Russians. We aim to erase the past until we try to remember it. When that happens... I will become a martyr, and I will be remembered."

Stunned, Don could not find any words.

Gurgen stood to leave, signaling the interview was over. As he opened the door, he turned back to Don and added, almost ominously, "Maybe the people who follow me—who walk in my footsteps... can achieve what I could not."

As the door shut, Don wondered if he'd just heard prophecy or paranoia. Either way, he could feel it—something had begun.

CHAPTER TWO

MOSCOW, RUSSIA
1995

THE WOMAN'S SCREAM TORE THROUGH the cramped delivery room, echoing off chipped tile walls and scuffed linoleum. The sharp scent of antiseptic hung in the air. She screamed again. It was a distraction, nothing more.

The senior nurse called out, "Where is the doctor?"

"She was called away. She'll return soon."

"The baby will not wait." This was not the first time the nurse had been on her own. Medical services in the country had gone to shit.

Oksana, exhausted and slick with sweat, screamed again. She wanted her husband, but they would not permit him inside the delivery room.

"Push, Oksana. Now—push!" the nurse commanded.

Oksana clamped down and pushed. Pain surged through her—sharp, relentless.

The nurse exchanged a knowing look with her attendant. This was going to be bad.

"Her blood pressure is falling. She bleeds... there must be a hemorrhage."

"Where is that doctor? *Chyort*!" But she already knew—she would not arrive in time.

"Push!" she urged. This baby needed to be born. "Push!"

The senior nurse shuddered. Any hope of saving the mother was slipping away. She had to save the baby.

"Push... push, dear one, push... for the baby... do not stop now!"

Oksana gritted her teeth and summoned the last of her strength. One final push. One final scream. Then she collapsed from exhaustion.

Finally, it was done—a beautiful baby girl. The senior nurse handed the infant off to be dried and stimulated. Then turned back to stem the bleeding—pressing sponges and pads. She massaged the mother's abdomen, a futile attempt to buy time.

When she had done all she could, she snapped at the attendant, "Quickly... bring her the child. To her arms, now." Both nurses knew the mother's time with her daughter would be short.

The nurses propped Oksana up in bed with pillows. Her breathing was shallow; her color chalky. One wiped her forehead with a cool cloth.

The attendant placed the newborn in her arms, almost reverently.

The infant girl gazed up at her mother.

Oksana whispered, "Will you ever know freedom, little dove?"

Please, Phil... keep our daughter safe from them, she

prayed silently.

The machinery hummed on as tension filled the room—while outside, Phil waited, unaware of the tragedy unfolding within.

She was growing weak now, the blood loss too severe. As Oksana studied her daughter's face, sadness and fear welled in her chest.

"You are loved, little one. I will always love you."

The past few months had been hard—cut off from her family, distanced from her work—she had clung tightly to Phil, her new husband. He had become her anchor, her calm.

On the worst nights, he would sit beside her and recite a Gaelic poem of augury, carried from his childhood. Soft and mournful, full of sorrow and fate, even when the meaning escaped her.

Now, as her world slipped away, the lines returned—gentle, inevitable.

She whispered:

"One 'tis 'en omen, something lost, two 'tis sorrow, count d'cost..."

Her voice trembled, barely audible.

"Three da spark, fire's light, four runs wild, free ta fight...."

As she drifted into unconsciousness—into the dark—her voice faded. The senior nurse leaned in and, with infinite care, lifted the baby from her mother's limp arms.

PART II

SEEDS ARE SOWN
2008 · 2013 · 2014

"Be patient and tough; someday this pain will be
useful to you."

-Ovid

CHAPTER THREE

SUNNINGHAM, ENGLAND, UK
2008

SEVENTEEN YEARS AFTER THE FALL of the Soviet Union, Russia prepared to invade South Ossetia, a breakaway region internationally recognized as part of Georgia. The local population was displaced, and diplomatic ties ruptured. Although a ceasefire was eventually signed, Russian forces never withdrew. Instead, they established permanent bases—cementing their presence and reasserting their influence over the region.

Some, it seemed, were still following the old playbook—while others undoubtedly operated silently in the shadows.

Across the Black Sea, on the far side of Europe, it was a clear day in Sunningham. Anywhere else, it might have felt gloomy. There was no sun—only a flat, dull-gray overcast. But at least it wasn't raining. The real action was on the ground, where everything was verdant and alive. The flora thrived in such conditions—and it showed.

A young girl, just turned thirteen, lived with her father in a large house at the end of the cul-de-sac. The house was far too big for just two people—or even three or four. Bigger was better, her father always said. In a country obsessed with status, size meant prestige. He was away on business, which wasn't unusual.

Raya had no memory of her mother—not even a name, not a photograph tucked in the back of a drawer. As she grew older, she began to ask her father. Gently. But each time she saw it in his eyes—the pain, the emotion he carried like a wound that had never healed. Instinctively, she would pull back, or he would quietly retreat to his study.

In time, he would tell her more. But for now, the pain remained too near the surface. She was certain he had made a sacrifice for her—a choice. That belief carried her, gave her strength. Her love for him would never wane. She learned to compartmentalize her feelings, to set emotion aside, to remain present when it mattered most.

Raya returned from the International Baccalaureate School on the bus and quickly finished her homework. She loved school and learned easily, so now she had the freedom to take out her bike for a ride. The newest nanny hadn't yet arrived, but that hardly mattered. They came and went like the weather. This one already knew Raya's routine.

Pulling her neck-length black hair into a ponytail, she slipped on a jumper. Her deep black eyes and strong brows framed an oval face—calm, composed, deliberate in every movement. Yet beneath her stillness, something was always coiled. Like a runner before the gun.

"Hello, Mrs. Robinson," Raya called, waving as she passed

the woman who lived a few doors down.

"Good afternoon, Raya," the woman replied. *That girl is quite a handful, always out roaming around. Where is her father?*

The tree-lined streets of Sunningham were wide enough for two cars—a rarity in a country of one-lane roads—and bordered by sidewalks and generous front gardens. Curved and coiled like a winding shell, they made you feel cocooned wherever you stood.

Every home was meticulously maintained, with trimmed gardens and vibrant flowers. The community had been built in an old forest, after much debate with the municipal council. You could argue about the ecology, but not about the outcome—it was a beautiful place to live.

Everyone was outwardly friendly. The homes were filled with diplomats, executives, experts, and expats—a neighborhood of peers, most working in nearby London. Conversation over the back fence was usually mundane. These people knew how to keep their secrets; they all knew the rules.

Raya neither noticed nor really understood any of this. She was simply excited to try the "double-jump."

Pronounced curbs curved into gentle ramps where each driveway met the street. Raya had been jumping these for the past year. She would ride down the sidewalk, build speed, shift onto the apron, launch off the curb, and land in the street. Enthralled, she repeated the maneuver again and again, refining her technique.

But the double-jump was different. It was farther down the road, where two driveways sat side by side—two sets of curbs in a row. Raya accelerated, hit the first curb, lost a little control, recovered, then struck the second. She flew higher than ever. At the last moment, she twisted just enough to avoid the mailbox. Her heart was pounding when she landed.

"Bravo!" called Mr. Kahn from his porch. "You are a pro—but don't hit the mailbox." *What an adventurous spirit.*

He said this every time. A semi-retired professor of economics, working mornings at the local university. Raya wouldn't have known this if her father hadn't made her apologize the first time she attempted the double-jump—and crashed, knocking Mr. Kahn's mailbox clean off its pedestal. He had been kind about it, and her father had paid to have it fixed.

As Mr. Kahn walked down from his house toward the street, he asked, "Are you off to see Ms. Mariya?" He had a peculiar habit of putting *Ms.* or *Mr.* in front of people's first names.

Raya ignored the "Ms. Mariya." To her, she was Masha ever since the crash. "Yes," she called back. "I'm off to see Masha."

A few weeks earlier, when the crash into the mailbox happened, Raya was momentarily stunned, sprawled in the middle of the road. Her bike had somehow kept rolling for nearly ten meters without her.

Then a woman started yelling—or at least that's what it sounded like to Raya. She spoke in a foreign language, rapid and sharp. Seeing Raya's confusion, she switched to English.

"Are you okay?" a woman asked as she ran over. "Where is your helmet?"

Raya sat up slowly, running her hands over her arms and

legs. A few scrapes and some road rash on her knee, but nothing was broken. She hobbled to her feet and retrieved her bike, inspecting it for damage.

"I don't have one," she said, puzzled by the question. "Why would I need a helmet?"

To Raya, the woman wasn't young but didn't look old either. She would be surprised to learn that the woman had just turned fifty-five. She wore a guard's uniform that fit as if it belonged on her. Her short brown hair was cut close to her head, and everything about her—posture, tone, presence— gave off a soldier's air.

"Because you crashed, little one. Your head is hard, but not that hard. What do you think I do here?"

Raya squinted. "I don't know... let cars in and out? Open the gate?"

"Da, that's true," the woman said, "but I oversee all security—and that includes your head. You will come back tomorrow. I will have a helmet for you. Maybe some kneepads too, if you insist on being a daredevil. You will call me Masha."

The next day, Raya returned—walking her bike this time. She entered the guard hut and was surprised at its state. Wires hung exposed, papers were stacked everywhere, and tools lay scattered across a workbench.

"What are you doing in here?" she asked. "What was wrong with the hut the way it was?"

"It is not a hut," Masha replied. "You should call it by its proper name. It is a security fortification."

Raya shrugged; she couldn't see the difference. "I think it's just a hut."

Masha continued, "It was not secure—flimsy wood, no real road barrier; it was not good safety. I insisted that we install concrete at the base, add security glass, and proper retractable security bollards. I am also reviewing the perimeter."

Raya had never felt unsafe before, but now she did. Still, Masha told her this was just good procedure. She pulled out a tin and offered Raya a candy.

"I like you, Raya. You will come visit me every day, and we will talk."

Raya felt obligated to do as Masha asked. Something about the way she said it made it sound less like a request and more like a fact. And Raya, without quite knowing why, felt it was important to agree. So she did.

Masha had spoken with Raya's father about the helmet. Later, Raya would wonder what they discussed—whether they had connected, and what, if anything, her father knew about Masha's past.

He wasn't upset—just annoyed with himself. That wasn't new. He often said, "I don't have the proper skills to be a parent," whatever that meant. Still, he seemed to like Masha and encouraged his daughter to visit her.

Over the next few weeks, they delved into many topics. Masha asked about Raya's schoolwork, what she was learning, and what sports she liked. Did she enjoy reading? Did she have friends—and what were they like? All the usual adult questions.

"What shall we talk about today?" Masha asked one afternoon as Raya pulled up and leaned her bike against a tree.

Raya had her own questions, but never felt she got satisfying answers. She thought for a moment, then asked,

"Why do you carry a gun?"

Masha paused before answering. "That is easy—for your security. For the security of the entire enclave. Important people live here, and because of that I have a special permit. There is much trouble in the world, but I am here to keep you safe."

"All this construction and these improvements," Raya asked, "isn't that enough?"

"No, Raya. Sometimes it is not enough," Masha said simply.

Masha was waiting for her after she left Mr. Kahn. Raya was excited to tell her how high she had jumped this time and how far she had flown.

The security renovation work was winding down. Masha asked Raya to sit while she tidied up. Despite the completed renovations, tools and scraps still lay scattered. The clutter seemed to bother Masha; it distracted her, making her quieter, more remote. All the while, she kept typing on her BlackBerry. That wasn't unusual, but there was something different in her posture—a tension that made Raya feel uneasy.

"So, your father is due home tonight," she said, eyes still on the screen. "Are you excited to see him?"

"Sure," Raya replied. It had been a week since he left on a business trip, and Raya had enjoyed being on her own. It felt grown-up. "I don't mind being alone as much as I used to, but it will be good to see him."

They talked for a while. Masha was trying to convince Raya to take up a second language. She said she was proficient in several, which came as a surprise. Masha rarely shared much about herself.

"I could teach you Russian, Polish, or Turkish, and we could converse each day."

"Wow, that's a lot to know—which is the best?"

"For me, Russian is best because it was what I learned first. It is also good for someone to know both English and Russian. A third language is even better. You will always have a job."

"Masha—I am only thirteen. I think I have time."

"Okay. Then to get into school. Do you want to go to university?"

At that moment, there was a strange noise outside—the screech of tires and the grinding halt of a van. Masha turned her head toward the window. Raya looked at the CCTV monitor.

Three men piled out of an old van, dressed in black, faces half-covered with scarves. They carried long guns.

"Get down against the concrete wall now. Make yourself as small as possible," Masha ordered Raya. "You will listen to me!"

Raya did as she was told but kept her eyes on the monitor. The men were shouting, waving their weapons. She could hear it now: "Jihad, Jihad, Jihad." Odd, what you remember. One of them wore a Magpie Union football scarf over his face.

Then the gunfire started.

Crack. Crack. Crack.

As Masha and Raya hunkered down, the sound of the automatic weapons seemed to go on forever.

Crack. Crack. Crack.

Raya caught the acrid scent of gunpowder as smoke drifted toward them. She wiped her eyes, suppressing a cough. Masha held her tight.

Crack. Crack. Crack.

Finally, the gunfire stopped. *Her ears were ringing.* And then—

Silence.

Raya's emotions were a confused mix of surprise and fear. Her body tensed with the instinct to run or scream—but she didn't. She held on to her emotional control.

Even so, the sound of gunfire would haunt her dreams for years.

"Stay where you are," Masha said, crab-walking to the reinforced door. Her eyes flicked to the monitor—she could see them, but they couldn't see her.

When the attackers stopped firing, they hesitated, as if unsure what to do next.

Masha stood up, pulled open the door, and walked out, exposing herself. You could see the surprise in the attackers' eyes.

Watching, Raya sensed time slowing down. She would later learn that the attack had lasted only a few minutes.

All three terrorists froze, as if waiting for what came next. They were no more than fifteen meters away—confused, unprepared.

Masha didn't speak. She just stood there, settling into a ready position, her hand on her weapon. Her face showed disgust, almost disappointment. It looked as if she wanted an apology. But if that were the case, they didn't get the chance to respond.

Like a scene out of a movie, she simply pulled her weapon and shot all three in the chest, just above the heart. Each fell to the ground immediately, like pins in a bowling alley.

Raya watched on the monitor in awe. When they fell, she got up from the floor and saw what came next through the shattered window.

Calmly, Masha walked up to each of them and delivered a second bullet—right in the middle of the nose, where there was less bone. All three were dead, and she never said a word.

Masha sighed, shook her head, and walked back to check on Raya.

"Are you okay, Raya?" she asked as they slid down the wall, holding each other. They sat on the floor—Masha pulled Raya into a hug and cradled her head in her lap, gently stroking her hair. The adrenaline was wearing off, and Raya began to shiver.

"What happened?" Raya whispered. "Why did they attack us?"

"I don't know," Masha replied. "Zealots are hard to comprehend. But you are safe with me... always safe with me. Do you know this?"

Raya realized she was shaking, but it was over now. She drew upon her own strength and the security of Masha. Masha would keep her safe. She nodded.

"You did well," Masha said softly. "You stayed composed. Kept your nerve. You did not scream."

The only sound Raya could hear now was her own panting breath. And yet, her mind felt still. Strangely still. It was an odd sensation—but somewhere beneath the shock, she felt proud. She didn't yet understand that trauma doesn't always strike all at once. Sometimes it seeps in slowly, finding quiet places to take hold—especially in someone as young as Raya.

Looking up from Masha's lap, it seemed like snow was falling—but it was only dust, drifting down from the ceiling. Sunlight streamed through the gunshot holes, the beams sharp and golden.

Unexpected as it was beautiful, she was glad the sun was out, and it was no longer a dull gray day. She wondered *what tomorrow would bring.*

CHAPTER FOUR

MAIDENHILL, ENGLAND, UK
2008

THEY SAY THAT IN CERTAIN parts of the world, if you want different weather—just wait an hour. But that's just an aphorism, and sometimes the weather comes and decides to stay. In Southeast England, you never knew what tomorrow would bring.

The sky turned sour overnight. An approaching gale built throughout the morning and showed no signs of letting up. The streets of Maidenhill were awash with that curious combination of grime and wet that left the cobblestones slippery.

Maidenhill was accessible during the day and less safe at night—a grittier version of the upmarket commuter towns dotted across the countryside. The High Street was unexceptional but had all the traditional merchants—banks, baristas, bars, and bookies. In the corners and alleyways, the smell of old urine and cigarettes was always present. Even the heavy rain could not wash away the tang and stench.

A young teen, beginning his first year of high school, lived on the outskirts of downtown with his mother, Gill, and his father, Avi. Home was the middle unit of an unremarkable, pale-yellow brick terrace—a kitchen, two bedrooms, and a lounge, the décor decidedly seventies-shabby. Down the road were the rail station, a kebab shop, and a liquor store.

Similar housing, built right up against the road, lined the local streets. There was barely enough room for a pedestrian to fast-walk down the asphalt sidewalk to catch a train into London. The windows stood draped with cheap damask cloth; the front doors stayed locked tight. Curious eyes were not welcome. People kept to themselves. Most were renters from somewhere else—another borough, another country, another life.

But Bram's small family had a heartbeat. There was genuine love—the inside jokes, funny faces, and affection for the local football club. That joy conspired to keep them together through all their faults and flaws.

Mum always said, "There is no bad weather, just bad clothing." But today, Bram questioned that wisdom. He was wet and cold as he shuffled home from school. Most days, his dad would come down and walk with him, but not today.

"If he's not at school to pick you up, stop by the Crown on the way home. See if his mates know where he is," Mum had ordered that morning. Never mind that it added a half-mile of struggling through the rain. Not for the first time, Bram thought to himself that *a kid should not be looking after a parent.*

Bram never knew his namesake grandfather, Ibrahim. He was a post-war immigrant from Jamaica who came to Britain in the fifties, securing work at the docks and surviving the taunts and inequities of second-class citizenry. The government promises were left unfulfilled. With resolve, he endured and built a home and a family.

Ibrahim's only son was Avi—Bram's father. Avi lacked the tenacity of his father, but not the ambition. This odd combination of attributes made him a dreamer—a jovial, loving father to Bram, who always believed better days were just around the corner. These hapless romantics filled the nation, expounding on the glory of the realm, sharing their woes over a pint, or laying a bet on the next sure thing.

Bram slogged up toward the Crown. This was his dad's local and the most likely place to find him. Outside, the front patio was festooned with cheap plastic tables and chairs, the rain slowly filling the dirty pint glasses left from the day before. The barkeeps were either too lazy—or too interested in staying dry—to come out and clean up.

As soon as he went inside, Bram saw Charley behind the bar. He knew Charley well enough—this was not his first foray to find his father. Avi had a regular group of friends who could usually be found sharing a pint in the corner booth.

"Hey, Charley, have you seen my dad?"

"Oh, hey, Bram. Haven't seen your pa for a few days... he and some of his blokes were onto something new—you know how they are."

"He didn't come home last night. Mum is getting worried."

"I'm sure it's fine. Tell your mum no ladies have been around—none of that lot in a position to go bird-watching."

Bram looked closely at Charley and said slowly, "I don't think that's Mum's worry."

"Yeah—you're right, Bram, sorry. Your pa is a proper geezer. He'll be along," Charley apologized.

"What about Billy or Alfie? Have they been around?" Bram asked.

"Nah. Like I said, they've got some new scheme working. Didn't include me. They were all very hush-hush... conspiring." Charley lowered his voice. "But I hear things. They were talking about 'helping to maintain national pride,' 'keeping people safe,' and 'honourable work.' Sounded dodgy to me."

So—the normal bravado, thought Bram. "Thanks, Charley. If you see him, please send him home. Tell him Gill's looking for him."

Gill was a local girl, raised with decidedly British expectations. Her family were plodders—no great aspirations, no great disappointments. A working-class family punctuated with populism: pray, keep out the riff-raff, honour the royals, and wait for the pension they were rightly due.

But Gill excelled in her studies and loved books—ideas and thoughts that maybe she could transform her life. She wanted more. Then she found it was not hers to have. Having a baby at nineteen didn't help—things just didn't fall her way.

Gill's family loathed the foreigner she was with and, by extension, her son. They hated themselves for lacking motivation, resented Gill for her determination, and chafed at their daughter's status as a fallen woman—irreconcilable with the perils of a changing world.

Sending Bram on his way, Charley said, "Tell Gill I'll keep an eye out for Avi. And send her my best."

Resolved to get home, Bram ducked through the door and

into the rain. He was a tall, stout boy—some would say he was well put together. Street-smart and naturally savvy, he loved to read (like his mother). He was the best of both his parents.

Life forced Bram to make some choices. He could have gone hostile, using his size, strength, and wits to get what he wanted from the world. Or he could have gone spineless, attaching himself (and his skills) to a local gang or bully.

But Bram went his own way—he found that a hard stare and a slow voice could be effective. Taking a moment to think before speaking had its own strength. His growing physique didn't hurt either. People were smart—they could see Bram had room to grow. He was becoming his own man.

He hiked up a small rise and reached the top of the street, where he could look down toward his neighborhood. Bram knew there was trouble at the first glimpse of the flashing police lights. The distinctive high-low sirens wailed as patrol vehicles sped in from different directions. Bram began to run.

He came upon the police line and could tell the action was close to his home. Two officers in neon high-visibility vests were corralling pedestrians away from the area. Both wore distinctive peaked caps with a black-and-white checkered band. Nobody in the crowd seemed to have a clue what was going on, but there was plenty of chatter.

He approached the nearest officer and asked what was happening. The officer quickly dismissed him: "Mind your business and stay behind the line."

It felt strange for Bram to challenge authority, but he pushed forward and said, "My mum could be in there. I need to know what is happening."

"Who are you?"

He gave his name and, almost immediately, a change came over the officer's face. The officer grabbed Bram, shoved him up against the wall, frisked him down, and said, "Come with me." The gawkers in the crowd all stared.

The two officers marched Bram toward a police van and shoved him inside. A detective was waiting for him there with his mother.

"Mum, what is going on?"

But she just sat there, unresponsive. He'd seen this before—when his mum was emotionally overwhelmed, her circuits kind of shorted out. She was in a state of panic, unable to pull herself free.

The detective asked, "When was the last time you saw your father?"

"Yesterday afternoon—or morning, I guess. Where is he?" asked Bram.

"Your father is dead," the detective said without sympathy. "Yesterday afternoon, under suspicious circumstances. There was an incident a few miles west of here... in Sunningham. We identified him only a few hours ago. This is now an active investigation."

Now Bram understood what was happening to his mum... and he felt like it was about to happen to him. His father was dead, and his mother was catatonic. Bram was fourteen years old and drowning.

The detective was talking, but Bram wasn't listening. "Do you know who he was working with?"

Bram came back to himself. "Working with?" His dad

hadn't had a construction job in weeks. Working on what? What did Dad do?

The detective droned on, asking about his father's affiliations, acquaintances, and passions. Bram couldn't comprehend any of it.

Then he looked at the detective and asked, "What is happening right now?"

"We are completing an intensive search of the house."

Looking at his mum, he realized she wasn't in a good way. She needed help. His feelings and emotions would have to wait; his trauma shunted to the side. Bram was compartmentalizing, even if he didn't know it.

He asked for a lawyer and was told he was not being charged. He asked where his father was and was told he needed to contact the coroner. He asked for a medic for his mother and got a bottle of water. He wondered what family he could call for help and realized there was no one.

They did not speak to the police again. His mother couldn't, and he wouldn't.

They passed the neighbors as they walked back to the house. There were glares from the crowd, not a kind pair of eyes to be seen. The house was completely ransacked: every drawer opened and overturned, holes in the walls where the police checked for hidden spaces, clothes ripped apart, linens torn to shreds.

Bram surveyed the carnage and began putting things in order. It was overwhelming. He pushed back the urge to cry. His job now was to save the life that was left.

His mother sat in the corner on the floor, staring into space. She was not well, and he realized she hadn't been for some time. Finding a glass, he got her some water, and she took a sip. *That was something.*

Bram could see his mum holding a paper in her hand. He gently took it and uncrumpled an advertisement for Crisis Actors Ltd. He had never heard of the business. Scanning the flyer, Bram saw phrases like "Help keep our Country Safe," "Honest Day's Work," and "Ensure British Security." Maybe it was what his dad had been onto with his mates.

He would ask his mother about it, but not today. She was far from ready. Feeling gut-punched, he slid down the wall next to his mum and hugged her. She didn't seem to respond or even know he was there. At that moment, Bram wanted so much to be comforted himself.

Out the now curtainless window, he saw the distant flashes of lightning above the trees. The slow rumble of thunder echoed down the road, and he could feel it under his skin. The day had not lied—a tempest had come and decided to stay.

The weight of the entire world sat on his chest. Bram would not be able to move or think for days. He was now alone in all the ways that mattered.

CHAPTER FIVE

SUNNINGHAM, ENGLAND, UK
2013

RAYA STACKED THE LATEST BOX on the driveway, ready to be inventoried. She looked up to see Mrs. Robinson approaching—dressed in her Sunday best. She walked with perfect posture and an air of obduracy, but Raya knew she was feeling melancholy. There was a gleam in her eyes.

The process had taken weeks—packing up the only home Raya could remember, all for a trip across the ocean. A sea freight container would carry most of their belongings to a storage facility. They could take only so much on a plane.

"I brought you some cookies," Mrs. Robinson said, handing over a tray. "I know we'll have a proper send-off, but I saw you packing and couldn't stay away. We're going to miss you very much."

Raya smiled. "Would you like some tea? One last cuppa?"

"Certainly, I'd love to. Where is everyone?"

"Dad is on his final trip. He'll be back next week—he'll only have a few days before we leave."

"And Masha?"

"Out doing Masha things." Raya paused, then lowered her voice. "She sneaks into London to visit the Orthodox Cathedral. She doesn't think I know. No idea why she'd keep that a secret... but you know Masha."

Mrs. Robinson pressed a finger to her lips. "I won't say a word... such a curious woman."

She stepped back to look at Raya. "Enough about Masha. Let me look at you."

Raya had grown slightly taller than average. Her olive-toned skin gave her a sunlit glow, even in shadow, and her black mid-length hair—usually tied back or tucked under a hood—had a way of coming loose at the worst, or perhaps best, times. With her athletic build, she looked like a professional tennis player.

"...A free spirit transformed," Mrs. Robinson said. "You've become a thoughtful—and, if I may say, a beautiful—young woman."

"Well, sometimes, I guess," Raya replied with a mischievous grin. "But you know me better than most."

"You'll be eighteen next month, if I'm not mistaken. A wonderful age to start a new adventure."

Raya offered a casual smile, her head tilting slightly. She wasn't sure how she felt about a new adventure, but she led Mrs. Robinson into the house.

A month earlier, her father had received a letter from Her Majesty's Immigration Service. His latest UK work assignment was ending, and he was expected to leave. His visa—and, by extension, Raya's—would soon expire. They were being asked to depart in the most British of ways: by post. Two expats headed home to America, their usefulness concluded.

For almost twenty-five years, he worked across Europe, the Middle East, and Africa. His base in Sunningham allowed him to travel freely. He freelanced for large consulting firms and excelled in bespoke procurement of IT systems and services. It had once been cheaper for companies to hire his expertise on demand—but recently, those firms brought the work in-house. Opportunities dried up.

He may have seen it coming, but for Raya and Masha, it was still a shock. Raya was deep in her college applications—some in the U.S., others scattered across the globe. Raya had planned campus visits with her father, but now time was compressed. The clock was ticking. They needed to find a place to live.

Raya and Mrs. Robinson moved to the kitchen, and she put the kettle on. Raya was quiet, reflective. Mrs. Robinson had become part of her life in recent years. So many in Sunningham had rallied around her after the incident. She loved them all.

Mrs. Robinson sat and waited. She could see Raya was elsewhere—thinking, remembering, woolgathering. She would wait.

Raya's thoughts drifted—*so much had happened*. It had been only four years since the terrorist attack, and everything had changed. She remembered the shift clearly.

It began shortly afterward: night terrors, vivid nightmares. The shock wore off, but the aftermath had only just begun. Her carefree determination hardened into a kind of quiet stubbornness. She decided she wasn't going back to school.

She no longer felt safe.

Her father, frantic with worry, knew it was more than he could manage on his own. He loved Raya deeply, but this—this was beyond his capacity. Business contracts needed fulfilling; responsibilities were piling up. When she was younger, he had hired help—nannies, minders—but they were part-time, short-lived, and ultimately forgettable. An independent Raya was a blessing. Together, they made it work.

But without school as an anchor, it would be impossible. He needed to figure out a plan—and fast. The solution came in the unexpected form of Masha. Raya couldn't quite remember where the idea came from. It just... happened.

Her father came to her and made a proposal.

"You feel safe with Masha?"

"Yes, of course."

"You feel close to her?"

"She saved my life."

"I spoke with her. She wants to help. Says she understands what you are going through."

"Um... okay."

"Would you like her to stay with us... for a while... until you feel... until you are older?"

Looking back, it had sort of materialized. It seemed so natural. So organic. Years later, Raya would understand this was all part of Masha's plan.

Two days later, Masha took the room next to hers. She brought only a few belongings, but her presence and aura filled the space. She was a commanding force.

The scheme was perfect at the start. They'd found a

homeschooling syllabus, and Masha took to it immediately. Raya discovered she had an aptitude for language, and Masha was able to instruct her. Masha also knew everyone in the community and, starting that first year, supplemented Raya's education with the local boffins.

In this most uncommon tutelage, Raya learned history, mathematics, music, art, and so much more—an enclave-driven education shaped by experts, spouses of experts, and other enthusiasts. Sunningham pulled together for this young girl and became better for it.

"Mrs. Robinson, remember the first time Masha brought me to your house? She was so excited to expand the curriculum."

"Oh yes, I remember thinking I would be such a boor, but you went through so much. I wanted to help—we all did. I'm not sure Mr. Robinson would have been keen on me sharing his squabbles and partisan backstabbing—so much more interesting than the policies of the MP from Surrey. It really was interesting, though, wasn't it?"

"It certainly was," Raya said fondly. "Thank you for those lessons... and for everything." She felt a catch in her breath. This was all happening so fast.

"But I didn't think it would work at first. You had become so shy, so withdrawn."

"Well, yes, if you remember, Masha had a plan for that."

In the days after the attack, Raya wanted nothing more than to crawl into bed and stay beneath the covers. She decided she wouldn't move. If she didn't move, then nothing bad could happen. It hadn't occurred to her then how much of herself she had already lost.

The next morning, Masha knocked on the door at sunrise. It was a Saturday, normally a day for relaxing. She told Raya they would be going out. They drove to Virginia Water Park to walk around the lake.

Originally a royal pleasure ground just south of Windsor Castle, Virginia Water was dotted with waterfalls, follies, ancient ruins, and enchanted woodlands. The five-mile circuit could be strolled leisurely, but they walked it twice at a brisk pace. Masha kept them moving. Raya didn't have time to enjoy the sights—she was too exhausted.

"You need to burn up the bad energy," Masha told her. "To get past your fear, you need to move. Activity is key."

That was the beginning of a daily routine: hiking or swimming, riding bikes—and sometimes horses. They talked as they exercised, often in Russian or Turkish. Masha pushed Raya to explain concepts she'd learned from the neighborhood teachers, to critique ideas, take positions, and solve math puzzles in her head.

All the while, Masha spoke—guiding, questioning, warning. She told stories of service and sacrifice, anchoring Raya in something larger than herself. Again and again, she reminded her: find your path. Make it meaningful. Stay loyal. Live with purpose.

"Do you remember the time you started screaming at Masha two summers ago?" asked Mrs. Robinson. "Right in the middle of the road? We were all flabbergasted." It had become the talk of the community, but she had never brought it up with Raya before.

Raya poured the tea. "You don't know the half of it," she said with a sly smile.

She remembered—it had been a long, punishing week, and Masha hadn't let up. Raya begged for a day to rest, just one, but Masha kept pushing. Her father was gone again, unreachable, and that left Masha in charge. Raya had had enough.

Masha rode beside her on a bike while Raya ran—legs aching, lungs burning, trying to match the pace. They were on the main road through Sunningham—broad and exposed, the worst place for a quarrel.

"I'm done. I am going home." Raya stopped in the middle of the road, hands on her hips, breathing hard.

Masha barked, "We are not done! There is one more kilometer to complete. Then we will be done."

"You're not my mother. Why do you even care? You can leave anytime."

Not shocked by the outburst, Masha simply asked, "What is the plan?"

"Just leave me alone. I am fine... my dad doesn't care, my mom is gone, I'm on my own. I can take care of myself." Raya finally vented her deepest frustrations.

"No, you are not fine, and that is not a plan. But this is good. You have found your voice. You think you've figured some things out, but with no strategy, you have no plan—and you have not used your brain."

"Arsehole!" Raya yelled. Then she turned on her heel and stormed home, not looking back.

A cold détente settled over the next few days. Masha knew not to push too hard. This was by design. Careful not to alienate

Raya, she waited for the right time to mend the rift and deepen their bond.

Raya was upstairs, stomping around like a storm trapped in a small room. Down in the kitchen, Masha was cooking, her jaw tight.

She took a breath, then called up, "Raya! Come down and help with dinner!"

"What are you making?"

"Khachapuri. You used to love it when you were younger. I thought it might help you feel better." Khachapuri was Masha's comfort food—a pastry dish she made from scratch, filled with a mixture of cheeses and topped with an egg. Masha stood kneading the dough.

"I never liked it. You liked it. I was just giving in to you... I always seem to give in... it's gross. I won't eat it."

Masha was surprised; she'd known Raya was still fuming, but this situation couldn't continue forever. She teasingly pulled off a piece of the dough and threw it at Raya. "If you won't eat it, maybe you should wear it."

Raya was stunned—Masha had never thrown anything at her. She grabbed a handful of flour and flung it back at Masha. It quickly escalated into a food fight.

Flour, cheese, and eggs covered both of them.

Raya finally relented and said, "You look ridiculous."

"So do you."

They laughed—the moment broke the tension.

"Now that dinner is ruined, let's get takeout curry," Masha said hopefully, "and maybe we can talk."

Words flowed, and feelings were mended. From that point

on, there was always some tension—but also an unspoken understanding of love. Raya became more headstrong, and Masha learned to manage their relationship more carefully. But now, when they fought, there was always reconciliation.

"You should have seen the food on her head," she told Mrs. Robinson, giggling as she refilled her cup.

"I bet you looked pretty funny, too."

"She's the most important person in the world to me. I hope she can get to the U.S."

This was a concern. Masha wanted to stay with Raya, but U.S. immigration would be complicated.

"Maybe your father will figure it out. He loves you more than you know. What he lacks in parenting, he can make up for in other ways." Then, realizing what she had said, Mrs. Robinson apologized. "I'm sorry. I shouldn't have said that."

"No, it's okay. Dad is just… Dad. I know this isn't normal, but I've grown used to it. Learning about me must have surprised him. I know he did his best. He's not the father of the year, but he loves me."

CHAPTER SIX

THE FOLLOWING WEEK, RAYA MADE her way to the going-away party held in her honor. After a hectic stretch, she was finally packed. The night was still as she walked down the familiar street—quiet, though her thoughts were anything but. By morning, she and her father would be on a flight to America.

Mr. Riku Tanaka greeted her at the door. His home, though without tatami mats and the usual custom of shoe removal, still radiated the quiet precision of Japanese aesthetics. It was gracious of him to host the event. Together, they moved toward the back garden—an exquisitely manicured space that felt more like a work of art than a yard.

"I imagine you're feeling melancholy," he said gently. "How are you managing?"

"I'm okay, I guess. I thought there would be more time."

"Life is like that," he said. "Remember to stay in the moment. This gathering is for you, and you'll want to carry the memory with grace."

Over the years, Mr. Tanaka had helped Raya with different forms of meditation. She found that quieting her mind allowed her to face some of life's complexities. She focused on cultivating acceptance and reducing avoidance, staying present. He was an excellent teacher.

"Will your father or Masha be joining us?" he asked.

"I'm sure they'll be along," Raya replied. "But I think they wanted me to have some time with everyone... on my own."

"Just so," Mr. Tanaka said with a gentle smile. "Go now—meet your guests."

Raya began her rounds. The entire neighborhood seemed to have turned out, standing in small groups, sharing drinks and stories. Across the stone patio stood a beautiful replica of a Japanese teahouse, bordered by a meandering stream that wound its way around plants and sculpted features. The setting was serene.

"We will miss you," said Mrs. Robinson as she approached.

"Thank you, Mrs. Robinson. I still can't believe I'm leaving tomorrow."

"I think you can call me Victoria now," she said with a warm smile. "We're more like family. It feels odd hearing 'Mrs. Robinson.' Promise me you'll visit. This will always be your home."

"Of course. There are plenty of direct flights—I've already checked," Raya replied with a smile.

Across the lawn, she spotted Ligia Garcia waving her over. Ligia, the nanny for the Adeoye family, had moved to Sunningham the previous year. She had been teaching Raya

Spanish in their spare moments. Now she handed Raya a drink.

"What's this?" Raya asked.

"Something you'll love—*Cava*. Champagne from Spain!"

They toasted and laughed—two young women amid the local gentry, feeling oddly at home among an older generation.

As the evening wore on, Raya continued her rounds. Her heart tugged in many directions: grateful, nostalgic, a little lost, yet quietly excited for what lay ahead. After so many heartfelt goodbyes, she felt emotionally frayed and decided to slip away quietly.

As she stepped toward the house, she spotted Mr. Edward Kahn standing just inside the doorway.

They went inside and settled on a couch away from the bustle. "You've made quite an impression on us. We were never this close as a community—until we found you."

"I'm glad I found you, too," Raya replied, her voice warm.

"Have you decided?"

"Yes. I thought about going to an Ivy, but chose a smaller school outside Philadelphia—Fairhurst University."

"Good, good. They have a fine reputation, and I'm sure you'll thrive. You already understand global economics better than some of my students. I hope my letter of recommendation was helpful."

Raya laughed. "It was great. I had so many I lost count. Probably the best list of recommendations any student ever had."

He smiled. "Are you sticking with languages?"

"Yes, and I'm adding a minor in psychology. I've come through... well, a lot. I want to understand people better."

"A good choice. It will help prepare you for life, and an excellent program will teach you the Socratic method. Psychology is a social science, like economics. I approve."

Mr. Kahn glanced around. "Ms. Mariya didn't make it?"

"No, I don't think so. I didn't see her."

He was thoughtful for a moment, as if collecting himself.

"I'd like to give you two gifts." He pulled out two slim hardcover volumes. "The first is a copy of the Magna Carta."

Raya raised an eyebrow. "Um... okay."

"Did you know we're only a few miles from Runnymede, where it was signed? One of the most important documents in the world—yet with barely a monument to mark the place. This," he said, offering her the book, "represents where you come from."

Raya accepted it with a smile, running her fingers over the cover.

"The second," he continued, holding up the next book, "is the U.S. Constitution. This represents where you're going."

He handed her the volume.

"These past years, I've helped as a tutor—"

Raya nodded.

"—but everyone here tonight has influenced you. Some more than others, I'm sure." He smiled faintly. "For me, teaching is the art of imparting knowledge while allowing students to interpret it freely, without bias. It's about letting them find their own path."

Raya recognized this in Mr. Kahn. He always asked her to deduce and unravel. It was up to her to figure it out.

"But now you're leaving, and you're not a student

anymore—you're my friend. So I'll tell you this plainly: to me, these documents represent something essential. Freedom, yes—but not in the political sense. Freedom of conscience. Freedom of thought. The kind that belongs to everyone, no matter where they begin."

He paused, watching her reaction.

"And they serve as a warning," he added. "Freedom is never secure. It must be protected—often quietly—through vigilance, through courage, through choice. So, keep your sense of independence. Guard it well."

Raya ran her finger along the worn leather spines of the books. Freedom. Independence. Until now, she had thought little about what those words truly meant. But she would. From this moment on, she would carry them with her—and reflect on them for the rest of her life.

"Ugh, okay. But why tell me? It feels a little heavy for someone who's not even eighteen yet," she said with a smirk, "especially since I haven't even started college."

Mr. Kahn chuckled. "Perhaps. But I imagine bigger things for you. And I'm in the habit of trying to influence those who might one day hold influence. Just... remember what matters—and what you're willing to fight for."

She was about to ask what he meant when Masha entered quietly, almost ghostlike. Her eyes met Mr. Kahn's for a second too long. He straightened, caught off guard.

"Put those aside for later," he said quickly, his voice soft but firm. "Reflect on what I've said." He stood and gave Raya a warm embrace. Then, with a glance at Masha—measured, unreadable—he turned and slipped back into the party.

Raya turned to Masha. "I didn't know you were here. Where have you been hiding?"

"Your father asked me to find you," Masha replied. "To remind you that the Uber will arrive early tomorrow."

As they departed, Raya cast one last look toward Mr. Kahn, who was rejoining the other guests. His figure shifted among the laughter and clinking glasses, but her mind lingered on the moment when he and Masha had locked eyes.

What was that about?

The next morning, the Uber pulled off the main road and climbed the ramp toward the departures level of Heathrow Terminal 5. The terminal rose above the tarmac like a scenic overlook. Wives, husbands, parents, and drivers all lined the curb, dropping off passengers bound for cities across the world.

Raya stepped out and paused.

A low ache of sadness tugged at her—leaving behind what she knew. But it was met with something else: a quiet surge of anticipation. She turned west. Philadelphia lay three thousand miles in that direction—the birthplace of America, and the beginning of her new life.

She felt ready. *Almost.*

Her father had secured an apartment in the city—close to Fairhurst, but not too close. It was well positioned along the East Coast and near where he had grown up. For him, it was a kind of homecoming. For her, it was a beginning.

Still, Raya worried about Masha. They shared a moment before the car arrived—bittersweet, uncertain. Masha's visa was still in limbo, and Raya didn't want to leave her behind. Not really.

She looked west again. Only fifteen miles in that direction lay Sunningham—the village that raised her, saved her, shaped her.

Ahead lay college. A new city. A country she barely knew. But Sunningham would always remain with her, folded into memory—a part of who she was, wherever she was going.

Masha stayed behind in the Sunningham house, sleeping on an inflatable mattress with little more than a suitcase, a few dishes, and the same sparse belongings she had brought when she first arrived. The lease hadn't yet expired—there was still time. She had endured worse.

The house was empty and quiet, its stillness sharpening the edges of her thoughts. There was work to be done, and now—for the first time in years—she had freedom of movement.

First order of business: contact her handler. Her link to the network had been silent for too long. The SVR was growing lax. The silence gnawed at her. Still, she knew the protocol. She knew the plan. And she would complete the assignment.

She needed to get to the United States—for Raya. The visa could take months. Her credentials had to check out. Her story had to hold. She would need help.

Blya. Nothing was ever easy.

The move to America had thrown her. She had imagined guiding Raya to a university in Europe, where Masha's own mobility was less restricted. The shift in geography created a new complication. But her resolve held. Staying close to Raya was non-negotiable—not just to support her, but to ensure she was guided, prepared, and developed for what lay ahead.

Another obstacle to overcome. She felt a flicker of anger. Control was slipping, and with it came the heat of frustration. She was grateful to be alone.

Beneath her composed exterior, emotions coiled tight. There were wounds she refused to examine—the man she had loved, and the betrayal that still haunted her. Another she had trusted but left behind. Each memory, a blade. Each pain, still raw.

She found herself breathing hard, her heart racing. She buried the thoughts—foolish sentiments. They would serve no purpose now. A life of secrecy left little room for regret.

Masha didn't pray. Belief, for her, was complicated. She longed for the comfort of faith, but it remained elusive—an echo of a past she hadn't entirely released. A tether to a life before the shadows.

But patience and fortitude—those were different. They defined duty. Something she could hold on to. Fiercely.

She would find a way.

CHAPTER SEVEN

WASHINGTON D.C., USA
2014

FRED AVERY SAT AT HIS desk, feeling old, fat, and incredulous. He was no longer the man he once had been, though he could still manage a five-mile run. The years had taken their toll, and he knew it. Over twenty years in the same position, and he still sometimes felt like an imposter.

Fred had a decision to make, and time was not on his side.

His office was a functional workplace, without the customary pictures on the wall of handshakes and smiles. There were no mementos on his desk that would link to any personal reminiscences. This was by design. He was impenetrable, without distraction—remote and clinical. It served his purpose, and the purpose of his function.

It hadn't started this way.

Recruited by the CIA out of college, Fred had an exceptional mind. His scores in visual cognition, pattern recognition, and critical thinking were exceptional. They considered his low empathy a useful trait. College wrestling prepared him physically and demonstrated his discipline. Fred loved his offensive style: take the shot, react, and re-attack. He loved the feeling of forward momentum.

The fierce individual accountability in those moments—a man on his own, facing an opponent on the mat. A metaphor for his future. The perfect platform for him to master himself. Fred studied hard, competed hard, and played hard.

His was the perfect profile for an agent in the field. Ruggedly independent, he started as an operator in remote, unimportant cities—training grounds. The chance to work the streets, develop assets, procure informants, and gather intelligence. He flourished and developed a reputation—a mastery of taking people apart and using them to the fullest advantage.

Fred made the right friends, the right connections. Rotations followed—recruitment, training, analysis, and support. Then came the leadership opportunities. He built a reputation as a reliable, honorable, and patriotic operative.

His future was secure—until it wasn't.

It started, as most things do, with a phone call. A plea for help from a person he had not heard from in years—Phil. A competitor. A fellow wrestler. They had clashed throughout high school and then into college. Phil was the opponent Fred could not beat.

Matches were always close, but Phil consistently came out on top. In rural Pennsylvania, wrestling was a tight-knit community where devotion to the sport demanded self-control, both in victory and defeat. Fred respected Phil, but he was fiercely competitive by nature. As their rivalry deepened, so did the undercurrent of simmering resentment.

Fred made a phone call and solved Phil's problem. Help had arrived, but not without strings attached. The agency collected favors like currency, and this was one more added to its ledger. With Phil's frequent work travel providing natural cover, he was an ideal resource for the agency—a convenient errand boy, decoy, or messenger, ready to be called upon when needed. To Fred, it was a suitable arrangement, but others saw it differently.

Maybe it was hubris—Fred believing he was above reproach. Perhaps it was simply a friend in need, asking for help—but that seemed unlikely. More likely, it was a chance for Fred to feel as though he was the one winning. Whatever the reason, it was a mistake.

There was blowback—he had overstepped his remit. The local station took offense, and pressure mounted from the home country in the form of a barrage of uncomfortable questions. Tensions flared, attachés were summoned, and the situation teetered on the brink of escalation. Then, miraculously, everything seemed to settle.

But once lit, the OIG (Office of Inspector General) fires were hard to douse. It began with a formal interview, then escalated into an investigation, and finally a reprimand. Fred learned an important lesson: there was a price for a poor decision.

He was reassigned to the general staff—a holding pen for those in purgatory. He had been trained to use people as tools, relying on his skills and instincts, with the mission as the sole driving force. Broken eggs were simply the price of success. He loved that clarity of purpose—and missed it now. These were hard times: the transition from the freedom and independence of the wilderness to the suffocating fishbowl of writing reports and sitting through endless meetings.

Then, after months, the Director came calling with a new and exciting opportunity. They knew each other, but Fred was not fooled about the nature of their relationship. The Director was as hard-nosed as Fred—and opportunities now always came with repercussions.

It was presented as a chance to contribute in a new and meaningful way, to use all his skills and relationships. His experience and knowledge made him uniquely suited—perfect for the job. But Fred knew it was his last assignment. This was where they sent someone no one wanted. To do a job no one wanted.

The organization within the organization, universally despised: Counterintelligence. The ones who imposed themselves and obstructed progress, constantly raising intrusive questions about mission security, the reliability of assets, and the risk of being manipulated as pawns in enemy operations.

The threats were real—everyone agreed. But there was a history, a legacy of bad actors who had been too zealous, too intrusive, and ultimately too obsessed. It was easy to draw from those histories. The argument went: we can handle our own internal audits; we're the ones closest to the action, and we know best. We did not welcome being second-guessed or told how to run our operations by so-called CI specialists who were not directly involved.

Fred took control of the department no one wanted but everyone needed. His wife told him not to make this his career, but she didn't understand that he was both stuck and stubborn. This is not for you, she cried. It will change you. In the end, Fred stayed—and she left.

There were some successes: an operation compromised in Bulgaria; an Army major leaking secrets to Venezuela; Belarusian agents attempting to infiltrate the Green Party; and an analyst passing intelligence to a new boyfriend—who in turn passed it to operatives in China. But none as spectacular as the arrest of Aldrich Ames in 1994. The FBI swept up Robert Hanssen and Ana Montes in the early 2000s, but those cases felt like echoes of an earlier era.

In the last ten years, however, nothing significant had emerged. Faced with ambiguity, every potential threat began to look the same. Fred was certain there were infiltrators in their midst—he could feel it. Yet they eluded him, and his failure to uncover them gnawed at his core. Over time, Fred changed. He too became obsessed.

He searched for ghosts in the mechanisms and cogs hidden within the machine. When had he drifted so far from the man he once was? Vibrant, energetic, sharp—Fred had thrived on the offensive. True counterintelligence work demanded time, resources, and patience, yet it was also decisive, daring, and bold. Now he found himself mired in defense, reacting to the moves of others instead of shaping the game himself.

A knock at the door. Samantha entered—Fred's new assistant, recently assigned. The eyes and ears of the Director. Fred knew it but said nothing.

She was young, tall, blond, and striking. Her beauty was undeniable, though she tried to subdue it with conservative clothes and tightly combed hair. Brisk and unblinking, she carried herself with the presence of a schoolmarm and the bite of an interrogator.

She went by Sam—perhaps a ruse to claim the kind of respect men received by default. There was a story there, but Fred knew he'd never ask.

Fred often wondered where her loyalties lay. *In a world of secrets, did she keep any for herself?*

Why tolerate it? Why not replace her? Fred knew how the game worked—they would only send in a replacement, or worse, replace him. And truth be told, she was what he needed: a sharp mind, an unshakable presence. An anchor to keep him focused.

Sam advised, "You need to decide soon. It won't be as effective if you wait."

"It can wait. We have time," Fred said, a hint of mischief in his voice.

Sam just stared. She knew his process—he needed to talk it through. *He could be rather annoying.*

"Do you know how this one started?" Fred asked.

"Yes, you leveraged a friend. A long time ago. And now maybe it turned into a thing. Maybe."

Fred tilted his head. "Do you think it's real?"

"You're the expert." Sam's voice was flat. "Hard to tell." She wasn't giving him an inch.

He frowned. "But the intel we're getting from the Israelis—

it could point that way."

"The Israelis are being coy," she said. "Same as always. They wrap it up in ten different ways to protect their source."

"What about this woman, Mariya Morozova? What did you find?"

"The visa application paperwork is pristine. We ran it through the computers, and the further back you go, the more it looks like a well-prepared legend. It lacks detail and depth, but it's very professional. The analysis pegs it at an 81.3% chance of deception."

"So, an alias. What else?" Fred prodded.

"Her sponsor also raises red flags. A U.S. security firm that was recently acquired by an overseas investor, through a shell company. Probably registered in Guernsey or the Caribbean— I'll need to double-check. Nothing definitive, though. It could be private equity making a move, or it could be a cover for something deeper."

"Would you let her in?"

Sam sighed. She knew he was going to keep pushing. "Seems like a reach. Too much risk. Outside your comfort zone."

"For me... because of my connection to the girl?"

"You spend a lot of time mitigating risk. But you rarely green-light counter-penetration ops." She gave him a look. "You play small ball. You play it safe. If this goes south, you're exposed. Are you really ready to make a move?"

She surprised him with her concern. But she told him what he already knew: he was playing it safe. "What about the girl? Is she part of this?"

"I also ran her through the computers," Sam replied.

"Really... an American citizen?"

"Let's call it research." Sam shrugged. "Didn't know what I'd find. But she's smart—college now. Strong in languages and analytics. Someone we might have recruited."

"Maybe we should put eyes on her. Pressure-test her. Anyone at the school we could use?"

"I'll look into it."

Tapping his fingers, Fred reflected, "Better to have her close."

"Just decide. I want to move this off my desk."

"Okay. We'll need a budget and resources. Do you think the Director will approve?"

"I think he's ready for you to 'get off your ass and find some spies.' His words, not mine. Budget season, you know—always hits CI first. We need a win. You need a win."

"Okay, that's pretty clear feedback." If this failed, he would be the tethered goat.

Fred felt the craving for action returning. Maybe it was time to take control—something bold and aggressive. Make the news, don't just report it.

"I'll give Don Chestnut a call, bring him in. He can run point."

Sam said, "We'll need a code name for the operation."

"Give me a day. If I don't have something tomorrow, we can let the computer choose."

"Fine. You've decided. Now live with it... and get a shave. You'll need to present this to the top floor."

◆◆◆

Later that night, Fred sat alone in his dimly lit office, a highball in hand. There was nowhere else to be. He was annoyed with himself—his indecision, his hesitation. He had let it happen. Worse, he had let it affect him.

His father's voice echoed in his mind, a mantra from childhood: *"You need to be your own man. Act and damn the repercussions."*

Fred sighed. He was a mystery even to himself—paranoid yet analytical, intuitive yet impetuous, cautious but reckless when it counted. He needed to pick a lane. *Did the Director see that? Was Sam his answer?*

Fred recalled Sam's blunt assessment: "You can't do this job if you're tentative."

His thoughts drifted to an early operation in India. Holed up in a sweltering apartment block, he had watched a bank executive take a bribe—laundering money for an arms dealer. The arrest was scheduled for the following day. He remembered the heat, the endless hours, and the strange pulse of excitement that ran through him.

Below, in the courtyard, children played a game. They outlined a rectangle in the dust, split by a centerline. Each team sent a "raider" across to tag as many opponents as possible before sprinting back to safety. If caught, the raider lost. All the while, he had to hold his breath.

The game was called *Kabaddi*—a physical contest of daring and stamina, pushing limits as oxygen ebbed away second by second.

Now, with a drink in hand, Fred understood why the memory had surfaced. The parallels were striking: daring, pressure, timing, exposure. The name clicked—it was perfect.

Operation KABADDI.

He took a long sip, letting the whiskey burn on the way down. He needed to reclaim that sense of clarity. No more waiting. No more reacting. It was time to go on the offensive.

He needed to be the *raider*—to gird himself, take a deep breath, and cross the line.

PART III

OVERCOMING IS BECOMING 2016

"What stands in the way becomes the way."

-Marcus Aurelius

CHAPTER EIGHT

BRAM FEELS THE CHILL OF a draft on his neck as the rear doors of the church open and shut. The scent of frankincense hangs in the air. Lights are dimmed, and the furnace has been turned low. He knows the usual signals to worshippers that the service is over.

He hears the vicar slowly walking up the aisle, the echo of his steps rebounding off the ancient flagstones and across the nave. Bram sits alone in the second pew. Beside him rests an urn with his mother's ashes. He had hoped to spend a little while longer alone.

"You are welcome to stay as long as you like," Vicar Hughes says.

"Thank you, Parson. You gave a nice service."

Bram knows him, but not well. His mother used to take him to regular Mass when he was young. That ended when his father died. Bram wonders if his mother would have wanted the service. She had lost so much of her faith, and of herself. As he reflects, he realizes the Mass was really for him. He wanted this closure.

Sparsely attended services are not uncommon for Vicar Hughes. The congregation is not getting younger, and time marches on. The parish provides a funeral for anyone in the community. Even so, he has never held a funeral service where only a son attended. Truly, they had been isolated from family and friends. Such a sad situation.

The vicar sits beside Bram to offer some comfort. "Your eulogy was very nice. You have a way with words."

Bram doesn't respond right away. After a pause, he says stoically, "I've been writing it for a long time."

They never held a proper funeral for his father. After the "calamity," as his mother called it, things never got better. Gill turned to the bottle, trying desperately to keep the rage at bay. Bram was the one who found and smashed the hidden flasks, trying to save what was left of their family.

Gill's pain eclipsed all others. Few escaped her scorn. In moments of mania, no one else mattered. She hurled furious, hurtful words. Bram bore the brunt of it, endured it—because someone had to. Because he still wanted to believe she could be saved.

But now it's time to go. He rises slowly, picks up the urn. He's reluctant to leave. This moment—quiet, still—is rare. A moment to breathe. A pause. Respite.

Two people wait in the back. They arrived near the end of the service and now stand in the vestibule. Both are uncomfortable in churches, for different reasons.

The first is Cilla James. Stern, unsentimental—at least

when they first met. She'd been through the social-work wringer and learned not to over-invest. You only have so much strength to give. But that hardened edge softened with Bram.

The first years without his father were the hardest. Cilla tried with Gill—countless talk sessions about getting help—but Gill was too far gone, lost deep in her grief. She traded the living for a bottle and a slow descent. She had found the abyss, and nothing would pull her back.

Cilla is now retired. Her being here says more than words ever could. She hates funerals and churches. She works in the realm of the physical, the possible. Her calling is to salvage what can be saved. And Bram, she realized, was not a lost cause. He was the reason you kept trying.

With her help, Bram got a job after finishing his eleventh year—a printmaker's assistant. It gave him a small income. Not enough—they still struggled—but it was something. For a while, he thought he might turn it into a trade. But that wasn't Bram's path. That path changed a year after his father's death.

Bram's thoughts drift back to that time.

He was walking home from the print shop after a long, sweltering shift. His body ached, and beneath the fatigue simmered a quiet anger. He had pulled away from friends, from what remained of his former life. His world had narrowed to a relentless routine: work, sleep, and caring for his mum.

This was not how fifteen-year-olds were supposed to live.

As he passed an alleyway, he caught sight of three boys about his age surrounding a smaller boy of twelve or thirteen. The boy didn't look scared, but he was certainly out of place. It was not Bram's business. He had his own problems, so he kept walking.

A few strides later, he stopped. Something was not right. Not right with the situation, and not right for Bram to let it pass. So he walked back and entered the alley. He approached the group and called out, "Hey fellas, what's up?"

He did not know these boys.

"No concern of yours. We're just chatting with our friend."

Bram felt an instant of understanding. This was a shakedown. "Oh—so everyone's friendly... that's good. So, what's his name?"

The three boys were about Bram's height but hadn't filled out. They looked at each other for courage. The leader had orange hair and was suffering from an extreme case of acne. He glared at Bram. "Piss off."

Bram ignored him, looked at the smaller boy, and said, "What's your name?"

"Adam."

"Okay. Adam, why don't I walk you out of here?"

The leader—Bram mentally named him Redhead—snapped, "Whoa, wait a minute, who said you were in charge?"

Bram shrugged and started walking, leading the smaller boy toward the exit.

Prodded by his friends, Redhead made a mistake—he put his hand on Bram's back and gave a push. Redhead didn't know it, but Bram was not in a good place.

Bram turned toward the boy, and without even thinking, answered. It was quick and compact. He could feel the middle knuckle of his right hand dovetail with the small cleft in Redhead's chin. It was a lights-out punch that put Redhead to sleep, clean and fast.

Looking down, Bram surprised himself with his own ferocity. He would normally talk himself out of fights, or his size made others reconsider. He had been lucky. But it was a good lesson: sometimes violence is necessary. The other two boys had picked him as their leader. Their courage spent, they ran the other way.

Bram turned to Adam and said, "That was not what I wanted to happen. I'm sorry you saw that, but sometimes we must fight back." As he looked down, he noticed Adam was wearing a kippah, so he added, "But you already know that."

He got Adam to the street and sent him on his way, then went home to deal with his mother. Before he left, Adam asked Bram his name.

"My name is Bram Vidal," he told him.

Cilla never learned about the encounter in the alley, but if she had, she would have been proud. He had found a way out of a bad situation, and he would keep trying. She understood Bram had a good heart and a strong mind. She also saw Gill's future and knew that, unlike Bram, she was headed down a blind alley.

Bram hugs Cilla and thanks her for all that she did, and for believing in him. Bram is now twenty-two, outside the system. Touched that she came to the funeral, he knows he may never see her again.

The second person to greet him is David Klein.

He shakes Bram's hand, and they walk. Bram had met him two days after the alley altercation, in the most unfortunate circumstances.

Gill was ranting and raving, pissed at the world and letting everyone know. Bram had been trying to calm her down when the doorbell rang.

"What do the lousy neighbors want?" she shouted. "Nothing but trouble. Tell them to bugger off!"

"Quiet, Mum, please. Let me get the door."

At the threshold, he sees a man dressed in black, diminutive in stature, with calm eyes. Bram explains that this is not the best time for a visitor.

The man seems undeterred. He introduces himself, saying, "I am Adam's father. David Klein. I wanted to thank you for helping him."

Bram isn't used to being appreciated, but he assures David it was fine. "I was happy to help. No one should be alone in that kind of situation."

Just at that moment, Gill decides to rage on. "Who is it? Tell 'em to shove off."

Distracted, Bram keeps his wits. Looking back into the house, he says, "I got it, Mum, just relax, give me a minute."

David, who seems to understand, says, "It took a bit of time to find you, and I learned about your situation. I understand it has been a hard year."

Bram is unsure now. *What is this man about?*

"Why are you looking into me?" Bram asks, his guard up.

"I didn't really 'look into' you. I wanted to find you. To thank you. But there was also information about your father. Not as much as I would have thought. Did they ever get to the bottom of it?"

"No, we never got any answers. But right now, I have other

worries."

Gill shouts again about the local wankers. "Who is it? This is my house." But she is fading.

David looks at Bram—observing, thinking. He knows this boy needs help, but should he take the chance?

"Well, thank you again." Bram begins to shut the door.

David raises his hand for him to wait and says, "It's just that I had a thought. I understand this must be distracting, yet you seem calm. My son said you were very calm against three bullies."

"Well, yes—it was okay..."

"I was wondering if... you would like a job."

Bram is confused. Is this guy looking to hire some local muscle? Thinking he's part of a syndicate? "I'm sorry, Mr. Klein, but I don't need any more trouble."

"I don't mean that kind of job. I mean an actual job with my agency—SIS. Surrey Investigative Solutions. We do background checks, missing persons, fraud investigations. It's all very legitimate."

"Thanks, but I have a job. I appreciate the offer."

David continues, "Lately I'm getting a lot of work serving papers—divorce documents, subpoenas, that sort of thing. It can get a little hairy, but if you can keep your head and handle yourself, well, that's half the battle. Plus, I think you could use a break. Like the one you gave Adam."

That was six years ago. And taking David up on his offer had been the best choice of his life. Over the past years, he had supported Gill, paid off some bills, and begun making a life. He built relationships with the local constabulary, lawyers, and hoodlums. He owned a reputation now—people knew him to be trustworthy. He wasn't crashing anymore. He was carving a path.

He had found David—or David had found him.

When it happened—four days ago—David was the one Bram called.

The moment he opened the front door and felt the quiet, he knew it was over. He felt it in his bones. He found Gill in the lounge, in her usual seat. The TV was off. She was gone—claimed by the hatred and disease that had consumed her.

This time, he cries. He really knows he's on his own. He had tried so hard not to lose another parent.

As David walks Bram to his car, he puts a hand on his shoulder and gives it a squeeze. "Take a few more days. You need some time."

Without pause, Bram responds, "No... thanks. I need the distraction of work... need to keep busy. See you at the office in the morning."

David nods. "One thing before you go. I got a call from an occasional client. An old contact. He asked specifically for you. Wants to meet. Said it was important."

"Okay, really, that is strange. Can you set it up for tomorrow?"

"Sure, shouldn't be a problem. He told me something strange, but this is an odd time to ask. It can wait."

"Go on," Bram insists. "Otherwise, I'll be up all night... wondering."

David looks at him.

"Well, okay. Did you know your grandfather was Jewish?"

CHAPTER NINE

MAIDENHILL, ENGLAND, UK
2016

THE FESTIVE BONFIRES AND FIREWORKS of Guy Fawkes Day have passed, leaving only echoes of celebration. The crisp scent of autumn is fading, replaced by a flat, sterile chill in the air. Occasionally, unseasonably warm days still arrive, as if the season itself is battling to hold on to the past. A time of change.

The offices of SIS occupy the second floor above a Turkish barber and a Korean nail salon. The shared lobby, modest and discreet, allows clients to ascend the stairs and approach the detective agency with a degree of anonymity. For those seeking even greater discretion, there is an alternative: a narrow back stairway leading to a grimy alley, perfectly suited for clandestine arrivals and departures.

David offered few details about the anonymous client, and several weeks passed before he finally arranged a meeting. Late in the day, the man slipped in through the back entrance, his footsteps quiet on the tiled floor. David led him into the conference room, his manner crisp and businesslike. Bram feels a flicker of anticipation, eager to learn more about his grandfather.

"Bram, I want to introduce you to Neshad Tal. He is a client I help from time to time."

"Nice to meet you, Mr. Tal." Bram shakes his hand.

"You can call me Neshad," he replies as he sits down.

David heads to the door to depart.

"You aren't staying?" asks Bram.

"No, Neshad asked to speak to you alone," David says as he closes the door.

Neshad and Bram sit across from one another. The room is small and stuffy. Unsure, Bram's heart races. His desire to ask about his family, his Jewish roots, is overwhelming, but he holds back. *Why am I here?*

"First, let me say I was sorry to hear about your mother... and father."

"Thank you," says Bram cautiously.

"I know this is all strange, and I will explain as best I can as we go along. But first, I want to ask you—what do you want?"

"I want to hear more about my grandfather, Ibrahim. Was he really Jewish?"

"I'll get to that in a moment. First, what about you?"

"What about me?" Bram asks.

"David says you are capable and have been with him for several years. He trusts you. But you are now on your own. What do you want?"

Bram looks at Neshad, brow furrowed. "I haven't thought about it. My mother just died."

"Life hasn't been kind, has it? Just when you've pieced

together something resembling stability, you find yourself utterly alone—left behind by those who mattered most. I don't say this to be harsh, but perhaps now is the perfect moment to decide what truly matters to you."

Bram at first offers no response, glaring at Neshad. "I want my old life, before all this happened."

"There are no time machines, no going back. What do you want now?"

"I want answers."

"That I understand. I would want answers too."

"I want to know who killed my father!" Bram says, his voice rising, surprised by his own emotion.

"It has been some time since your father died, but I can hear the pain in your voice."

"It feels like yesterday to me."

Neshad seems to relax. "That is why I am here—to give you that opportunity. I want you to investigate your father's death."

"What? You said it yourself... it's been years. Why?"

"You are older now, and well positioned to take this on. Sometimes things change... and for reasons I will not completely share with you, I want it done without my involvement."

"You want to remain anonymous? Who do you work for?"

"Smart boy. Yes. I can't tell you everything, but I can tell you a story. You can put together the rest."

"Huh—okay, I'll listen. But this is all very bizarre."

"It starts in the distant past. Four hundred years ago, Iberian Jews escaped the Spanish Inquisition—a very traumatic time, as you might imagine. They fled in many directions. One of those routes led east to the Caribbean and finally to Jamaica. There, they found a home and became integrated into society. By the seventeenth century, Jamaica was almost twenty percent Jewish—a prosperous community."

"This is all ancient. What does this have to do with me?"

"The people I work for keep tabs on these kinds of things. During World War II, Jamaica took in nearly fifteen hundred Dutch and Polish Jewish refugees—an act of compassion, no doubt, but not without challenges. After the war, things took a downward turn, and many Jews found it harder to find work. So, as has happened in times past, they began searching for a new place to live."

"Mr. Tal," Bram asks, "why are you telling me this?"

"Please, call me Neshad. Allow me a moment to continue. In 1948, a boat called the *Windrush* arrived in Tilbury, UK, carrying hundreds of Caribbeans. They answered the call to rebuild post-war Britain. Many additional émigrés arrived after that first ship, but they would forever be known as the *Windrush* Generation."

Bram is pulling the pieces together. "Was my grandfather on the Windrush?"

"No, he arrived later. But we have records of his arrival."

"So, I'm Jewish?"

"Well, your grandfather was. You are of Jewish descent, but you didn't grow up practicing Judaism. You could convert, if you choose."

"They never told me."

"I want to hire you. You are in a unique position to help me. I want you to find out why your father was killed."

"Off the books."

"Yes. I can cover your expenses and provide some minor support. But I want this to be seen as a son investigating his father's death."

"Why?"

"Does it strike you as odd—the son of a Jewish immigrant involved in a terrorist plot?"

"My father was not a terrorist." Bram remembers the flyer he found.

"That is what I want you to find out."

Bram is still unsure. *Who is this guy? What does he really want?*

"David will receive the cash. He will use that money to pay you. A son looking into the death of his father—all perfectly normal."

"And I just investigate. What if I decide not to?"

"That is your choice. But you said you wanted to find out. So go find out."

"How soon do you need a decision?"

Neshad pauses. "I think you have already made a decision, don't you?"

"How will I contact you? What if I find information?"

"I'll stay in touch with David. You keep him informed. I'll meet as needed, but not here—never again here."

Neshad Tal departs the way he arrived, out the back.

After the meeting, David checks in on Bram and asks if he wants to take the air. They decide to walk down the street to a Pret a Manger for a cup of coffee. More importantly, it's an opportunity to talk outside the office.

"Who is that guy?"

David sighs. "An associate. I can't tell you much more."

"Do you know what he wanted... why he chose me?"

"I have an idea, not all the details."

"But you know him. What do you think? Is he serious?"

David pauses before answering. "Neshad is always serious—of that, you should be clear. You should trust what he says... mostly."

Bram looks at David. "What does that mean?"

"Is this what you want, Bram? Do you really want to know what happened?"

"Yes, I think so?" *Have I decided?*

"You should be certain. Working with Neshad will take you down the rabbit hole. With him, there's always more beneath the surface than it seems."

"I can tell—this is so weird."

"Listen. Right now, you have a rare chance to start over—completely fresh. Nothing is tying you down. You could go anywhere, do anything. Stay here and work for me, or explore something entirely new. You have options, but make sure this is truly what you want. The answers you find may not be what you're hoping for—or expecting."

"Did something like this happen to you?"

"Yes, and no. I didn't lose my parents the same way you did, but I was compelled to help. And once you are involved, you can't be uninvolved."

"Won't I always wonder what happened? It'll eat at me."

"Yes, yes, it will."

"Then I've decided. I choose to find out."

"Good. You may have found yourself in some deep waters. That's okay—life happens that way. But make sure you get what you need and find your answers. Don't get sucked into someone else's play. Do you understand?"

"I think I do."

"From now on, anytime we talk about this, we choose a different place. Outside is preferable. If you want to chat, come into my office and ask me a question, but shake your head no. I'll get the idea."

"This seems all hugger-mugger."

David says, "You can do whatever you and Neshad agreed on, but we still have other work. I have a business to run. So find time in between assignments, or on weekends."

Bram nods.

"Best put together a log—take notes, record dates, observations. Use your personal computer. Make your commentaries, pose questions. This will take longer than you think."

"And Neshad—what about him?"

"Oh, I'm sure he'll monitor your progress."

CHAPTER TEN

THE CAMPUS OF FAIRHURST UNIVERSITY buzzes with activity as students prepare for the Thanksgiving holiday. It's a peculiar three days when everyone rushes to finish their work, eager to avoid anything lingering over the break. The promise of rest looms, but so does the impending pressure of final exams upon their return.

The Department of Psychology occupies an old granite building perched atop the hill that dominates the academic campus. Its imposing structure stands stark against the clear, brisk sky. At the bottom of the hill, the trees are bare, leaving the landscape desolate and exposed.

Raya climbs the steps to the scholastic offices, her chest tight with unease. The note was simple: *Come see me.* Curt, almost cryptic, without explanation or context. The uncertainty gnaws at her.

She feels like a study in contradictions—one moment a little girl summoned to the principal's office, the next incredulous that she could feel this way at all, wanting to recapture her carefree spirit. She recognizes the duality within herself and tries to shake the feeling. But self-awareness only amplifies her irritation.

It is her fault. She uses this feeling as a tool, a compulsion that drives her forward. It gets her out of bed at dawn, pushes her to submit assignments days ahead of deadlines, and keeps her going to the gym on days she would rather relax.

Earlier, she tried to burn off the tension in a spin class, pedaling harder than ever. Her legs ache, her chest heaves, and her muscles scream for relief. Afterward, she sits cross-legged on the mat, eyes closed, forcing herself to focus on her breathing. It helps her regain focus.

She knocks. Her knuckles rap harder than intended against the wood. Through the narrow window in the door, she sees him. He isn't busy—not in a meeting, not even on the phone. He sits there deliberately, making her wait. She can feel it in the measured pace of his movements, the way he ignores her knock, as if testing her patience.

Finally, he calls through the door. "Please, come in and take a seat."

Raya enters and takes one of the two chairs in front of his desk. His office is neat and spartan—so unlike the stacks of books and dusty papers she's seen in the offices of other professors.

Dr. Calhoun is a stern man—precise, measured, and utterly lacking the warmth one might expect from a therapist. Every movement feels deliberate, controlled. Intimidating.

He steeples his fingers and asks, "I don't think you've

visited me before."

"No. This is my first time."

"Why is that, do you think?"

Raya shifts in her seat, uneasy. "Not sure. Never had a reason, I guess." *It's a big class, and not that difficult.*

"Are you enjoying your senior year?"

"Sure, it's fine." She feels on guard. Irritation flares briefly, but she reins it in.

"Well, I wanted to talk about your recent paper. It was interesting. You seemed unusually comfortable with the ambiguity of the topic."

Raya nods. "Yes—I found it interesting."

"And you experienced no difficulty completing the assignment?"

"No, I don't think so. It felt like an ordinary assignment."

He studies her face for a moment too long. "You brought a curious approach to your writing. Different from your peers."

A pause. Raya frowns. "How so?"

"Well, it was nuanced. Sophisticated, even. But more importantly..." He tilts his head. "I don't think you wrote it."

"What do you mean?" *So this is what I was feeling*, Raya thinks.

Dr. Calhoun doesn't blink. "I think you either had help... or used someone else's work. I've seen parts of this writing before."

"You think I plagiarized my paper?"

"Oh yes," he says, calm and certain. "I'm confident you did."

Raya takes stock. *Remain calm*—either this is a nasty man

pushing buttons for his own gratification, setting her up for some future unsavory request, or he truly thinks she copied someone else's work.

"...I have asked you in to make an offer. Admit that the work is not yours, and you will receive a 'D.' Otherwise, the paper will fail, and your final grade will be severely impacted."

Raya snaps out of her reverie. What would Masha do? *Clarity before action.*

Gather info—slow things down.

"I'm sorry, Dr. Calhoun. May I clarify a few things?"

Gain confirmation—ask clarifying questions.

"Did the paper meet the objective?"

"Yes, it did that very well. But it was not your work."

"Was the writing substandard?"

"No, the writing was excellent."

Look for weakness—understand motivation.

"And you have not proven your assertion. You have not found the so-called source material."

"Not yet. But I will. I've read it before—I'm certain."

"Were there other, higher-performing papers in the class?"

"The paper you handed in was the best in the class."

"And there is no other accommodation we could make?"

"That is not going to work."

So, he's not a pervert. *Operate asymmetrically. Look for options.*

"I could complain—take it to the dean."

"Well, that won't work. I won't change my mind."

"There's no other way to boost my grade?"

"No."

"So, my only choice is to admit to something I didn't do... or fail?"

"Yes," he replies smugly.

Delay response if possible.

"I didn't cheat on your paper. I need some time to think," Raya says, feigning emotion, her voice pitched higher. "Why are you doing this? I did nothing wrong?" She has the germ of a plan but needs time.

"Think it over. Use the holiday. But I want an answer on Monday."

She departs without shaking hands or looking back.

Act with fortitude.

Raya takes stock of herself. She is in control, grounded by the resilience she has built over the past few years. Now she needs to summon her determination. She will not be pushed around by anyone—least of all Dr. Calhoun. The decision settles over her like armor. She will get started right away.

Phil Rogers is in the kitchen when the doorbell rings. He wipes his hands on a dish towel and calls out, "Masha, can you get that?"

Raya has arrived after a short train ride—only thirty minutes from school—followed by a brisk walk through one of Philadelphia's oldest neighborhoods. Linden and sycamore trees line the streets, their bare branches swaying gently in the crisp autumn breeze. Phil's home is a beautifully restored 18th-century row house, its brick façade steeped in history and charm.

The neighborhood may not be old by English standards,

but it carries a picturesque character and a palpable sense of history. Only a few blocks away stands Independence Hall, where the First Continental Congress convened—a cornerstone of the American story.

Masha greets her at the door with a warm smile. They embrace tightly—the kind of hug shared between people who know they matter to one another. Weekly coffee dates and regular phone calls have kept them close.

Masha has finally resolved her visa issues, though the process took far longer than expected. Raya was shocked by how difficult it proved—America isn't the land of easy immigration it once seemed to be.

Raya steps into the warm, inviting space, the aroma of roasted turkey and spices filling the air. Her father has purchased a pre-cooked bird and all the trimmings from the local Whole Foods. She knows Masha will think it all so decadent, but he isn't much of a cook. And everything will be so much better if all he has to do is heat it up.

Over dinner, they trade updates.

Raya is preparing to finish the semester. She alludes to a challenge in her psych class, but insists it's nothing she can't handle. Conversation shifts to her volunteer work—part-time, but meaningful. She talks about how much she enjoys helping people, the energy of working in the grittier parts of town, and the feeling that she's making an impact.

Masha lives outside the city, managing a gated community west of Philadelphia—similar to her job in Sunningham. Her company, Bremen-Sarp GmbH, has recently asked her to take on an expanded role. They want her to provide additional support to other communities while also stepping into a consulting capacity. She takes pride in her work and anticipates more travel.

Phil is settling into a semi-retired life: working on his home, walking the streets, enjoying the amenities of a large city. He does some consulting, but mostly he enjoys his free time. Much to his daughter's chagrin, he has been dating, though nothing serious. Unlike most retirees, he has little interest in travel. He has traveled enough in his lifetime.

After dinner, they clear the plates and settle into the living room—a cozy space with a warm, inviting fireplace. The flickering flames cast a soft glow across the room, illuminating the small couch in front of the hearth and two wingback chairs to either side.

Phil pours everyone a glass of port, the rich aroma mingling with the faint scent of wood smoke. They settle into their seats; the mood shifts as casual conversation gives way to something heavier. This is the real talk Raya has been dreading.

"Have you thought about my suggestion?" Phil asks.

"You want me to do consulting—I'm not sure."

"Well, what could be better, given your degree?"

"I never imagined doing what you do, Dad." She loathes the idea of sharing a career with her father.

"I could help get you interviews."

"I thought you wanted to go into government... something secure," Masha says.

"Nothing secure about the government," Phil mutters under his breath.

Masha continues, "It would be great for you to work in the

State Department—or something international."

"I like the idea of working internationally," Raya replies.

"You know, you can get international experience in other ways—just look at my career."

Raya winces.

Masha notices Raya's reaction to Phil's comment—he isn't helping his cause.

Finally, Phil asks, "Well, Raya, what are you thinking?"

"I enjoy helping the people at East Penn Legal Services. They'll take me on full-time, but the pay isn't great. I enjoy being in the city... outside of an office and *independent.*"

Masha feels her temperature rise. Raya needs to be heading down the right path. A local charity won't do.

"That won't bring you international travel," Phil says.

Masha adds, "And where will it lead? These groups shut down all the time."

Raya can only shrug—*everything is a risk.*

Phil offers, "You know, there are big organizations that do similar work. Maybe the United Nations would be a place to start. They do all types of work helping people—poverty, women's rights, medical care, you get the idea."

Raya thinks that's an idea—*maybe.*

Masha makes one more pass. "And where will it lead?"

"Well, whatever you do, you need to think about it soon. Only one more semester," Phil says.

They all rise as it's getting late. Masha reaches for her coat.

Knowing how hard he's tried to be a good father, Raya gives her dad a hug. She still has one more thing she wants to talk about with him. She had hoped to arrive before Masha so they could speak privately, but it didn't work out that way.

Raya whispers in his ear. "Do you think we could talk about Mom sometime? I think I'm ready."

"Sure, honey, of course."

As the women leave and Phil retreats to the kitchen to clean up, his thoughts spiral. An NGO would be fine, he reasons—safe, purposeful. Just stay away from the damn security services. *Don't fall into the same trap I did.* The thought tightens his chest.

And then there is the matter of Raya asking about her mother. *Why now?* Why, after all these years, does she need to dig up the past? He doesn't want to have that conversation— not now, not ever.

Walking side by side toward the train station, where their paths will eventually diverge, Masha thinks maybe an NGO could work—it's a process, and it could help get Raya where she needs to be.

Raya thinks it's time to get back and deal with Dr. Calhoun.

CHAPTER ELEVEN

EVERY MONDAY, FRED SITS IN his secure office reviewing a rotating selection of operational cases. Sam meticulously manages this routine as part of their regular cadence. They can't cover every case in a single day, but over the course of a quarter, this governance cycle ensures nothing slips through the cracks.

Today's docket brings them to KABADDI. Sam frowns. It's an unusual name for an operation—one Fred hasn't bothered to explain.

Fred notices Sam's reaction but says nothing. He leans back in his chair and issues a calm directive: "Bring in Don."

Don is an old friend and a key figure in Fred's inner circle. Years ago, Fred recruited Don into counterintelligence—though Don preferred to call it being "pulled in." Their shared history is complicated, forged by secrets neither man will share—but both understand.

Now, with Don on the brink of retirement, he serves as

Fred's sounding board—a steadying influence in an environment where trust is currency. Don's years of experience make him the perfect person to navigate the nuances of cases like KABADDI. Don Chestnut arrives from the outer office and takes a seat.

"Okay—where are we?" Fred asks.

Don settles into a chair. "We've been surveilling Mariya Morozova for over a year. Upon entering the U.S., she took a position with Bremen-Sarp GmbH, a German security company. They manage threat assessments, do some IT work, and have a limited personal-protection capability. They also administer secure residential communities throughout Europe and parts of Asia. This seems to be their growth area; they've recently taken on some new contracts in the U.S."

Fred looked up, surprised. "And we still don't know who owns Bremen-Sarp?"

"No. They hide behind shell companies, and all the directors are lawyers."

Sam asks, "Who lives in these communities?"

"It is interesting. They all seem to house important people across the spectrum—business leaders, government officials, people with influence."

Fred proposes, "Maybe that is the threat? What does Ms. Morozova do for them?"

"She manages the operations at a facility near Philadelphia," answers Don.

"Did you find out any more about her early years? I seem to recall there were concerns about her background."

"Before arriving in the U.S., she immigrated to the UK

through Poland. Seems her family originated somewhere in Russia, but no clear records."

Fred expresses his frustration. "What good are all these systems if they can't tell us anything? Keep looking."

Sam reminds him, "Computers are useful, but only as good as the information available."

Fred looks at Don and asks pointedly, "And her activities—anything troubling you?"

"She is clearly performing SDRs. We've lost her several times, but we don't have our best watchers. Her last surveillance detection route took her across three trains, a taxi, and a large shopping mall before we lost her. No international travel since she arrived, but she could travel anywhere in the U.S. by car."

Fred locks eyes with Don. "You know what I'm asking. Could this be it—the first signs of the Doctrine of Patience?"

Sam raises an eyebrow. *Doctrine of Patience? Another secret.*

Don hesitates. He doesn't like this discussion happening in front of Sam. He makes a mental note to speak with Fred later—in private.

"We haven't found anything on her phone or laptop," Don continues. "If she's in contact with a handler, we haven't figured out how. With encryption these days, everything's a moving target."

Sensing Don wants to move on, Fred asks, "What else?"

"She meets regularly with Raya Rogers. She came over a few years after Raya because of the visa hold. They stick to public places—gardens, art museums, coffee houses. They are very close, almost mother-daughter close. Since the incident in Sunningham, they've become inseparable."

"Hmm... what about Raya? What have we found on her?" Fred asks.

"This gets a little tricky. We have some wiggle room, but we can't actively watch Raya without a warrant. The FBI would have a fit."

"Okay, we need to figure that out. What do we know now?"

"She's finishing her senior year at Fairhurst College. She speaks several languages but focuses on Slavic Studies and minors in Psych. She sees her father, Phil, irregularly, but there don't seem to be any relationship issues. She does volunteer translation work for displaced communities. That could be an avenue for foreign communication."

"That would be speculation," Sam says.

"Just spitballing here," Don replies.

Fred raises his hands to signal everyone to relax. "The question is, how does this relate to Ms. Morozova?"

"She calls her Masha," Sam says.

"Who does?" Fred asks.

"Raya calls Mariya Morozova by the diminutive Masha—a term of endearment," Sam answers.

Trying to regain control, Don says, "The big question is, where are Raya's loyalties? Does Masha influence her, or is she the cutout—or even a handler? That would be very unusual for someone her age. Or maybe it's nothing."

"What about Dr. Calhoun at the university? Did you talk to him?"

"Yes... well, he went a bit rogue."

"What are you talking about? We were lucky she was in his class. All he had to do was give us his impressions."

"He may not have been our best choice—he decided to call her in and press her."

Fred, annoyed, says, "We never asked for that—did she get spooked?"

"Maybe—but not in the way you think. She took care of Dr. Calhoun herself."

"How?"

"Turns out she had plans of her own. After their initial meeting, she returned and asked him to reconsider. He refused. She mussed her hair, disheveled her clothes, and slammed the door as she left. Unknown to Dr. Calhoun, it created a scene outside his office. She pushed her way out of the building, bumping into other students without saying a word."

Sam nods. "Something people would remember."

"Yes. She went back to her dorm and made a video on her phone describing her experience—how she felt Dr. Calhoun was pressuring her for 'favors,' how distraught she was, and creating a record."

"I don't see this ending well for Dr. Calhoun," Sam says.

"No. The following Monday, she returned and explained to Dr. Calhoun what she had done. She planned to post the video and file a complaint with the administration. Without an 'A' on the paper, she would release the video—more to follow."

"And what did he do?" Fred asks.

"He told her it wouldn't work, that he would be exonerated. She agreed—but predicted his reputation would be destroyed. She said it in a cool, calm way that unsettled Dr. Calhoun. No woman would ever take his class again."

Fred winces. "She hit him where it hurt."

"Yes. He relented and gave her the grade."

"But was he right? Did she plagiarize the content?" Fred asks.

"Hard to tell, maybe. It's so common, with so many papers to write. It would be hard to prove, but she probably took some liberties. They all do."

Fred looks at Don knowingly. "Eleventh Commandment."

Don replies, "Don't get caught."

"I like her," Sam says.

"What was Calhoun's assessment? Was his reckless approach worth it?

"She has a comfort with uncertainty, stayed levelheaded in a tense situation. He assessed her as resilient—she can take a punch, hard to knock down."

"You think?" Sam chimes in.

Don continues, "Decisive. Once she chose to act, she acted with alacrity. The one thing he couldn't comment on was her patriotism—her loyalty is unknown."

"So where does that leave us?" Sam prods.

Fred suggests, "Why don't we simply kick this 'Masha' out—cite some visa issue, let someone else deal with it."

Sam looks straight at Fred. "You wanted to find out."

"What do the Israelis say?"

"Their current analysis is that nothing has changed from the prior analysis," says Don.

"Very helpful," Fred remarks.

"Reading between the lines, they're telling us to stay on it."

"So—options?"

"Status quo, increase surveillance, or kick out Ms. Morozova," Don suggests.

"We still need to deal with surveillance on Raya—our hands are tied," Sam reminds them. "We could turn her over to the FBI, let them decide if they want to pursue it."

Don hesitates, then says, "There's another option. We could bring Raya into the CIA—as a recruit. She has the requisite skills. It would allow us a much higher level of scrutiny without raising flags. If she were one of ours, we could polygraph her till the cows come home."

Fred looks up, surprised. "Seriously?"

"Let's be aggressive."

Sam nods in approval.

"Put her through the paces—orientation, training, interrogation. I can mentor her through some low-level ops. If you want me to assess her loyalty, this will give me the chance to find out," Don says.

Fred pauses to think. *This is what he asked for, right? Is this something—or nothing?* He decides to trust his instincts. Maybe it's time to have a serious talk with the Israelis.

"Okay. Make the approach."

Don suggests, "I could take Sam along. After Raya's last interaction, she may be skittish around a man in authority."

And it gives me a chance to vet Sam, he thinks.

Sam looks up, surprised at Don's suggestion. "You want me in the field?"

Fred smiles. "You'll do fine. Besides, you're the one who thinks this is a good idea."

Unconvinced, she says, "Sure."

"And one more thing," Fred says.

"What's that?" Don asks.

"Fire Calhoun... never use him again."

PART IV

FINDING FOOTING
2017 · 2018

"Your purpose in life is to find your purpose and give your
whole heart and soul to it."

-Buddha

CHAPTER TWELVE

SOUTHEAST PENNSYLVANIA, USA
2017

AS THE NEW YEAR BEGINS, Sam and Don drive north from Washington D.C. to Fairhurst University. The car speeds along a salt-crusted stretch of I-95, cutting through frozen farmland. Their conversation circles around how best to approach and recruit Raya.

They rule out emails or phone calls—Raya might not respond, or worse, dismiss them entirely. Besides, they don't want to leave a trail. If they're going to reach her, it has to be done carefully.

"You should make the contact," Don says casually, eyes on the road.

Sam glances over, caught off guard. "Why me? You're the expert."

"Don't you think I might scare her off?"

She smirks. "You're not that scary."

They settle into uneasy silence.

Finally, Don says, "If you don't want to do it, I understand."

Sam turns her gaze to the window. "You don't think I'm capable."

"Uh... no. I didn't say that. You just seemed... reluctant."

"Whatever."

Don keeps his eyes on the road. "What does that mean?"

"I mean,"—she turns back to him— "you don't have confidence in me."

Baffled, he says, "I'm the one who suggested it."

She lets out a short, skeptical humph.

Unsure if she's serious or just testing him, Don decides to probe. Maybe it's time he understood her better.

"So... what's your story, anyway?"

She looks down at her hands, guarded. "What do you want to know?"

"Well... you're sharp. You've got instincts. You could be doing more—you've got a presence that could work in the field."

"You mean I'm pretty."

He hesitates. "Sure."

She shakes her head. "Men are all the same."

"I didn't mean..."

"No?" She sighs. "You want to know why I work for Fred? Fine. When I joined, I asked for the support ops track—logistics, coordination. I didn't want to be in the field. I wanted to help the people who were. That was the dream."

"What happened?"

"The Director at the time took one look at me and reassigned me. Said I was 'too polished' for the back rooms. Translation... eye candy for the front office."

Don grimaces. "He always liked to be surrounded by...

charm."

"Right. And just like that, the dream derailed. Eventually, the Director offered me the *opportunity* to be Fred's assigned assistant. He wanted someone to keep an eye on Fred—his problem child. I saw it as a way to get away from a creep."

"Fred doesn't strike me as someone who needs a babysitter."

"No. He can be an ass, but he doesn't play favorites."

Curious now, Don asks, "And do you? Do you act as the Director's eyes and ears?"

He looks at her, waiting to see how she'll answer.

She stares back without answering, holding her cards close.

A pause.

Then, softer, she says, "When I was a kid, I was always sidelined. My parents assumed I'd marry young, have kids, stay close. They never asked me what I wanted."

Don doesn't speak—he just listens.

"My sister was the star. Everyone adored her—including me. She had everything under control... she was so focused."

"What was her name?"

"Josephine. I called her Joe... sometimes G.I. Joe." She smiles, just a little. "She understood I had dreams—dreams I couldn't share with our parents."

"A hidden life."

She smiles faintly. "She used to call me Cam, like a chameleon. She joked I'd make a better spy than she ever would. That kind of stuck."

"Where is she now?"

"Gone." Her voice tightens. "She joined the Marines. There was an 'operational misadventure'... whatever the hell that means. Anyway, she's gone."

Don lets the moment sit before pressing again.

"So—life's been unfair?"

Sam starts to answer, "That's not—"

He cuts her off. "And rather than take this opportunity, you're going to stew in it—hiding behind that scowl?"

Sam glares at him, but there's no real heat behind it. *Maybe he's right.* She exhales, relents. "What would I need to do?"

"We'll find a setting where it feels organic. Casual. A conversation, not an ambush. Trust me—Raya's more likely to talk to a woman. Someone her age. Someone who doesn't look like the government."

"You know, times have changed." Sam scoffs in mock indignation, though worry flickers at the edges of her voice.

"Yes," Don replies. "But people haven't. And this isn't about principle—it's about approach."

She nods slowly, but doubt gnaws at her. She's not a field operative. She's never pretended to be. Could she really pull this off—without blowing it?

As the highway unwinds ahead, Sam isn't wondering whether Don believes in her—she's wondering if she believes in herself.

Walking past St. Mary's Church, Raya catches sight of three Benedictine nuns strolling side by side, their black-and-white habits stark against the blue sky.

She stops momentarily, struck by the sight. You don't see

that too often, she thinks, trying to recall the last time she saw a nun on the street.

A memory stirs—her father's voice, his warmth, the weight of her small body sitting on his knee, curled against his chest. He told her stories, reciting strange old poems filled with shadow and meaning.

She stands like a statue, frozen, as an old nursery rhyme from her childhood bubbles up from the depths of her mind.

When thrice-black meets white,
Signs stir softly through the night.
Wary—
the turn of time unfolds.
The light shifts,
and the future—
is foretold.

Something about the moment feels heavy with meaning. Shaking it off, she reminds herself, *I'm in the home stretch now.*

The last semester has been brutal, and dealing with Dr. Calhoun tested her resolve. Raya is finally beginning to feel like she can breathe again. She pulled off her plan, and true to his word, Dr. Calhoun delivered—her grade is secure.

As she approaches the gym, she doesn't notice the tall man standing outside—a man used to being unseen, blending into the flow of life. His posture is relaxed, but his eyes are alert. If she did see him, he would look up and meet her gaze, nodding briefly in acknowledgment. Anything else would seem unnatural.

She pushes through the gym doors. Inside, she heads to the locker room to change. Today is her cardio day—she plans to hit the treadmill.

Across the gym, Sam spots Raya heading for the treadmills. She watches as Raya begins her run, her movements steady and focused.

Sam's stomach churns with nerves. How is she supposed to strike up a conversation, introduce herself, and convince Raya to meet Don—while making it all seem casual?

She tells herself she hates lying, hates deception. But the truth cuts deeper: she's lying to herself.

Sam grips the water bottle in her hand, knuckles white, completely out of her depth.

Raya notices the striking woman step onto the treadmill beside her. She sneaks a few sidelong glances but keeps her focus on the steady rhythm of her run. She isn't interested in small talk.

After a few quiet minutes, the woman speaks. "Hi—I'm Sam."

"Raya." Her tone is polite but flat—a clear signal: *leave me alone.*

"You live around here?"

"Yeah." Raya doesn't elaborate. Her eyes stay forward, earbuds still in place.

Sam hesitates, visibly uneasy. *How do I not screw this up?* She fidgets, then blurts, "I know. I... I was hoping to meet you."

Raya is nonplussed as she processes what Sam just said. Her stride falters slightly. She turns, confused. "Wait—what? Are you following me?"

"No—well... kind of," Sam admits, instantly regretting it. "Not like that. I just... I'm sorry, this is coming out all wrong."

Raya tenses, glaring at the woman beside her. "What's this all about?"

"I was hoping we could talk. Just for a few minutes—if you've got time."

"What do you want?"

"You're not in trouble," Sam says quickly. "It's nothing like that. My partner and I... we have a proposition. I think you'll want to hear it."

No way, Raya thinks. She's not meeting this woman or her mysterious "partner." Not a chance. "I don't think so," she says flatly, stepping off the treadmill and heading for the exit.

Sam panics. "It's a job," she blurts. "I swear—that's all. My partner can explain better."

Raya stops, turns slightly, balling her hand into a fist. "You don't ambush someone at a gym. You send an email. Call. Like a normal person."

"You're right," Sam admits, breathless. "We didn't want to scare you off—but I did anyway. I totally screwed this up. Still... please, just give us a chance to explain."

Raya studies her. Sam's nervous, but not threatening. And something about her—earnest, a little out of her depth—feels real. Still, Raya stays cautious. The world's full of schemes, and she does need work.

She lets the silence stretch, then says, "Fine. There's a bench in the center of the green, facing Franklin Hall. I'll be there tomorrow at noon. I'll have eyes on me—friends."

Sam exhales, relieved. "Thank you. You won't regret this."

Raya walks off without another word.

Sam watches her go, heart still thumping, thinking *she's a natural*. She's about to find Don and tell him the meeting's set—but she hesitates. He's the one who pushed her into approaching Raya. Let him sweat a little. She turns back toward the treadmills. She'll finish her workout first.

Let him wait.

Sitting on the bench, Raya surveys the surrounding grounds, scanning the shadows. She instinctively tightens her grip on the bag. Footpaths crisscross from building to building. Students head to their next class, or maybe lunch, moving in all directions. This is a well-chosen spot—private enough for a quiet conversation, but public enough to make her feel safe.

The man is smart enough to approach from the front rather than suddenly appear from behind. Tall, thin, athletic. As he nears, she realizes he is older than she thought. Midwestern executive vibes—confident, comfortable in his skin. A man with the drive to achieve.

He holds out his hand. "Hello, I'm Don."

"Don what?" She shakes his hand.

"Don Chestnut. And you are Raya?"

She gives him a knowing look. "I think you know who I am."

He smiles slightly. "Pleased to meet you. May I sit?"

Raya nods. "Where is your friend?"

"I thought we could chat alone." He settles in next to Raya.

She studies him for a moment before tilting her head. "She mentioned a job. What firm do you work for, Mr. Chestnut?"

Don exhales, a faint smirk tugging at the corner of his

mouth. "Ah, well... right to the heart of the matter. I do, in fact, work for The Firm."

A student sprints across the quad, right in front of the bench where they sit, startling Raya. Backpack bouncing with every step, late for class.

She breathes in sharply. Raya has read enough spy thrillers to know he means the CIA. This has taken a turn, and she needs to take it seriously. "How can I help you?"

"I wanted to talk, to see if you're interested in pursuing a career with us. We don't usually actively recruit—we have procedures—but sometimes we go outside that process."

Was it only a few months ago when she spoke with her dad and Masha? What had she said... *wanting to help people, travel internationally, have a sense of independence.*

The wind picks up, rustling the trees, sending stray leaves skittering across the pavement.

"You're recruiting me to be a secret agent?"

"We have lots of jobs that aren't spies. And we're called officers, not agents."

"But why me? I'm nothing special."

"Don't underestimate yourself. You read, write, and speak Russian and Turkish. I understand you're also conversant in Polish and have some Spanish."

Raya smiles. "So, you're looking for a translator?"

Don shakes his head. "You've lived and traveled internationally, you excel in analytics, and you maintain a high level of physical fitness."

"Okay."

"All this would create interest in any potential candidate.

But I'd add that you survived a terrorist attack. And when you applied to Fairhurst, you submitted some of the best school recommendations we've ever seen—one of them from the likely next British Foreign Minister."

She smirks. "You mean I'm a suitable candidate?"

"If you're not the candidate I'm supposed to talk to, then I'm not sure who is... plus, you're feisty—which, believe it or not, can be an asset."

Raya reflects for a moment. *I know what this is. But do I want it?*

She meets Don's gaze. "What would I do for The Firm?"

Don leans back slightly, considering his words. "Honestly? I'm not sure. We hire for talent, then find the best fit."

"Would I get trained?"

He chuckles. "More than you could imagine. We tailor the training to the individual, but it won't be easy. You'll have months of homework—probably more than you expect."

Raya folds her arms, thinking it through. "How do I know if it's right for me? How did you decide?"

Don studies her, his expression unreadable. "I didn't. Not really. The job found me. It was a different era—I came out of the military. I'll tell you this: it's the best job in the world. Mission-driven, surrounded by smart people. Few regret their choice. But it's a hard life, filled with secrets. It's not easy."

Raya watches him closely. "You would do it all again?"

Without hesitation, Don nods. "Absolutely. You learn to balance your own curiosity and initiative with collaboration and responsibility. We have a purpose, a commitment to protecting U.S. interests, and we take that extremely seriously."

Don fixes her with a hard look as he says this last part.

She lets the words settle. "What happens if I say yes?"

"You still need to go through the application process. We'll screen you, run medical tests, and check your background. If you pass, we'll offer you a position—provisionally."

"And if I don't pass?"

Don shrugs. "Then we don't offer you a position. You never hear from us again."

Raya pauses, weighing his words. *It would be good to talk this through with Dad or Masha.*

As if reading her mind, Don leans forward slightly. "One more thing—you know this is secret. You can't tell your roommate, your parents, your significant other... anyone."

Raya frowns. "So, what would I tell them?"

"We have plenty of cover stories, and we'll find one that fits you. But don't get ahead of yourself. Your job now is to finish school and graduate."

Her instincts scream caution. *Take your time. Think it through.* Advice rattles in her ears—from her father, from Masha, from others.

But even now, sitting on a bench in the middle of the university green, surrounded by strangers drifting past, she knows—this is something she wants to try.

Would she be willing to give up some degree-of-freedom for something bigger—maybe something more important?

What about her independence?

She can't answer. But there's something here that feels right.

✦✦✦

A few months later, Raya has good news to share. It's her first chance to test out her cover story, to bring her legend to life.

She calls her dad, Phil, excitement clear in her voice, and announces that an NGO called Orava International Relief has hired her. It's a Polish organization focused on supporting communities in the Black Sea and Baltic regions, with an emphasis on displaced persons, immigration, and education.

Her language skills—and the fact that she's lived abroad—impressed them. Best of all, their U.S. office is in D.C., just a train ride away. They refer to themselves as OIR.

Every father loves to see his daughter happy, and Phil is no exception. She's finding her own way, becoming the adult every parent hopes their child will become. And she's happy. She's found a path that gives her both fulfillment and a future.

But over the following months, that happiness morphs into something else.

It starts innocuously enough with a phone call. OIR needs to conduct a background check. Could Phil provide some information about Raya's mother? Odd, but not unreasonable—or so it seems.

Then comes Raya's difficulties when he asks for specifics about the organization. She can't provide much detail. She knows little about the overseas arm, how it's funded, or even the name of the CEO.

What unsettles Phil most, though, is a vague memory he can't shake. Years ago, during a mission, he was tasked with delivering materials to a contact in Krakow. The contact worked for an NGO. He thinks its name might have been OIR.

What has his daughter gotten herself into?

When Raya shares the news with Masha over coffee, Masha's excitement is obvious. She beams, her enthusiasm spilling over as she congratulates Raya. To Masha, this feels like confirmation that her guidance has been working. This job with OIR is exactly what Raya needs—something to move her in the right direction, to set her life on the right path.

Already, Masha's mind is working, mapping out how to turn this opportunity into something bigger. She leans in, her voice full of encouragement and conviction.

"This is perfect for you, Raya. You'll get firsthand experience with global issues and see the challenges other countries face. It's preparation for what's next. Think of it as a stepping-stone—a way to move into government, into a position with genuine power and authority."

Raya listens, nodding, but something inside her shifts. A faint pang of uncertainty rises in her chest, unwelcome and persistent. For a moment, it feels like this isn't her accomplishment at all—it's Masha's. Maybe it always has been. After all, Masha is like a mother to her, guiding her choices and shaping her future.

But whose future is it, really?

Raya stirs her coffee, unable to push the question away. She's made her choice; now she'll have to navigate Masha's expectations as they come, even if they don't match her own.

CHAPTER THIRTEEN

MAIDENHILL, ENGLAND, UK
2017

Even as Raya makes plans for her future, Bram feels stuck. Across the Atlantic, he knows he should begin his own journey—but it feels less like moving forward and more like drifting.

He always imagined that living alone would bring freedom, but he's learned it comes with its own challenges. Sorting out his life has taken far more time than he expected, especially in the wake of his mother's death.

The end of their family home's lease forced him to pack up and sift through decades of memories. Finding a new apartment—a place that feels right for a single man—became another hurdle. There's been no time for reflection, no room for grief, no space for repair. Only the next task, the next responsibility.

He still has his job with David, with all its relentless, mundane demands. But lately, even the simplest chores feel heavy. Grieving. Adjusting. Working. And beneath it all, the gnawing sense that he's failing his father.

Only a few months have passed since Bram sat down with Neshad and agreed to investigate. But he still hasn't started—not really. His work with SIS remains confined to whatever David assigns him: deliver this document, watch that house, follow this man.

He's not a cop. And this—this feels different.

He tries asking David for advice, hoping for clarity. But something in their relationship has shifted. David feels more distant now, more... transactional.

"How do I do this? He died years ago," Bram asks, unsure.

David's response is blunt. "Start at the beginning. Each step will show the way forward."

Bram presses. "I thought maybe you might guide me in this..."

David cuts him off. "Look, this is your journey, not mine. I've got my own challenges. You agreed to this—it's yours to figure out."

Frustrated, Bram clenches his jaw. *David has challenges.*

He mutters, "I should've never said yes."

David doesn't flinch. "Your parents died too early. That's not fair. But you've found your footing. Maybe you missed some of the guidance you should've had. Being a man means keeping your word—honoring your commitments, even when it's hard, even when it demands sacrifice."

Bram tries to lighten the mood. "Is this your version of tough love?"

David softens. "Maybe. I find myself doing it with Adam, too. He's younger than you... but he hasn't lived your life. I slip into tough-father mode, and it rubs off on how I treat you. It's not fair—to either of us."

Bram holds his gaze.

"I'm not your dad, Bram. I'm your employer. I care about you, but it's time you took on the responsibilities of an adult. No more hand-holding."

It stings—but Bram knows he's right. It's time for him to be his own man.

That evening, Bram sits staring at a blank page. He takes a breath. If he's going to start, he needs to define what "the beginning" actually is. He decides to write a report—an investigative journal. Stick to the facts. Collect the data. Analyze.

Step one: gather everything he can. Request police reports. Visit the site. Talk to the people who were there. Before he can act, he has to ask the right questions. That's the real challenge—knowing what to ask, and where the answers might lead.

He doesn't realize it yet, but the investigation will span the next year. And by the end, he'll come to understand things about himself, his family, and the world—truths he can't yet imagine.

◆ ◆ ◆

The Journal of Bram Vidal

<u>February</u>: I request all the police reports.

Since my father is dead (and I don't have power of attorney), I can only request a report about

myself. I hope my interaction
with the police pulls in some
relevant details—maybe the names
of officers I can track down. It
will take weeks, at best, to get
a response.

I also go through my father's
belongings, looking for any signs
of radicalization. I have no
recollection of him ever
referring to, or using, firearms.
The police conducted a
comprehensive search, so I expect
they already took anything
incriminating.

In my possession is a flyer for
Crisis Actors Ltd. I don't know
what this is, and I can't find
any record of the company online.
No references to these kinds of
jobs being recruited. I never
questioned my mother before she
died—an oversight on my part.

Questions:
>   Was my father radicalized?
>   If yes, who was his
>   contact?
>   What was the purpose of the
>   attack?
>   Was he trained—and where?
>   Who is Crisis Actors Ltd.?

<u>March</u>: I visit the Sunningham site.
I drive to Sunningham, down the A330 via London Road. The site is difficult to find, set back from the main roadway with a nondescript entrance. As I approach the security gate, I notice multiple cameras. A guard comes out to meet my car and asks my business. I state my purpose as an investigator with SIS.

I'm told this is private property and asked to leave. I inquire after the names of the residents but am refused. I also request permission to enter on foot and walk the area, but that too is denied.

I inquire about the guard's name. He tells me it is Mr. Jones (not sure if it's real). On his uniform is a patch in the shape of a shield with the letters BSG. I take that to be the security company managing the property.

I park my car on a siding just outside the entrance and walk part of the perimeter. The area is heavily wooded, but a high

fence runs along it, again with
cameras mounted above. Entry
would not be easy—or possible—
without being observed.

Mr. Jones comes out again and
orders me to leave or he will
call the local authorities. I
depart without further trouble.
This is my first time seeing the
site, and I can't imagine how my
father ended up here.

Questions:
    Who are the people living
    in such a secure location?
    Who is the company BSG?
    Why was this site the
target?

I stop at a nearby Costa to see
if anyone from Sunningham comes
in for coffee. It seems like a
likely spot—well placed in a
retail strip near the enclave.

I slip the barista a quid and ask
him to signal me if anyone he
knows from Sunningham comes in.
No one does for an hour.

Finally, a young woman orders a
latte, and I get the nod. Her
name is Ligia Garcia. Posing as

an estate agent doing recon for a
client, I ask about the area,
schools, and so forth. Then I
broach the subject of the
terrorist attack.

She says she was not in the UK at
the time of the attack, but now
works in a domestic position for
one of the families (she will not
share their names). She has heard
stories from neighbors about the
attack and, of course, knows Raya
and Masha. When I inquire
further, she becomes
unresponsive.

With no additional patrons coming
in, I depart.

Questions:
    Who is Raya?
    Who is Masha?

April: Received police report.

I receive a heavily redacted
report from the Thames River
Police Department. There are a
few clues, including the name of
the detective my mother and I
spoke with—Detective George
Fernsby.

A second reference appears to a responding officer, Lewis Chapman, at the scene. This may have been included in error (not redacted), but I'll take any luck I can get.

It's clear the police concluded my father was a terrorist and were working to establish if he was part of a broader conspiracy. Their aim: prevent further attacks and secure evidence.

Some detail is included about the van he was driving (GB plate BD51 SMR), but not its origin. There are also references to cameras, but I suspect securing video would be aspirational at best.

No other details of importance. The case is quickly escalated from Thames River PD to the Southeast Region Terrorism Task Force. No further details are provided about the outcome or the continuing investigation.

It seems it may have been moved into a cold case file. No clear motive was ever established.

Questions:

How do I find Detective
George Fernsby?
How do I find Officer Lewis
Chapman?
How can I track down the
van (BD51 SMR)?
Is there any video evidence
I could still secure?

<u>May</u>: Interview with Officer Lewis
Chapman.

I decide to interview Officer
Chapman, the first responder to
the scene in Sunningham.

I know Detective George Fernsby
will be a harder conversation
(based on my first experience),
so I want to gain as much
information as I can first.

Tracking down Officer Lewis
Chapman is easier than I expect.
Through one of my work contacts,
I even manage an introduction. He
suggests meeting outside the
precinct, so we agree on lunch at
a local pub.
My cover—as an SIS investigator
doing work for a client—doesn't
fool Chapman for long. He
immediately pegs me as the son of
Avi Vidal. Even so, he isn't

adversarial. In fact, he seems
sympathetic to a son looking into
his father's death.

From our conversation, Chapman
explains he arrived at the scene
and interviewed the guard—the
shooter—Mariya Morozova. She was
a cool customer, giving only
short, one-word answers.
According to Chapman, her defense
of Sunningham was extraordinary—
less a firefight than an
execution.

He confirms the case was quickly
taken over by the Southeast
Region Terrorism Task Force. The
local force wasn't happy but
complied. Detective George
Fernsby, who had interviewed me,
was particularly outspoken about
the handover and was reprimanded.
He is now retired.

I ask who the residents of
Sunningham were, but Chapman has
no specifics. He also can't say
whether my father was
radicalized; he wasn't on the
case long enough to gather those
details.

Video is not in the police
report, and Chapman tells me I'll
never get it from BSG. They have
too many lawyers. He does
mention, however, that the police
collected a copy of video footage
from a Mr. Edward Kahn. A camera
on his home had a view of the
attack. If I can find him, I
might be able to get something.

Another useful detail: Detective
George Fernsby is apparently a
regular at the White Hart pub.
That may be my best chance to
speak with him.

Questions:
        How do I track Mariya
Morozova?
        Who is Edward Kahn, and
        does he still have the
        video?
        Does Detective Fernsby have
any answers?

June: Visit Charley Deegan.
I return to the Crown to find
Charley, the bartender, and see
if he has more information.
Charley knew my father, and he
saw him the night before the
incident. Turns out he's better
informed than I thought.

I show him the flyer from Crisis
Actors Ltd. His reaction is
immediate—he recognizes it.
According to Charley, a woman had
been going around to local pubs
looking for candidates. He
doesn't recall anyone else who
got involved—just my father and
his friends. He'd heard rumors of
others being approached, but
apparently only my father's group
took the bait, whatever the
scheme was.

Charley describes the woman.
Dressed sharply in a pencil
skirt, she wore dark oversized
sunglasses and a headscarf
holding in her hair. "She looked
like a celebrity," he said.
Probably a disguise.

She told them there was quick
money to be made under the table,
with the possibility of more work
down the line. They were hooked.
Charley says he was glad not to
get involved.

But as we talked, Charley started
acting coy—I could feel it. I
pressed him for anything else he
remembered, anyone else he

recalled being involved. He clammed up.

"I don't want to be involved," he said. "It's been almost ten years. Just let it go."

It feels like something is unsaid. He's hiding something.

Questions:
    Who is this woman
    recruiter?
    What is Charley hiding?

July: Interview Detective George Fernsby.

I finally tracked down Detective George Fernsby at the White Hart after several attempts. He looked like a shell of a man—possibly dealing with medical issues. He sat drinking alone, only a handful of patrons around. Yet even in decline, he hadn't lost his bluster.

Once he realized who I was, he turned dismissive. Told me I was lucky to even be in this country. He was an easy character to push; most like him are. I knew from Chapman that he was retired, and

I hoped he didn't have any mates
in the room to back him up.

I started by asking why he failed
to investigate. How did such a
"smart" man not solve this case?
When he claimed it had been taken
from him, I pressed harder. Told
him he was full of excuses. Lazy—
or incompetent.

I told him he could have kept
going, that he could have found
answers if he'd tried. Instead,
he left it to other, more capable
men and women.

I added that I'd heard they ran
him off the force—that he was
nothing but a drunk and a blight
on society. That set him off.
I'll admit, I enjoyed a bit of
payback for the way he'd treated
my mother and me.

But I wasn't there just to needle
him. This entire investigation
had ended in nothing, and I
needed answers.

That's when he snapped back: "You
people are always protected. I've
seen this before."

I pushed him. "What did he mean?" He said the same thing had happened to a fellow officer in Lancashire—always the government stepping in before the men on the ground could get answers.

"I would have had this solved, given the chance," he muttered, still bitter.

He kept raging, but nothing else useful came out. A few of the other patrons were starting to take notice, and I knew if the police were called, justice might come at the end of a baton.

Bluster or not, it was clear I wasn't going to get anything more from this fuming man. I stood, leaving him to his anger. He was still railing about immigrants taking his job as I walked out. I don't intend to speak with him again—and I was glad to be done with him.

❖❖❖

Bram feels like he's wading through mud—progress is slow, with no real sense of accomplishment. Everything stays hidden behind a veil, and the frustration of his investigation weighs heavily on him.

Two steps forward, one step back. Each small truth

uncovers only more questions. He's moving forward, but toward what, he still can't see.

Yet he refuses to stop. Determination drives him—the need to solve this mystery, for himself and for his father.

One step leads to the next. And always, David's words echo in his mind.

CHAPTER FOURTEEN

UNDISCLOSED CITY, EUROPE
2017

Neshad steps off the train as the doors slide shut behind him. A quick glance left, then right—no one else disembarks. Without hesitation, he sprints up the stairs from the platform and crosses to the other side. As the next train pulls in and begins to depart, he boards, staying sharp, scanning for any signs of a tail.

This is his third circuit. Four stops later, he disembarks, hails a cab, then abruptly orders the driver to drop him at a crowded shopping plaza. He keeps his pace measured, watching storefront windows for reflections of anyone who might be following. Ducking into a dress shop, he slips out the rear exit and continues on foot.

Flying directly back to Tel Aviv would've been faster, he admits to himself.

But speed isn't the priority—staying clean is.

Neshad understands the critical importance of this SDR (surveillance detection route). Operational security is paramount, especially today.

His destination is an industrial park. He boards a bus, disembarks several blocks before the site, and walks the rest of the way. The barren sidewalk stretches ahead, flanked by warehouses, quiet, with only the low rumble of lorries making deliveries. CCTV cameras track his every step, ensuring no one could tail him undetected in this desolate environment.

As he approaches the building, he spots the signal—a streetlamp burning brightly in the middle of the day. Final confirmation: he's clear.

The structure is unremarkable, a windowless warehouse indistinguishable from the others surrounding it. Neshad steps inside, surrendering his computer, cell phone, and smartwatch at the entrance. Stripped of every digital tether, he carries only the files he came to review.

He is escorted to a secure room—an impenetrable box within a box, mounted on industrial springs to eliminate vibration. The walls are coated with noise-canceling material, with the faint hum of static filling the air. No notes are permitted; he will be searched thoroughly before leaving.

This is a SCIF: a Sensitive Compartmented Information Facility. A fortress of intelligence, designed to ensure the most critical secrets remain safe from interception. A sanctuary for information—the Holy of Holies, the sanctum sanctorum of espionage.

Mossad maintains only a handful of such facilities worldwide. The intelligence reviewed here is guarded with unrelenting vigilance, the stakes often measured in lives. For operatives like Neshad, stepping inside carries an unspoken promise: to protect the assets within, even at the cost of their own life.

Neshad pores over the file in front of him. The agent's codename: KNOLL. Their real identity? Still a mystery, even to him. All he knows is that KNOLL remains one of Israel's most valuable assets—embedded nearly half a century inside hostile territory. The sheer dedication it must take to maintain such a cover for so long humbles him.

The latest intelligence from KNOLL offers no fresh revelations. Their caution, however, is part of what has kept them alive. Every scrap of information is calculated, designed to protect sources and methods as carefully as their own identity.

The operation they've flagged is codenamed SEMYA—a name so secret it is never spoken outside the SCIF. Its purpose remains elusive. What is clear is that it is not new; it has been active for years, growing, shifting, adapting. KNOLL's persistence suggests SEMYA is significant—perhaps more so than anyone realizes.

One name keeps surfacing: Mariya Morozova. But is she a key architect of this operation, or just a minor piece on a much larger board?

Direct contact with KNOLL is out of the question. Communications are sporadic, deliberately delayed to minimize risk. It frustrates Neshad—he finds it hard to accept. The margin for error is razor-thin. Still, a thought nags at him: *what if KNOLL has been compromised? What if the intel is deliberate misdirection?*

KNOLL's recruitment predates Neshad's tenure. Can there really be no handler in place, no direct oversight? It's rare, unsettling even, but it's the reality he inherited. Emergency protocols must exist—code phrases, crash meetings—but activating them would mean taking a massive gamble. And KNOLL hasn't failed them yet. For now, he waits.

But waiting does not mean inaction. Neshad needs answers, and his instinct has always been to move first, to act. With actionable intelligence scarce, he feels compelled to launch his own operation. If KNOLL can't deliver the truth, then Neshad will find another way.

Mariya Morozova remains in his crosshairs, but she's still out of reach. Neshad keeps nudging the Americans, feeding them signals to keep their interest alive. He knows, though, that without solid intel their attention will inevitably drift to other threats.

Then there's Bram—a wildcard. Neshad keeps him at arm's length, yet he sees the potential. If he can steer Bram in the right direction, the boy might uncover the answers no one else can.

The question still gnaws at him. A question KNOLL has never answered.

What the hell is SEMYA—and what are they planning?

CHAPTER FIFTEEN

RAYA FULFILLS DON'S ADMONITION AND graduates in June. By August, she's stepping through the gates of CIA Headquarters in Langley. The Agency wastes no time.

Her first days mirrored those of countless recruits—orientation sessions, policy briefings, endless lectures on organizational history and core principles. At a glance, it could almost pass for onboarding at any large corporation.

Almost—except for the relentless undercurrent: patriotism. Not the abstract kind found in textbooks, but the drilled, uncompromising demand for loyalty.

What Raya doesn't realize is that her training isn't only about preparing her for the job. Unlike the rest of her class, she is under quiet, constant scrutiny. Every exercise, every test, is designed not just to sharpen her skills but to probe her allegiance. Is she simply an ambitious young recruit—or a piece in a larger game the Agency has yet to expose?

The initial lessons strip away any illusions of glamour. Most of the work is tedious, slow-moving, and often leads nowhere. But when an operation succeeds—no matter how small their role—every officer is expected to take pride in the result.

From the very beginning, Raya is subjected to more testing than she anticipated. Polygraphs establish her baseline responses and probe for deception. Psychological evaluations measure her stability, resilience, and the traits the Agency might exploit—for good or ill. Physical assessments push her in oxygen labs, measuring VO_2 max, metabolic rate, and endurance.

Then came the development of her cover. Her new position at Orava International Relief was more than a front—it was a tool. One she would need to sharpen quickly. On paper, it suited her: humanitarian work, foreign aid, high mobility. But the assignment gnawed at her. Being embedded in a relief organization felt hypocritical. She wanted to do good. Using that goodwill as camouflage felt like a betrayal.

Maybe she could tell herself *there was a way to do both*. But she knew better. She cut the thought short, scolding herself. *Stop it. Focus.*

They waste no time putting it to use, performing covert background checks. This is when the real unease sets in. The agency digs into her past—speaking to her classmates, her professors, even her former colleagues at East Penn Legal Services. They ask about her father, her mother, and even Masha.

All the while, Raya wonders what they're saying about her. And more unsettling still—why does she have the gnawing sense that something is wrong, even if she can't yet name what it is?

✦✦✦

Her training shifts east to Chantilly, Virginia, to the CIA University (CIAU). Here, she finds herself in familiar surroundings—back in a classroom setting. The only difference is that her dorm is a hotel room.

The pace is relentless. There are no easy classes. Instructors drill her in the art of conveying information precisely and dispassionately, teaching her to write reports the CIA way—concise, factual, stripped of emotion. Her language skills are tested in rapid-fire dialogues with seasoned experts, each exchange designed to expose flaws and force mistakes. There are no praises, no reassurances—only evaluation, constant and unyielding.

They push her analytical skills with complex, morally ambiguous case studies. Group discussions follow, deliberately structured to provoke conflict. Her classmates are all alphas, each determined to come out on top. Every exercise ends the same way—more assessments, more scrutiny.

She learns how to conduct interviews, detect deception, and apply coercion when necessary. The goal is simple: results. She studies the motivations that drive potential targets—whether financial, ideological, or rooted in personality traits like pride, greed, or over-inflated egos.

Some lessons surprise her. The CIA encourages meditation, a practice she hadn't expected but instinctively embraces.

She draws on the techniques she learned from Mr. Riku Tanaka back in Sunningham—a life that now feels like a distant memory. Meditation helps her silence the noise, focus her mind, and process the relentless pressure of training.

Evenings and weekends are spent in small-group exercises. Instructors push them to work together, testing who can balance individual initiative with collaboration. Raya watches others struggle, but she feels herself growing stronger. With each challenge, her confidence deepens. For the first time in a long while, she feels exactly where she should be.

CHAPTER SIXTEEN

MAIDENHILL, ENGLAND, UK
2017

BRAM REFUSES TO GIVE UP. Progress sometimes comes from unexpected places—a passing remark, a forgotten detail in a file, a chance encounter with someone who knows more than they're willing to admit. He widens his net, searching for new angles.

One step leads to the next.

The Journal of Bram Vidal

<u>August</u>: The wives of Billy and Alfie.

I finally manage to arrange a meeting with the wives of Billy Pussett and Alfie Reid—Dad's two mates, also killed during the shooting. Nearly ten years have passed, but for both women the emotions are still raw.

Gloria Pussett drifts between
withdrawal and sudden bursts of
energy. The spurts, though rare,
can be useful, but just as often
they're confusing.

Ronna Reid proves more open, even
helpful. She has carried enormous
pain but has moved forward with
her life. Still, she's the one
who insisted on bringing Gloria
along. Clearly, she's a good
friend.
Ronna hosted us at her home, and
as she poured tea, we reminisced.
The three of them had been good
mates—fun-loving, gregarious.
What the hell happened? Why was
there never a proper
investigation or outcome?
We spoke only briefly about the
mysterious woman who had
recruited them. Just the mention
of her unsettled Gloria. Both
women confirmed there had been
training, though the location
remained elusive. Ronna recalled
Alfie saying it was within an
hour's drive and near "some other
shooting." She admitted she
didn't know what that meant.

I asked about their husbands'
beliefs—had they been reading

online propaganda, expressing new
ideas, showing sudden changes in
behavior? Both insisted there had
been none of that. No signs. No
warnings. The only thing they
were "radical" about was Magpie
Union Football Club.

Talking with these women felt
strangely cathartic. But just as
I was about to leave, Gloria
asked a question that stopped me
cold.

"What about poor Leo?"

Who? It turns out Leo was also in
the group. Gloria said Billy told
her, but that Leo was erratic.
Then Gloria added, "It was just
odd that he would show up dead a
week later." Apparently, he liked
the bottle and the betting hall,
so who knew what really happened.
Still, that was new information.
It seemed the police never made
the connection, as no one ever
talked to them about it.

Neither woman had any additional
information to share, so I
departed.

Questions:

Where did they train?
Who is Leo, and what
happened to him?

September: Officer Lewis Chapman
Beginning to reach my
investigative limits, I reach out
to Officer Chapman. I hope that
if I give him specific questions,
he will help. I've reviewed my
notes and identified the areas
that feel most important. I want
to keep it simple. There are
hundreds of questions I could
ask, but I've boiled it down to
four.

1. Officer Chapman gave me
   the name of the security
   guard during the attack,
   Mariya Morozova. But I
   have no further
   information about her.
   Was she simply doing her
   job, or was she directly
   involved? The
   professional precision
   of the killings suggests
   there may be more to her
   story.
2. The van feels like an
   underappreciated clue.
   Where did it come from?
   Was it rented, stolen,

or purchased? There must be a trail—some record tying the vehicle back to the case.

3. Where did they train? Ronna mentioned the site was within an hour's drive and near another shooting. I need help narrowing this down.

4. Who was Leo? According to the wives, he was part of the group and died a week later, but I need details. Did he ever speak with the police—and if not, why?

Officer Chapman said I had made good progress, but he didn't think the questions would lead anywhere. There was no way the security guard was involved. The van, he insisted, would reveal nothing. And as for the training site—why would it matter where they trained?

He was more interested in Leo and said he would investigate it.

October: Track Masha and Raya through Ligia Garcia.

I reviewed my notes and decided to dig deeper into Masha and Raya. I didn't have their last names, but I knew the lead had come from Ligia Garcia.

At SIS, we had a trick for tracking people down when serving subpoenas. People often hid from agents, but their online footprint could still give us access to their daily routines.

So, I created a fake Facebook account under the name of a Spanish expat living in the UK. I sent a friend request to Ligia. She accepted without hesitation. Through Ligia's updates and photos from her visits home to Spain, I found several shots of Sunningham. From them, I pieced together details about her life there—caring for the children who were her wards. More importantly, I learned about Raya Rogers. An expat, she had returned to America after her time in Britain. A young woman now in the U.S., attending college. There was nothing about Masha, but Raya was a lead.

Questions:

> How could I talk with Raya
> Rogers? How would I
> approach her?
> Could Raya lead me to
> Masha?
> Could Masha be Mariya
> Morozova?

<u>November</u>: Find the training site.
Officer Chapman called to say
they may have located the
training site. The area wasn't
private property, but rather a
secluded track in the woods.
According to a report, the local
constable ran off some kids
partying there. When Chapman read
the details—an isolated spot with
an old shack and bullet casings—
he realized it could match.

He instructed me to look for an
old dirt road about half a mile
before the entrance to the Old
Guard Rifle Club. Ronna had
recalled Alfie mentioning they
trained "near some other
shooting." This lined up
perfectly.

When I arrived to meet Officer
Chapman, the site was deserted.
The setup was unusual—someone had
built a mock-up of the Sunningham

guard gate. Chapman explained
they found some old brass strewn
around the site. Some of the
recovered casings were from live
rounds, while others were blanks.
All noise, no bullet. It didn't
make sense.

Seeing the structure up close, I
was struck by how closely it
resembled the one in Sunningham.
The base was poured concrete,
sturdy and intact, but the roof
was riddled with holes and
practically collapsing. The lower
section showed only minor damage.
Whoever fired here had focused
their shots high.

We circled the site, but found no
further clues. I admitted to
Chapman that I couldn't make
sense of what had happened here.
He had no explanation either.

December: Revisit Charley Deegan.
I found out about Leo before
Officer Chapman. I wanted to
press Charley—he had always been
evasive, and maybe he knew more.

When I walked into the Crown, he
saw me right away. His eyes
dropped, and he shuffled down to

the far end of the bar. He was
avoiding me.

I called him on it, told him he
seemed upset about being left
out—but I could sense there was
more behind it.

He started talking about my mum,
Gill. Turns out he'd dated her
before my dad, and he was clearly
still smitten. He admitted he
regretted not going to the
funeral but said it would have
raised too many questions. He
hadn't wanted to be a burden,
hadn't wanted to answer anything.
I pushed him, kept at it. Told
him that—for Gill's sake—this was
his chance to help. I thought it
was about being excluded by the
boys.
I was wrong.

Before I could ask, Charley
surprised me by bringing up Leo
Fraley (I finally had a last
name). He said Leo had been
scared. Then Charley asked if I
knew Leo was murdered.

He told me the story: after the
attack, Leo came to him in a
panic. He said he'd missed the

text from the woman they called
Hilde (Charley wasn't sure if it
was her first or last name). He'd
missed his chance to take part,
and he knew she'd be angry.
According to Leo, Hilde was a
hard woman.

Leo had described her as
extremely secretive—she never
appeared without dark glasses.
She trained them at a site
somewhere to the southwest, deep
in the woods, a place I now knew.
She put them through their paces.
They learned firearms, but she
insisted on loading every weapon
herself.
They were given black camouflage
gear and taught to act like
terrorists—screaming things like
"Jihad!" They all thought it was
ridiculous.

According to Leo, it was all for
show. The purpose was to stage an
attack as part of a training
exercise, supposedly to help
prepare first responders. It was
meant to be a regular business,
and they believed they were on
the good side.

She had provided the van, telling
them she would send instructions
through a self-destructing
messaging app called Confide.
That alone should have been a red
flag. When she was ready, they
were to pick up the van and drive
to an address she would provide.

Leo, drunk from the night before,
slept through the text. He missed
his opportunity. When he later
heard about the attack, he went
into hiding. He even asked
Charley to put him up, but
Charley refused. Leo admitted it
had all made sense to him at the
time—but once he realized what
had happened, he knew it was a
scam.

A week later, they found Leo in
an alley. Covered in grime,
living rough, his throat slashed.
According to Charley, the police
dismissed it as a random crime
and never connected the dots.
Charley has been living with that
knowledge ever since, wondering
if the woman they called Hilde
had been the one to kill him.

I relayed Leo Fraley's story to
Officer Chapman, but I left
Charley's name out of my report.

Bram sits alone in his apartment, the soft glow of streetlights slipping through the blinds. Christmas has come and gone. No one to celebrate with. The silence presses in, thick and unrelenting, forcing him to sit with his thoughts.

Has it really been more than a year since my mother's death?

He stares at the blank walls, his mind drifting back over the years. *What if things had been different?* The question lingers, but brings no comfort. Bram isn't bitter—not exactly—but beneath it all, he is angry.

Angry at his father for reckless mistakes. Angry at his mother for leaving when he needed her most. Angry at Hilde and whomever she worked for—their actions casting a long shadow over his life. And angry at the police, whose incompetence let everything spiral so badly out of control.

He reaches for a pad of paper, his hand steady as he scrawls a simple note—a promise to himself: he will figure this out and find those responsible.

Life has thrown more at him than most could bear, but Bram has survived it all. He has learned to draw strength from the struggle, to keep moving forward even when the path ahead is shrouded in doubt.

Now, as he folds the note and tucks it away, he can only hope that strength will carry him to the end—to the truth, to the answers that have eluded him for so long.

Bram, his expression unreadable, steps into David's office without knocking. At the sound of the door, David hastily minimizes his computer screen.

Strange. David has never hidden anything from me.

"What are you working on?" Bram asks.

David doesn't meet his eyes. "Just some personal business."

Bram studies him, unconvinced. Ever since their conversation the previous year, he's been cautious around David—choosing his words carefully, keeping his own counsel.

I need to be my own man.

David looks up from his desk, a faint smile forming—as if to soften the moment—but it fades quickly when he sees Bram shaking his head slowly, deliberately.

Bram isn't smiling. His voice is calm but firm. "Might be time for me to speak with our friend."

David pauses, reading between the lines, then nods. "I'll let him know," he says evenly. "It may take some time."

CHAPTER SEVENTEEN

VIRGINIA, USA
2018

THE CIA GIVES RECRUITS A FEW days over the holidays to visit their families—to practice their cover stories. Each one must learn how to deflect questions, avoid missteps, and refine their legends.

Raya frames her training as just another academic program, carefully polishing the details. She tells her father she'll soon be traveling to Sofia for an international conference, working with OIR to promote reforms in the Balkans.

"Thanks, Dad. I'll be swamped—workshops, translations, endless meetings. And with all the travel, it'll be hard to connect. You probably won't hear from me much."

"I'm sure cell phones still work," Phil replies, doubt edging into his voice. "But you know best."

She feels his skepticism.

Masha is even more probing, but Raya keeps her answers vague—mentally noting the questions, then pushing the worry aside.

"That's terrific!" Masha gushes. "Where are you staying? What airline are you flying? Who will be there?"

"I don't have all the details yet," Raya replies evenly. "OIR's travel services are handling everything."

It surprises Raya how quickly Masha seems satisfied. It feels strangely out of character. Normally, Masha is sharper, more probing. Instead, she seems caught up in how OIR might boost Raya's career.

None of it matters for now. Raya reminds herself to stay focused. The next phase is coming. She's heard whispers among recruits about "going south." No phones. Strict operational security.

The real training is about to begin—in southern Virginia.

Heading south doesn't mean a scenic trip to Colonial Williamsburg, where tourists stroll through a living museum of America's plantation past. It isn't a carefree visit to Busch Gardens, with its roller coasters and faux-European charm. Raya is heading somewhere very different—an old pig farm.

Camp Peary sits along the York River, a tributary feeding into the Chesapeake Bay. Legend has it that after World War II, the camp commander decided to raise hogs on base—an ill-advised private venture on government property. The pigs are long gone, but the nickname stuck. To this day, the CIA's elite training ground is known simply as the Farm.

For Raya, this is it—the real thing. Not everyone makes it through. Washouts happen. Probationary periods are sometimes cut short. Some recruits are injured, even killed. But for those who survive the gauntlet of the initial training, the moment of arriving at the Farm is a milestone—a rite of passage.

This is where the world of spy novels and Hollywood thrillers comes to life. Raya trains in the art of clandestine operations: bump passes, dead drops, bolt-holes, and signal sites. She learns how to plant a bug—and how to know when someone has planted one on her. She learns to track a target, whether working solo or as part of a team, and how to vanish when the tables turn. Weapons handling, evasive driving, emergency exfiltration—the skills pile up, each more demanding than the last. Above all, they drill her relentlessly in operational security.

Richmond becomes their testing ground. Simulated surveillance exercises push recruits to think on their feet. They practice counter-surveillance, navigating the city while hunting for watchers—or trying to shake them. Each scenario grows more complex, laced with loyalty tests, moral ambiguity, and split-second choices. The scrutiny never stops.

She learns the recruitment cycle—the deliberate, methodical dance of spotting, assessing, developing, and ultimately controlling an asset. She studies the secret lives people lead: their hidden guilt, their shame, their pressure points. How to find them. How to use them. And perhaps most unsettling of all—how to confront her own secret self.

For some recruits, it's overwhelming. Task saturation, they call it. But for Raya, it feels natural, almost inevitable—like she's been preparing for this her entire life. In a way, she has. Masha. Her father. Both agents of a sort. She just doesn't know it.

Yet even amid the grueling pace, she hears whispers of something more. Something beyond the standard curriculum. Enhanced training.

Upon arrival, each recruit received three pieces of information: a name, a place, and a date. No explanations. No context. A computer randomly generated and assigned these details. It was their job to keep these secrets—never to be shared.

Throughout the training, instructors tested them—sometimes casually, sometimes aggressively. Who's your contact? What's the location? When's your next meeting? The recruits learned never to answer, no matter the circumstances, no matter the pressure. They were being conditioned and desensitized for the real test.

Raya is in Richmond, deep into an SDR exercise—one of the longest and most punishing of her training. For hours, she moves through the city under cover of darkness, working to evade three other recruits assigned to hunt her. The operation stretches across alleyways, bus terminals, footbridges, and service corridors. Every sound feels amplified. Every passerby might be a watcher. The pressure never lets up.

It isn't until 0300 hours that she finally feels clear—no tails, no signals, just silence and the heavy pulse in her ears.

After reporting to the instructor, she returns to her room. She's spent—mentally and physically drained from hours of vigilance. She sets her alarm with unsteady fingers, kicks off her boots, and climbs into bed.

Sleep claims her instantly—dark, dreamless, absolute.

By 0430 hours, they place a hood over her head and frog-march her out of the building. They throw her into a van, hands cuffed, feet bound. The drive feels endless. Eventually, the adrenaline fades, and she drifts into sleep.

When she wakes, she is naked in a cool, damp cell, lying on an old, moldy pad. The only light filters through the doorjamb. She can just make out a bucket in the corner and a dirty shift lying on the floor. She slips it on and thinks—*and so it begins.*

The chill in the cell deepens, pulling her toward unconsciousness. But each time she begins to nod off, powerful lights blaze on, strobing for several minutes. *I'm being watched.*

She loses track of time. Guards push food through a narrow slit at the bottom of the cell door. She eats it all—briny water and dry bread. *Eat what they give you. Force it down.*

Raya finds a grimy stone in the wall and scratches a mark with her fingernail. *Day 1.*

She has a job. First: survive. Then, escape. She will dole out information slowly, knowing everyone eventually breaks. Start slow, she tells herself. Look for a crack. Watch the guards. Track their patterns. Spot their weakness. Remember everything. *Survive first.*

They finally come for her and lead her into a brightly lit room. Intimidating white subway tiles line the walls—clean, sterile, merciless. A tray of instruments rests under a cloth cover. A drain gapes in the center of the floor. Strapped to a chair, she cannot move. The stuff of nightmares.

A large, burly man enters, his face hidden behind a balaclava.

"Who's your contact?"

She thinks he looks like a fat ninja. "I don't have a contact. I'm a translator for OIR."

He slaps her hard across the face.

"What's the location?"

"Location of what? What are you talking about?"

He forces her head down, pressure grinding into her spine.

"Don't fuck with me. What's the date of the meeting?"

Raya realizes this is more than she expected. Who are you? What do you want? Her rational mind insists they can only do so much, that it can only last so long. *I just have to outlast them.*

Back in her cell, she meditates—the only tool in her arsenal. Another tray slides through the slot. She eats everything. I need calories. She makes a scratch on the stone to count another day. To her surprise, there are already two marks. She doesn't remember making the second. Convinced she must have misremembered, she adds a third. Day 3.

By Day 5, Raya is unraveling. Confusion and exhaustion blur the edges of her reality. Her mind drifts between memory and fiction, her own narrative twisting with fragments of books she's read and movies she's seen. Colors pulse unnaturally bright; sounds slice through the air with razor-sharp clarity. When she moves her hand in front of her face, trails of light linger in its wake. She knows she's losing her grip, but she can't fight it. *How long can this last?*

By Day 8, she is broken. The fat ninja—as she has come to call him in her mind—crouches in front of her. His voice is casual, almost bored.

"Who's your contact?"

Raya blinks. No defenses left. No walls to hide behind. The answer slips from her lips before she can stop it.

She braces for the next blow, the next demand—but instead, what he asks makes no sense.

"Who does Masha work for?"

Raya frowns, her mind struggling to grasp the question. Masha?

"She works for some security company?" she answers hesitantly.

The ninja's eyes narrow. "Is she a spy?"

The words make no sense. Raya lets out a weak laugh—the kind that escapes when the world stops making sense. "A spy? For what?"

"What is her mission? Where was she trained?"

"I don't know what you're talking about. Masha is no spy."

Silence. The ninja studies her, his gaze sharp, unreadable.

"How are you helping her?"

She stares back, her exhausted mind searching desperately for meaning. "Helping her? Helping her do what?"

Raya does not know how long the questions last. Back in her cell, she tries to meditate, but she is past any level of concentration—existing on autopilot. *What is she missing?* Even her addled mind knows this is bizarre.

What she knows and doesn't know blend together... ideas born of hidden knowledge just beyond her grasp... a secret self... known only to Masha. She is losing her mind. She suddenly wishes she knew her mother.

The next day, the questioning continues. Her tormentors have been changing the scratches on the rock. Raya thinks it is Day 9, but it has only been four days.

CHAPTER EIGHTEEN

WASHINGTON D.C., USA
2018

TWO PIZZAS AND A SIX-PACK of beer are Fred's idea of a working dinner. Because Sam ordered the food, she has a salad. Fred doesn't notice.

Fred is pontificating. "Do you know how many people have security clearance in the U.S.?"

"About four million, I think," replies Sam.

"Yes, but only around a million have top-secret access. Half a percent of American adults. Seems small, but it isn't."

"No, sir." Sam knows saying anything more would only fire him up.

"All our adversaries need to do is find one and convince them to turn—for money, for ego, whatever. We have over a thousand active investigations, just a fraction of what must be the total. Do you think we'll catch them?"

"No, sir." *This is the paranoia that affects them all*, thinks Sam.

Don comes in and takes a seat. "Either way, you take the

blame, so you might as well take your shots."

"You're right about that—I do. They're everywhere. Even friendly governments harbor unfriendly spies. Dangles, doubles, and false-flag operations lurk around every damn corner."

"Job security," Don offers with a smirk.

Fred ignores him. "We use persistence. We build capabilities. We try to draw in our own, look to turn theirs, watch for mistakes, cross-check and cross-check again. With all we do, we must fail a lot. I'm tired of it."

He's on a roll, thinks Sam.

Don knows there is nothing else to add and simply nods.

They all sit in silence for a minute or two before Fred turns to him. "Is Raya still in the hole?"

"Yep," says Don.

Fred senses Don's frustration. "What have we learned? It was inspired to repurpose the simulation. You deserve credit?"

"Nothing. She knows nothing. I don't want any credit." Don is angry at himself.

"You're probably right, but don't punish yourself. We need to make hard choices. Did she hold out long?" Fred asks.

"Better than most. The drugs we added to her food didn't make it easier. Maybe there's another way she can lead us to Mariya Morozova. You never wanted to use Raya's father, Phil, to get to Masha. Why not?"

Fred replies, "He's not trained, and I think he's cooked. He might not keep it together. Raya is stronger."

Sam smiles.

"I still want you to test her. Take her out into the

wilderness. See what lurks in her brain. Fill her with some of your wisdom."

Fred and Don both know that getting into someone's head takes a close connection—time spent together under stress. They have the physical and mental scars to prove it.

"She's going to be pissed after what we put her through. Am I the best choice? I recruited her."

"Hmmph." Sam snorts, reminding them both that she made first contact.

Fred isn't convinced. "You might be surprised. She'll have questions... see if you can guide her down the golden path. Be there when she comes out."

They release Raya from the cell after five days. The lawyers in Langley insist this is as far as they can push any recruit. Medics take her to Medical for a complete checkup and give her an IV for hydration. Then they let her sleep. They don't put any limitations on the time—every recruit recovers differently.

Following a debrief and an interview with a psychologist, they permit Raya to return to her room. Doctors have given her a clean bill of health—she will rejoin her training after a few days.

Raya assesses her feelings. She knows this is something she can face and is proud she handled it. Memories, now foggy, of the interrogation confuse her. So many unanswered questions. She'll worry about that another day. The expressions on the staff tells her all she needs to know. She is one of them now. She has survived the crucible.

As she approaches the dormitory, she sees Don sitting on

a bench outside the front door, waiting for her. Suddenly, Raya feels overwhelmed with emotion. She misses her father and wishes she could speak with him.

Don steps toward her and gently wraps his arms around her. Raya doesn't resist. She's crying now—finally letting go of everything she's been holding in all week.

He's seen this before. He felt it himself, years ago.

"It's important to know what could happen," he says softly. "This was just a taste."

"I know," she murmurs through tears.

"Didn't you want to be a secret agent?"

"I never said that," Raya blubbers.

"Well... do you?"

"Maybe."

He gives her a light squeeze, then steps back enough to meet her eyes.

"Then we need to figure out your special powers."

She nods, still sniffling.

"The only way to do that," he says, a smile tugging at the corner of his mouth, "is on the road. Want to go on a field trip?"

CHAPTER NINETEEN

MAIDENHILL, ENGLAND, UK
2018

SPRING HAS YET TO ARRIVE, but as so often happens, winter grants an early reprieve. A warm, clear spell settles over the town, a brief taste of what's to come. Bram takes full advantage of the day—the kind of day that calls for a leisurely walk along the River Thames.

Here, before the river winds its way through Windsor, snakes through London, and eventually spills into the Channel, it is the very picture of idyllic England. Trees shade the path, gently rustling in the breeze, while the Queen's swans glide gracefully along the water, dotting its surface.

Dragonwick Lock, a favored stopping point for locals and visitors alike, buzzes with quiet charm, offering fish and chips to those enjoying the scenery. Nearby, Bram spots Neshad. Without breaking stride, he makes his way over and falls into step beside him, their movements synchronized, as though they were old friends meeting for a casual chat and a bit of exercise.

The world feels serene—the steady rhythm of their steps mirrors the unhurried flow of the river. Bram updates Neshad, unaware that Neshad is already well-informed. He needs Bram to follow the clues on his own, to uncover his own answers.

"You've made good progress. What do you know?"

"I know my father wasn't a terrorist—just a dupe, an actor recruited to play a part. He must have thought he was doing something good. He certainly wasn't radicalized, and I'm pretty sure this has nothing to do with him being Jewish."

"Just a pawn in some wider conspiracy?"

"It makes no sense. Why shoot up a security shack?"

"No discernible motive? Why did the attack take place? Who benefited?" Neshad prods.

"I have no idea, and no way to find out."

"What about the woman—Hilde? She handed out the flyers, trained them."

"I don't even have a picture, but you're right—she was the start of this."

Neshad continues to press. "And you think Masha may be Mariya Morozova? Can you track her down? Seems like there's more to her story." He already knows who Masha is, but doesn't tell Bram.

"Maybe I can find her, through this girl, Raya. I was able to use her friend's Facebook."

"That was very creative. Good work. What else?"

"I know there was a video. A Mr. Kahn, who lives in Sunningham, has a security camera. The police said it showed the attack."

"Get the video."

"I could use some help. You said you would provide me with support." Bram feels exasperated. He wants to punch through Neshad's calm exterior.

"Yes, I did say that. But for my own reasons, I want this to come from you."

"So... nothing? No help?"

"I didn't say that. I need the help to come from sources that are not my own."

"What does that mean for me?" Bram is exhausted. He has reached his wit's end and wants to know what Neshad knows.

"I know a guy."

"Great—can he help?" Bram brightens.

"Yes. He certainly can help. His skills are essentially unlimited, but they come at a price."

"I thought you would cover the cost."

"Yes. Well, I will pay any monetary expense."

"But you said—"

Neshad cuts him off. "He's a kind of middleman. He has a vast network of helpers... and they can do extraordinary things. However, he's a complicated, eccentric person."

"When can I meet him?" Bram presses.

"Just listen for a moment—it doesn't work that way."

"How does it work?"

"First, he's freelance—very security-conscious. He'll contact you. Second, and this is important, he collects future considerations. Sometimes he calls them future boons. You'll need to agree."

"What are you talking about?"

"Like I said, he's eccentric. It's part of his fee. He'll expect you to repay the debt of his help."

"And I have to pay this myself?"

"With your help to him in the future. He takes it all very seriously. His sense of things is odd, but he's effective."

"Am I promising my soul to the devil? What if I don't comply?"

"No, nothing that exciting. He'll just stop helping—and he'll stop you from getting help anywhere else. His network is enormous."

"That doesn't sound too bad."

"Look, I may have made this sound more sinister than it is. But I want you to take it seriously. You need his help, so don't fuck this up."

"What's his name?"

"Who the hell knows his real name—but they call him Jynx."

A week later, Bram enters the office, exhausted. Business has been brisk for Surrey Investigative Solutions. The operation has grown over the past few years—and with it, so has Bram Vidal.

He spent the previous night on a stakeout and, that morning, delivered incriminating photos to their latest client. David has been giving him more work and more responsibility, but it's inconsistent. Sometimes David micromanages every step. Other times, he's nowhere to be found.

Bram isn't surprised when Adam, David's son, calls out, "There's a package for you."

Adam is finishing his final year at university, and David seems eager to bring him into the business. Adam mans the phones from time to time—especially lately, as David is away more often.

"Where's your dad?" Bram asks, reluctant to pry.

"Don't know. He said he had some things to take care of. Woke me up this morning and told me to open the office."

Strange. "Is everything okay with him?"

Adam doesn't seem concerned. "Sure. He gets this way sometimes—comes and goes."

Bram decides to let it go, though unease crawls at the edges of his thoughts. He walks to his desk, not expecting anything. A nondescript box wrapped in brown paper sits there. His name is scrawled across the top in block letters with a Sharpie.

He calls back to Adam. "Did this come in another box? There's no label or postage—just my name."

"Nope. It was sitting in front of the door this morning. No address, no stamp. Someone must have left it."

Bram's worry sharpens. If David were here, he'd never allow an unverified package inside. But Adam brought it in, not knowing better.

Cautiously, Bram approaches his desk. There's nothing to do now but look. He opens the box slowly. Inside lies a BlackBerry KEYone mobile phone. Bram recognizes it instantly—a specialized device, equipped with encrypted hardware and advanced security to prevent hacking.

Taped to the phone is a handwritten note:

Keep this phone charged, and with you at all times.
I will contact you through the Signal app.
Jynx.

PART V

ANSWERS BEGET QUESTIONS 2018

"Patience is the greatest of all virtues."

-Cato

CHAPTER TWENTY

BRAM IS DETERMINED TO GET out of his own way. Work has become exhausting, and the pressure he puts on himself to solve his father's case is taking its toll. He feels it—trouble sleeping, trouble focusing.

On Saturday morning, he heads into Windsor, hoping for a break. The streets are thick with tourists gathered to watch the changing of the guard. A regimental band plays as onlookers crane their necks for a glimpse.

But Bram can't settle. Other thoughts crowd his mind.

He walks down the hill along Thames Street toward Eton. On his left, shops and restaurants cater to the crowd. To his right, the high granite wall of the castle looms over the street.

At the bottom of the hill, he turns right toward the Home Park, where open fields stretch out beside the River Thames—a quiet place to think.

There he spots a group of men playing recreational cricket, the long, slow game perfect for a lazy afternoon. He decides to sit and watch.

Bram finds a large willow tree offering generous shade, and as he leans back against its trunk, he hears the sharp trill of a phone.

It takes him a moment to remember.

He fumbles in his backpack. He's been carrying the phone for a week, nearly forgetting it was there—until now. He pulls it out, unlocks it with the passcode, and taps the Signal app on the fourth ring.

"Well now, looks like you're in need of a bit of help."

"Hello? Who's this?" Bram asks.

"Ah, are ya soft in the head? It's Jynx. Who else would it be?"

"Sorry, you caught me off guard."

"Pull your head out of the sand, will ya?"

"Right... sorry about that. Can we meet?" Bram asks, eager to test the information Neshad gave him.

"You know how I do things. Didn't he lay it out for ya?"

Bram glances around, scanning for anyone nearby who might overhear. But he's alone.

"He did, but I'm still a bit confused. Can you go over it again?"

"Ah, Jaysus, I thought you were sharp. Didn't he say you were clever? You pullin' a Columbo on me now?"

"A what?" Bram knows exactly what he means but plays dumb.

"Never mind that. You and me—we never met, right? Here's how it works. I go by those in the know. Without 'em, I'm useless to you. But if I've got you in my pocket, I can sort some other poor fella's mess down the road. See?"

"All right... so the more I ask, the more I'll owe?"

"Stop makin' it sound harder than it is, for fuck's sake. I'll ask for a favour, and you'll do it. That's it."

"What kind of favours?"

Jynx breathes out slowly in frustration. "Might need a bit of info you've got and don't fancy givin' up. Might need a safe place for someone to kip—no questions asked. Or maybe I'll have you meet a lad and pick up somethin'. Whatever I ask, you'll sort it. Simple as that."

Bram hesitates. He's always prided himself on doing the right thing—or at least trying. But this feels... wrong. Worse, he'd have no say in it. It wouldn't even be his choice. He wants answers, but is this the way?

"Look, son," Jynx says, his tone softening a hair, "I've been at this a long while. Sometimes people like me solve problems when no one else can—or won't. That's the price. Feel guilty about it? Go light a candle at Mass. You're out of options, lad, so stop actin' arseways."

"How do you manage it, then?"

"I've me own rules, see? I don't live me life worryin' about things being banjaxed. I do what suits me—things that interest me. I don't rob things; that's small-time. Information? Sure, that belongs to everyone anyway. I don't cheat—the Good Lord's not fond of a liar. And I don't fight anyone bigger than me—though I'll tell ya, I'd be hard enough to find if someone tried."

Bram can't help a wry grin. "Can you teach me about this... world?"

"I'm not runnin' a charity, boy, but it's not a bad ask. Maybe you've the head for it, maybe not. But you're in the tall grass now, and you'll need someone watchin' your back. You need to get some supervision."

Bram decides he likes Jynx. For all his bravado, this is a man worth cultivating. He senses a sympathetic soul. How does one become a concierge to the dark side, a doorman to information?

"So, are we agreed? What do you need?" Jynx asks.

Bram fills him in on the details of his investigation. "Let's start basic. I want a picture of Hilde—last seen on a certain High Street ten years ago. I want the video from Mr. Kahn of Sunningham. And I'll need background on Raya Rogers and Mariya... Masha Morozova—what they do, where they live, contact information."

"Startin' small, yeah? A good start, but it'll take a bit of time. Let's see what turns up." Jynx has a soft spot for marginalized people. It was one reason he helped Neshad. And Bram was on the outside, trying to find his father's killer.

"Oh, and one more thing," Bram adds, a grin practically dripping off his words. "Can I call you Jeeves?"

"Ah, piss off." Jynx chuckles to himself, deciding he likes this one. "Don't be messin' with me now. I'll be in touch."

CHAPTER TWENTY-ONE

SOUTHERN GERMANY
2018

RAYA AND DON HITCH A ride on a C-17 Globemaster bound for Germany, packed tight with materials for U.S. European Command in Stuttgart. The space is cramped, but the trip offers the advantage of traveling incognito—not to mention saving a few dollars, which the accountants at Langley always appreciate. With luck, they won't be in the country for more than a few days. This is strictly an observational assignment.

Strapped into webbed seats along the fuselage, the ride is anything but first class. Neither of them complains. For Don, this is routine. For Raya, the thrill of getting out into the field overshadows any discomfort.

They try to talk over the roar of the engines, but conversation is impossible. Upon landing, they requisition a car and drive north toward Wiesbaden, home to the U.S. Army Europe and Africa headquarters. Nestled within the barracks— locally known as the Kaserne—is a clandestine CIA operations center.

It's still early in the day, but exhaustion weighs on them after traveling through the night. They're told to wait—nothing will happen until late evening. When the time comes, they'll get the call.

◆◆◆

They drive into Mainz; a city nestled along the Rhine River.

"Tell me more about this man," Raya says.

"His name is Oraz. His wife is Jeren. Don't worry about last names," Don replies. "He's connected to the 2016 coup attempt in Turkey. They've been on the run ever since. But the Turks are closing in, and Oraz is getting spooked. We've got word they'll try to exfiltrate from Albania soon. This is a chance for you to learn."

"We don't have a play. Why do we care?"

"There's a man living in upstate Pennsylvania. Turkey believes he orchestrated the coup. Oraz has a connection to him. They've tried to lure him back to Turkey—filed multiple extradition requests, maybe even an assassination attempt. Turkey could use Oraz to get to him. For now, we're on the sidelines. Turkey is... complicated for the U.S."

"Did this man orchestrate the coup?"

"That's beyond your remit. You're here only to observe."

"Who's bringing Oraz and Jeren out?"

"A group called the Nordic Centre for Freedom, runs out of Sweden. They help Turkish dissidents escape through the Balkans. Oraz and Jeren plan to seek asylum in Sweden—if they make it."

"Do they have the capability to run an operation like this?"

"We'll see. They have a few solid operators, but they're

limited. The Turkish government is using every method and tactic to bring their 'escaped enemies' home. They want to send a message."

Don and Raya wait for the call.

Walking through the old city of Mainz, time seems to slip away. Down narrow lanes and along cobblestoned streets, they pass through history.

Don offers, "I'll tell you a story. There was a man, and he had a good life. He was in the Army, on track, doing well. One day, a friend asked him for a favor. He needed some information. It was a small thing. So, the man helped."

"Sounds like a good friend," Raya says.

"A few weeks later, the friend asked for more. The man hesitated. But the friend pushed—offered money. The man's wife wanted a new car. He couldn't afford it. So, he took the money and helped again."

"So maybe not that good of a friend."

"It always starts small. A crack. An innocuous request. Then you're over the edge. Have as many vices as you want—lie, drink, cheat—but never get caught with your hand in the candy jar. The moment you take that first piece, they own you."

"Do you know this man?"

"No. But we'll see him soon. He's trying to escape Albania for the West. It'll be interesting to see if he makes it. I wonder if, given the chance, he'd still help his friend."

They wait for the call.

Along the Kirschgarten, they stop for dinner at the Brauhaus: schnitzel, an oversized pretzel, a quiet table. Conversation flows.

Raya finally brings up a question that's been nagging her. "Some strange questions came up during my simulated interrogation."

"What kind of questions?"

"About my friend Masha. If she's a spy."

Don deflects. "I don't know anything about that. Is she?"

"No," Raya says firmly.

"How would you know?" Don presses.

"I guess I don't. But she isn't, okay?"

"Okay. What about you? Is Raya your real name?"

"I'm not sure."

"Ah yeah... you came over from Russia... maybe your dad changed it?"

"Dad saved me. That's all I know." She doesn't know how he did it—only that he got her out of Russia, to the West, and to safety.

They talk, sharing stories. Raya tells him about the attack in Sunningham. She opens up.

And still, they wait for the call.

Later, they find a small stall serving rich, aromatic coffee. Both are running on fumes, awake for nearly two days. They sit, sip, and keep talking.

"So," Raya asks, "what happened to you? Why aren't you in the field?"

"I'm getting old, too old for real field work."

Raya doesn't buy it. "And?"

"Someone identified me."

"What does that mean? Are you on a hit list or something?"

"Here's the dirty secret: we're all known. Everyone knows

who the spies are—on every side. But we pretend not to. Until someone's outed. Then everyone acts surprised."

"And they say you're compromised. No longer a field officer."

"Exactly. When everyone knew all along. It's all Kabuki theater. We keep the veil on so the game can continue. But once that veil drops—your usefulness goes with it. Sometime soon, they'll nudge me toward retirement."

Raya nods.

Don's phone rings. He listens.

"Time to head back to the operations center. It'll begin in a few hours."

The room is dimly lit and cool. Don and Raya sit along the back wall in seats bolted to the floor. They are merely spectators. Ahead of them, three concentric arcs of desks with monitors—classroom style—all face two large projections: one with a map, the other with a live feed of the marina.

"Ten-hut." Everyone rises as the COMCAP enters the room. No names are given.

"Sitrep?"

"We have a Global Hawk prowling the Adriatic coast—no visuals on the package. Local contact reports they are en route to the port. They hope to board a cargo ship out of Durrës."

"And the ship?"

"The Aurora Star is still in berth. Visual confirmation of smoke in the stacks—they're preparing to depart."

"Advise when we have eyes."

As they sit in the back, watching, Don asks, "What do you

think will happen?"

"I don't know," Raya replies.

SITOPS reports, "Monitoring the chatter—confirmation package is traveling along the SH4, the *Rruga Pavaresia*."

"The Independence Road—how appropriate," whispers Don.

Raya turns to him. "I didn't know you spoke Albanian."

Don thinks *there's a lot you don't know about me.*

SITOPS reports, "We have visual, pulling up on the main feed now."

The main screen displays the video in night-vision green, the resolution precise and detailed. Two individuals travel in a battered Škoda Felicia—Oraz and Jeren—hoping to reach freedom.

"What do your instincts tell you?" Don asks.

"I don't know enough, but it feels like they lost their nerve—can't take it anymore. They're ripping off the band-aid."

Don nods. "You think they decided to make the run? Take the risk?"

"Maybe. My gut tells me they won't make it. This feels wrong."

"That feeling needs to be your special skill. You can be action-oriented, detail-oriented, cautious, smart, or quick—but above all, you need to be right. Every agent has to feel the Op, feel the street, feel the moment, and trust their instincts. You need to find your intuition."

"Can you train for that?"

"Nope. But if you don't find it, you won't last long."

SITOPS reports, "We have two cars traveling toward the

package at high speed."

The video widens, the field of view increases. Two Mercedes close the distance.

"Analysis. Can they make the port before they are intercepted?" COMCAP orders.

"Negative. They will be overtaken," reports DATACOM.

They all watch as the two cars pull alongside the Škoda. The camera zooms in. Raya sees the determination on Oraz's face—hands gripping the wheel, eyes forward. She thinks about the hope and fear he must be feeling.

One of the pursuers pulls ahead of the Škoda, clipping its front bumper. At the same moment, the second car rams it from behind, sending the Škoda into a spin and off the road. The lead Mercedes speeds away, but the second lingers. A series of bright flashes erupts from its front end—moments later, the Škoda's gas tank explodes.

They all watch the screen in silence.

SITOPS reports, "We are picking up cellular traffic. Local motorists are calling the accident in to the police. Reporting two charred bodies."

More silence.

SITOPS reports, "Police on the scene. Reports indicate a car crashed into a barrier at high speed and exploded. Two DOA."

More silence.

SITOPS reports, "Visual on the Aurora Star. Mooring lines cast off. Departing berth, heading for open sea."

More silence.

Finally, COMCAP announces, "I'm calling it. Stand down."

They all rise as he departs through a side door.

Raya stares out the window as they drive to the base for a flight home. The ride back to Stuttgart is dark, and the weight of what they witnessed presses on her.

Without really thinking, she says, "They wanted to be free."

When Don doesn't respond, she presses. "Do you ever think about it? What would it feel like to be... completely free?"

Don lets out a dry laugh. "Free? That's a fairytale, Raya. Freedom's a word people toss around because it sounds noble. It doesn't exist."

"You don't believe in it at all?"

"My whole life, someone's been pulling the strings—a boss, a government, events, circumstance. Hell, even your own secrets control you. People fight like hell for freedom, but it's rarely real. There's always something—or someone—dictating what you do next."

Raya speaks quietly. "That's a bleak way to live."

"Maybe. Or maybe it's honest. The trick isn't chasing freedom—it's figuring out which leash you can live with."

Raya falls silent, turning Don's words over in her mind. He's right—*true freedom is impossible. But independence... her thoughts, her decisions... no one can ever take those away.*

CHAPTER TWENTY-TWO

MAIDENHILL, ENGLAND, UK
2018

BRAM WALKS INTO THE RESTAURANT with his parents, the warmth of the moment settling around him like a familiar embrace. They are close, brimming with the joy that comes from shared success. In his hands, he clutches his diploma—he's just graduated from college.

They take their seats, laughter and celebration filling the space. His father lifts his glass for a toast, his mouth forming words Bram can't quite hear. A strange buzzing noise. He tries to speak, but no words come.

He turns to his mother—suddenly, he's somewhere else. The hard bench of a police van presses against him. Cold metal walls. The familiar, suffocating weight of panic. He knows this place.

He looks back—his father is gone. His mother has disappeared. He is still alone.

Bram jolts awake, his breath sharp in the darkness. He reaches for his phone. A text from Jynx. He has an update. Bram connects to the Signal app, his pulse still racing from the dream.

Jynx has set up a voice-only conference call; the screen remains dark. Bram leans back, eyes on the black void, wondering—again—what Jynx actually looks like. A shadow with a voice.

"You're a right pain in me arse, y'know that? These things ye ask for weren't easy."

"Tell me it was worth waking up for," Bram mutters.

Jynx lets out a breath. "Oh, it's worth it, right. Shake yer head awake, will ya? D'ya wanna know or not?"

"Tell me."

"First up—I'll pull up the video from Sunningham."

Bram waits for his phone to refresh.

"Me man managed to hack Kahn's computer... dug up the video he sent off to the law. That Kahn fella's as slippery as an eel—but sure enough, that's a tale for another day."

As Jynx talks, a video starts on Bram's phone. He sees a view of the guard shack. A young girl pulls up on her bike and talks with the guard. Then, a van rolls up. The doors swing open, and men spill out. Bram knows straightaway which one is his father—the Magpie FC scarf is a dead giveaway. Gunfire erupts, but something is off. They're firing high—aiming at the roof.

"This is the rough bit, lad. Steady yourself," Jynx says.

Bram watches as a woman steps out of the hut and shoots all three.

"Fuckin' Mozambique Drill."

"What?"

"Look it up. Two to the body, one to the head. She only

needed one chest shot, though. Proper pro. Trained for close-quarters combat."

Bram sits stunned. He never imagined it could be so ruthless.

"That," Jynx says, "is Mariya Morozova—goes by Masha. The lass on the bike is Raya Rogers."

"Can you pull photos and enhance the image? It's pretty grainy."

"I'll sort it. Send ye a full packet. You ready for the next bit? Gets even better."

"Yes." But Bram can't stop thinking about his dad.

"Next up—'tis Hilde." An image appears on Bram's phone. A woman walks down the street in office attire, a silk scarf covering her hair. Contrary to the description he had, she isn't wearing dark glasses.

"Where did you get this?"

"It was a mission. Had a man comb through hours of footage. He walked that street, mapped every bloody security camera. Proper legwork."

"But this is a still image."

"Aye, well spotted. We nabbed it off Globe-Map's Street View archives. They've got a timeline feature—we got lucky. Bit of code work, and we cleaned it up."

Bram frowns. "I don't recognize her."

"Don't ye? She's hidin' her look, wearin' heels—but take another gander."

On Bram's phone, an image of Mariya—Masha—appears next to Hilde.

"They are remarkably similar."

He studies the side-by-side images. "You think they're the same person?"

"There's a right chance."

Bram is stunned. "What does this even mean? What the hell happened?"

"That's for you to figure out. Are you ready for the next bit?"

Bram hesitates, then says, "Go on."

"We've little on Masha—nothin' online worth a shite—but a few bits we can stitch. Looks like she tailed Raya an' her da over to the States. Workin' now in Pennsylvania, same security lot that minds Sunningham."

"So, a dead end," Bram mutters, frustration rising.

"Not 'less you find Raya. You reach her, you've got Masha in the net."

"Okay... so where is Raya?"

"Right, this is the bit where things turn interestin'."

"How?"

"She wrapped up uni last year, she did, an' landed herself with an NGO—Orava International Relief."

Bram exhales. "And?"

"And looks like OIR's a front—could be SVR, could be CIA, some agency playin' cloak-and-dagger."

"How do you know?"

"You questionin' me now?"

Bram stares at the ceiling, astonished. "You're saying she's a spy?"

Jynx clicks his tongue. "Christ, how would I know that? But aye—maybe."

"Shit."

"Right—ye'll need to tread careful here."

"How the hell am I supposed to reach out to her?"

"Easy, lad. You text her. Straight with her—give yer own name, tell her you're SIS. Let her check ye out. Say you've dug up somethin' about the attack in Sunningham. Say you want to share it."

"And you think she'll meet me?"

"Best done in person. Let her pick the time, the place. Put her in charge."

Bram exhales, rubbing a hand down his face. "I feel like a creepy stalker."

At their next meeting, Bram declares, "I need money... traveling money."

"What for?" Neshad asks.

Bram explains. He believes the key is this woman, Masha—Mariya—who may also be Hilde. This is a revelation to Neshad, but he doesn't react.

"So, you want to meet Raya?"

"Yes. What if she tells me to meet in New York or in Europe? I don't have the money for an international flight. Hotels are pricey."

"Okay, I get it. But let's see if we can keep the costs down. I'll talk with David and get you a starting stake."

Bram is exasperated. "Whatever—you said you would pay, now you've got me begging. It doesn't seem like your employers are struggling for cash."

"No. But you'll learn that every employer wants to keep costs down. Just keep your receipts."

"Fine."

"One more thing… keep this conversation to Raya, then let's talk."

"Why?"

"Just don't engage this Masha until we have more intel," Neshad says. "She may be more than she seems."

What Bram hears is: *This woman is dangerous.*

CHAPTER TWENTY-THREE

DUBLIN, IRELAND
2018

"EXPLAIN IT TO ME AGAIN... why are you in Ireland?" Masha demands.

"I told you already. I'm part of the Orava International Relief contingent. We're trying to figure out the impact on the Western Balkans. The deadline is coming. Does Brexit help or hurt?"

"How is this possible? It makes no sense—they are not near each other."

Raya explains, "Everything is connected. The Irish border is in dispute. The Scottish want out of the UK. It's a mess. The outcome will be a big factor in our outreach and support for the Balkan states."

"Bah, you make everything complicated. Why are you not home? I miss our coffee."

"I'll be home soon, and then we can have lunch together."

"I don't see what this has to do with the Balkans," Masha

says.

"There's lots of push and pull. Negotiating trade deals takes time. Everything could fall apart quickly—it's a fiasco."

"Okay, but that's not a problem in Bosnia, Serbia, or Montenegro. Why do they care?"

"If the EU remains united, Germany stays strong—likely a good outcome for the Balkans. But if unity cracks, efforts to expand the coalition could stall, giving secessionist movements an opening. That could mean the loss of financial and political support, leaving Britain to step up—doubtful, given their own troubles."

All Masha hears is blah, blah, blah. She tunes out the details—it's all noise to her. What matters is staying connected to Raya. Without their regular meetings, she feels the distance growing.

"Still, I worry. You are far. You are busy. And I feel... forgotten."

Raya realizes Masha is lonely. She wonders if Masha has any friends at all. Raya is getting her first real taste of operational life. To maintain her cover, she needs to solidify her position within OIR. With it, she will gain access to parts of the world useful to the CIA. But it takes a toll—building a legend, professionally and personally.

Raya softens. This is the balance. "I know. I promise when I'm back, we'll have that coffee and catch up properly."

"Maybe I could help—if you tell me more about what you do. Who you're meeting. What you do for them."

A warning flare sparks in Raya's gut—that instinct Don talked about.

When she doesn't answer, Masha presses, "Don't forget, I am always here for you."

Raya forces a smile into her voice. "I know, Masha. I won't forget."

Raya yawns as she sinks back in her chair, trying to shake off the drowsiness of the conference. It's only day three, and her mind keeps drifting, woolgathering.

She can't stop thinking about Germany—the tension of the operation, the brief moments of connection with Don. Everything feels different now, as though she's looking at him through a lens. She feels like she can trust Don... but does he trust her? Can she truly trust anyone?

Real life doesn't work in clean lines. It's murky, full of half-truths—especially in their line of work. Instinct is the only thing to rely on when everything else is uncertain. That's what Don told her. She knows she needs to hone that skill.

One thing, though, she's decided: Don. She will trust him. Her gut tells her that. But who else?

Her father—*yes, definitely*. She's certain of him.

Masha? Maybe. Their relationship is shifting in ways she doesn't understand. There's something there, something unresolved. She needs to dig deeper. There's more to Masha's past, and Raya is determined to find out what it is.

Then there's Sunningham.

Mrs. Robinson—always so supportive. They email regularly. Mr. Kahn and the others... they're like family. She'll need to visit soon. She can't afford to lose touch with them, not now.

She replays Mr. Kahn's gift in her mind. Independence. *From what? What was he trying to say with that strange look toward Masha? Were her memories playing tricks on her?*

Her thoughts swirl. *What else had Don implied? Was she disposable—someone to be used for a purpose and then cast aside? Did they really operate that way?*

How could she protect herself?

It feels like she's standing at a crossroads. To survive—and to succeed—she knows she'll have to trust her instincts and her own judgment above all else.

Alone in her room, Raya prepares for bed. She plans to meditate on all the thoughts crowding her mind. Tomorrow will bring another round of lectures, forums, and workshops. She wonders at all the bickering and banter—how will they ever solve this mess? The monotony of the work is setting in. She's ready for an actual assignment.

Her phone pings—a text:

>> *Hello, my name is Bram Vidal. Is this Raya Rogers?*

She stares at the message, thumb hovering over delete. Another spam.

>> *I work for a firm in the UK called Surrey Investigative Solutions.*

She waits. The screen shows the sender still typing.

>> *I have some information about the attack in Sunningham. My investigation turned up some interesting details. I was wondering if we could meet. I'd like to share it with you.*

Raya replies:

>> *What information?*

The reply comes quickly:

>> *It would be better if we met. You pick the place and time.*

Raya rereads the texts, intrigued by Bram's message. She wonders if this is another CIA test, a trap set up by the agency. She dismisses the thought. The proper procedure would be to report this as an unexpected interaction—but her gut tells her otherwise. For now, she's not telling anyone.

She pulls out her laptop and runs a quick search. SIS's website lists Bram Vidal as an investigator. The site looks legitimate, but she knows it could be a fake. With a few more searches, she finds what she needs. She has the makings of a plan.

Raya smiles to herself as she types, feeling roguish—craving a distraction, eager to test her skills.

She sends:

>> *Are you up for a little travel this weekend?*

CHAPTER TWENTY-FOUR

THE IRISH SEA
2018

ABOARD THE *EDITH ELIZABETH*, **RAYA** stands on the promenade, watching passengers disembark at Holyhead. The regular Saturday ferry from Dublin to the UK is nearly empty now, but she remains onboard. A steward approaches, politely reminding her it's time to leave.

She reaches into her bag and pulls out a return ticket. "I'm just riding the ferry," she explains. "Can I wait for the next departure?"

The steward gives her a puzzled look, clearly wondering why anyone would spend four hours crossing the sea only to turn around. With a shrug, he moves on, leaving her to her solitude.

Raya wanders the now-empty passenger decks. She hadn't expected a ferry to be so luxurious—restaurants, lounges, duty-free shops, even an arcade and a small movie theater. But with the ship at port, everything is closed. Anyone who might have been following her has disembarked.

An hour later, she returns to the promenade, watching as new travelers queue for the return trip to Dublin. Pulling out a small pair of binoculars, she scans the crowd. Amid the sea of passengers, she spots a young man in a blue Chelsea FC jersey—just as she instructed. An unusual choice in a place dominated by Liverpool and Manchester fans. She knows he took the train from Reading that morning and, like her, plans to take the ferry round-trip.

Satisfied, she retreats to a quiet alcove and settles in to wait.

During the first leg of the journey, Raya sat in the lounge, nestled in a comfortable chair at a small table. Through the high windows, she watched the sea roll by, dark and endless. Then movement caught her eye—a small pod of orcas gliding off the port side.

Nearby, an elderly man pointed them out to a young boy— his grandson, most likely. "They must have separated from the larger pod," he mused. "Orcas never travel in such small numbers. They're looking for their family."

Raya's reaction was different. She never liked orcas. There was something unsettling about them—the way they played with their prey, toying with it before the kill. All she saw were four killers on the hunt, their black-and-white camouflage turning them into ghosts in the water. Hard to spot for both predator and prey. Unfettered killers, ruthless and precise.

She stalks Bram before making her move—watching his movements, reading his body language, noting how he interacts with other passengers. She's looking for signs: deception, awareness, anything that might give her pause. She still doesn't know exactly what to expect.

Bram is tall—taller than she imagined—and built in a way that suggests strength, but not the kind honed in a gym. His is a lived-in strength, quiet and functional, like someone accustomed to carrying weight without complaint.

Finally, she steps forward. Like any good hunter, she catches him off guard.

He's nervous but steady. It's her eyes that hold him—dark, alert. Her mid-length hair, dark as wet stone, frames a face that stays calm even when her mind is racing. There's elegance in her restraint and a quiet power in the way she carries herself—like someone who knows exactly when to strike.

Bram collects himself, squaring his shoulders as he takes her hand. "Thank you for meeting me."

"Come with me." Raya presses a finger to her lips, signaling silence.

He nods and follows.

She leads him to a quiet corner she's chosen carefully—against the bulkhead, where the windows overlook the choppy water. She sits with her back to the wall, ensuring she has a full view of the room. He takes the seat opposite her, his back to the other passengers.

She studies him. He doesn't posture or push. He simply watches her, measured and calm. His skin is a warm brown tone, his eyes darker still—sharp and observant. His hair is cropped short, neat, as though he doesn't have time for vanity.

Reaching into her bag, she pulls out a satchel and gestures to his phone. He hesitates only a moment before handing it over, placing it inside the bag she holds open. Her own phone is already there.

"Any other electronics?" she whispers.

He shakes his head. "No."

She would prefer to search him, but there's only so much she can do. Instead, she trusts her instincts. He doesn't have the look of an operative, though he carries himself with quiet confidence.

"Can we talk now?" he asks.

She nods.

"Faraday pouch. Very clever. Who are we worried about?" He has already decided not to ask directly about the CIA.

"Just being cautious. I don't know you."

"Right. I'm Bram Vidal. I work for Surrey Investigative Solutions. We're investigating the assailants at Sunningham."

Curt, firm: "Why?"

"One of the families asked us to look into it. You should know they weren't terrorists."

On guard now, she scoffs. "Looked that way to me."

Bram holds steady. "To a lot of people, it did. But they weren't. They were fools who became victims."

"They shot at me."

Bram is sympathetic but stays focused. "I know. That must have been horrifying. Do you know why?"

"No."

"I didn't think so. The reason for the attack is still a mystery."

"So, why are you here?"

"I was hoping you might connect some dots for me. Let me

lay it out."

Bram tells the story: the woman Hilde, the flyer, the crisis actors, the training. The story of Leo and the trauma left behind.

Raya is still uncertain what to make of it.

Then Bram tells her about Avi and his Jewish heritage—how unlikely it would be for him to act as an Islamic terrorist.

She sees his point.

"I've got video. The security guard was very efficient."

"And you got this video? How?"

"I have a source helping me. His name is Jynx." Bram immediately regrets sharing the name.

Raya's reaction is incredulous. "Jynx, huh?"

She won't let him show the video, but Bram has brought some photos. The first is a close-cropped shot of Hilde, with only her face visible.

"Do you recognize this woman?"

"Yes, that's Masha."

He pulls out another photo showing the full image—her walking down the street. "And this is the woman, Masha?"

Raya stares at the photo. Masha is almost unrecognizable, but it is certainly her. "What does this mean? Why is she dressed that way, in a wig?"

"She's in disguise. This is Hilde—the woman who recruited the men. The woman who sent them to attack that security hut. Why would Masha pretend to be Hilde?"

"I don't know." She is shaken.

Bram can see she's becoming emotional. Whatever happened, Raya wasn't part of it. He decides to drop his last piece of information. "One of the men killed was my father. Will you help me figure it out?"

"I need a drink. Do you want a drink?" She rises and heads for the bar.

Over the next hour, they review Bram's information again and again. She hears the passion in each retelling of his father's murder. Raya checks her instincts. She looks at Bram and decides he is worth her trust.

She voices her own concerns—nagging doubts about Masha that can't easily be explained. How Masha never had a firm grasp on her past. Was this even about her?

"Do you think this tracks back to your coming from Russia?" Bram asks.

Raya thinks it sounds crazy, but too much feels like coincidence. Her mind is flooded with information, thoughts, images. She needs to pull it together. "I don't know, but I want to find out."

Bram is the first to say, "We don't know what we're dealing with. We need to be careful."

Raya recalls a novel she read and says, "Moscow Rules."

Bram nods. They are both being coy—she hasn't revealed the CIA, and he has chosen not to mention Neshad.

"What can I do?"

"I don't know, maybe... see if you can find out more about Masha. She always said she came from Poland, but the family was Russian. There may be a record. Maybe your friend Jynx can help?" Raya suggests with a smirk.

"I can check. I don't think his initial search went that far. He has some capabilities."

"Good." Raya wonders if she can use the CIA to help but quickly dismisses the idea. *I need to figure this out on my own. There is something else going on.*

"What are you going to do?"

"I need some time. I need to talk with my dad about my mother... and I need to talk with Masha." *Masha and my mother—what is this all about?*

"How do we communicate?"

"Not by email... or phone."

"What about the Signal app?"

"Let's go old school for now. I'll mail a letter to your office at SIS with instructions on where to meet next."

The ferry horn blasts, signaling their approach to Dublin. Time for Raya to disembark—and for Bram to begin the journey back home.

"Are we really doing this?" Bram asks.

"We both need some answers. Let's find them. I'll try to get back to the UK as soon as I can."

They both stand. Bram hesitates, then reaches out to Raya. They share the awkward embrace of two people who have only just met, yet have forged a tentative connection—the hug of colleagues, cautious but genuine.

For Raya, Bram is something to consider. Maybe she can trust him. She needs to let her instincts work their magic. Trust—for her, it's always the pot stakes in any relationship.

But for Bram, it's different. Emotion tugs at him while he's still searching for his own sense of self. She's beautiful. And smart. His thoughts feel primitive, raw.

It's been a long time since he's had a hug.

CHAPTER TWENTY-FIVE

Moscow, Russia
2018

THE ROUTINE OF A SOLITARY man can become everything. But when routine changes, a man's thoughts can wander, become confused. For some, it creates a sense of inevitability. For others, uncertainty and fear. It can shift one's view of the world—and their place in it—suddenly and without warning.

It was late in the evening. When things change, it is always best to stay late. He leaves his office building and steps into the night. Few of the lights that should guide his way are working. This is the dark forest—the area surrounding the SVR headquarters in the Yasenevo District, south of Moscow.

Just an anonymous man traveling home on a train from an anonymous office. This is his routine. His life has become mundane. The ride along the Kaluzhsko-Rizhskaya line takes thirty minutes to reach the stop near his home: a one-bedroom apartment in a desirable neighborhood. A privilege of rank—one he could soon lose.

For the man on the train, there is only regret. Regret he has harbored for decades, regret he has tried to forget. The only thing keeping him going now is the hope of one moment of relief—a chance to make amends and complete his personal mission. If that chance is gone, it may be time to leave... or to make some other choice.

Change and time play on a man's mind. A life filled with choices and secrets. A life of dedication and sacrifice.

Yuri wonders: was it all worth it?

When Yuri arrived at work that day, a new man was in charge. Evgeni Antonov—his mentor of over forty years—had been unceremoniously removed. Evgeni was no longer the Director, and Yuri's own position was suddenly in doubt.

The President had demanded results and appointed a new man to deliver them: Ivan Kirillov. Ambitious, young, and restless. A disrupter in the mold of tech entrepreneurs and hedge fund CEOs. An aggressive man who valued action over substance—and who would deliver results at any cost.

Yuri was reassigned to a new office. He packed his things without protest, walking the long hallway away from the center of power. The shift was unmistakable—his work was no longer considered foundational, his position no longer one of prominence.

He had started at the Foreign Intelligence Service when he was young, back when it was still the First Chief Directorate of the KGB. He was there when it became the SVR in 1991, rising steadily alongside Evgeni Antonov. He wonders where Evgeni is now.

For the moment, Yuri seemed safe. Ivan Kirillov, the new

Director, had bigger concerns and more immediate targets. He would see Yuri as superfluous—necessary, but unimportant. That would give him time.

They called Yuri the *Dvoretskiy*—the Butler. His domain was the Directorate of Support. He did not run operations; he sustained them. He secured safe houses, built legends, and ensured surveillance ran smoothly. The unseen scaffolding of countless missions. The man who would never seek credit. And in such a role, very little happened without his knowledge.

It would not last. A new Director would want a new staff, bringing in loyalists who would erase the old guard without a second thought. Yuri had seen it happen before. He had spent years building his position, carefully navigating the corridors of power, but he knew how fragile it all was. One wrong move, one shift in the political winds, and everything he had worked for could be swept away.

Yuri was prepared—always prepared. Contingencies layered upon contingencies. He had survived this long because he never let his guard down. Still, there was one thing even his careful planning could not fully protect—his other life.

For almost as long as he had served the Russian state, Yuri had also been an asset for Israel. A double life, a dangerous game played in the shadows. For now, there was no choice but to persevere. To watch, to wait, to survive.

Yuri grew up poor in a country where poverty bred toughness and survival demanded obedience. His father was a soldier— distant, strict, loyal to the Soviet state. From an early age, Yuri understood that strength and discipline were the only ways forward. He was smart, physically imposing, and deeply aware of how the world worked. He studied hard, kept his head down, and learned to move through the system without drawing unwanted attention.

But his family carried a secret, one that could destroy everything they had built: they were Jewish. In Soviet Russia, that wasn't a minor detail—Jews faced widespread discrimination. His parents never acknowledged their faith openly. Fear kept them silent. Even as he grew older, Yuri learned to suppress that part of himself, burying it beneath layers of patriotism and ambition. He had no other choice.

His first job in the Soviet system was a lowly position as an errand boy. He was a nobody, a nameless functionary running papers, making coffee, cleaning up after those who mattered. But Yuri understood everyone started somewhere. He listened more than he spoke, observed more than he acted. He learned the internal dynamics of power—how men climbed the ranks, and how they fell.

Then came Evgeni Antonov—a state prosecutor, only twenty-eight, with a sharp eye for talent. A man with connections, a man on the rise. Evgeni recognized something in Yuri: his intelligence, his quiet efficiency, his unwavering ability to follow orders. Under Evgeni's mentorship, Yuri advanced, moving from meaningless tasks to real responsibility. He was slowly becoming someone worth noticing.

That was when he met Anna, unlike anyone he had ever known. Beautiful and ruthless, she exuded control in every aspect of her life. She had just returned from a difficult assignment, the details of which were classified. Yuri knew enough to recognize the weight she carried. But there was something else, too—a secret she could not hide forever. She was pregnant.

Their marriage was as much a strategic move as it was a personal one. She needed a husband; he needed access. Anna was one of Antonov's favorites, a woman trusted within the state's highest circles. Marrying her solidified Yuri's place in the system, granting him further legitimacy. Together, they were the ideal Soviet couple—loyal, intelligent, dedicated to their country.

Anna gave birth to a daughter, Oksana, but motherhood changed little for her. She remained focused, committed to the cause. Her work was more important than raising a child. Anna had a gift for infiltration, for slipping into circles of dissidents and uncovering hidden threats. She was relentless—a master of deception, and utterly loyal to the state.

But Yuri's loyalties were already divided. A young Israeli agent named Hevel Biram was the first to approach him. Yuri hadn't known his name at the time, but the resources of his office eventually revealed his identity. Hevel recognized Yuri's potential—and his growing position within the Soviet structure. He also knew his secret heritage. Hevel became Yuri's first and only handler, the only man he trusted.

At first, Yuri did only small favors—passing along minor details, helping Jewish operatives move undetected. Risky, but manageable. Over time, though, the favors became assignments, and the assignments became a mission.

As the years passed, Yuri and Anna drifted apart, though their marriage remained intact. Divorce was out of the question—it would raise too many suspicions. Instead, they lived parallel lives, each keeping their own secrets.

Yuri moved beyond being a Sayanim—a local asset assisting Mossad operatives—and became something more. He was now Katsas, a full-fledged intelligence officer, actively working against the very system that had given him everything.

Over time, Yuri's perspective shifted. He saw the cracks in the Soviet system, the Russian people's desire for the oppression to end. The world was changing, evolving. But Anna was unyielding. She saw the West as weak, corrupt, and a danger to everything she had sacrificed for.

She harbored the secret of their daughter. It played on her mind, reshaping her own narrative of the past. She despised the idea of reform, seeing it as a loss of control—a betrayal.

For Yuri, hope still lingered. For Anna, there was only the mission. And in Russia, losing sight of the mission meant losing everything.

◆◆◆

As he exits the train for the walk home, he wonders: are they watching him even now, waiting to see if he is loyal? Yuri relies on routine, on monotony. It has kept him safe for so long. He does not walk the street in fear. He knows anything that might happen is beyond his control—a man resigned to his fate. This was his choice. But deep down, he harbors a single sorrow.

He is angry with himself for one sacrifice he made. A regret that will not fade: losing a daughter he raised as his own. It was necessary, but it cut in a way no one else could understand. Yuri did not have the luxury of sharing this pain. He bears the torment alone.

Yet Yuri has planned well, and redemption may still be possible. He just needs to soldier on. He will send another update through channels to the Mossad. They need to act—or he will.

CHAPTER TWENTY-SIX

IT IS A TRADITION FOR families in Philadelphia to rent a beach house on the New Jersey shore for a week between Memorial Day and Labor Day. The appeal lies in the proximity to family-friendly boardwalks and beaches, with cool sea breezes offering relief from the city's sweltering summer heat. Year after year, families reconnect with their seasonal neighbors, forming traditions and lifelong memories.

Others, however, prefer to skip the summer crowds. Once school is back in session, the shore transforms into a quieter retreat. With the ocean still warm from the summer sun, September becomes the perfect time for retirees to take advantage of lower rental prices and a more peaceful atmosphere. Their days are spent reading, dozing in the afternoon sun, and letting the rhythmic crash of the waves lull them into complete relaxation.

Phil rented the top floor of a duplex a block from the beach—a cozy two-room apartment, perfect for him and Raya.

After months of relentless travel and the strain of living a double life, she needed a break. The intensity of her training had taken its toll, and even the Agency encouraged her to take time off to recharge.

For the first two days, they moved cautiously around each other, adjusting to the rhythms of sharing space again after so many years apart. Mornings began with pork roll and egg sandwiches from a local deli, and evenings ended with seafood takeout and walks along the boardwalk. They turned in early, lulled to sleep by the distant crash of waves, and rose with the sun.

On the morning of the third day, they packed their beach chairs, an umbrella, and a cooler before settling in near the water. The tide receded from their toes as they sat in companionable silence; the ocean stretching endlessly before them.

"Dad, tell me about Mom."

Phil knew it was coming. Raya had been hinting for some time—she wanted this conversation. He wasn't sure he was ready. "You know what happened. Your mom passed away when you were born, and you came to live with me."

"But how?" She finally had him alone, without distractions. Raya needed answers, and she planned on getting them.

"What do you mean?"

Raya let out a breath, exasperated. "How did you two meet?"

"That's a long story."

"I've got nowhere to go. Tell me... please."

✦✦✦

Phil leans back in his chair and shuts his eyes. Behind his eyelids, a kaleidoscope of colors swirls, shifting and blending like an old film reel spinning into a flashback. The past rushes toward him—vivid and unstoppable—pulling him into another time, another place. He takes a slow breath, steadying himself. If he is going to tell it, he might as well get it all out.

"I wasn't yet thirty, I remember that... I'd established myself on a project for an IT firm. Funny, I can't even recall their name now—the things we forget. Anyway, I was useful, and they asked if I'd be open to a new project in Russia. A new adventure."

"I remember it was raining and balmy—must have been September. I'd flown in from the UK, where it had been hot all summer. The British papers were full of the Queen's planned October trip to Moscow, and I was heading to the same place."

"Working in London had been different, but working in Russia—truly in another culture—was jarring. I didn't speak the language, but everyone was eager to meet a 'Yankee.' They were all trying to figure out this new capitalism. Money was flowing. It was the dawn of a new Russia, and excitement was everywhere. The project was a joint venture between a U.S. firm and the Russian state. Speed mattered. Relationships mattered. Graft mattered."

"There were parties—lots of parties. Late nights followed by hard days. Repeat. And our government—the U.S. government—was front and center. The embassy sponsored social events, and they asked me, as an American, to attend."

Raya wonders what this had to do with her mother, but she has all the time, so she listens. Learning more about her dad than she ever knew.

"But," Phil continues, "this was new to me, and I was cautious. I grew up at a time when Russia was our enemy. I don't even remember the reason for the gala, but I was there in my tuxedo, expected to socialize. Your dad looked pretty sharp, if I do say so—but I was out of my element. So, I sat by the bar drinking expensive French champagne, doing my best to play the part. But you know me... that's not my forte. I've always been better at the work than at rubbing elbows."

"That's when I saw Oksana Yuryevna Dadianova for the first time. Your mother was beautiful—dressed in a black sequin cocktail dress. She was a vision. Dark hair in a bun, an oval face, deep black eyes. She wore a pout that only made her more attractive. She was young—young enough that I should've kept my head. But there was something in her bearing, in her eyes. She felt like an old soul."

"I was probably staring. I know I was staring. We'd catch eyes, then I'd turn away. And then I realized—she was doing the same thing as me—trying to hide in plain sight."

"I offered her a drink. Her English was good, but she spoke in that very direct way Russians often do when learning the language. She said she had a man she needed to meet. I thought she was telling me to get lost, but she stayed. She asked me to go for a walk. I was smitten—and confused. I didn't put the story together until later."

"Anyway, we went for a walk. The air had cooled, carrying the crisp bite of evening, but the Moskva River shimmered under the moonlight. The Kremlin stood illuminated in the distance, looking almost unreal—like something out of a postcard. She took my hand, her fingers cold but firm, and drew close, pressing against me as we walked in silence. Later, we went back to my hotel... and that is as much as I'll say about that."

Raya chuckles, then stops. She can see the story saddens her father. "I get it, Dad. I won't pry."

Phil continues, "I saw her a few times in those first weeks. She told me she worked in security—the *politsiya*—but I didn't understand. I imagined her as a secretary or a traffic warden... she said everything so cryptically."

"In time, I learned she'd been at the party to cozy up to a 'valued target'—to meet and develop him, a test of sorts. But she didn't go through with it. She went with me instead. She told me the security services were a mess. It was 1994, and there were many conflicting views of *perestroika* and the new reforms. Most in the service felt forgotten. There was bitterness. Anti-Western sentiment was still rampant."

"Oksana had a family contact who helped her get the job, but I never met the family. They'd pushed her into the service, and she resented it. I believed they were estranged. They wanted the past. She was young, hopeful, and craved a better future."

Phil stops talking for a moment, preparing himself for the next part. Raya holds her breath, waiting.

"I still remember that day a few months later, walking with her through Gorky Park. The sky was overcast, the air crisp with the bite of approaching winter. She was tense, her silence heavier than usual. I knew her well enough to sense when she was brooding—but that day, it was different. She hated her existence. Hated the endless games, the deception, the constant vigilance that came with her work. The life she had chosen—or perhaps the life that had been chosen for her. But it wasn't just that. There was something more."

Phil falls silent again. Raya waits.

"She told me she was pregnant. Everything changed in a moment... I was in a daze. What would happen? Could she go to her family, tell her employer? I was afraid they would insist on terminating the pregnancy."

"Instead, she was resolute—defiant. I drew strength from her when it should have been the other way around. She told me, 'If I have a boy, I will name him Mikhail. And if it's a girl, she will be Raisa.' It wasn't simply a choice of names. It was an act of revolt—a punch back against the establishment that controlled her life."

Raya wipes a tear from her eye. "So, Raya is from Raisa. I never knew. Why didn't you tell me?"

Phil just smiles at his daughter. "I'll get there..."

They both look out at the ocean as the tide begins to turn. The ebb has ended, and the waterline slowly creeps back toward them—a quiet but relentless force. Like the passage of time, the pendulum has shifted. The distance that once defined them is closing with each revelation.

Raya glances at Phil, watching the lines on his face soften in the fading light. He's always been a supportive, loving father, but somehow distant—separate. With the salty breeze and the rhythmic pulse of the sea, something is shifting.

"Our solution was to marry. Neither of us knew what we were doing. It was smart in how it worked out, but we had no real plan. Was I going to stay in Russia? Would she come to the U.S.? We weren't thinking."

"I should have asked myself if I was the 'valued target.' Was getting married her objective? Was she really pregnant? But I didn't. I was sure we were in love. I certainly was in love."

"It all happened quickly. The ceremony at the Department of Public Services lasted only a few minutes. Afterward, when most couples would celebrate with friends and family, we ate a quiet dinner at a local restaurant. When she told her family, she was ostracized. To them, she was a traitor."

"Dad, I'm so sorry. That must have been awful." She never knew her mother—and never realized her father had endured so much.

"I moved into her small apartment, waiting for the big day. I was working so hard then, helping her at night. We grew closer as her family grew more distant.

They wouldn't even acknowledge me, let alone meet me. I would recite old Irish poems from my youth, and she would tell me about the times she spent with her father. They'd been very close. His betrayal was the most painful. I like to think they might have reconciled, but she never got the chance. You know she died in childbirth."

Raya is listening intently. She knows the facts, but never the details.

"I never really grieved Oksana properly. There wasn't time. You were my priority. How to get you home? I was married, yes, but this was Russia—it took time. I was frantic. I knew you were my child. But what would happen to you?"

Phil is crying. He has hidden these memories and feelings

from himself for so long, but it feels cathartic to let them out. At the same time, it feels disloyal to be free of the weight.

Raya suggests they take a break. "Let's take a walk."

They wander along the tideline where the sand is firm, pretending to look for shells and not talking. The silence between them is thick with unspoken thoughts.

Raya sees the pain in her father—but also senses his quiet relief, a burden released.

Phil turns to her, his lips parting as if he might say something. Instead, he only nods—a small, almost imperceptible gesture of understanding.

Strolling together along the shoreline, they find a new connection—closer than they had ever been.

Raya realizes how strange it is, how pain and loss can draw people together in ways that years of normalcy never could.

When they return to their chairs, Phil takes a deep breath.

"Those first days were the worst," he says, his voice quieter now, as if speaking too loudly might summon the ghosts of the past. "I was at the hospital, but I didn't speak Russian. When the nurse finally came out, I didn't understand a word she was saying. Her face told me everything. I lost her."

He swallows hard, staring past Raya, lost in the memory. His voice drops to a whisper. "... Five d'chance, toss 'em bones, six a mark, cut 'en stone. Seven ta flee, ne'er turnin' back, eight a choice, ye heart turns black..."

Raya tilts her head. "What's that, Dad?"

"Oh... nothing. Just an old poem I used to tell you when you were little. Your mother used to like it..."

She feels a flicker—something stirs inside her. A quiver of memory, just out of reach.

Before she can ask more, he moves on, continuing his story.

"But by some miracle, you survived. And that should have been a relief, but instead, it was terrifying. What would happen now? I didn't know her family. Would they claim you? Would you end up in some orphanage, growing up without me? Would they even recognize me as your father?"

Raya can feel his unease, his leg bouncing against the sand.

"I knew one thing for certain—I had to get you out of Russia." His jaw tightens. "The embassy was useless. They didn't want to ruffle feathers... commerce was king. My employer was sympathetic but unhelpful. Everyone said their hands were tied. I was out of options, grasping at straws. And then I remembered him."

Raya's heart pounds. "Dad, who helped you?"

Phil rubbed a hand over his face before looking at her again. "A guy I knew in college. We had a complicated relationship—grudging respect, a rivalry. I'd heard rumors he was working for the government, maybe in a covert role. I wasn't sure whether he would help. I wasn't sure if he could help."

"Getting you out was... complicated. This man had connections. He got you a passport, one with an entry stamp already in place. I never asked how. I didn't want to know." His eyes darkened. "It took weeks. You stayed in the hospital while I waited. Every day, I went through the motions at work, pretending nothing had changed. But I was preparing. I bought you clothes, formula, and cloth diapers. I packed only the essentials for myself—I wouldn't be taking anything else."

"The day we left..." He hesitates, his fingers tightening into a fist. "I walked into the hospital for a normal visit... and took you. They knew me—I was there every day. But when I walked out with you in my arms, when the nurses realized, they panicked. I could hear them yelling for me to return. A car was waiting, idling at the curb. The moment I got in, we were gone."

Raya realizes she is holding her breath.

"We switched cars to reduce the chance of being followed. I had a ticket out on the next flight. Time was tight—we were cutting it close. The airline listed you as an infant-in-arms, not as a separate passenger. We assumed the hospital would call the authorities, but by the time anyone connected the dots, we'd be airborne. That was the plan."

"But then came passport control." His lips press into a thin line. "I've never been so afraid in my life. The officer took my passport, flipped through it, and looked at me. Then he looked at you. You were so small... so quiet. My heart was pounding, but I forced myself to stay calm. If they asked questions—if they pulled us aside—it would all be over."

"They had already changed your name to Raya on the passport. Your mom had never taken my last name. There was nothing for them to match against. He stamped my passport and waved me through."

Phil let out a shaky breath. "Sitting on the tarmac, waiting for that plane to take off, was the longest wait of my life. I didn't move. Didn't breathe. Not until we were in the air, and I saw the lights of Moscow disappearing beneath us. Only then did I allow myself to believe we'd made it."

He looks at her, his expression unreadable. "Anyway, he helped. I got you out... it was worth it."

Raya suddenly feels a shiver of understanding. "But there was a cost, wasn't there?" She already knew where this was going.

Phil exhales slowly. "He didn't do it for free, did he?" A small, humorless smile tugs at his lips. "I've been paying that debt ever since."

Raya stares at him, her mind racing. "What was the cost, Dad?" she asks, her voice barely above a whisper.

"It's a secret I can't share."

"Then swear me to secrecy."

Phil gives her a long, searching look. No—he wouldn't make his daughter swear. And he suspects she has some secrets of her own. Then finally he nods. "I am... sometimes... an agent for a Western intelligence agency. I use my international work as a cover. I scout, help agents, and courier information. Nothing glamorous."

Raya feels her stomach twist. She had always known—had always sensed—that her father wasn't just a simple businessman. But this... this was something else.

Phil sighs and looks at her with something close to regret. "I was so young, Raya. So angry. I resented him. I resented everything. Maybe that rubbed off on how I raised you." He swallows. "But I'd do it all again. Because I got you out."

"It's okay, Dad. I understand. You did it for me."

"It was so hard," he admits. "And then... somehow, it was so easy."

For a long moment, neither of them spoke. The weight of the story settles between them like the pause between breakers rolling in from the ocean.

Later, Raya sits out on the second-story deck. It is almost 3 a.m. The streets are quiet, and Phil has long since fallen asleep. It is a time of contemplation—a secret time. The moonlight reflecting off the ocean hides the stars from view, but she knows they are there. She wonders if she made a wish, would it still count?

Should she tell her father about her work—about how she serves the same agency that saved her life? And changed his? He has shared so much. Maybe she should come clean. But she made promises, and she intends to keep them.

Would he have understood her concerns about Masha— the attack, her origins, the endless questions? Things were still too vague, and she doesn't want to create unnecessary conflict. She needs to confront Masha herself and get answers. *But is she ready?*

Could she have told him about Bram? About his determination to understand his father? Raya realizes they are both searching for the same thing—the truth of their pasts. No, this is for them, for now, Bram and her. Her instincts tell her there is more to come, more to uncover. If she shares this secret, it will no longer belong to her.

She does none of these things. For now, she chooses silence—not out of deception, but preservation. The bond with her father is fragile, new in a way she hadn't expected. She won't risk shattering it before it has the chance to take shape.

So, she lets the night hold her secrets. The stars keep watch. And the moon, resolute, stands sentry. For now, that is enough.

CHAPTER TWENTY-SEVEN

MAIDENHILL, ENGLAND, UK
2018

BRAM SHIFTS IN HIS SEAT, stretching his legs as best he can in the cramped space of the car. The street is quiet, the glow of a single streetlamp casting long shadows across the damp pavement. It is late, but he will stay a few more hours—this job requires patience.

Tonight's job is simple. David has asked him to monitor a woman, track her movements, see whom she is meeting. And tonight, she is in a house—a married man's house. The lights are still on, the curtains drawn. No movement yet.

Bram exhales, rubbing a hand over the stubble on his jaw. He is bored. Stakeouts were all waiting and watching—hours spent in silence, with only his thoughts for company. And tonight, his mind keeps circling back to Raya.

The meeting had been nothing like he had expected. She was controlled, precise, slipping seamlessly into tradecraft as if it were second nature. She had taken charge of the conversation, guiding it without arrogance. It surprised him.

His first thought was that she was so American—bold and self-assured. But the more he thought about it, the more he realized she defied the stereotype. His information had genuinely surprised her; he could see that. And yet, she remained composed—he'd caught the flicker of sympathy. There was something deeper there, something he hadn't anticipated. A connection.

Bram sighs, dragging his focus back to the house. Still no movement. A flicker of light in an upstairs window catches his attention. A shadow moved. The woman? Maybe. Maybe not. He'd give it more time.

But as the quiet night stretches on, his thoughts refuse to settle. Raya, Masha, his father—and his endless pursuit of answers—one tangled knot after another. He understood what happened to his father, but not why. Unanswered questions had always consumed him, driving him forward, pushing him to sacrifice everything. No real friends. No lazy afternoons at the pub watching a match. No family vacations or weekend trips. No real life.

As he turns the thought over in his mind, he realizes something unsettling. All that time, he hadn't missed it. This is *who I am*, he thinks. A loner chasing ghosts. Maybe this is his purpose. He isn't so sure.

Bram's phone rings. A call from Jynx. He answers on the Signal app. "Why is it you always call me late at night?"

"Keepin' ya on your toes, so I am."

"You got my text?"

Bram had sent a message to Jynx right after meeting Raya:

>> *Need deeper dive into Masha. Raya indicated she was Russian but came through Poland as a child. Can you widen search?*

"Wouldn't be callin' if I hadn't, now would I? So, how'd the meetin' go with the lass?"

"It was good. She was... interesting. She didn't mention being in the CIA, and I didn't ask."

"Did ya tell her 'bout me?"

"I told her I had someone helping me out, but nothing about Neshad. And David knows nothing."

"Smart lad, holdin' back. Quid pro quo an' all that. Keeps things balanced, like."

"I don't think I need to do that."

"Ah, why the hell not?"

"It wasn't like that. She was straight with me about everything. Told me about her mother. She didn't have to do that."

"Keep yer head straight, boyo. Ye ain't courtin' her."

Bram stammers, "I... I know that. What do you take me for?"

"Ah, feck, she's got into yer head, hasn't she? I can hear it in ya. Be careful now."

Bram sighs. Jynx barely knows him, but there is no dodging his intuition.

"Smitten, are ya?" Jynx teases.

Bram hesitates. He had spent years keeping his emotions in check—staying distant, detached. But Raya feels different. "Yeah. Maybe."

Jynx doesn't needle him further. Instead, he gets straight to the update on Masha.

"She's clean," Jynx says. "Too clean."

"What does that mean?"

"Did a proper deep dive, like ya asked. Nothin' of consequence—no past before the last few years. No work records in Poland, no birth certificates, no residency papers. Even them supposed ties to Bremen-Sarp GmbH, Sunningham's security firm—nothin' useful."

"How often does that happen?"

"Never. An' that's the problem. Past don't just vanish on its own, not without help. An' if Masha's past is wiped this clean, well... that means someone powerful made it happen."

Bram clenches his jaw. He needs something tangible. A real lead.

"So, I tried somethin' new. Got a fella who's handy with facial recognition. Dug into the old archives, went back further... way back."

A grainy photograph loads onto Bram's screen. Two people standing side by side—a man and a woman. The software matched the woman's face to Masha. But the name attached to the photograph wasn't Masha. It was Anna Lomouri.

"Who is she?"

"Who's to say? All I got is her name. But the caption dates the photo—1974. Says 'Case 42.' An' the man next to her? Evgeni Antonov. Back then, he was a Russian state prosecutor. Now? High up in the SVR. Proper nasty bunch, them. She must've been wrapped up in Case 42."

The implications twist Bram's stomach into knots.

"Case 42?" he asks. "What was it?"

"Can't say for sure. The case is sealed, no details. But if she was in deep back in '74, then she's been in the game a long time."

Bram scrolls back to the photo, staring hard at the woman in it.

Was Anna Lomouri also Masha? So many aliases. Was it possible?

"Listen, lad. I like ya, I do. But I'm worried for ya. Need to watch yourself with this one. Tread careful now."

Bram doesn't respond. His mind is racing, trying to make sense of the discovery. A woman resembling Masha had been involved in a major Russian prosecution—a case significant enough for her to be photographed beside a man who later became a powerful Russian intelligence official.

"It doesn't add up. It can't be Masha." But deep down, he isn't sure anymore.

"Just be careful, lad. That's all I'm sayin'."

Bram looks back at the house. All the lights are off, and the woman's car is no longer in the drive. He'd missed her leaving. What a waste of time. *What will I tell David?*

He signs off from Jynx and drives home.

Jynx rolls along in his caravan, the hum of the tires on the asphalt a familiar comfort. He thrives on the open road, on the endless possibilities that come with it. Born into a family of travelers, he had never taken to the tight quarters, the constant closeness. He is a nomad—solitary—roaming on his own terms.

Something about this job has Jynx intrigued. There is more

happening than meets the eye. Whatever Bram has stumbled into, it is bigger than it seems. And Jynx, ever the opportunist, wonders how he might turn it to his advantage.

Still, now and then, he thinks about the future. The work never stops, and lately, the idea of taking on a helper has crept into his mind. Bram comes to mind first. The kid is sharp, unattached—if he can keep his head straight, he might just be a good fit.

His phone chimes—another request. It never ends. He exhales, already scanning for a good place to pull over. Time to set up shop, find a hotspot, fire up his LAN, and get to work.

CHAPTER TWENTY-EIGHT

KENNETT SQUARE, PENNSYLVANIA, USA
2018

IN THE EARLY 1900S, THE du Pont family acquired a stretch of land near Brandywine Creek, a picturesque expanse along the Pennsylvania–Delaware border. Drawn to its natural beauty and vast wilderness, Pierre du Pont envisioned more than just a private retreat. What began as a simple flower garden soon evolved into a grand country estate, meticulously crafted to celebrate the harmony between cultivated landscapes and untouched nature.

Yet this land carried a long and storied past. Once the hunting and fishing grounds of the Lenape people, it later became a vital stop along the Underground Railroad, known as the Long Woods—a place of refuge and passage for those seeking freedom.

It opened to the public in 1921, preserving its legacy while inviting visitors to explore its wonders. Over time, the estate expanded and came under the stewardship of the Longwood Foundation, growing into a world-class arboretum and botanical center that earned international recognition for its extraordinary collection of flora.

Today, meandering trails wind through the grounds, leading visitors past hidden follies, intricate water features, and breathtaking recreations of ancient gardens, many inspired by European landscapes. Restaurants and cafés provide quiet corners for reflection, but the heart of Longwood remains its dedication to plant conservation and botanical research.

It is a place of beauty and contemplation—perfect for a peaceful stroll or an intimate conversation amid nature's grandeur. And it is here, among the whispering leaves, that Raya chooses to meet Masha.

Raya's call had not been unexpected. Masha knew she was back in the States, visiting her father. Still, a pang of jealousy struck her—she was no longer as important as she once was, not as important as she needed to be. Yet she told herself she was happy now. Raya wanted to see her.

They walk through the park, the late afternoon light filtering through the trees and dappling the stone paths beneath their feet. Raya pulls out a map, tracing a route with her fingertip.

"Let's circle around to the Italian Water Garden and then head to the Conservatory. I want to see the bonsai trees."

Masha nods, letting Raya lead. She doesn't notice the couple trailing them at a distance—just another pair of visitors, a stroller pushed between them. Beneath the blanket, a parabolic microphone disguised as a sleeping child.

Masha glances sideways at Raya. "How was the beach? Did you enjoy spending time with your father?"

"The Shore," Raya corrects. "It was good. I needed a break."

"And your work? Did you solve Brexit?"

Raya huffs a quiet laugh. "No... nobody can solve Brexit."

She forces herself to stay relaxed, but her muscles are taut and her mind is racing. This is a delicate game, a conversation where every word has to be chosen with care. She has questions she is afraid to ask outright—about the things Bram uncovered. About whether Masha was Hilde. The questions from the fat ninja. She needs to catch Masha off guard, to push without making it seem like a push.

They pass the Canopy Cathedral Treehouse on the right, the Large Lake stretching out to the left. The familiar landscape made Raya nostalgic.

"Longwood always reminds me of Virginia Water. Our long walks. Why don't you ever go back?"

"I'm here now, near you."

A deflection. Raya tries another approach. "How's work at Bremen-Sarp?"

Masha's eyes flick to her. "It's fine. But I miss our time together. You should find a job here, closer to me. Work for a senator or a congressman... you'd be happy helping people."

Raya keeps her tone light. "I help people now. I love what I do."

"You could do better." There is an edge to Masha's voice, a sharpness that makes Raya's pulse quicken.

They reach the Italian Water Garden, the path curving over

a small bridge that offered a view of the sculpted fountains. Raya seizes the moment. "Why are you always trying to get me into a different job?"

"I'm not. I want what's best for you."

Masha feels a flicker of unease. *Has she been too obvious?* She needs to guide Raya, but it has to seem organic—like it is Raya's idea.

Behind them, the couple pauses by the railing, pretending to fuss over the stroller, their attention fixed elsewhere.

Raya is struck by Masha's persistence. *If she only knew I worked for the government already.* She tries another angle. "My work lets me travel. I can see you anywhere. You always say you're lonely... you could go home."

Masha stiffens. "Who says I'm lonely?"

"You do. Every time we speak." Raya feels as if she is volleying in a game of ping-pong.

Masha exhales, her voice quiet. "Raya, my parents are dead. I am old."

They walk past the Sylvan Fountain, the meadow spreading out before them in soft greens and golds. The sight reminds Raya of the French countryside, of those rolling landscapes that always feel untouched by time.

She looks at Masha. "But your extended family, your friends? They're in Europe, aren't they?"

A pause. "Sad times," Masha says finally. "I don't want to relive them." *Why is Raya asking me about my past?*

Masha is pulling back. Raya can feel it. The shift, the instinct to retreat. She presses forward anyway. "I feel you don't trust me. Why don't you ever tell me where you're from? Your life in Poland? What town did you live in?"

Masha does not respond. She just keeps walking through the winding trails, heading towards the Topiary. The finely trimmed hedges reminded Raya of an English garden.

The couple begins moving again, trailing at a careful distance.

Raya pivots. "I was thinking about Sunningham. When you killed those men. Where did you learn to do that?"

Masha's steps falter slightly. "Raya, that was long ago. Why do you ask now?"

Raya shrugs. "All those hours on planes, traveling—I think about things. It's been on my mind."

"There's nothing to tell." Masha's tone was firm. "I don't want to talk about it."

"But someone must have trained you. How did you learn to shoot like that?"

Masha's fingers curl into a fist. "I can't tell you."

"Can't?" Raya catches the verbal slip. "Or won't?"

Masha scrambles for an answer. "I mean, I have promised myself never to talk about that part of my past."

Raya doesn't buy it. Masha is too smooth, too careful. *She isn't lying, she's withholding.*

They turn toward the café, passing the beer garden. The couple shadowing them follows, mirroring their movements, always just far enough away.

Masha exhales sharply. "Raya, enough. You're upsetting me."

Raya tries again. "I promised to visit. Now you are complaining."

"All this talk of the past. I don't like it."

"Relationships require two-way communication."

Masha scoffs. "Your generation worries too much about the past. You should focus on your future."

My future, not yours.

When they reach the restaurant, neither of them is hungry. They order hot drinks instead, sitting in silence, the tension lingering between them.

Raya had thought she'd be able to untangle what Bram told her—the questions from the interrogation. But her instincts tell her Masha is lying. Don said I needed to trust my instincts. She looks across the table at the woman who had been like a mother to her for so many years. *How much of that was real?*

On the other side of the table, Masha feels the frustration gnawing at her. She is losing control of the situation. She needs to be careful, to pull Raya back in—slowly, deliberately. This isn't a sprint. It's a long game.

Raya forces a smile, trying to smooth over the cracks. "You know I love you. I want us to be close."

Masha hesitates. She is stubborn, but in the end, she gives Raya the words she thinks she wants to hear. "I am always here for you."

Behind them, the couple trailing quietly observed, recording every word.

CHAPTER TWENTY-NINE

Tel Aviv, Israel
2018

NESHAD'S APARTMENT BUILDING STOOD IN the heart of Neve Jaffa, a district steeped in history where old-world charm blended seamlessly with modern sophistication. The neighborhood was a tapestry of Mediterranean architecture—earth-toned buildings with arched windows and ornate wrought-iron balconies, their shutters painted in vibrant hues of blue and green.

Stone-paved alleyways wove between whitewashed facades, bougainvillea spilling over stucco walls, their magenta blossoms catching the late afternoon sun. Clay-tiled rooftops, weathered by time and sea air, overlooked narrow streets infused with the scent of fresh-baked bread and citrus.

He loved returning home. It was more than an apartment; it was his sanctuary—a place where he could remind himself why he did this work, why it mattered.

Walking through Neve Jaffa, he absorbed life unfolding around him: the laughter of children echoing off limestone walls, mothers chatting beneath a café awning, the aroma of strong coffee mixing with salt from the sea. A relative peace. But peace here was always tenuous, fragile—something to be cherished, yet never trusted. He had seen how quickly it could shatter.

The enemy was never far. Bombs on buses. Missile strikes from the north. There would always be another war, another attack. Vigilance was their only defense, and complacency a luxury they could never afford.

He was born into chaos—a time of great uncertainty for Israel. A nation still reeling from war, questioning whether the world would stand with them or let them fall. The echoes of Munich, the weight of Entebbe, and the whispers of betrayal and survival formed the backdrop of his childhood. His parents were patriots—believers in service—and they instilled that same duty in him from an early age.

It became clear quickly that he had a gift: the ability to remain cool under pressure, to think three steps ahead while others reacted in the moment. It was an asset—and the agency took notice.

Missions came quickly, each more dangerous than the last, and he excelled. Not just in execution, but in instinct. An office job and desk would never have suited Neshad. A free spirit, he thrived in the field, where things were real, where every decision carried weight.

Neshad traveled to Israel at least twice a year for regular meetings with his superiors and, occasionally, a direct audience with the Director himself. He had come up through the ranks alongside the current Director—both forged in the same crucible of operations, bound by years of shared victories and losses. Their relationship was strong but measured. They trusted each other. Yet in this world, trust was never complete—everyone carried their own secrets.

A nondescript Bauhaus building, clustered among similar structures and hiding in plain sight, housed the headquarters of the Central Institute for Intelligence and Special Operations—better known as Mossad.

The façade was a carefully crafted illusion; its interior had been rebuilt and modernized many times. Beneath the surface, layers of steel and concrete formed a near-impenetrable stronghold, capable of withstanding missile strikes or car bombs.

Ordinary-looking windows were, in fact, blast-resistant, and hidden barriers in the corridors could lock the building down in seconds.

Neshad steps into the Director's office, the familiar scent of leather and aged wood greets him like an old friend. Hevel rises from his chair, a rare smile breaking his usually stern expression. They clasp hands before pulling each other into a brief, firm embrace—a nod to their unspoken understanding.

"Good to see you, old friend," Hevel says, gesturing toward the side of the room where a small bar cart stands. "Drink?"

Neshad nods, watching as Hevel pours two glasses of deep amber liquid. No formalities here—no stiff seating across a desk. Instead, they settle into the well-worn armchairs by the window, a setting meant for candid conversations.

Neshad takes a sip, letting the warmth settle in his chest.

Hevel studies him for a moment before speaking. "I've read your reports."

"And?"

"I understand your need for answers. But you must be cautious... the information we get from KNOLL is profound. We must protect the asset."

"What if we do nothing with the information?"

"KNOLL is too important. We can't put that at risk."

Neshad sees Hevel is invested. "What is your relationship with KNOLL?"

Hevel takes a slow sip of his drink while he decides. Neshad was always intuitive—sometimes too intuitive. Finally, he says, "I recruited KNOLL. A long time ago." And then he tells Neshad the story—or at least, a story.

For the first time, Hevel lets on that KNOLL is a man and not a woman. Neshad had assumed, but never certain.

"It has been a long time. You must be worried about his mental state."

"Of course I am. Living a double life that long damages a person—but we manage with what we have."

"And you are his handler?"

"No. I trust KNOLL. He sends us what he can, when he can. He is under incredible pressure."

"It's not how we do things. Why do you allow it?"

"KNOLL is in a sensitive position. His situation creates complications. He is heavily surveilled. We... I made the decision."

There *are* protocols for a reason. Neshad will not push it further, but he doesn't like it.

"There is a meeting this afternoon I want you to attend," Hevel says. "Keep your head. A new batch of intel has come in from KNOLL. The cryptographers are working to decipher it as we speak."

When Neshad arrives, he realizes this is no ordinary meeting. Escorted into a large SCIF, he is met by a long conference table and several people he doesn't recognize. When the heavy door shuts, he feels the subtle shift in air pressure, the isolation of the sealed room.

The Director addresses the team. "I don't need to remind anyone, but I will. KNOLL is our most important and productive asset. The information shared in this room must be protected at all costs."

Everyone nods in agreement.

"Let's begin. Our latest reports indicate a change of status with KNOLL."

The room stirs. The air is hot, unmoving, almost oppressive.

"This communiqué is concerning, though still cryptic. We know KNOLL is well-placed within the SVR, but we have never confirmed his actual position. His information has always been accurate—but we must remain skeptical."

Neshad wonders how the information finds its way to them. It remained a mystery—one that gnawed at him. How *can we* operate like this? It contradicted everything he had been taught, everything he believed intelligence work should be.

"What we know is that there has been a change in the directorate," the Director continues.

"A new leader has been assigned. We will need to confirm, but it appears Evgeni Antonov has been replaced by Ivan Kirillov. KNOLL will be seen as part of the old regime. This new leader will likely make changes."

At the back of the room, analysts whisper to each other. Soon they will scour every scrap of data, drafting white papers on the possible implications.

Neshad asks, "Do we think this indicates a shift in policy?"

"We don't know," the Director replies. "But any change to SVR leadership would come from the President."

"Are we going to exfiltrate KNOLL?"

"KNOLL is not asking for an exit. But we should review our plans in case conditions change quickly. This communication is different—based on its size, its quality, and the unusual request he has made." Hevel raises his hand. "Before you ask, I'll get to that in a minute."

In a nod to Neshad, Hevel adds, "We must evaluate it all. We need to ensure KNOLL is not compromised. Vigilance is everything."

Neshad suggests, "We should look to weaken this new man, Ivan Kirillov. A new leader will have a short leash and high expectations."

Hevel agrees. "We'll watch for an opening. If an opportunity arises, we must be prepared to act."

An aide distributes a single sheet of paper to everyone in the room.

Hevel continues, "KNOLL has also indicated that SEMYA is active—and about to go operational. This may be the reason for the change in leadership."

"What you see before you is a translation of a document KNOLL included in his report."

Neshad scans the page. The date suggests a long-term plan, one in motion for years. The gears turn in his head. Could this be the key to understanding Sunningham?

He says, "If this is going operational now, it's been in the works for a very long time."

"We don't know what it is yet," Hevel cautions. "We'll need time to evaluate."

But Neshad knows instinctively, this is the key—if he can just piece it together. The document mentions no specific countries, only inferences. Multiple assets. His experience tells him America and the world's democracies will be in the crosshairs. It could happen anywhere. And if it is what he thinks, it's ruthless.

Hevel continues, "As I mentioned, KNOLL has made a very specific request. I don't fully understand the implications. But he wants a meeting."

The room falls silent. A heavy pause. The kind that carried its own weight.

"He does not want to meet with us," Hevel finally adds. "He specifically asked for a woman named Raisa Dadianova. I don't know who she is. He claims he needs to meet her—says he will only share more information with her. Our job is to find her, assess the situation, and determine the risks."

Neshad's mind is already racing ahead. Hevel hasn't connected the dots yet, but Neshad has a gut feeling—an instinct honed from years in the field. Too many coincidences. Raisa Dadianova... Raya.

He keeps his expression neutral, but inside the pieces are clicking into place. If KNOLL is asking for Raya, this is bigger than any of them realized.

CHAPTER THIRTY

MASHA DRIVES NORTH ALONG THE Northeast Extension of the Pennsylvania Turnpike. Her grip is firm on the wheel, her mind already on the task ahead. Wintervale Ski Area lies a few hours north of Philadelphia, tucked into the Pocono Mountains—a perfect meeting ground, isolated yet crowded enough for anonymity. As always, she takes a circuitous route, doubling back to check for signs of surveillance.

Along the way, she stops at a sporting goods store, selecting a ski jacket and matching bibs in the season's latest styles. A few different hats, several pairs of gloves—variations, disguises in plain sight.

It has been only a few weeks since her meeting with Raya in Longwood, a meeting marked by mixed emotions and confusion. Now, her handler has signaled for an unexpected meeting. *Something has changed.* It had been some time since she last heard from her contact, and that alone put her on edge. But she will not let that show. Not in front of him.

Masha spends the morning skiing, weaving effortlessly down the various runs, her body moving with the fluid precision of someone who learned long ago. Skiing has always been a release — the speed, the control, the freedom. Here, she can almost forget the weight of the world.

Between runs, she adjusts her appearance, switching hats and swapping gloves. The resort has been making artificial snow for days, with fresh powder covering every surface. Any operative tracking her will have a difficult time; she has become just another skier among the throngs, anonymous in her movements. That is why places like this work—the very nature of the environment is a shield.

She glances at her watch. Time to move. Masha skis toward the double chairlift leading to the summit of Ursa Mountain, blending seamlessly into the crowd of skiers waiting in line. Timing is everything.

A man nearby slides in line next to her, casual, unhurried. His movements are controlled and deliberate.

"Do you know the way?" he asks.

"It's a short trip to the stars."

"And the time?"

"I was always partial to seven."

The exchange is smooth. Code phrase confirmed. No more words until they are safely in the air. She knows him only by his codename—KODIAK.

Over her years in America, they've met intermittently, but it has been months since their last encounter. That's unusual. That could mean something. Everything means something.

The lift chair scoops them up, carrying them into quiet

isolation. The ground falls away beneath them, and the icy wind presses against their faces. They get straight to business.

First, had either of them been followed? Masha would never have approached the lift if she were not certain she was clean. But protocol is protocol.

Second, they determine their next meeting location, confirm emergency code words, and update signals.

The resort stretches out below them, pristine slopes bathed in winter sunlight — a peaceful façade masking the reality of their clandestine meeting. The chairlift carries them higher, farther from listening ears.

KODIAK doesn't waste time. "Report."

Masha keeps her expression neutral. "All is proceeding as planned. Tell the Director the БЕТА is progressing." She shifts slightly, adjusting her gloves against the chill. "Why have you contacted me?"

KODIAK's reply is blunt. "Evgeni is out. The new Director is Ivan Kirillov."

For a moment, Masha feels weightless, not from the altitude but from the news. Evgeni... gone? Her mentor, her friend. The man who shaped her, guided her, protected her. She thinks of Yuri—where is he now? He has always been loyal to her and has kept her secret. But he belongs to another time, another life. The past is not a refuge she can afford.

She forces herself to focus. "Who is this man? I've never heard of him."

"One of the President's protégés. Kirillov expects results. Timelines are moving up. He wants action now. You need to move to the next step—operationalize Raya."

Masha's mind immediately returns to her conversation with Raya, the uncertainty that has settled between them. She knows she is losing her grip on her, but pushing too soon could risk everything. "She's still in process. To be effective, she needs to transition into a government role."

KODIAK scoffs. "Idiot. She's already in government."

Masha's stomach tightens.

"We have your reports. She works for OIR. We recently discovered it is a CIA front. How did you not know? You're failing your mission—growing soft," he says with derision.

The words cut deep. Masha realizes she focused on OIR's advantages, but not its bona fides. She should have dug deeper.

She masks her reaction. "Don't be stupid. I had my suspicions, but I couldn't confirm without exposing myself. And who would I have told? There's been radio silence for months. You should have provided this information. It's Moscow's failure, not mine."

KODIAK doesn't acknowledge her challenge. "You need to change your approach. Accelerate."

Masha inhales slowly, steadying herself. Raya working for the CIA explains so much—her questions, her guardedness. This is a disaster. Or maybe... an opportunity. She has been too careful, too tolerant. This changes nothing. If anything, it makes it easier. Raya is already in a position of influence.

She narrows her eyes. "Is there anything else you haven't told me?"

KODIAK hesitates before replying. "Kirillov wants to complete the testing to determine if the process will work. We have other candidates in the pipeline. We need to resolve whether the method is viable."

Masha's grip on the safety bar tightens. "I'll take action." She needs to focus on Raya. Shape her. Control her. Any choice will be painful, but she will do what is necessary.

KODIAK's voice drops, the warning unmistakable. "Kirillov expects results. If he doesn't see them, he will terminate. Eliminate all loose ends. SEMYA is draining too many resources. It's costing too much."

Masha barely blinks, but her mind races. Not subtle. Kirillov is already considering purging the operation, cutting off all involved. They're getting nervous. What's changed? Would Kirillov really abandon such an important project? Or have priorities shifted?

The ride takes less than ten minutes. As they reach the top, they separate without another word, skiing in opposite directions.

Halfway down the slope, Masha veers off the main run, stopping in a secluded patch where she will be unseen. She inhales sharply, steadying herself against a tree, then removes her jacket and turns it inside out. Reversible. Different colors. A different style. She swaps gloves, changes her hat, and replaces the goggles covering her eyes. Masha presses her palms against the cold bark of the tree, feeling its rough and jagged shell. She realizes she is crying. Why?

She handled the meeting as best she could, yet she must acknowledge her deficiency. The situation with Raya has not been handled as it should have been. She is failing. And now, she has to press Raya. She has to force her into the fold by any means necessary.

She is not crying for herself, but for what she must do.

Masha loves Raya. It did not happen at the start. From the beginning, she had been determined to remain detached. The mission demanded it, and she was still angry with her own daughter. But over time, she softened, becoming dedicated to Raya.

Her devotion to the mission, however, was absolute. And she could not have both. The duality of her loyalties is fracturing her, and for the first time, she feels it slipping beyond her control.

She clenches her jaw, rage flooding through her—not just at herself, but at everything. The isolation. The manipulation. The way she has been left in the dark—like she is nothing. She feels herself spiraling. The more she thinks, the deeper she falls into the black. She wipes her face, exhaling hard. She pulls herself back from the edge, as her training has taught her. Raya must be controlled. No matter the cost.

CHAPTER THIRTY-ONE

HEATHROW AIRPORT, UK
2018

BRAM IS DREAMING AGAIN. HE was thinking about Raya's upcoming visit when he dozed off, and now Raya is with him. They are wandering the London Underground, searching for an exit they can't find.

Stairs up, stairs down. False turns. Detours leading nowhere. Bram feels panic creeping in, while Raya remains calm—as if she knows the way but will not say.

The shrill ring of his phone yanks him awake.

"Wake up, ya great lummox. Time to earn yer keep."

Bram groans, fumbling in the dark. "What the hell are you talking about?" He knocks over his alarm clock, groping for a shirt.

Jynx doesn't bother explaining. "I need eyes on a couple of fellas. Now."

Bram wiped the sleep from his eyes, switching on the light. "I'm in bed. What time is it?"

"Doesn't matter what time it is. I done you favors, now it's time to square up. Get yer arse outta bed and head toward Heathrow. Call me when you're on the road."

The Mossad Operations Center never sleeps — a 24/7 nerve center staffed with young men and women monitoring intelligence feeds from every corner of the globe. Several hours earlier, an alert came from an intercepted transmission near Guildstead, England. A flagged conversation. Keywords: "Dissident," "Elimination," "Novichok."

The Southeast Region Terrorism Task Force is already mobilizing. British authorities are scrambling to make sense of the incident—a poisoning, no name given on the open channels. But Mossad's analysts do not need the name. They already know it is Dmitri Beridze.

A Russian dissident. Stateless until recently, when he was granted UK citizenship. A man with powerful enemies. And now he is dying. British authorities suspect a nerve agent— Novichok, the Russian President's preferred method of silencing enemies. A sloppy but unmistakable signature.

Dmitri Beridze is unlikely to survive. A neighbor offers a description of two men loitering around his house. No names, just details: big men, heavyset, professionals. That is enough. Within an hour, Mossad is ahead of the UK Security Service.

They identify two recent entrants to the country on Polish passports. Their passport numbers are sequential—an amateur mistake. Mossad has seen this pattern before: fake identities used by Russian operatives.

They track the men. They are heading towards Heathrow. A reservation at a low-budget hotel—Best Quality Inn. But British intelligence does not yet know where they are. The duty officer contacts Neshad immediately. Unfortunately, he is in Liverpool on a different assignment. It will take him hours to reach the site. He needs eyes on these two suspects now, and he has no nearby resources.

Neshad wants these two men—he has a use for them. He calls Jynx for help. He needs visual surveillance. Neshad needs time to get a team in place.

Bram doesn't know any of this. He is simply on his way to watch two men sleeping in a hotel. It is 1:00 a.m., and he is still groggy. He takes the ramp onto the M4 East toward the Colnbrook Bypass and calls Jynx. "I'm on my way. What do you need?"

"Once you're on Bath Road, keep an eye out for the Best Quality Inn. Don't be goin' in it, just park up where you can see the front exit. I'll send you a description of the two gobshites. They should've arrived before you."

He sees the sign and pulls into the parking area—clearly a commuter hotel for those taking early flights. Bare bones, no amenities.

"I'm here," Bram says. "What's next?"

"Just watch, that's all. No feckin' heroics, they're dangerous men."

"That's all you're going to tell me?"

"That's right."

Bram sits in his car, parked in a dark corner away from the dim glow of nearby streetlamps. The place is dead. Then, movement—two men enter the front lobby. Big, broad-shouldered. They fit the description.

Bram thinks, *at least I have a visual.*

After an hour of waiting and watching, Bram feels exhausted. His eyes burn from staring at the hotel entrance. He shakes it off and refocuses.

Again, movement. One of the men steps out of the entrance alone. Bram's pulse quickens. Should I follow? Or stay with the second guy?

He grabs his phone—no signal. "Damn it." No way to get advice quickly from Jynx. Bram hesitates. If I stay, and the other guy leaves too, I lose them both.

He makes a snap decision: follow the one. The man walks slowly toward his car, looking around but not noticing Bram. Once the man shuts his car door, Bram starts his engine, keeping a safe distance. The parking lot is deserted—too easy to get spotted.

The man pulls out and speeds down the road. Bram reacts late and soon trails at a distance. The man accelerates toward the intersection before the light changes. Convinced that the man saw him, Bram stops at the red light. He can see the taillights fading in the distance.

As the light turns green, Bram guns the engine to close the gap. He does not plan on losing this man. As he nears the car ahead, the man switches lanes without warning, then turns abruptly.

Bram's heart pounds. He knows I'm following him. Slowing, Bram nears the turn and sees the man pull into a gas station. Bram's stomach clenches as he follows and circles to the rear of the parking lot. Is this a trap? Am I making a mistake?

The man parks in front of the 24-hour mini-mart and walks

inside. Bram watches him through the windows. Through the glass, it looks like he's shopping. A few minutes later, he emerges, holding snacks and a couple of bottled waters. Bram exhales.

Bram tails the man back to the hotel. Calming now, he knows the route. His heart rate slows as he wipes sweat from his forehead. His phone buzzes—Jynx.

Bram relays the events of his chase.

"Jaysus, you nearly got yourself spotted, didn't ya?"

"Shut up."

A sharp knock rattles his window. Bram jumps, startled. Turning, he is shocked to see Neshad.

Bram unlocks the car, and Neshad climbs into the passenger seat. Bram instantly knows this is more than he thought. Neshad's presence changes the air inside the car.

"Give me an update," Neshad says.

Bram relays what he has seen and done. Neshad nods, eyes fixed on the darkened hotel windows.

"You did well."

"Why are you here?"

Neshad ignores the question. His phone buzzes, and he reads the text. "They've landed."

Bram tenses. "Who's 'they'?"

"Extraction team."

A black van pulls up in front of the hotel. Neshad steps out and approaches the driver. Bram watches him gesture toward the windows, identifying the room where the two men are staying.

Suddenly, the van doors slide open. Three men step out.

They carry duffel bags and a gas tank. They hustle into the hotel — ghosts in the night. Bram wants to ask questions but says nothing.

Fifteen minutes later, two body bags are loaded into the back. No struggle. No sound. Bram wonders if they are alive or dead. The van pulls away, headed for the private airstrip terminal. By dawn, the team will be in the air, en route to Tel Aviv—as if they had never been there at all.

Bram sits motionless, hands locked around the wheel, his pulse pounding in his ears. The van. The bodies. The gas masks. It all happened in minutes. *What the hell just happened?*

The world outside feels too still, too normal. The hum of distant traffic grows as dawn approaches—travelers oblivious to what has unfolded. His breath is shallow, every nerve still wired with adrenaline, as if his system hasn't caught up to the fact that it's over.

The passenger door opens. Neshad slides in, silent, controlled. Not a hint of tension in his posture, as if this were just another job, another routine night.

"Go home, Bram."

Bram turns, staring at him, searching for something—an explanation, a debrief, anything. "That's it? That's all I get?" His voice sounds distant.

Neshad holds his gaze, unblinking, his face a mask of quiet certainty. "That's all you need. For now."

Without another word, Neshad steps out of the car and disappears into the shadows. Bram watches him go as the darkness swallows him whole. What the hell just happened?

◆◆◆

At Mossad headquarters, the two men have nowhere to run. No country to call home. No agency coming to save them. They are ghosts now—disavowed, abandoned, left to fend for themselves in a room where the walls never speak, but always listen.

They face the full weight of the interrogation machine—a slow, methodical dismantling of their will. No bright lights, no shouting—just quiet, relentless pressure. Debriefed. Interrogated. Broken down piece by piece.

They are given choices—none of them good. Every alias, every cutout, every dead drop, every coded message—they will reveal them all. And in the end, they will confirm the inevitable truth, the truth Neshad wants: Kirillov ordered the hit.

But that alone is not enough. Mossad doesn't want just confirmation—they want details. They will extract the full story: how Kirillov rushed the operation, how he cut corners, how his own arrogance led to their capture.

They will describe his carelessness, his miscalculations, his desperation to prove himself. And when they finally break, every word will become a weapon, sharpened and precise.

Mossad will not move against Kirillov directly—they don't have to. Instead, they will feed the right pieces of information to the right people. Let his enemies inside the SVR whisper about his failures. Let the Kremlin doubt his reliability. Let it filter through to the President, to question his judgment.

A man like Kirillov doesn't need to be eliminated. He needs to be turned into a liability. And in Russia, a liability never lasts long.

CHAPTER THIRTY-TWO

KING OF PRUSSIA, PENNSYLVANIA, USA
2018

JUST 20 MILES NORTHWEST OF Philadelphia sits a town with a peculiar name—King of Prussia. Its origins trace back to a colonial-era tavern, named in honor of Frederick the Great of Prussia, a nod to the region's early German influence.

Today, the town is best known for housing one of the largest shopping malls in America, a sprawling commercial hub that has fueled rapid development. Glass offices, luxury apartments, and high-end restaurants now stand where farmland once stretched.

A place of growth, convenience, and opportunity, it has become one of the most desirable places to live in the greater Philadelphia area—a modern center, built on history and commerce.

Masha's apartment in King of Prussia is sleek, modern, and efficient—a fortress of comfort and security, just as she intended. A doorman at the entrance, secured indoor parking, a gym, a heated pool—every convenience of modern living. It was an excellent place for a woman like her: safe, discreet, and surrounded by amenities.

It is also a lonely place. She has always managed well on her own, but solitude has a way of creeping in, especially now. The conversation with KODIAK still gnaws at her.

Everything about SEMYA required patience. Candidates needed time to be shaped, to be guided into positions of influence. A handler had to be their compass, their sole source of support and discipline—ensuring that when the moment came, there was no turning back. It was a system cold in its efficiency, merciless in its execution.

And now, Kirillov wants it rushed. The demand is impossible. Rushed work led to failure, exposure, disaster. If she pushes Raya too hard, she will lose her. If she does nothing, she will be blamed. Masha paces her apartment, going over scenario after scenario. There is no clear path forward.

If she confronts Raya directly about her role with the CIA, she will be exposing her own duplicity. Raya is already drifting, already questioning. Masha is losing her. And if she lost her, Raya would be in danger. Kirillov has made that clear enough.

Masha's frustration twists into something more potent— anger. Anger is useful. It is a steadying force, a way to regain control. Anger drives you forward. Keeps you from drowning in uncertainty.

Masha spent her life calculating every move, controlling every outcome. But now? Now she was tired. Sixty-five years old and beginning to feel it. The sharpness was still there, but her body was betraying her—slower to recover, slower to react.

She needs a diversion. Something to shake the unease that had settled deep in her bones. Something decidedly uncalculated. Decidedly American. She isn't one for indulgence—self-control is the cornerstone of her life. But tonight, she wanted to abandon that discipline, if only for a little while.

Masha craves something that goes against everything she believed in—excess, comfort, frivolity. A place where she can sit back, let the weight of the past slip away, and for once, not think. She is not herself.

She scans the endless list of restaurant choices but ultimately settles on The Chamber Grill, a high-end steakhouse with a dark wood interior and a well-stocked bar. A place where she can disappear into a glass of Chianti and let her mind go quiet.

She orders her wine and takes slow sips, letting the deep red settle on her tongue, the tannins drying her mouth. By the second glass, her face was warm, flushed—by the third, she starts to relax.

Masha notices the television above the bar. A breaking news segment. A poisoning. An international manhunt. Masha isn't paying much attention until she catches a glimpse of the CCTV footage flashing across the screen—two thugs, faces grainy.

Then, they show a picture of the victim. Dmitri Beridze. Masha's breath catches in her throat. She has not seen this man in forty-five years. This man that set the course of her life.

Her stomach twists; her vision swims. The restaurant, the voices, the weight of the past—everything crashes down all at once.

She feels herself sway before the world goes black.

The first thing Masha feels is pain. A dull, insistent throbbing at her temple. She forces her eyes open. White lights. The sterile smell of antiseptic.

She blinks, trying to remember—the restaurant, the news, Dmitri, the fall.

Then a voice. Familiar. Soft but firm. "How are you feeling?"

Masha turns her head slightly. Raya sits by the bed, watching her with a mix of concern and quiet frustration.

Masha's throat is dry. "Like a truck hit me. Where am I?"

"In the hospital. You took a nasty fall. You've got quite the shiner... fifteen stitches."

Masha exhales sharply. "It's nothing. I'll be fine." Then, more cautiously, "Why are you here?"

Raya sighs. "Because you put me down as your emergency contact. Since you never tell me about anyone else in your life, who else would be here?"

Masha doesn't respond. Because it is true. Raya is the only person she has. The room feels too bright, too exposed. With the hospital monitors beeping loudly, and the weight of everything presses heavily on her chest.

She lets her eyes close again, exhaustion pulling her back under.

Just before sleep takes her, she murmurs, barely above a whisper, "I only want the best for you."

CHAPTER THIRTY-THREE

LONDON, ENGLAND, UK
2018

RAYA DEPARTED THE DAY AFTER Christmas—Boxing Day, as the British called it. She was ready to leave. She told herself she looked forward to seeing her friends in Sunningham. But there was something else, too: she was eager to reconnect with Bram.

Before leaving, she spent a few days in King of Prussia, caring for Masha after her fall. The woman who had once been her anchor now felt like a riddle. Masha wouldn't open up to her, wouldn't meet her gaze. The tension between them hadn't eased—it had only thickened.

They exchanged gifts, but it was awkward. Raya not only wondered about Masha the spy but also grew increasingly concerned about Masha's erratic behavior. She seemed at war with herself.

On Christmas Day, Raya visited her father — alone, just the two of them. For the first time in years, their relationship felt different. Closer. As things with Masha grew more uncertain, the long-standing tension with her father seemed to wane.

He was becoming more important now that she finally understood him: the sacrifices he had made, the life he had given up to save her. That night, she stayed at his house. They sat up late, talking. No tension. No guarded words.

For Raya, it was wonderful. For Phil, liberating.

Before leaving the U.S., Raya planned. Her first instinct was to stay with the Robinsons in Sunningham—Victoria and her husband had always been like family. She called, expecting an easy confirmation.

"We'll be so happy to see you! But when are you coming?"

"Two days after Christmas."

A pause. "Oh, poo... we'll be in France for the holiday break!"

Raya sighed, adjusting her plans in real time. "No worries, I'll figure it out."

"You should stay in the city first, then come out to Sunningham on Sunday. Monday is New Year's Eve, and we're having a party! You'll see all your old friends."

Raya hesitated. "I have nowhere to stay—it'll be impossible to get a hotel."

"Oh, don't be silly! Stay in our pied-à-terre in the city. We won't be using it."

That, at least, was a perfect solution. She would have time to meet Bram and still spend New Year's with her friends.

"That works great," she admitted. "I have a friend I want to meet."

Immediately, she regretted saying it.

"A friend?" Victoria's voice sharpened with curiosity. "Is this romantic? I want to meet him."

"Nothing like that."

"Pshaw, everything is like that."

Raya could practically hear the excitement bubbling in Victoria's voice.

"I have an idea. You're young and pretty—you should have dates. Consider this an early Christmas present—I'll set up a dinner at one of our clubs."

"Victoria—"

"No, no, don't argue! Let me work out the details—you'll love it. I'll find somewhere romantic. A private room. A perfect evening in London. You absolutely must have a date in London at Christmas—it would be so unromantic to have it anywhere else."

Victoria was giddy with the idea, already planning. Raya knew there was no stopping her now.

Raya's flight touches down in the early morning, one of the cruel tricks of eastward international travel. Depart at night, arrive at dawn. Too short a flight for proper sleep, yet long enough for her body to feel as if it had been dragged backward through time zones.

She summons an Uber and heads into the city, watching as the gray morning light creeps over the Thames. Her rhythms are off-kilter, her body still tuned to another time. Days will pass before she feels normal again. For now, she needs sleep.

Raya collapses into bed, intending to rest for an hour, only to wake in the dark. She has overslept. It will haunt her for days.

Nothing to be done about it now. She pulls on her coat, steps out into the crisp winter air, and lets her feet carry her through the city.

Tonight, she has to admit, there is nothing quite like Christmas in London. The city wears its history like a festive cloak—the land of Dickens, the home of Prince Albert, who gifted the world the Christmas tree. At the Royal Albert Hall, choirs fill the grand space, their voices soaring, wrapping the audience in warmth that feels timeless.

The Royal Botanical Gardens at Kew twinkle with endless lights. The Christmas markets bustle with laughter and mulled wine, while the London Eye turns slowly above the frostbitten city, offering glimpses of Tower Bridge dusted with snow.

She takes it all in: the magic, the romance, the sheer beauty of it all.

Bram follows Raya's instructions to the letter. She sent him a note in the post—a time, a route, a location. No digital footprint. No traceable message.

He takes the train to Waterloo Station, walking along the Southbank toward the reconstructed Globe Theatre. Just as she directed, he crosses the Millennium Bridge, the pedestrian span stretching over the Thames toward the grand dome of St. Paul's Cathedral.

Timing is everything. As planned, he turns right at the cathedral, moving toward Festival Gardens, a quiet oasis lined with benches. He takes a seat, exhaling as he scans his surroundings.

He won't wait long.

Raya watches from a distance, tracking his movements, practicing her tradecraft. She isn't worried—not really, not about Bram. If this were some kind of CIA trap, she'd have sensed it by now. But the habit is hard to break, and something still gnaws at her instincts. Is someone watching?

She studies the surrounding faces, looking for patterns, for anyone familiar from the bridge. But if they wanted to tail her, she knew she'd be out of her depth. Enough. She takes a breath and moves toward him.

He sits on the bench, waiting. Broad shoulders, lean frame. Not bulky. Not flashy. Solid—like something built to last. She realizes people must underestimate him, missing the quiet resolve. But there's a loneliness there, too. Bram is more than she remembered.

She suddenly feels nervous.

Bram looks up as she approaches, a flicker of warmth in his expression.

She is striking because she carries everything—loss, anger, purpose—with a quiet dignity. Her smile is warm and open. But it's her dark eyes—steady and perceptive—that miss little, always calculating. They give away nothing unless she wants them to. He looks at her as if she's a lit fuse. Not because he's afraid, but because he doesn't want to miss the moment she goes off.

He stands, offering his hand. "It's good to see you," he says stiffly.

She takes it, feeling the firmness of his grip. "Did you have any trouble with my instructions?"

"No, easy enough. Very cloak and dagger..." Bram grins.

He realizes he is exactly where he wants to be.

She smiles. "I guess I was jumpy after our last meeting. I wanted to be careful. But I don't feel that way now."

"Are you staying in London?"

"Yes... I wanted to see the city for the holidays."

"So... where are we going?"

"We have a reservation at a club—the Windsor House. A friend set it up for me."

Bram raises an eyebrow. "Are we on a date?"

Raya hesitates. "No... well, yes, if you like. My friend Victoria will be happy to think so."

Bram flushes; heat creeps up his neck, betraying the composure he tries so hard to project.

"Hmmm..." Raya adds playfully, "You'll need to improve your look. I know just the place."

Bram glances down at his pea coat. He's wearing a nice jumper and slacks. But she's right—that won't do at a fancy club. He hails a cab.

They end up at the John Lewis department store, across from Cavendish Square Gardens. Raya helps Bram pick out a dinner jacket, a crisp shirt, and a tie.

He has to admit he's enjoying spending this time with her. He turns to Raya and asks sheepishly, "Is all this necessary? We could find a pub."

She adjusts his collar, her fingers brushing his neck. "Don't you want to look good for our date?" she teases.

Bram swallows, suddenly self-conscious.

"You look brilliant," she adds with a small smile.

Bram doesn't know how to respond. He simply nods. For

the first time in a long while, he feels something simple. Real. Is this what normal relationships are supposed to feel like?

With time to spare before their reservation, they wander down Regent Street, beneath the dazzling Christmas lights strung across the road. The city feels alive—romantic. Somewhere along the way, Bram realizes, they started holding hands.

He doesn't let go.

The Windsor House Club is a vision of British sophistication—brass fixtures, mahogany trim, plush wool carpets. The maître d' looks Bram over, taking in his newly acquired attire. He is well dressed—but not club dressed. The scrutiny lingers for a moment before passing. The Robinsons arranged the booking—their reputation carried weight.

The host leads them to a private dining room, with one table set for two. A waiter arrives to take their drink orders. Everything is covered by the Robinsons. When the waiter closes the door, they can finally speak freely.

Raya opens up to Bram about her father, his revelations, her escape as a baby from Russia, and her mother. She updates him on Masha, the strained conversations, and the lingering doubts. Something is there, she knows. She just doesn't know what.

Bram listens, engaged and supportive. He helps her slow down, reflect.

Then he shares his own story.

The story of Heathrow. The story of Neshad. The night Mossad disappeared, two Russian agents. His fear that he saw something he wasn't supposed to. The unanswered questions.

His father. His mother. The guilt that still lingers.

Raya reminds Bram that his father's death was not his fault, nor was his mother's. Both were tragic. If anything, he should be angry. She relies on her instincts. She trusts Bram.

Raya orders a bottle of Pinot Noir. Bram, usually a beer drinker, decides to share. He figures he should match the occasion.

The wine works quickly, loosening the edges, lowering the walls. Bram feels at ease—but something nags at him. Raya has still said nothing about the CIA. In his head, he hears Jynx's voice: Quid pro quo, mate. He doesn't want to ruin the moment, but he needs to know.

He exhales, then steps over the ledge. "Is there anything else you can tell me? About your concerns with Masha?"

Raya tenses. "What do you mean?"

"Are you sharing everything?"

A beat. "No. Not everything," she admits. "But everything I can share. I've made promises I intend to keep. But I swear—I would tell you if I could."

Bram studies her, unsure what to think. Should he ask her outright about the CIA? He considers it, then lets it go.

Raya wants to tell him everything — about the CIA, her training, the interrogations, the questions about Masha. But she can't. She has sworn an oath.

The waiter breaks the silence, returning to take their order.

Raya knows she needs to keep the conversation moving. "What about you? Are you holding anything back?"

"No," he answers honestly. The realization stings.

Bram feels hurt that she's holding something back, even

while he's putting everything on the table. But he reminds himself: she has a reason.

They fall into an awkward silence, both realizing the same truth. This is bigger than they ever imagined.

Raya leans forward, trying to mend the rift. "I may have some options. People I could talk to. But that will open a can of worms." She could go to Don and tell him everything. *But what if the CIA is part of it?*

Bram exhales. "We're kinda stuck without help, don't you think?" He considers pushing Neshad for more, but doubts his trustworthiness.

For now, neither can come up with any better options. They both know they aren't walking away.

Raya asks for patience. She needs time to think about her next steps, to consider everything.

Bram agrees—there isn't much more he can do, anyway. He's relieved his questions didn't push them apart.

He escorts Raya back to her borrowed apartment. As they walk, he wonders: *Where is this leading?* She captivates him. He can feel it. He thinks—hopes—she might feel the same.

But stepping inside feels wrong. This is only their second meeting. If they cross that line, there's no going back. They reach the entrance.

An uncomfortable pause.

Bram exhales. "I should head back. The train won't run all night."

Raya hesitates. She doesn't want to be ungracious. "Would you like a nightcap before you leave? I'm sure the liquor cabinet is stocked."

Bram doesn't move. "No... I don't think that's a good idea."

She nods. "I understand." Then she smiles. "I had a nice time."

"Me too. It's just..." He trails off.

"What?" She looks at him expectantly.

"I don't want to mess this up. Give you the wrong impression."

"Wrong impression?"

A sigh leaves his lips. "That I don't want to continue this." He gestures toward her. "Because I do."

He moves in closer, his posture telling her everything his words don't. She opens her mouth to respond, but he only smiles, nods once, then turns to leave.

Praying he had done the right thing, Bram hailed a black cab.

The driver, sensing his mood, glances at him in the mirror. "Blimey, guv! Trouble an' strife, or is it yer sweetheart givin' ya grief? You look proper done in—like ya just been kicked down the apples an' pears."

Bram exhales. "I'm all right. Hoping I made the right call is all." He hesitates. "I should've kissed her."

The driver smirks. "Chin up, mate—plenty more fish in the sea, eh? Could always be worse. Always another one 'round the corner!"

Bram looks out the window as the cab pulls away, unconvinced.

As she steps inside, the doorman tips his hat to Raya—a silent sentinel, watchful and respectful. The lobby unfolds before her, a picture of refined opulence. The Robinsons truly live an extraordinary life. She takes the lift. Small and old, it belongs to another era. More than two people would be a crowd. It rattles softly as it ascends.

Exiting, she still has a short flight of marble stairs to climb. The hallway stretches long, lined with ornate sconces casting a warm, golden glow every few feet. This building is one of substance, of stature—built to protect, to endure. It should inspire confidence. A warm embrace.

But Raya feels none of that. She feels what's missing. The absence. The emptiness. She closes the door behind her, exhaling into the echoing silence of the apartment. Leaning against the heavy wood, her heart still beats a little too fast. She wonders at her emotions.

Then a realization—this is a place for two.

A thought—*maybe she should invite Bram to the Robinsons' New Year's party*. The feeling of loss recedes.

CHAPTER THIRTY-FOUR

WASHINGTON D.C., USA
2018

FRED IS HAVING A TOUGH week. The holidays are always difficult, ever since his divorce. He can only thank God there were no kids. The early darkness, the bitter cold, the never-ending pressure from the top—it all weighs on him. Fred needs a win. The world offers plenty of problems and few answers.

To make matters worse, everyone in his department wants time off. This new generation—*no commitment*. Work-life balance. *Bah*. Intelligence work never stops, but they're all eager to slip away to family and friends. Fred is unsympathetic. He's been holding things together all week.

Now it's New Year's Eve, and everyone is hoping to get out early. They all know the rules: no drinking, no extravagant partying, everyone's on call. But he will be short-staffed. Maybe he should keep them late—remind everyone who's in charge.

Fred continues to review the never-ending stacks of papers, reports, timelines, interviews, and analyses. There's a knock on the door, and it slowly cracks open. He sees Sam cautiously look in. She has a big smile. He turns back to his work.

"What are you so happy about?" Fred grumbles.

"I have a present. I come bearing a gift."

"What gift?"

Sam's voice brightens. "Someone else for you to turn your fury on... a respite for us lowly workers."

"I'm not that bad."

Sam raises her eyebrows and makes a mock guffaw. "Ha!"

Fred looks up and finally smiles. "Okay, what do you have?"

The tension of the week eases a little. Sam says, "You'll never guess who wants a meeting?"

"I hate guessing," but Fred asks anyway, "Who?"

"Neshad. He says it's urgent."

Fred throws up his hands. "It's about time we got some answers... he keeps telling us something. I just can't figure out what the hell it is."

Sam thinks to herself, *he's in rare form today.*

"Let him wait, get a taste of what he put us through."

Hesitating, she asks, "Are you sure that's a good idea?"

Fred exhales. He needs to be pragmatic. "No... I'm not sure. Neshad is cautious. He's never come into the office in D.C. What does that tell you?"

"That if he's calling for a meeting here, it really is urgent," says Sam.

"Damn... right, what does he suggest?"

"He says you should pick the place."

Running his hand through his hair, Fred mutters, "An early

peace offering. He must also want something."

"If you say so."

"We need somewhere quiet, out of the way. Ideas?"

"How about a walk along the Potomac? You two sitting on a park bench overlooking the water. Or huddled on the steps of the Lincoln Memorial. Oh, I know. How about Rock Creek Park?"

"Don't be a smartass. Those places are under surveillance by every service in the world. Nobody's having a private conversation in any of those locations."

"I know, I was making a joke," says Sam, thinking, *he really does get uptight when it's serious.*

As if on cue, Fred replies, "This is serious. I need somewhere quiet, out of the way."

Sam considers for a moment. "I know a place. It's perfect. It's an old conference center along the Rye River, closed now. No one could follow you. There are multiple back roads, lots of exits. I know the caretaker of the old estate. It's called Hill House."

"How the hell do you know about this place?"

"Rude—my grandfather, Henry, is the caretaker. It's all set up for meetings, but they're refurbishing the grounds. Won't reopen for a few months, but it's perfect for a private meeting."

"Okay, we have a location—rural, impossible to spy on. Just him and me."

"I could have the place wired," suggests Sam.

"Don't bother. Neshad's a pro, he'll want to walk and talk."

Sam nods. Annoyed, she doesn't even get a 'thank you.'

Fred returns to his papers. "And get Don in here. I want a

briefing."

✦✦✦

Before he can enter Fred's office, Sam grabs Don in the hall. "Just a heads-up—he's in a snit," she warns.

Don grins. "Thanks, not my first rodeo with Fred. I'll be okay, but chime in if I get into trouble..."

"Right, put my head on the block. I've given you fair warning." She's done her part. Now, she looks forward to watching these two old friends spar.

Fred is in an operational mindset, his old wrestling attitude taking over. Before a match: cut distractions, conserve energy, train effectively, gather knowledge. When the match starts, commit fully to winning.

A root canal would be more pleasant than dealing with Fred when he's like this. Don knows exactly what to expect—Fred will come out hot, pressing hard from the start. Don has his own strategy. Parry. Give ground when necessary, but never fully submit. Let Fred burn energy, saving the key piece of intel for the end. Hold for a tie or, at worst, a respectable loss. Let the boss have his moment—but never capitulate.

Sam will never understand it. How two grown men could argue, fight, practically go to war in a meeting—and then, hours later, act as if nothing had happened.

But that was the nature of men like Fred and Don. They'd known each other too long for it to be any other way.

Fred opens strong. "KABADDI is on the move. Neshad wants a meeting. We've moved past dipping a toe in. Past easing into the waters. We are in dive-headfirst-through-a-brick-wall mode."

Don has a bad start, asking a stupid question. "What does he want?"

Sam stares at him, not sure if he's received the message.

Fred's voice is pure ice. "Well, Don, if I knew that, I wouldn't need your help, now, would I?"

Don recovers. "He hasn't given us shit on Mariya... Masha, but if he's coming, he'll be willing to trade. Something has changed."

Fred nods. "I need a review of where we stand. Have you or your watchers found anything useful?"

Don's body tightens. "You are in a mood today." He will need to tread carefully.

"Just give me the update."

Don fills him in, starting with Raya's sojourn across the Irish Sea.

"So, your team in Ireland just jumped off the boat, with no thought that she might employ some tradecraft. Halfway to Liverpool before they realized they'd lost her. Meanwhile, she's riding the ferry back to Dublin with her phone off... nothing to worry about there..."

Don winces. He knows Fred is right, but they didn't have the top team following Raya.

Sam is also wondering what Raya is doing in the middle of the Irish Sea, but she's smart enough to stay quiet.

Don offers, "Our surveillance had more success at Longwood Gardens. They got audio of the conversation."

"Yeah. I read the transcript... two people bickering... nothing useful. I still don't know what the hell is going on between these two... can someone please give me an explanation?"

Don offers, "It doesn't sound like Raya and Masha are on the same page."

Fred is getting annoyed. He wants something concrete. "Very insightful," he says bitingly.

Don knows better than to respond.

Looking over his notes, Fred remarks, "Then these two geniuses lost Masha in the woods."

"She went skiing. There was no way to follow."

"She was heading north, buying ski gear along the way. Could *Jack and Jill* not have anticipated something was up?" Fred had taken to calling the watchers Jack and Jill.

"They didn't know how to ski."

Fred gives Don an icy stare.

Sam, meanwhile, is smiling on the inside—she loves it when someone else is in the hot seat.

Don is feeling the pressure. He pulls out his trump card. "We had more success in London with the updated software on Raya's phone. We could hear most of the conversation." He thought to himself, *except in the club*, where they only picked up some of the conversation.

Fred brightens. "This is new. Where's the transcript?"

"I was reviewing it when you called me in. I'm not just sitting on my hands."

Fred is unmoved. "Give me the highlights."

As Don gives him the overview, Fred shakes his head.

"So, this Bram... we think Neshad enlisted him to investigate? Why not do it himself?"

"Reduced exposure, maybe protecting his source. Neshad

knows more than he's telling."

"And he found Raya? How?"

"His father was one of the terrorists in Sunningham... probably a false-flag operation run by Masha. He's enlisting Raya to help figure it out."

Fred is stunned at the progress Raya and Bram have made. "Sounds like Neshad is pushing them in the right direction... he's crafty."

Don nods.

Fred smirks. "Looks like they're making more progress than you."

Don ignores the jibe. "Bram and Raya are both concerned about Masha, but they haven't put the pieces together."

Fred rolls his eyes. "Neither have we. What do we make of the rendition at Heathrow? Is it part of whatever this is?"

"We know the Israelis have two hitmen. We don't know what they plan to do with them. Sounds like a very professional operation."

Fred wryly responds, "I'll be sure to ask Neshad. What about the man they killed?"

"Why they killed Dmitri Beridze is a mystery. Back in the '70s, he got into trouble in Georgia—spent time under arrest. No surviving family. He had a sister, Polina. She was also arrested, but it seems she may have died. After his release, Dmitri relocated to Poland, keeping a low profile."

"The same place Masha claims she's from?"

"Right. But we have no record of them colluding. The dates don't match up. He arrived after she was supposed to have moved to the UK."

Irritated, Fred demands facts. "That means nothing. What kind of trouble was he in?"

Don winces. "He was part of an artistic circle—writers, painters, activists. Printing pamphlets, protesting. The usual 'do-gooder' types. He would've had contacts."

Sam surprises herself by asking, "So why murder him?" Then, thinking, why am I helping him?

So locked in with Fred, Don almost forgets she's in the room. He wonders: *Is she breaking the flow, interrupting Fred to help me?* He gives Sam a wink of thanks.

Don answers, "Hard to say. They let him out of prison, so they must not have seen him as a threat. Maybe they used him to track others. Maybe he was a double agent. Maybe he started publishing things the Kremlin didn't like. Maybe he knew something he wasn't supposed to. All speculation."

"A lot of maybes." Fred regains control of the conversation, shooting Sam a stare. "Okay, so a possible rabbit hole. Let's stick with what we know, or don't know. Neshad is working with Bram, looking into Masha. He must have a reason."

"Do you think Neshad will tell you?"

"The only things we have in play are Raya and Masha."

Don hesitates, *starting with a positive.* "On the upside, Raya is clean. We need to figure out how to use her to our advantage."

Fred, having known Don for too long, asks, "And the downside?"

"Masha is currently on a plane. Heading to a security conference in Dubai."

PART VI

RUST AND RAIN
2019

"He that can have patience can have what he will."
-Benjamin Franklin

CHAPTER THIRTY-FIVE

Moscow, Russia
2019

YURI KNOWS HE IS GETTING old. His body does not respond the way it used to. His mind feels sharp, but that could be an illusion. He has things he needs to do, and too often, they are things he hates to do.

His position within the Directorate of Support grants him access to systems few others can touch. But in Russia, no one operates without scrutiny. He understands that. He plans for it. But like any organization, when the boss is away, the opportunity for some flexibility emerges. Kirillov is out of the country on business, so the timing is right.

Every month or two, he would arrive early or stay late, subtly reinforcing the image of a diligent worker—someone willing to go beyond his remit for the good of the state. Over time, small favors for senior officials yielded a collection of access credentials.

Their easy surrender of login credentials amazed him—all in the name of efficiency. He never forgot those details. And he used them when it suited him.

This morning, he left his apartment before sunrise. The train is nearly empty—the city draped in bitter silence.

At headquarters, the security guards wave him through without question. Routine. Expected. If anyone later reviews his movements, they will see nothing out of the ordinary—just a man solving problems, cleaning up inefficiencies, doing his part for Russia.

He makes his way to the computer room. He never uses his personal terminal.

The space is dimly lit, humming with the low murmur of servers. One workstation, tucked into a recess along the far wall, offers a partial shield from the door's line of sight. It isn't perfect, but he has chosen it carefully—it's the best option for what needs to be done.

Raya will have to come to him. On the surface, it seems risky. Moscow is a fortress of surveillance, with cameras on every street corner. But in order to achieve his objective, he will need to speak with her, to explain.

He can't leave the country without permission—his role is not fieldwork, and he will be watched. But here? Here, he has control. He can move unseen. He can get her in and out.

First, her biometrics. Facial recognition in Russia and at its borders is near infallible. The system doesn't just analyze a single feature—it maps distances between eyes, the contours of the nose, and the prominence of cheekbones. Early models used only a few points of reference. Modern algorithms map over a dozen nodal markers, evolving with each scan.

Scarves, glasses, subtle surgery—none of these tricks

would fool the system. But Yuri can. His solution is simple: swap Raya's digital identity with someone else's.

A young woman from Spain, a housewife he found through a Facebook profile. Their features match closely enough. It's unlikely that she will ever set foot in Russia. Yuri's modifications will ensure that any scan of Raya will register as this woman instead.

Perfect.

Then—

"What are you doing?"

Yuri's spine stiffens, but his face remains unreadable as he turns.

A young technician stands in the doorway. Too quiet. Too close.

Yuri's mind races, cataloging details: Early twenties. Fresh-faced. Uncertain.

"Ah," he says smoothly, as if he had simply been interrupted mid-task. "Anton, if I'm not mistaken?" Yuri makes a point of knowing everyone's name, a rare trait among senior leaders in the SVR.

The boy hesitates. He isn't expecting that.

"Sorry, sir. Yes, sir," Anton stammers, flustered. "Anton Popov, sir."

"New, aren't you?" Yuri's voice is steady, curious, but firm.

"Yes, only a few weeks. Assigned from my army unit."

Perfect, thinks Yuri. This boy has no real contacts. No actual relationships. No one to watch his back.

Yuri's expression darkens. "What do you want?"

Anton swallows. "I didn't recognize you. I thought... maybe

you needed assistance?"

Yuri lets the silence stretch a fraction longer than necessary. Then, with quiet authority, "No. If I required help, I would ask. I am quite capable." His tone is sharp. "But you are interfering with my work. See that I am not disturbed."

Anton's posture stiffens. "Understood, sir." He turns and leaves quickly, closing the door behind him.

Yuri exhales slowly. Sloppy. He hadn't heard the boy enter. A reminder—he needs to stay sharp. He imagines Anton now, lingering near the doorway, standing guard out of misguided duty.

No matter. Never one to waste an opportunity, Yuri goes back to work.

Finishing Raya's biometric adjustments, he pivots to another task—laying a foundation for a future fall. Yuri performs classified searches, deliberately suspicious queries, and adds anonymous message board comments. All under Anton Popov's credentials.

A quiet trail of breadcrumbs, time-stamped, coded, and irrefutable. Maybe he will never need it. But if he does? The system will have all the proof needed.

Yuri always plans ahead. He always covers his tracks. In Moscow, that is how Yuri survives. While others might not be so fortunate.

CHAPTER THIRTY-SIX

ON A GOOD DAY, THE flight from Philadelphia to Dubai takes eighteen hours, with multiple stops. For Masha, it stretches to nearly thirty. The American Airlines flight to Frankfurt is delayed, causing her to miss her connection on Qatar Airways to Doha. She scrambles to find a last-minute Lufthansa flight—direct, at least.

Her body still aches from the fall—the stitches on her scalp throb and itch beneath the bandages. Although the swelling around her eye has faded, a dark purple bruise still mars her face. She knows she looks awful—healing is slow when you're older, and she'll be sixty-six later this year.

Travel in the best of times is taxing—today, she is miserable.

But the signal from KODIAK is clear: attend the Security Expo. She is registered, and they have secured her a pass. She sees through the deception. This isn't about the conference. She is here to meet someone.

Later, on her return flight, she will reflect on the absurdity of it all—*all that time wasted for a fifteen-minute conversation.*

The heat is oppressive, and she curses herself for packing poorly. No one is waiting for her at the airport—no car, no escort. The message is unmistakable: she is here for their convenience, not hers.

Masha checks into her hotel and heads to a desk in the ballroom foyer to collect her conference credentials. The woman at the desk barely acknowledges her, reciting a practiced spiel about the cocktail party that evening. She looks up, truly seeing Masha for the first time—her bruised face, the bandaged wound. She winces.

"Will you be attending?" the woman asks hesitantly.

Masha does not know when or where she is supposed to meet her contact. She will just have to endure the indignities and wait. "Of course," she replies, forcing a thin smile. "I wouldn't miss it."

She has no interest in cocktails and small talk, but she needs to maintain appearances. Her contact could approach at any time. She forces herself to stay for an hour, making the necessary rounds, keeping her exhaustion at bay. But no contact comes.

The next day, she attends the conference. She buys more appropriate clothes—light sundresses—to endure the stifling heat. The keynote speech is long and droning. She struggles to stay awake, her mind drifting.

Her thoughts turn inward. Her past. Her choices. *What is important? Is it still important?*

She remembers the betrayal. The pain. She thinks of

Oksana. *Then Raya. How did it come to this?* Everything has been so carefully planned, yet now...it's unraveling.

Her mind circles back to the two men who always haunt her thoughts—the one she treasures, her first and most passionate love, and the one she trusts, who stood by her when she needed it most. And now there is this new man, a man who is making her life difficult. A man she will grow to despise.

For Masha, the conference is a waste of time. She wants to leave. *Why is she here? Why do they treat her like this? She has always been loyal. Why?* As the day comes to an end, Masha dines alone. Tomorrow is another day.

By the time she is ready for bed, insomnia has taken hold. The melatonin she so carefully took before her flight is useless. She curses the jet lag—her internal clock still clings to Eastern Standard Time.

Her body begs for sleep, but her mind refuses. *Dmitri—why kill him?* She didn't even know he was in the UK. The thought unsettles her. She feels exposed. Unimportant. Disposable. She lies in bed ruminating—staring at the ceiling.

Frustrated and restless, she decides to walk along the esplanade. It's two in the morning, but she needs to move. The air is cool and dry, calming her nerves. Crime is nearly unheard of in Dubai—no one dares risk the consequences in the Emirates. Maybe she will stay and watch the sunrise.

Ahead, a man stands beneath the colonnade, dressed in a white dishdasha, a traditional headscarf draped over his shoulders. At first, she assumes he is simply enjoying the night air, perhaps setting up a stall for the morning vendors. Then, he discreetly signals her to come over.

She hesitates but walks toward him, unarmed but not defenseless. Anyone foolish enough to try mugging her will not find an easy target. She doesn't recognize the man, but his expression tells her everything. This is the man she is meant to meet.

When he speaks, his Russian accent is unmistakable. "Hello. Thank you for coming."

She studies him. "Kirillov, I'm guessing?"

He glares at her. "No names."

"Fine. What do you want?" she asks, exhausted. This man is interfering with her life.

"You should show me respect."

She exhales, remembering herself. He is right. She nods in deference.

He sees her bruises and smirks. "You look like shit."

"I take a fall. Nothing to worry about. It allows me to spend time with Raya."

"And?"

"And what?"

His expression darkens. "Don't play stupid. You have your orders. Have you compromised her? Applied pressure? Have you done anything useful?"

"She's close," Masha says carefully. "But the timing isn't right."

"Then make it right," Kirillov snaps, "...or I will."

She looks around. They are alone. "You bring me all this way just to tell me that?"

"I needed someplace... neutral. And I want you to hear it from me. You will do as instructed."

A chill runs down Masha's spine. "Why are you pushing this so hard? Psychological analysis says to wait for the right moment."

Kirillov bristles. "None of your goddamn business."

He knows patience is the cornerstone of the program, but he is under pressure from the Kremlin. He promised results. A more disruptive approach. Now, he must deliver.

She tries one more time. "You know this will put everything at risk."

"We're already at risk," he hisses. "I order the elimination of that traitor in Guildstead. He was a nuisance to the President, but more importantly, he was asking questions, trying to track you down. I do you a favor."

What Kirillov doesn't say is that the Israelis captured his two operatives. He has already seen the interrogation footage, sent through back channels. He hopes it has not yet reached the President. He promised progress, but he's had setbacks, and now he's dangerously close to failing.

Masha stiffens, her heart beating quickly. Kirillov killed Dmitri—*the man she had loved. Why was Dmitri looking for her?*

He continues, not noticing the emotional impact on Masha. "And there's another—a boy poking around, the son of one of the three flunkies you killed. I'm watching him closely. You don't want more bloodshed due to your incompetence."

Masha forces out a weak, "Fine. I'll move things along."

Kirillov narrows his eyes. "You have a job to do. Get it done. Put her through a third crisis, if necessary, but get it done. The President wants to finalize the program. He wants a level of confidence."

He needs proof of concept. One success to validate the program, to silence the skeptics. *Why is everyone making this so damn difficult?*

Masha exhales. "I need to get back. I need to see Raya."

Kirillov softens, pulling the loyalty card. "Good. You're part of something important, Masha. You should be proud. Raya is the beginning. Times change. Priorities shift. Programs evolve. This is about more than you know—we need to refine the process for those who will follow."

Masha isn't fooled. The praise is another tactic. Inside, she is panicking. If Kirillov is pushing this hard, it means he is willing to break her—or Raya.

As if reading her thoughts, Kirillov adds, "Be ruthless. Do your job."

In the morning, Masha departs. She needs to figure out what to do. She has few options and so many questions.

CHAPTER THIRTY-SEVEN

WYE RIVER, MARYLAND, USA
2019

THE 90-MINUTE DRIVE FROM WASHINGTON to Wye River Refuge takes Fred across the Chesapeake Bay and into Maryland. The stark overcast sky blends with the gray water, a dull palette, open to the whims of an artist.

As he reaches the far side, he enters the tidal plain—fields of wheat and tobacco stretching between cattle farms. Scattered across the landscape, clusters of ancient oaks, beech, and holly stand solemn and enduring, their gnarled branches weaving a patchwork of shadow and light.

Large estates born of a different era dot the landscape, broken up by the occasional modern subdivision. As Fred gets closer to his destination, the roads become narrower, snaking through the countryside in search of dry land. He enters an area more feral, more natural, a habitat for the wildlife.

Osage Orange trees line the road to his final destination — large, gangly, and unruly, bristling with sharp, untamed thorns. It is gloomy and dark, rain threatening, a portentous feeling, a heavy moment.

Hill House stands in stately elegance, a testament to the refined simplicity of Federalist architecture. Its red brick façade, crisp white trim, and clean lines are accentuated by five evenly spaced windows stretched across the front, their black shutters neatly framing the glass like a row of watchful eyes.

Fred does not know what to expect, but this is not the modern conference center he imagined. This is a place designed for heady negotiations over port and cigars. A diplomatic refuge from a time long past.

An elderly man greets him at the door.

"Hello, you must be Mr. Fred Avery?"

"And you are?"

"Just the caretaker. I understand you'll be using the facilities for a few hours. My granddaughter said you needed a quiet place to talk."

"Oh yes, you must be Sam's grandfather. Henry... right?"

The caretaker nods in response. "Yes, we call her Samantha."

As Fred follows Henry down the hall, a grandfather clock looms at the corridor's end, its dark Roman numerals stark against the white face.

BONG.

The chime strikes the hour, reverberating through the house. A sharp jolt of adrenaline shoots through Fred's veins. The tension he's been holding tightens further. This whole meeting has an ominous feel.

He clenches his jaw. Two hours. If we don't finish by five, I'm walking.

Henry interrupts his thoughts. "Sorry about that. It's quite loud."

Outside, tires crunch against the gravel as a car pulls up the driveway. Neshad has arrived. Game time. After an awkward handshake in the foyer, Henry ushers them into a small study. Two high-backed chairs front the fireplace.

"The bar's stocked," Henry says. "I'll bring food in a while."

Fred nods. "Perfect. Thank you."

The dance begins.

Fred offers Neshad a drink. As he settles into his chair, he asks, "Why have you been ignoring me, Neshad?"

"I have been sending you what I can."

"But now something has changed?"

"In our business, things are always changing."

Fred leans forward. "What do you want? You've been leading us down a path for years, but we don't know the destination. What can you tell me? I need trust."

Neshad exhales. "I know. I've been constrained."

"By whom?"

Neshad is cagey. "More like, by what? Circumstance."

"So why am I here?"

"As you might have guessed, I need your help."

"With what? Be specific."

"You Americans," Neshad smirks. "Always straight to the action."

"If you're trying to get my help, this is not the way. This is a waste of time." Fred stands, as if to leave. They both know it's an act.

Neshad raises his hand in mock surrender. "Patience...

please. Can we both agree Masha is an asset with unclear allegiances?"

"Yes, she certainly acts that way. Probably SVR. And you used us to investigate her. Why?"

"We knew she was in play and have confirmed it's the Russians. Just not why."

Fred's eyes narrow. "And now?"

Neshad's voice lowers. "We don't have all the details, but the strategy is clear. They compromise certain individuals, steer them into positions of power, grooming them, shaping them. And when the time is right, they manipulate them... turn them into assets. It's a long game, maybe an effective one."

"Nothing unusual there. We both look for people to recruit... scientists, politicians, analysts... anyone with access to secrets."

"We think they're starting earlier, younger, more connected, looking for future assets."

"Seems ambitious, even for the Russians."

"Yes, we suspect its creation stemmed from a time of desperation. The early nineties were a time of chaos. The USSR was dead... *perestroika* was alive. Not everyone was happy with the state of affairs. Those old spies would never let a crisis go to waste."

"Churchill, right?"

"Yes."

"Fuck." Fred wondered to himself: Did I know that something like this would exist? Is this why I let KABADDI play out when he could have killed it?

Neshad watches him. "We think it's becoming active."

Fred's pulse ticks up. "How? Your elusive source?"

Neshad's jaw tightens. "A source so valuable we can't risk exposure. We must protect this individual at all costs."

"So, you used me and the CIA? Is that why you're feeding us scraps... hoping we figure it out on our own?"

"Yes... using your own sources and methods, it would not track back to our mole."

"But you couldn't just bet on us, could you? You needed more than one iron in the fire. We know you used another cutout to investigate... you found this boy, Bram, and you used him."

Neshad is surprised that Fred knows of Bram Vidal. "Yes, I have been using him. But don't get high and mighty with me. You used Raya Rogers the same way."

Fred stiffens. "How do you know she's ours?"

"The OIR front? It's been blown for some time. You need to keep up with the times. You're almost as sloppy as the Russians."

Fred is stunned at this revelation, but he moves on. He does not want to lose momentum. "What changed?"

Neshad asks, "This new man, Kirillov. You know of him?"

Fred is coy. "We have reports. He's a wild card..."

"He is of a new breed. The President put him in place to shake things up. He's taking this directive very seriously."

Fred pieces it together. "Is that why you compromised those two thugs who killed Dmitri Beridze?"

Neshad's face betrays nothing. "What do you mean?"

Fred is irritated. "Did you use them to help chip away at Kirillov's credibility? I saw the video. Are you protecting your source by weakening Kirillov?"

Silence.

Then, after a long moment, Neshad rises and walks to the doors leading to a veranda. Rain falls softly outside. The scent of ozone and petrichor thickens in the air. "Let's view the grounds before it rains in earnest."

"Sure, I never worried about getting a little wet." He knows Neshad wants out of the building. They walk across the trimmed lawn and sculpted shrubbery toward the estuary, lined with pines. There's not a soul in sight.

"I'm giving you my trust," Neshad says. "Because I need yours."

Fred is smart enough to say nothing. Now is the time to listen.

Neshad tells a pared-down version of KNOLL. "We have a source near the highest levels within the SVR. A source that was placed nearly five decades ago. A unique situation, as the information flows to us, but without control. It's a one-way street. We have effectively no contact with this source. We constantly assess whether our source is compromised, but we've never been disappointed."

Fred is truly impressed, but he understands the caution. Their source could be a counter-espionage operation against the West. Just the same, he would very much like to have access to such a person.

Neshad continues, "The asset is meticulous in protecting their identity. The only person who knows is the Director of Mossad, and he would die to protect this source."

"And now your source wants something, something you can't provide?"

"This man, who has given his life to our cause, has made a request. A request that presents us with an opportunity."

Fred feels the hair on his neck tingle and asks, "What something does he want?"

"Not something, someone. He has insisted on meeting Raisa Dadianova."

It takes him a moment to put it together, but Fred finally says, "Raya?"

It starts to rain in earnest, and the two men scramble back to Hill House. Inside, the fire crackles, the room warmed by its glow. A spread of food waits on the table, untouched.

BONG.

The grandfather clock strikes five. Fred is past his self-imposed time limit, but now he's getting answers. He knows he'll be here late. This is the real conversation, the one that matters.

Neshad starts, "You can share this with no one, not even your Director. We need to run this from Israel. We need to own the operation."

Fred counters, "We have greater capabilities."

"And we will use them if needed, but our Joe is in Russia—I need control."

Fred's voice hardens. Posturing. "My Joe is Raya, and I'm not agreeing to anything without a good reason."

"This is bigger than one person. If they're operating at scale..." Neshad exhales. "It's hard to imagine the scope."

Fred leans forward. "Then tell me everything."

"No. Not yet." Neshad is firm. "Our source is the only one

with the information. We understand we need Raya to make this happen, but we protect them both by keeping this need-to-know."

"Not good enough. I won't give up control."

Neshad presses. "Hevel won't budge unless we run it ourselves."

"What do you mean, won't? Is this a fully baked plan, or are you selling me a story?"

"We are always selling, but he is cautious."

"And this won't work without our help."

"He does not trust you have your house in order. He feels there could be a leak."

Fred smirks. "I could say the same about you."

Then, quieter, almost resigned, Neshad says, "I'm out on a limb here. You know how that feels—between a rock and a hard place."

Fred exhales sharply. "Fuck." He does know. Too well.

Neshad sees the shift and presses forward. "Besides, this helps you. If this is as big as I think, the U.S. will have to run it through the FBI. You don't want to lose it. We don't have that problem. Moral ambiguity doesn't slow us down." He gives Fred a pointed look. "We live in a world where the strong do as they will, and the weak do as they must."

A silence settles. Both men understand the nature of their business. Neither man is ready to commit.

Finally, Fred breaks the silence. "We need a third option."

Neshad nods. "Something we both can sell back to our respective leadership."

"How would it work?"

"We could create an ad hoc team—Mossad and CIA oversight."

"Governance?"

"You and me, but the team operates independently."

Fred nods slowly. "I need veto power. I'm taking the risk."

Neshad looks up. "You mean Raya's taking the risk."

Fred meets his eyes with a sharp look. Both are men of this world, where hard choices must be made. If the operation goes south, Raya will be the one left hanging. Neshad will protect his source; Fred will protect himself. Neither wants to think about the consequences.

Neshad relents. He needs Fred on board. "Fine. You get veto on this... but we can reassess any future operations. That needs to be shared."

Fred pushes harder. "Full disclosure. Everything. Including the fruits of Raya's visit to your elusive source."

"Look," Neshad says, his voice low, steady. "We all have information. You, me, Raya, Bram—even some others. Pieces of the puzzle. Some are bigger than others. Some flawed."

He lets that sink in before continuing.

"Once the team is in place, and sequestered, we go full disclosure. Everyone. No exceptions. No half-truths. We share what we know. We compare, we cross-check, we pull apart the lies. Then, and only then, do we put together a working assessment."

"How long?" Fred is already thinking of the difficult choices he will need to make.

"A few weeks, a month. We are waiting on an update from our source with instructions. Once we get that, we will be on the clock. So, who knows?"

"I can't dedicate that much time, especially not outside the U.S."

Neshad doesn't hesitate. "Find someone to be your liaison, but we run the infiltration out of Israel."

Fred considers. "And if this expands? If we need additional operations?"

"After that, we can talk about future locations."

"You have a place in mind?"

"Yes. A military base southeast of Haifa. We'll be secure. We can safely bring a team together."

Experience tells Fred this will someday be an issue. "We need to have a firewall. I don't want this biting me later."

"On that, we agree."

"So, a joint operation. Very small, people we can trust. We task them with helping infiltrate Raya, meeting your elusive asset, and getting the intel."

"Yes, that's it in a nutshell. I may have some unique resources to bring to the table. But we don't share anything about the infiltration until we're together—I don't want any leaks."

Fred nods and adds, "We need deniability, and you're right... this needs to be airtight. But I have to give my Director some details."

Both men are already thinking of whom they can use.

Fred stretches, his body stiff from sitting. He surveys the food—charcuterie, cheese, fruit. He pours himself another drink, letting the whiskey burn its way down.

He shakes his head. "I imagine selling this to my Director.

He'll see a fishing expedition."

Neshad smirks. "Tell him it's big-game fishing."

Fred exhales. "If I can get him on board, will Hevel agree?"

Neshad leans back. "Get your house in order. I'll get mine."

Then Fred nods. "I guess the die is cast."

Neshad nods in return. "Maybe... everything always seems so clear at the start, before it turns to shit."

They find Henry, the caretaker, to let him know they are leaving.

Henry comes into the room and begins to straighten up. "I hope you both had a productive meeting. Didn't expect it to run this late."

BONG.

The grandfather clock strikes eleven.

Fred shakes Henry's hand. "Neither did we. Thanks for your hospitality."

Outside, the rain has slowed. As they walk to their cars, Fred glances at Neshad. "You know," he says, "Churchill had another quote I like."

Neshad raises a brow. "What's that?"

Fred smirks. "If you're going through hell, keep going."

CHAPTER THIRTY-EIGHT

MAIDENHILL, ENGLAND, UK
2019

THE TIME HE'D SPENT WITH Raya before her departure had been one of the best times of his life. New Year's Eve at the Robinsons' felt like stepping into another world—a blur of laughter and music, of clinking glasses and twinkling lights that shimmered like possibilities.

For a few precious hours, he'd let it all go—his doubts, his relentless sense of loss. He'd been fully present, and it felt like freedom. The wine had given him a warm, buoyant haze, and the music pulsed through him, vibrant and alive. He'd never felt this way before, as though he truly belonged somewhere—and he didn't want to lose that feeling.

Raya introduced him to her circle of friends, her energy infectious and her joy in their company disarming.

It was easy to see why people were drawn to her—why he was. Even Ligia had been there, the woman he'd met in a coffee shop almost two years earlier. She'd barely given him a second glance, and he couldn't help noticing how distant she seemed, lost in the everyday worries and simple joys that seemed to come so easily to others, but always felt out of reach for him.

They drifted through the party, sometimes together, sometimes apart—but always, somehow, finding their way back to each other. And when the clock struck midnight, they were side by side. He could still feel the warmth of her arms around him, the press of her body grounding him in that moment. And finally, before he left, he'd gotten his kiss—soft, lingering, charged with promises neither of them dared to speak aloud.

For Bram, it had been the best day of his life. Yet as he departed that night, a familiar weight pressed on his chest, warning him that good things never lasted. He couldn't shake the fear that this, too, would vanish, leaving only memories and longing. But he vowed to fight that fear—and do everything he could to keep hold of what he'd found.

As the weeks passed, Bram held on. She was thousands of miles away, back in America, yet still woven into his everyday life. They texted constantly, their conversations flowing as easily as they did in person. They avoid the case, steering clear of the shadows that loom over them both. Instead, they text about the little things—what they ate for breakfast, the strange quirks of people they've met, the mundane details of life that somehow feel sacred when shared.

He wonders when they will see each other again... but is happy that he found someone he could trust. But as much as he likes where things are heading, doubt still creeps in. The answer eludes him. He knows only that, for the first time in a long time, he isn't alone.

Bram walks down the street, the crisp winter air brushing against his skin. The pavement glistens with the remnants of last night's frost, crunching softly beneath his shoes. Despite the cold, warmth blooms in his chest. He's in a bright mood— an unusually light feeling settles over him.

He exhales, watching his breath curl into the cold air before disappearing.

A flicker of movement catches Bram's eye—a shadow falling in step beside his own. He tenses, instinct flickering before recognition settles in. Neshad.

"Hello, Bram. How are you?"

He hasn't spoken to Neshad since Heathrow. He responds cautiously, "Good. You?"

"Let's take a walk," Neshad says — more an instruction than a suggestion.

Ignoring his tone, Bram falls into step beside him. "You sure love to walk."

"Safer that way. Harder for anyone to listen in on my conversations with you."

Bram just nods.

"You've done well, but maybe you've reached your limit?"

Unsure how to answer, he replies, "I know how my father was killed, and who's responsible. But I don't know why."

It sounds feeble in Bram's own ears.

Neshad prods. "Do you still want to know? You could end this now. We don't always get to know everything in life. Maybe this is as much as you need."

Bram thinks of Raya—her willingness to ask her superiors

for help. Maybe there's more to uncover. But he's not ready to share that with Neshad. "No. I want to know. I've come this far."

"Right. Thought so. That's why I'm here."

Bram wonders at all the subterfuge. "You know what happened, don't you?"

"I have an idea... but no, I don't have all the answers."

Bram's irritation spikes. "Just tell me!"

Neshad ignores his outburst and shifts the conversation. "I'm taking a stake in Surrey Investigative Solutions."

Bram's mind whirls. "Wait... what happens to my job? And David?"

"David is staying on. It's a solid operation, and it gives me a useful cover. Allows me to keep an eye on some things."

Bram's spirits sag.

"You ever talk with David about this operation?"

"No, David isn't interested. He's got other things on his mind."

Running a hand through his hair, Neshad smiles.

There's a long pause before Bram speaks again, unsure what it all means. Finally, he asks, "So, what happens now?"

"I may have something for you. You know things, you have perspective, you handled yourself well."

Swallowing hard, Bram asks, "Even at Heathrow?"

"Especially at Heathrow... under tough circumstances."

They reach a corner and wait for traffic. Pedestrians queue to cross, and they fall into silence, waiting to be alone.

Finally separated from the crowd, Bram asks, "What is this... something?"

"If you want to stay on, you could be part of a team I'm

putting together."

"Will this lead me to answers about my father?"

Neshad shrugs. "Maybe. Nothing's certain."

Bram throws up his hands. "Always circles within circles with you. You can't tell me anything straight?"

Neshad answers firmly. "No. You have to decide before you get all the information. This is a small team. Think of it as a cell... compartmentalized."

Bram nods slowly. "Easy to deny."

"Yes, easy to deny and easy to control."

Bram wonders if he should take another chance—the way he did with David and SIS, and earlier, with Neshad.

Neshad scans his surroundings, then quickens his pace. "If you sign on, you'll be traveling. You could be away for a while."

Bram thinks again of Raya. They both want answers. It won't be easy, but maybe this is the way forward. "Will I still have my phone?"

"We'll see... you won't be able to tell anyone where you are or what you're doing."

He thinks of Jynx. They've been talking about the future. Bram can see a path forward with Jynx—a different life. Jynx's words echo in his mind: Keep your head, boy. Bram doesn't want to go it alone.

Bram suggests, "What about Jynx? He already knows what I know. He could be an asset."

Squinting his eyes, Neshad considers it. He needs a third man, and Jynx could be useful. "Maybe. We'll see. I have some assets of my own. Yeah... I'll have to think about that. He has a problem with keeping secrets."

"So, can I think about it too?"

"No," he snaps. "Get your shit together. I'll talk to David and sort things out about your job."

Bram thinks to himself: If my job's already gone, I may have plans of my own. For now, he'll let Neshad think what he wants.

Neshad keeps walking after parting ways with Bram. The kid is right—he likes to work and walk. The movement keeps him sharp and helps him think. He thrives in the rhythm of the streets, the pulse of the city in motion. He pulls out his phone and opens the Signal app, dialing a familiar number.

Jynx answers after the second ring. "What d'ya want?"

Neshad smirks. "Is that any way to treat an old friend?"

"Every time ya feckin' call, I get the short end of the stick."

Neshad chuckles. "That's probably true. I do my best, but sometimes things work out that way. Maybe this time is different?"

"Aye, not likely. One can always hope, but seein' yer name pop up on me phone don't make it any feckin' easier."

"You could change that, you know. Come in from the road. Work for me full-time."

Jynx scoffs. "Hah. I like me freedom, me own way of doin' things. Thanks all the same."

"But you're getting older, my friend. It catches up with you. Don't tell me getting up in the middle of the night is as easy as it used to be. Or dealing with morons who can't follow basic instructions. The idiots who don't comply, who don't get the arrangement. That must wear on you."

Jynx exhales through his nose. Damn Neshad. Like a mind reader. He had been thinking those things—about slowing down, about passing the torch.

"And what of it?"

"All I'm offering is some security. A transition plan. A chance to build in some contingency. And in exchange, I get your special skills."

"Hmmm," Jynx mutters, not impressed. "Looks like ya already got yer hands on me talents as it is."

"True. But this way, you'd have options. A break, if you ever wanted one. A successor, if you needed one."

Jynx's mind wanders. Bram—the kid has grown on him. Their late-night talks. The way Bram shared his life: New Year's Eve, Raya, the warmth of her friends, that first kiss. How Bram buzzed with excitement, only for it to fade into quiet longing when she left.

Jynx scowls. It should be impossible. "Are ya feckin' listenin' in on me calls now?"

Neshad smiles, even though Jynx couldn't see it. "Maybe."

Jynx rubs at his temples, his patience wearing thin. "What exactly is it yer after?"

"I'm putting together a small team for an operation. Your skills could be invaluable."

Jynx doesn't even blink. "Keep me out of it."

Neshad sighs—he had been expecting that. "There'd be a certain amount of autonomy. And I could make things hard if I had to. But I don't want to do that. It's always better when things go smooth. You know how I hate complications."

"Are ya threatenin' me now?"

Neshad pulls out his ace. "Your friend has already joined."

Jynx stops dead. "Bram? Feck off. No way." But deep down, he knows. The lad has a stubborn streak in him, that pull to dive headfirst into shite he shouldn't. That need to protect.

"I need someone who knows what they're doing," Neshad presses.

A sharp, bitter laugh. "Go ask yer mate David. Sure, ya already got yer claws in him."

"David is not going to be involved," Neshad says. After a pause, he adds, "He doesn't have your contacts, your skills."

Jynx closes his eyes, jaw tight, cursing under his breath. "Christ," he mutters. "Do I even have a choice here?"

"Not that I can see."

Silence stretches between them. The kind of silence when both men already know the answer.

Jynx sighs, shaking his head. "Feck."

Bram's phone buzzes. His stomach clenches when he sees Raya's name flash on the screen. Too late for good news. She usually calls earlier—her time zone is five hours ahead, and by now, she should be asleep.

He answers immediately. "Raya?"

"Thank God," she exhales, her voice shaky. "I'm happy to hear a friendly voice."

His pulse quickens. "What happened?"

"I spoke with Masha today. She's crazy."

Bram sits up straight, tension creeping into his shoulders. "What did she say?"

"She told me she was in Dubai for a few days." Raya's voice

wavers. "What the hell, Bram? She was just in the hospital."

Bram's grip loosens slightly. If this were merely about Masha traveling, then maybe—

"Bram," she says, her voice thinner now. "I need to tell you something."

His stomach tightens again. "Okay."

Silence. A long, heavy pause. Long enough for his mind to go dark with possibilities.

"Are you there?" he presses.

"Yes." She hesitates, then says, "Remember when I told you I'd tell you everything? But that I made promises I intended to keep?"

"Yeah."

"Let's say for a moment that I am what you thought I am. Would that change anything between us?"

Bram's chest tightens. He forces himself to answer without thinking too much. "No. I trust you."

A beat of silence, then, "Masha asked me if I was in the CIA."

His breath hitched. "And are you?"

"Bram, don't ask that."

Shit. He spoke too quickly. "Right," he says, kicking himself.

"I asked her what she meant," Raya continues. "Told her she must be tired, confused. But she was so focused." Raya took a shuddering breath. "She asked me who I was loyal to?"

Bram's fingers curled into a fist. "And?"

"I told her I was loyal to my dad." Raya's voice grew quieter. "And before I could even mention her, she lost it. She started screaming, 'What about me?'" Raya swallows hard. "I told her I was loyal to her, but she was off the rails. She said I should be most loyal to her. That she raised me. That I was abandoning her."

Bram exhales sharply. "That sounds bad."

"It gets worse." Raya's voice drops even lower. "Masha said she knows I'm in the CIA. She wants me to tell her everything."

A chill runs down Bram's spine. "What did you say?"

"I asked her how she could know that. I asked her, 'Who are you?'" Raya lets out a bitter laugh. "That set her off. She started ranting about our being a great team. Something about bridging divides."

Bram's skin prickles. "Are you safe?"

"Yes... I think so." A pause. "I got out of there as fast as I could. I'm meeting my employer tomorrow. I'm going to tell them everything."

Bram breathes out, nodding to himself. "Good."

"I am getting pissed. I feel like things are happening to me, to us, that are outside our control. I don't like this feeling of being used."

He wants to tell her about Neshad, the deal he's made, the choice he's already half-swallowed. But the words catch like jagged glass in his throat. Raya's voice—her uncertainty, the weight pressing down on her—it was too much.

Later, he promises himself.

For now, one thing is clear—if the only way to protect Raya is to help Neshad, then that is what he will do. No matter the cost.

CHAPTER THIRTY-NINE

FRED SUMMONS DON TO HIS office the morning after his meeting with Neshad. When Don arrives, Sam shows him in, and they sit in chairs across from Fred's desk. Don sits erect, legs crossed, the consummate professional. Sam taps a pen absentmindedly against her notepad. Fred leans back, opens his desk drawer, and pulls out a tennis ball. He squeezes it in his right hand, then flips it to his left. Back and forth. Each time, he gives it a few slow, deliberate squeezes. Sam isn't sure if he's relieving stress or getting ready to wring someone's neck. Don knows it's a diversion—it helps Fred think.

"Sam, I am going to ask you to step out. I need to talk to Don alone."

She looks up, surprised. "Um, okay. Whatever you need."

Both men wait as she departs, gently closing the door behind her.

Don doesn't flinch. "Let's hear it."

Fred doesn't waste time. "I want to debrief you on my

meeting last night. You were right, they have been using us to reduce the exposure to their asset." Then Fred hits Don with the bombshell. "They want Raya to meet their source... in Russia."

"What... that makes no sense."

Fred knows he promised Neshad not to disclose this information to anyone but his Director, but he trusts Don. He knows that if he is going to use Don as his liaison, he will need to know everything. "Apparently, this is a request from their elusive agent."

"But why? They aren't telling us everything."

"Of that I am certain, but this could be a significant opportunity. I can't ignore it." Fred walks Don through the conversation— "I made a deal. We are going to create a small team to run this outside normal channels. It will be sequestered in Israel for security."

"You worried about leakage?"

"Yes... and blowback. This will offer some protection. You are the only one who knows about the request for Raya to visit this asset. You can't reveal it until Neshad tells the team."

Don watches Fred closely and nods. "So? What's the play?"

Fred squeezes the tennis ball hard, then meets Don's gaze. "I need you to quit your job. Retire."

"What... why?"

Fred leans forward. "I need you on point, but I also need deniability. If this turns to shit, the only one left hanging will be Raya. I can spin up a story to cover our tracks—rogue officer chasing the truth about her mother... something like that."

Don shrugs at Fred's cold calculation. At fifty-five, only a year or two older than Fred, he knows this will be his last assignment. Every officer thinks about retirement, but actually leaving the service is tough—becoming a civilian pushes you out of the loop, creates a hole. He's seen it happen to others. Life in the service is difficult, but the life after can be brutal.

But this felt right. He could consult, stay loosely connected. Maybe take on some side projects. Leave the right way, on his terms.

"Alright." He exhales. This is the life he chose. And he needs to make sure Raya gets home safe. "I was going to retire soon, anyway."

Don's snap decision surprises Fred; he expected a fight. He presses forward. "Neshad is putting together his team. It will run out of Israel. You can take who you need, but keep it small. Anyone joining will need to leave the service."

"Is that why you asked Sam to leave this conversation? You wanted me to have the freedom to pick myself?"

"Yes. She knows everything about KABADDI. But she may be reporting directly to the Director. I'm not sure what you need. She may not be right for this. She would need to resign. She may not want that... you can feel her out, or pick someone else. I leave it with you."

"How soon?"

"Neshad believes he'll get an update from his source with instructions in the next few weeks. After that, you'll need to move fast."

Don exhales, rubbing his chin. "Next step—we bring in Raya?"

"Yes," Fred replies, "do that right away." He glances at the ball in his hand. He knows so much could go wrong. It's a risk, but he's already made his choice.

Raya wakes with a start, her chest tight, breath uneven. She slept late.

Rain streaks the window, the sky a dull, grim expanse. Thunder has rattled the walls all night, and in between the cracks of lightning, her dreams have twisted and churned, leaving her restless.

Masha's mind is unhinged. The memory of last night tightens around her like a noose. Threatening. Paranoid. Raya heard the sharp edge in Masha's voice, the desperation masked as control. *What is she doing?*

An ominous weight settles in Raya's gut. *What have I done?*

She grips the sheets, staring at the ceiling. She's been careless, letting emotion cloud her judgment, letting her guard down. Bram.

Raya exhales sharply, pressing a hand against her forehead. She alluded to it—to what she does, who she works for. Hadn't confirmed it outright, but in the world they live in, allusions are enough.

I'm an idiot. I need to get ahead of this.

Grabbing her phone, she dials Don.

He picks up on the first ring. "Raya."

Her voice is steady, but her pulse pounds. "I need to talk to you."

A pause.

Then, calm as ever, Don says, "I was just about to call you."

Raya swallows.

Don continues. "It's time we had a real conversation... come in. I think it's time."

Raya doesn't understand. Don has been cryptic, telling her only to come in. Now, sitting across from two men in a windowless room, she feels the weight of something she should have seen coming.

The older man leans forward. "Hello, Raya. My name is Fred Avery." Fred studies her, measuring her reaction.

Don adds, "This is my boss. He has had an eye on you for some time."

Raya wonders what that means, but she doesn't like it.

Fred asks, "You wanted to see Don? You called him. What did you want to tell us?"

Raya shifts in her chair. She is in a pickle. She hoped to confide in Don. Now, she is giving a report that she is not prepared to make to a senior leader. Damn.

Don sees her discomfort. "Raya, Fred and I have known each other for a long time. You can trust him with anything you would tell me."

Raya realizes this is too important and decides to share everything. She holds nothing back. Her meeting with Bram, about his father, the investigation, the revelation that Masha is Hilde, the confusion she and Bram share, and the most recent meeting with Masha. Letting all her fears pour out.

Fred and Don sit and listen in silence.

Raya turns to Fred. He looks... impressed? Surprised even at the progress she has made. But there's something else. Her instincts again. A second layer of intrigue just beneath the surface. He's still figuring things out, still deciding... and then, like a switch flipping, she sees it clearly.

This is the asshole who has been using her. And used her dad. The realization hits her hard, a familiar old truth settling in like an unwelcome guest. She remembers her conversation with Don. You are useful until you are not.

Fred sees the change in Raya's expression... sees her working through the implications.

Her voice is sharp. "Did you recruit me into this to test me?"

Fred doesn't flinch. "We make choices. We didn't know then what we know now."

"But you have been doing this to figure it out. Investigate Masha and me?"

"Yes," Fred concedes.

Something inside her snaps. She shoves back her chair, standing abruptly. "Then I quit." She turns toward the door, fury rising in her chest.

Fred's voice stops her. "Before you leave, let me ask you something?"

She freezes but doesn't turn around.

"What would you have done?" Fred asks, his tone even. "We had some scraps of information, but nothing concrete. No other avenues. No other options."

She exhales sharply. "I would have found another way."

"That is naive." He doesn't sugarcoat it. "This is what we do. We use people to get answers. You know that from your training. And we had to know if you were involved."

She replies with gritted teeth, "I wasn't."

"We know that now. And I can assure you—if I believed otherwise, we wouldn't be having this conversation."

She turns back slowly, arms crossed. "And now things have changed?"

"Yes," Fred says. "But I can't tell you more if you're resigning. I need one-hundred percent commitment to the mission."

Raya's eyebrow raises. "A mission?"

"Well... yes."

A long silence stretches between them.

Then Fred shifts tactics. "Would you like to be part of a small team working to figure this out?"

Raya doesn't respond immediately but continues to stare at Fred.

"If you agree," Fred continues, sensing an opening, "we relocate. Another site. A team of people who each know parts of this puzzle will come together to determine our next steps."

"And I will get answers?"

"Of that, I am sure," Fred replies.

Raya thinks of her conversations with Bram, the elusive Neshad, the help he was getting from Jynx.

She knows—without a doubt—that Bram will be involved in this somehow. Raya won't leave him alone in it, realizing that he is where her loyalty lies right now. They need her. She wouldn't be here unless she was critical. But she's angry, tired of being a pawn in someone else's games. She needs to talk this out with someone—she needs to talk to her dad.

Raya replies coldly, "I'll think about it." She turns and

walks out of the office.

When Don finally departs Fred's office, Sam is sitting at her desk. She looks up, uncertainty in her eyes. She knows she's been excluded, but not why.

As Don passes, he gives her a wry smile. She waits a moment and then follows him to his office. As he walks down the hall, he can sense her presence. He enters, and she follows closely behind, shutting the door.

"What is going on?"

"I can't tell you that."

"Can't or won't?"

Then he surprises her by telling her, "I am leaving the agency."

This hits Sam like a brick. Through all the feuding and banter, she felt a kinship with Don. She feels abandoned.

"And you can't tell me why?"

"No."

"But it has something to do with Raya and KABADDI?"

"Maybe."

"Well, whatever. It's bullshit. You have a career—Fred should have more respect than to cast you out. I could talk to him."

Don is genuinely touched. Maybe Fred underestimates Sam's loyalty.

"Look, I can't tell you what I'm up to, or why, so please don't ask."

Sam looks at the floor and mumbles, "Okay."

Don switches gears. "What about you? You've made a

career here too. You don't want to go off half-cocked and say something you'll regret."

"I know. It's just that... this felt like something important. And I was part of it, and now I'm not."

"That happens in this business. You should know that."

"I do. I'm tired of all the politics. I want to do something useful."

"So why not leave and do something you want?"

"Hah, you make it sound so simple. I like to work hard, and I can be effective in my own way. I don't want to be the leader. I want to be the person helping the leader. That's difficult to find."

Don thinks for a moment. "That's a very honest self-appraisal. So, for the right opportunity, you would leave the CIA?"

Sam hasn't thought that far ahead, but nods, "Yes, I would, for the right chance to be part of something consequential."

"You should go back, do your job. We'll talk more before I leave."

Don has some thinking to do.

CHAPTER FORTY

Phil Thinks About Getting A dog. He spends too many nights on the couch, flipping through channels, numbing himself with late-night television. The commercials for shelter adoptions are relentless—big, soulful eyes staring out from cages, the soft, pleading music lingering long after the screen fades to black.

Maybe he's getting sentimental in his old age.

He knows the time he spent with Raya is part of the reason. The relief of finally sharing his secrets has lightened him, lifting a burden he hadn't realized was weighing him down. It washed over him, pulled him under, and when he surfaced, he felt... free.

For the first time in years, Phil feels at peace.

His body seems to know it too. He sleeps less, but his energy levels are rising. He wakes before dawn, eager to move, eager to see the world in a way he hasn't in a long time. This is his second act.

He walks to the Delaware River, savoring the cool morning

air, the sound of water shifting against the shore. His pace is lively, with a small bounce in his step. He pictures a dog walking beside him, leash in hand, stopping to sniff at lampposts and greet strangers.

Maybe he'll tell the boys—the men he meets every morning. He enjoys their company, their stories of faraway places. No need to explain geography to men who have lived it.

He turns south toward The Rook's Nest Café, his usual coffee shop. The place has a warm, lived-in feel. The scent of espresso and baked bread wraps around him like a familiar coat. His friends are already there—men like him, men of the world.

Across from the counter, six chess tables stand waiting, their black-and-white boards set, pieces arranged like soldiers before battle. Phil has always liked chess, but he never excelled. He remembers his first visit, the hustlers beckoning him in with an easy grin, offering a friendly game, letting him win—building his confidence before the real game began. A rite of passage in this place.

But he learned. He started watching chess videos, studying books, and even taking a few lessons. Today, he hopes to test his new skills. He settles in, sipping his coffee, absorbing the low murmur of conversation. He talks about his plans for a dog, relishing the comfortable rhythm of the morning.

The café empties after the rush, leaving only the scrape of chairs and the occasional clink of porcelain. The younger, noisier crowd won't arrive for hours. He prefers the morning.

Eventually, he heads home. He slips in his earbuds, letting the jazz standards of his youth carry him down the quiet streets.

322

Life feels good.

Then his phone rings. Raya.

He smiles as he answers. "Hey, sweetheart."

"Hey, Dad." Something in her voice is off.

"What's wrong?"

He takes the alley—a shortcut he's used a hundred times before. The dumpsters and scattered trash are a minor inconvenience to shave off a few blocks. His routine has become just that—routine.

"Where are you? Sounds like you're outside."

"Just walking home from coffee. I'll be through the front door in a few minutes."

"I'm going on a trip," she says, hesitating. "I'll be out of town for a while."

Phil frowns slightly. He hears the tension in her voice, the unspoken worry. She wants to talk. "Relax, honey. You go on trips all the time."

"I know, Dad. This one might be different."

Phil quickens his pace. "Well, I want to hear all about it. I'm a few blocks away. Let me get home, get settled—use the facilities. I may have had too much coffee. Then I'll give you my full attention."

He reaches the corner and pauses, waiting for a few cars to pass. The street is quiet. No other pedestrians. He stands still, presenting a silhouette against the cityscape.

"Okay, Dad, call me when you get in, okay? I love you."

"I love you too, Ra..."

But Phil will never speak to Raya again. He never hears the silenced shot.

A sharp, burning pressure blooms in his throat. His hand flies up, fingers pressing against warm, wet blood as it spills through them, soaking his shirt. He stumbles, confusion clouding his mind. His knees buckle.

The phone is still in his hand. He can hear Raya say, "Dad, Dad... are you there?"

He wants to say something—to tell her he's okay, to ask for help—but no words come. Gasping, his lungs refusing to fill.

Phil falls to the pavement, slowly drowning in his own blood.

CHAPTY FORTY-ONE

PHIL IS LYING ON THE pavement in Philadelphia, a block from his home.

Raya, still in Washington D.C., calls the police the moment the phone connection is lost. She knows his general location and gives the dispatcher a frantic description of what happened—mugging, heart attack, stroke? She doesn't know. The dispatcher tells her to stay where she is and wait by her phone.

Hell with that. She grabs her keys and heads north.

The drive is a blur. After hours of riding in silence, focusing on the road, she nears his neighborhood. Her phone rings. A detective. He speaks in a clipped, careful tone, but doesn't tell her what happened. Simply requests her to come to the precinct.

That's when she knows.

Her father is dead.

At the station, they lead her to a small, cold, windowless

room. A detective sits across from her, with a social worker at his side. The words hit like bricks. Phil had been shot. Killed.

The questions come next.

"Do you know who might have done this?"

"No."

"Did he have any enemies?"

"Not that I am aware of."

"Anything that might help us?"

"No."

But Raya's mind screams a different answer. Masha. Her name burns through Raya's brain like acid. No proof, no evidence—just certainty. Her hands clench into fists. Bitch. She wants to find her. Wants to wrap her hands around her throat. The grief hasn't hit yet. Only rage.

The social worker leans in gently. "Do you have family or friends we can call?"

Raya blinks. Reality sets in. She is alone.

"Do you have a place to stay?"

She can't think. Can't make sense of anything. She stares at the wall, body frozen in stunned rigor.

"I can set you up in a hotel?"

Raya pulls herself out of the spell. "No, I will stay at home... at my father's house."

The social worker steps out to make a call.

Her first clear thought: Bram. She dials.

He picks up immediately. "Hello?"

Her voice shakes. "My dad has been shot. Killed."

The moment freezes in stunned silence.

Then, steady and resolute, Bram says, "Tell me where you

are. I'm coming."

"You don't have to. I'll be fine."

"Raya, you don't have a choice. I'm coming." He knows exactly what she's feeling—how deeply she needs support, and how much he wants to be the one to give it.

"Okay," she replies without really thinking.

"I am so sorry, Raya." He wants to say more. How important she is to him, how much he cares for her—but everything he thinks to say feels forced. He will let his actions speak for themselves.

She gives him directions, barely registering her own words—or his—before the call ends.

Bram doesn't hesitate. He taps into the travel fund Neshad set up and books the first available flight. Back row, middle seat, nowhere for his long legs to stretch. None of it matters. Nothing will stop him. The earliest flight is the next morning, so he won't arrive in Philadelphia until early afternoon. It will be a long flight for Bram, full of worry.

Raya slowly looks around. The interview room is spartan—just a desk, two chairs, a box of Kleenex, and a bottle of water. She doesn't touch any of it.

She is past denial. Her father is gone. Now, there is only anger.

The social worker returns. "You need to be somewhere better than this," she says. "I've spoken to my manager. I can stay with you as long as you need."

Raya barely reacts.

"I can go to my dad's," she finally says. "I have a room."

The woman hesitates. "Are you sure that's best? You're

fragile right now."

Raya exhales. "That's where I need to be."

"Then I'm coming with you. You shouldn't be alone tonight."

Raya doesn't argue. She blindly follows the woman into the hallway and out the door.

✦✦✦

Phil's house is the same. But it isn't. She walks through the rooms slowly, her fingers trailing over surfaces, searching for something—anything—to anchor herself.

The social worker gives her space, heading to the kitchen to see what's available. Raya will need to eat.

Raya enters Phil's home office. What is she looking for? She doesn't know. Remembrance? A connection? Proof that he was here. Mementos of the past.

She searches for pictures. In his desk drawer, she finds one. A woman with dark eyes and sharp cheekbones.

For a split second, she thinks it's Masha. Her stomach lurches in disgust. Then, she flips it over. Oksana, 1994. Her mother.

Raya stares, stunned by the resemblance. She looks like me. A wave of guilt washes over her. She had finally reconciled with her father. And now, when they were finding their way back to each other, he is gone.

She puts her head in her hands and cries, releasing a small fraction of the pain and fury she feels. Somehow, she feels guilty, but that makes no sense. She doesn't want answers— she wants her dad back.

✦✦✦

The first days after Phil's murder were pure pandemonium. Don was the first to hear. His immediate reaction mirrored Raya's: Masha.

Don updates Fred. Both men are seasoned operatives, all too familiar with the tragedy of loss—agents disappearing, or worse, coming back in pieces. But now, they're in operational mode. Cold calculation. Both know this could destroy everything they've been working toward.

Would Raya choose to quit, or would this drive her to seek answers and join the operation? Would she be strong enough to travel to Russia—a plan she didn't even know existed? Would she be stable enough? Professional enough? Anything is possible.

It hits Don hard. He knows Raya, has spent time with her. He feels a personal connection to the pain she's enduring. Without hesitation, he travels to Philadelphia.

Fred reacts differently. Phil was a CIA asset—and a friend, of sorts. Phil wasn't perfect, but he was one of theirs. Despite all his faults, Fred is old school. He takes care of his people.

He doesn't know if Phil's murder was a random act of violence or if it's tied to their operation. Either way, someone has disrupted his plans. And someone will need to pay.

Fred gives one order: "Keep Masha out of any police investigation. We cannot compromise the operation."

Don cautiously surveils her home. But Masha is gone. Her apartment stands empty—abandoned. She's on the run.

Bram arrives the next day. Raya opens the door, and for a moment, they just stand there, staring at each other in stunned silence. Then, without a word, they fall into each other's arms, holding tight as if the world itself might tear them apart.

In that instant, everything shifts. The playful spark that had once defined their connection burns away, replaced by something fierce, raw, and unbreakable. Raya needs Bram—his loyalty, his quiet strength. And Bram needs Raya, driven by an instinctive urge to protect someone who might love him for it.

The funeral arrangements are handled by others. Raya doesn't have a large circle of friends, but she does have Sunningham. She calls Victoria Robinson—the woman who has been more of a mother to her than Masha ever was.

Victoria doesn't hesitate. She insists on coming. Others in the community want to come, too.

But Raya knows it's a mistake. Too many questions. Too much attention. She is slowly regaining her strength, but for now, she needs to focus.

"No," she says firmly. "Right now, I have Bram. I promise I'll visit Sunningham soon, but not yet."

Victoria Robinson reluctantly agrees, but there's an undeniable tension in her voice.

Raya is already thinking ahead. She needs answers. She needs to continue the operation. Sunningham can wait. There's work to be done.

After consultations, it's decided that Sam and Don can attend, posing as work friends.

Raya is relieved to see Don, and surprised to see Sam. She hadn't expected her to show up. Others are there too—people Fred knew, neighbors outraged by the shooting on their streets, members of Phil's chess club.

But there's no sign of Masha. She's off the map. Raya half expects to look up and see her there, lurking in the shadows, but the woman is nowhere to be found. No response to any of Raya's messages. Masha is gone, and to Raya, that's enough. She is dead.

The gathering is small, a far cry from the life Phil had lived—quiet, almost pitiful in its size. A man who had once been full of stories, of victories, of battles fought on the chessboard and in life, is now reduced to this.

As the last guests leave, Raya stands beside Bram. She's grateful for his presence—his quiet support, the steady warmth he brings. She draws strength from him in ways she hadn't known she needed until now.

Raya isn't weeping. She doesn't fall apart, not yet. She's found a deep well of resilience, a silent strength rising inside her, the kind that doesn't crack under pressure.

And now—she's ready to act.

CHAPTER FORTY-TWO

WASHINGTON D.C., USA
2019

FRED SITS AT HIS DESK, STARING at the blinking light on the secure line. He already knows who it is. He already knows what it is about.

He picks up. "Go ahead."

Neshad doesn't bother with greetings. "KNOLL made contact. The plan for Raya's entry into Moscow is set."

Fred leans forward, pressing the bridge of his nose. "And?"

"There are specific steps she needs to follow, and contingencies in place. We need to move now."

Fred closes his eyes for a moment. *Damn it.*

"She just lost her father, Neshad."

The pause on the other end is only a second long, but it speaks volumes. Then, in that cold, pragmatic tone, Neshad says, "Doesn't matter. The timeline is set. We have two weeks. The dates are fixed. No way to shift them. Either we act, or we lose the window."

Fred lets out a slow exhale, his fingers drumming lightly

against his desk. He knows the answer before he even asks, but he asks anyway.

"So, Hevel is on board?"

"Reluctantly. He doesn't have many options, but he's worried about the team we put together. Says it's rubbish. He still wants to run the operation from our headquarters with our people."

Fred scoffs. "You know that's not going to happen."

"I told him." There is a smirk in Neshad's voice. "We have a saying—Mit vos men hot, muz men zikh farnoogin."

Fred allows himself a small smile. "With what one has, one must make do."

But his amusement is fleeting. The phrase is too fitting.

His mind is already back in the Director's office—reliving the difficulty of that earlier meeting. Fred sat across from the CIA Director, feeling the weight of the man's stare.

"How does this work when you're not in control?" the Director asked, his tone flat, unreadable.

Fred straightened his shoulders. "I'll have Don embedded in the operation. He will be operating as a contractor, reporting to me. He'll maintain our position."

The Director leaned back. "And Sam?"

"I left the choice of assets to Don. He asked her to join."

"Will she also be leaving the service?"

Fred kept his voice flat. "She made that choice."

"All right," said the Director, moving on. "Best outcomes? Risks?"

Fred had the answer prepared. "Not our first rodeo. High upside, manageable risk—for us, anyway."

The Director's gaze didn't waver. "And for Raya?"

Fred hesitated. "If she's caught, she has a cover story—a daughter searching for her mother. No direct ties to us."

"That was before her father was murdered. Seems events have overtaken you."

Fred's jaw tightened.

The Director continued, his voice measured. "So let me get this straight. She's just some woman on a personal quest. But now also a grieving daughter. You don't think that changes the equation? Are you sure she's up for it?"

"She's up for it... aren't we always blindsided?"

"If you send her in, you have to be willing to cut her loose. You'd lose control. The Israelis will have to bring her home, and they won't... they'll protect their source."

Fred fights his own frustration but accepts this is the only way to get answers. He has to make the hard choices. "I know."

"Can you stomach it?"

"We operate in a dangerous world. We take risks. We build contingencies. Sometimes we win, sometimes we lose. The risk is worth it."

The Director exhaled. "I usually tell my officers to let me know if they need help. Don't wait until you're bleeding out... get ahead of it." Shaking his head, he continued, "But in this case? I don't want to hear a damn peep."

Fred knew what that meant. His ass is on the line. He pressed forward. "This is our shot. If there's a large-scale infiltration on American soil, we've missed it. I've missed it. This is our chance to see it from the other side."

A long silence. Then, finally— "You have a weak hand,

Fred. Not our best assets. But," the Director said using the oft-used phrase, "we must make do."

Fred left that meeting feeling chewed up and spit out. But it didn't matter. The operation was still on.

"You still with me?" Neshad pulls Fred back from his woolgathering.

Fred exhales, returning to the present. "Yes. You're en route?"

"Hevel told me to get the plane and come pick you up. I'll be there in 48 hours."

"I'll introduce you to Don Chestnut when you get here. He will be my representative in this endeavor."

"You have his trust?" asks Neshad.

"Completely. I've known him for a long time. And he trusts me enough to resign, creating a buffer. You will appreciate him—he is old school. He is also bringing a woman named Sam, who has been read-in to the operation. Not sure what she will contribute, but she is loyal to Don."

"Fine, send whomever you like. We are partners, after all. So, you have three?"

Fred nods to himself. "And you're including Bram?"

"Already at the funeral. We can pick him up on your end. We'll pick up the other member of the team in Ireland on the return flight."

Fred lets out a breath, rolling his shoulders, wondering about this additional team member. Don can deal with that. "Get the team together, figure out what everyone knows, build an assessment, prep Raya for an infiltration, and get her out safe. What could go wrong?"

"Everything."

Fred knows operations have their own momentum. Go fever. They are filled with the contradictions of bravado and fear. The small compromises made to any plan. If you let them add up, you faced failure.

But Fred holds the veto, so it would all fall into his lap, disaster or success. It will be up to him to make the final decision.

CHAPTER FORTY-THREE

NESHAD QUIETLY RECLINES IN HIS seat as the Dassault Falcon slices through the night sky over the Atlantic, his mind already leaping ahead to the weeks to come. Every decision, every move—critical. Below him, the ocean stretches, endless and dark. A void.

In a way, it mirrors the operation. A mission built on gaps and shadows, pulling together people who barely know one another, each holding fragments of the truth. As the aircraft enters American airspace, he closes his eyes to gather his thoughts.

He orchestrated all of this, forcing their hand. Yuri may have demanded to see Raya, but Neshad is the one making it happen. It's not much of a plan. But he's driven to know—to know what Yuri isn't telling him. The truth behind SEMYA.

It's a bitter business, filled with lies and deceit. Would he risk his *own* operative the way he's asking the CIA to risk Raya? *Probably*. Sometimes, hard choices are the only way to get real results.

While he is flying, the team is gathering.

The first to arrive at the airport are Don and Sam. Don picked up Sam at her apartment in his black SUV. He eyed the pile of suitcases she had lined up at the curb.

"Damn, Sam. You moving in?"

She crossed her arms. "I don't know how long we'll be gone."

"Long enough to need three suitcases?"

Sam doesn't answer. Instead, she loads them while Don sighs.

He reminded himself—she has never been involved in something like this—she isn't convinced she belongs here. *She will have to learn quickly.*

When Don first spoke to Sam about the operation, she asked. "Why would you need me? What value can I bring?"

Don didn't hesitate. "You read people. You see what I don't. That's your job."

She frowned. "So, I... observe?"

"Yes. And no." Don looks directly into her eyes. "If you notice something, say it. If you see a connection, don't hold back. But no snark, no cynicism. This isn't a game of one-liners and gotcha moments. Everyone will be operating outside their comfort zones."

Sam exhaled. "And if I'm not sure?"

Don's voice hardens slightly. "Then tell me privately. But don't hesitate."

"What else?"

Don measures her reaction. He sees he has her attention.

"The first problem we'll face is trust. Neshad, Bram, this guy Jynx—they don't know us, so they won't trust us. Your job? Make friends. Create a space where people talk freely. Be the glue."

Sam nodded in acknowledgment.

"The second problem is fear of conflict. We need to push into the danger zone of disagreement without letting it turn into a pissing match. Challenge assumptions, but don't let anyone shut down. Keep people engaged."

She smirked. "So... don't piss anyone off."

Don studied her for a long moment. *Did I make the right call, including her?*

He trusted his instincts. "You'll do fine."

Bram and Raya arrive next, after taking the Acela Express high-speed train down from Philadelphia.

The decision to go, to join the team, was easier than either of them expected. They wanted answers—and they deserved them. If taking part was the only way to get those answers, so be it. But they are determined to act as a team, to work together, and to avoid making choices they'll regret.

Once decided, everything falls into a blur of logistics and preparation. They spent the time securing her father's home—cleaning out the refrigerator, doing laundry, covering the furniture.

Raya hires a private security company to install new locks and surveillance cameras. They will monitor the property remotely and conduct weekly inspections. She doesn't know when she'll be back.

When they finally have time alone, it is tender but awkward. Raya grieves, and Bram holds space for her, quietly offering his support. It draws them closer, even as the weight of death hangs between them like a wall.

There is a pull—a yearning for the comfort of physical closeness, the escape that intimacy might bring. But neither moves toward it. Both understand this isn't the time, the right moment. Acting on their desire feels like it would betray the solemnity of their loss. Neither is ready to cross that line.

Fred arrives as Neshad's plane touches down on the private runway of Dulles International Airport, its sleek frame gliding to a controlled stop.

The aircraft is registered to a private company buried beneath layers of shell entities and private syndicates, designed to leave no trail. Neshad intends to stay invisible. As the plane taxis toward the private hangar, he instructs the crew. "We won't be here long. Keep the plane ready for departure."

Fred greets him at the entrance. "Welcome to the U.S."

Neshad shakes his hand. "Are we all set?"

Fred nods. "The team is assembling in the outer office. I'll introduce you in a minute. But first—let's make sure we're on the same page. Are we all set?"

Neshad keeps it simple. "We bring them together. Everyone does a data dump. Whiteboard the various theories and speculation—strip it down to the facts and build a working timeline."

Fred frowns. "You don't have much time."

"No." Neshad agrees. "They'll have to move fast. And with this mix of personalities? It won't be easy."

Fred exhales sharply. "Lean on Don. He's good at managing egos. He can be your special sauce."

Neshad smirks. "Then let's get started."

After handshakes and brief introductions, they all board the jet.

Fred stands near the cabin entrance. One last moment before wheels up. His final words before they depart, and he heads back to his office: "You all want answers. But none of them come until you're together and speaking freely. Until then, nothing operational. Not here. Not now."

They all nod.

"Use the time to clear your head. Get your personal messages out of the way. This is a work trip. Once you leave, you're out of pocket. No distractions."

Onboard the plane, Bram and Raya take the back seats. They talk little. They don't need to. She feels safe with him. He feels needed.

Neshad, Don, and Sam settle in, each lost in their thoughts. *What will they learn? How will this end?*

None of them knows.

The plane is well-provisioned and built for long-haul operations. The seven-hour flight to Dublin will be followed by a second six-hour leg to Israel—a long journey with nowhere to hide. Conversations on any plane are never truly private. Their cabin is small enough that even whispers are not an option for secrecy.

After an hour, Don decides to take the opportunity to set the tone, start breaking down barriers. He glances at Neshad, who looks jet-lagged but alert, and leans in slightly. "What can you tell us about Jynx?"

Neshad sighs, rubbing his eyes. Too many hours in the air. Too many moving pieces. Neshad is quiet for a moment but understands the need.

Sam observes the interaction and sees what Don is trying to do.

Neshad considers his answer. Jynx is a wildcard, but a valuable one. "He's a unique character," Neshad says. "You'll see what I mean soon enough."

At the back of the plane, Bram perks up. Raya sleeps. The mention of Jynx catches his attention. Bram has been ignoring everyone, focusing on Raya. He has only ever spoken to Jynx on the Signal app. He is interested in seeing what he looks like.

They all settle in for the journey. Reading, sleeping, ruminating.

Finally, the plane begins its descent. Smoothly landing at a regional airfield outside Dublin and taxiing toward the far end of the airport.

Raya stirs, stretching slightly before glancing at her watch. "Why are we landing? We can't be there yet."

Bram tells her, "We need to pick up the last member of our team."

She remembers, "Jynx, what's he like?"

Bram laughs. "Don was asking the same question while you slept. You'll find out soon enough."

Outside, the low murmur of an argument carries through

the cabin walls.

"Yer sure me caravan'll be safe, aye?" Jynx's voice—raspy, edged with suspicion.

"I promise we will lock it in the hangar." Neshad's tone is firm but patient.

"An' keep yer filthy paws off it. If any of yer lot so much as breathes near me things, I'll know."

Neshad pauses and answers, "No. You won't know."

The cabin door opens, and Jynx steps inside, smelling of cigarettes and rain. "Jaysus, didn't know we were goin' first class."

All heads turn toward him.

Bram comes forward first. He didn't know what to expect. Jynx reminds him of Leonard Cohen—gruff voice, dark clothes, fedora tilted at a roguish angle. Tattoos crawl up his wrist, disappearing under his sleeve. He carries two full cartons of cigarettes, like a man planning for war. Before Bram can offer his hand, Jynx takes him into a bear hug. He's stronger than he looks. "Ah... Bram, me boy! Grand ta finally see ya in the flesh."

Bram is surprised. He assumed Jynx would be an introvert, a ghost who preferred distance. Instead, he is the loudest man in the room.

Jynx looks around the cabin, first turning his attention to Sam. "An' who's this fine-lookin' lass?"

Sam is taken aback by the older man, but remembers her coaching. "Uh, hello, I'm Sam. I work with Don."

Jynx ignores Don and says, "Ah, well met. 'Tis always better in fine company, sure, isn't it?"

Sam blushes slightly but holds her ground.

Jynx doesn't wait for a response and looks toward the rear of the plane. He spots Raya. "And you, my darlin', must be Raya—the cause of all this commotion." He turns to Neshad with a wink. "Two stunners. Fair play, lad. Ye know how to put a team together."

Raya doesn't flinch. She isn't sure about this newcomer. Raya knows Bram and Jynx are friends of a sort, but she still meets his look with steely eyes. "And you must be Jynx. I hope you bring something useful to this wandering party."

Jynx tilts his head, amused. "Right ye are. Born traveler, ready to help. Feels like home already."

Neshad finally breaks in. "Now that you've charmed the ladies, let me introduce Don."

Don offers his hand. He knows this sort, all bluster and shenanigans. Neshad must have included him for a reason. Time to keep an open mind. Practice what he preaches. "Good to meet you... Jynx. Should I call you Jynx?"

A big smile forms on Jynx's face. "'Tis kind of ye ta ask. I like it, keeps a man a bit less known, if ye get me drift. If I ever truly trust ya, maybe I'll tell ye the story."

Don doesn't push. He will need to figure Jynx out but now is not the time.

Jynx asks about David. "No, David on this crew, then?"

Neshad gives him a small smile. "No, he won't be joining."

Jynx laughs. "Hah. He was always a wanker. Prob'ly better off without him."

Bram is surprised. He didn't know Jynx and David had history, let alone that there was bad blood. *What is it with David?*

Sam, too, catches something unspoken in the exchange. A layer beneath the words. But she can't decipher it. Not yet.

They slowly regain their footing and take their seats. Now that Jynx is aboard, they won't waste any more time. Jynx takes the open seat next to Sam, and they head off for a landing strip southeast of Haifa. An airbase surrounded by miles of open desert, secure from prying eyes.

As soon as they take off, Jynx lights up a cigarette. The cabin erupts.

Sam leans over and, half scolding, says, "I don't think you are allowed to smoke on the plane."

Jynx exhales casually. "What are ye gonna do, arrest me?"

She thinks, so he is the rogue element in their little traveling circus. She puts her hand over his and asks, "Will you refrain on my behalf? I would certainly appreciate it from such a handsome man."

Jynx freezes for half a second. Then smirks. "Ah, appealin' to me better nature, is it? Now that's cheatin'. Fine, I'll finish this one... let's see how long I can last."

Sam decides to be flirty and responds, "I am sure you can last a long time."

Jynx is dumbfounded, but finally responds, "Jaysus, I think I'm in love."

Don, sitting a row back, smiles in satisfaction. He is glad he trusted his instincts. Sam is holding her own.

Long flights always have rhythms—conversations that start and stop, long silences stretching between bursts of discussion.

Eventually, Sam grows restless. She turns to Jynx. "Tell me

your story?"

"What do ye wanna know? I'll tell ya anythin'."

"I am sure you will."

Jynx smiles. "Alright, so. I come from a band of Travelers."

Sam frowns. "Like Gypsies?"

"No, cailín. Just a Pavee. Us Irish are different blood stock from the Roma."

Everyone on the plane is listening.

"What was it like?"

"Ah, we'd cross the back roads of Ireland, caravans rollin' behind us. Some of the older ones still used horses. We'd find a place, set up camp—'til the locals, or the peelers moved us on."

"Oh, that does not sound very romantic."

"It gets old, I'll give ye that. In time, I figured out I had a gift—the blessed skills every Irishman needs—a silver tongue, a quick hand, an' an unshakable hatred for the law."

Sam arches her brow. "Am I safe sitting next to you?"

Jynx grins. "Aye, I'd say so. I'm loyal to me own. An' for now, that means this crew."

"So why leave? I understand you usually operate alone."

"Ah, I was always one for me own company. Couldn't feckin' stand bein' penned in with a crowd of gobshites flappin' their jaws all day. Too many extroverts, too much noise—gives a man a headache."

As she leans back, she tries to imagine anyone more extroverted than Jynx. She closes her eyes for a moment, thinking—he is out of his mind.

Another pause in time as everyone retreats into their

thoughts.

The plane lurches slightly as a pocket of turbulence rolls through the cabin. Sam stirs awake, glancing sideways. Jynx sits relaxed, legs stretched, hands folded on his lap.

She restarts their conversation. "What do you do now?"

"Ah, now there's the million-quid question, isn't it? I fix problems—sort things out, make 'em go the way they ought to."

"How do you do it?"

Jynx gives her a sideways grin. "I work me relationships, y'know? Use 'em like a tool—get the right folks movin' in the right direction."

Sam prods. "Seems complicated... I am not sure how that works?"

He breathes loudly through his nose, glancing around the cabin. "Neshad reckons I should tell all me stories to you lot—ye grand mavens of the spy world—but I'll keep some secrets, if it's all the same."

A pause.

"Though maybe I'll give ya a wee bit. Keep me end of the bargain."

Sam nods.

Jynx leans forward slightly. "First thing ye need to understand—real influence? It don't come from who ya know."

He lets that hang for a second.

"Everyone says that. And it's shite."

Sam crosses her arms. "Alright. So, what is?"

Jynx's eyes gleam. "What matters is who knows you."

The words settle like a slow-moving current through the cabin. Even Neshad, seated a few rows away, turns slightly.

"Okay, but you get information for people?"

Jynx shrugs. "Sure. That's easy. An' a waste."

"A waste?"

Jynx smiles. "People with coin don't be needin' me for that. Information's as common as muck—floatin' round everywhere, just waitin' to be plucked."

He pinches his fingers together like pulling feathers off a bird.

"Want the plans for a new device? Join a university faculty or enroll someone ye pay, they all share. Need intel on a place? Rent time on a keyhole satellite. Wanna outflank a competitor? Just buy their feckin' company."

Sam frowns. "So, where do you come in?"

"Me real talent, now? It's givin' a wee bit o' encouragement. The right nudge, for the right person, at just the right time an' place."

His voice remains calm, measured.

"I see to it that the right stamp lands where it should, the right detail slips into the contract, the right fella gets the job. The swing vote on the board of directors goes your way. A well-placed whisper can turn the tide of a whole feckin' deal. I don't go chasin' information—I bend the world 'til it fits."

Everyone on the plane is listening to Jynx as he holds court.

He smiles. "The hand o' God 'is grand, sure—but wild an' fickle as the wind. Me? I bring a touch o' certainty, somethin' no amount of prayin' will ever match."

Sam is stunned. "And you can do that?"

"Given the time an' the will, any eejit could do it. But not everyone's got the stomach for it."

CHAPTER FORTY-FOUR

MOSCOW, RUSSIA
2019

IVAN KIRILLOV LIVES BEYOND HIS means—not out of necessity, but because he deserves it. The access, the luxury, the power. He believes himself destined for it.

The world is full of men who replace substance with aggression, who bully their way forward without attention to detail. Kirillov is one of them. He is manic, egotistical, and allergic to accountability. His failures are never his own—they are always the fault of others, of weak subordinates, of jealous rivals.

Yet, despite his recklessness, he has a gift. Kirillov paints visions, spins fantasies of the future—and sells them to bankers, politicians, and power brokers. Reality is secondary.

Unlike his predecessor, who thrived in the shadows, Kirillov craves visibility. He needs the stage, the audience, the applause.

At university, he cheated, used people, and then discarded them. He found the weak and wrung them dry. Relationships were transactional, fleeting, disposable. Only money and power mattered.

After college, he fails spectacularly. Multiple startups, all disasters. He over-promised, under-delivered, and spent lavishly until everything collapsed in scandal and debt. But in modern Russia, failure is fashionable. Fail big enough, and the right people assume you are due for a win. His stock rises.

What Kirillov truly excels at is raising money. He spins dreams into capital, tells hedge fund managers what they want to hear, drives up valuations—then bails before the fall. High risk. High reward. No self-reflection.

His wealth and reputation grow. He buys his way into elite circles. He isn't an oligarch—yet. But he is close.

His home, an opulent apartment along the Sofiyskaya Embankment, overlooks the Moskva River. From his window, he can see the Kremlin's golden domes, the heart of Russian power.

Close, but never inside. And that gnaws at him.

Kirillov steps out of a limousine, a model on his arm, when his phone buzzes. He knows the number and answers.

A single word: "Come."

Kirillov stiffens. Even at his level, he understands the layers of power. The man calling him is a man working for the man. Which means this is serious.

He turns to the model. "Change of plans. Get back in the car."

"Where are we going?"

He ignores her. Tells his driver the location.

Kirillov, ever the showman, brings her along. A mistake.

They drive south towards Rublevka. This is where Russia's true elite live. The unmapped suburb—its name whispered in the corridors of power. The land here is among the most expensive in the world. A place of palaces disguised as homes. A place where the powerful disappear behind walls taller than their ambitions.

As they near the estate, Kirillov's bravado slips. But he is a man with the power to overcome. He regains his footing quickly, reminding himself of his unique skills. He wouldn't be here if they didn't need him.

The limousine crunches along the gravel driveway, winding through immaculate gardens, past stone fountains lit from below, casting eerie shadows on marble statues.

The mansion itself is a masterpiece—a Georgian Revival estate, its pillars gleaming white against the night. A house for a prince. A king. A tsar.

When they arrive, a stone-faced security man approaches and opens his door. "You should go in."

Kirillov grips the model's hand. "Come on. Let's see who needs my help."

The guard doesn't move. "She stays."

Kirillov stops cold. "What?" A chill runs up his spine.

"She stays." It isn't a request. The finality in the man's tone makes it clear this is not a discussion.

He lets go of her hand and walks inside alone. For the second time that night, Kirillov feels something he rarely does: uncertainty.

He is led down a grand hallway. Dark wood. Heavy silence. Off the center hallway, he is ushered into a side study—small, almost claustrophobic compared to the grandeur outside.

And waiting for him, behind a polished mahogany desk, is a man who needs no introduction. The President's Chief of Staff. A man with more power than most ministers. A man who can end careers with a whisper.

Kirillov opens his mouth, ready to launch into his well-rehearsed charm.

The Chief of Staff speaks first. "Why are you wasting my time?"

Pressure. Immediate.

Kirillov blinks. "I... uh, what do you mean?"

The man's stare could strip paint from steel.

"I've seen the tapes of those two idiots you sent after Dmitri. Novichok? It should have been quiet. You're embarrassing us."

Kirillov flushes. He knows. He tries to regain control. "If I could just explain to the—"

"You will not meet with the President. You are barely worthy of a meeting at all."

Kirillov's stomach twists.

"But..."

"No." The voice is a gunshot. "Do. Your. Job."

Kirillov's hands clench into fists. He feels small. A child before a disappointed father.

"You have already failed... I have reports you are still failing."

Kirillov's mind races. "Reports? Reports from who?"

The Chief of Staff's expression doesn't change. "I have eyes everywhere."

Kirillov's paranoia blooms. A traitor. There is a traitor in his midst.

The Chief of Staff demands, "SEMYA is still in play, yes? When will you have confirmation? The President wants to move forward. You promised results."

"You will have them."

"I better, for your sake."

Ignoring Kirillov, the man looks down and begins working. Kirillov immediately understands that he has been dismissed.

By the time he reaches his limousine, Kirillov has tamped down his rage—replacing it with calculated fury. Someone is working against him. Someone is feeding information to the wrong people.

And Masha. *Why hasn't she acted? Why isn't she using Raya's grief?* The reports are troubling. Raya is being consoled by Bram Vidal. Masha owes him a report. If she has gone rogue, she will regret it.

But first—the traitor.

Kirillov opens the limousine door.

The model, oblivious, looks up expectantly. She is waiting for good news.

Kirillov smiles. She is in the wrong place at the wrong time. On another night, she would be wined, dined, and worshiped.

But tonight, she will be his outlet. She will learn what it means to be near power, but never have it.

Tonight, she'll pray for the mercy of a man who has none to give.

PART VII

CONVERGING CURRENTS
2019

"Where two rivers meet, the water is never calm."

-Ugandan proverb

CHAPTER FORTY-FIVE

Secure base outside Haifa, Israel 2019

ON A WINDSWEPT RUNWAY, THEY finally land, kicking up sand and loose gravel. The dry brush and flat desert surround the isolated base; sunbaked clay scents the air. The distant roar of departing jets echoes across the compound, but their section of the base remains eerily calm.

A low, rectangular dormitory awaits them. Its exterior is unremarkable, built for function, not comfort. Inside, the layout is tactical—a circular formation of individual rooms, each door facing a central common area. At its heart sits a large conference table, with a projection screen at one end, flanked by worn leather couches and sturdy chairs.

The atmosphere as the team enters is thick with exhaustion. They are all tired. They need time to shower, rest, and collect themselves. Everyone needs a moment alone. As they each head to separate rooms, Bram and Raya look at each other. A choice.

The past week has been difficult, pulling them closer. Their relationship has grown, though neither has put it into words. Raya has become stronger, more assertive. Steadier, surer of herself. Bram is still finding his way. Hesitant, less secure in their newfound romance.

She meets his eyes. She reads his thoughts. "Stay?"

Bram exhales, tension he didn't realize he was holding leaking from his shoulders. "Yeah."

Neshad and Don huddle, voices low, debating how to proceed.

Don pushes for transparency. "We tell them everything... now. Trust is fragile. If we don't start with it, we'll never get it back."

Neshad hesitates. "If we reveal too much, too fast, people react emotionally. We need them thinking, not panicking."

Don shakes his head. "Keeping secrets won't work. It will backfire. Trust me."

When they reconvene over dinner, Don's position will prevail. Dinner is plain but filling—stew, bread, and black coffee. They've received their phones back, but there is no signal.

Jynx scowls, holding his dead phone like it's an insult. "Why in the name of Christ doesn't me phone work?"

Neshad sighs, expecting his reaction. "The building has countermeasures—electronic interference. No signals in or out."

Jynx leans back, unimpressed. "And I'm just supposed to take that, am I? I need the feckin' thing to do me job."

"Please focus," Neshad says. "We'll revisit it later."

Jynx flicks his lighter open, then closed. Open. Closed. A

slow, deliberate show of his agitation. He lights a cigarette, hoping someone will complain.

Finally, they clear the dinner and gather around the conference table. The stark fluorescent lighting buzzes in the background. The air is thick with tension.

Don leans forward, resting his arms on the table. "Here we are. We all have pieces of the puzzle. First order of business—put it all on the table."

Jynx exhales smoke. "Right, so, easy done—let's tip it."

Don holds up a hand. "The challenge isn't dumping information—it's how we interpret it. We all have our own theories. Bias. Things we think are irrelevant could be crucial. We need to separate facts from assumptions."

Bram frowns. "Why does that matter?"

Sam, trying to be helpful, jumps in. "It's like a trial. We're both the witnesses and the jury. And a judge always says—don't deliberate until you have all the evidence."

Don nods. "Exactly. We don't filter. We lay it out first. Then we analyze."

Jynx, ever skeptical, leans forward, eyes narrowing. "Fine. But what's the play here? Why drag us all to this hole in the desert? What's the proper job? What's bein' kept from us?"

Don glances at Neshad. It's time.

Neshad stands, adjusting his jacket. "We have a source in Russia. Codenamed KNOLL. He's been in place for nearly fifty years."

"That's a fierce bit o' commitment, so it is!"

Raya's gaze sharpens. "Man or woman?"

Neshad hesitates.

Jynx catches it instantly, his smirk dangerous. "Ah, now, what happened to all that talk of full transparency? You're already bendin' your own rules, are ya?"

Neshad exhales. "Fine. He's a man. I don't know his real name."

They all nod. Trust is still tentative.

Neshad continues. "KNOLL has been warning us about a long-term Russian program called SEMYA. It started in the early nineties. We know Masha is involved."

Bram stiffens at the name. Raya's hands tighten into fists.

Don interjects. "That's why we recruited Raya. To see if she was involved. To understand what she knew."

"And why I asked Bram to look into his father's death," adds Neshad.

Jynx is sure he has found a flaw in the argument. "That makes no sense at all. You've got all the assets in the world, yet you're dancin' 'round the edges. Why not get straight to it?"

"To protect KNOLL. Too big, and it could leak, putting him in danger. This way, it looked like a son searching for answers," Sam answers.

Silence. The weight of that settles.

Raya stares at them, her expression locked in stone. She had known, but hearing it spoken aloud still stings.

Jynx clears his throat. "So that's why you were sniffin' about in their lives. Even so, that don't explain the bigger picture. You didn't need the whole bloody lot of us for that."

Don looks at Neshad again.

"Two reasons," Neshad says. "First you figured out—security. We don't know who we trust."

Raya's temper flares. "You still think one of us is a spy? After all you put us through?"

Sam's voice is quieter but just as sharp. "Do you?"

Don interjects before it spirals. "No one here is accused of anything. But having you all in a controlled environment is safer. No leaks. No interference."

Bram leans forward, voice edged. "But eventually, we leave?"

"Yes," Neshad concedes. "But before that—KNOLL has made a request. Almost a demand. This is the second reason."

The pause is heavy. Everyone leans in.

"KNOLL wants to meet with Raisa Dadianova. In Russia."

For a beat, no one reacts.

Raya jerks back, realizing what he has said, her breath catching. "What? What are you talking about? I don't know this KNOLL."

Then Sam blinks, the realization hitting her like a gut punch. "Wait. Raisa Dadianova? Raya?"

Bram shoves back his chair. "No. Absolutely not. She's not going."

The room is on edge. Don raises a calming hand. "No decisions yet. We need to weigh the risks, the possible outcomes—"

"No. She can't. It's too dangerous." Bram cuts him off.

Raya's voice is ice. "Maybe I get a say in that?"

Bram feels embarrassed, but when he looks over at her, she smiles at him.

Sam tries to defuse the tension. "We agreed—no debate until we have all the facts."

No one knows what to say next. Finally, Neshad breaks the silence. "No one is leaving this base until the mission is over. No leaks. No interference. We decide this—together."

Jynx leans back in his chair, flicking his lighter open, then closed. "What's our timeline? When's this KNOLL fella expectin' to clap eyes on Raya?"

Neshad exhales, pensive. "There is a window that opens in ten days."

Jynx whistles low. "Quick, is it? Grand."

"It's what KNOLL set." Neshad's voice is firm.

Bram, arms crossed, shifts in his seat, agitated. "So, move it."

"We can't."

"That makes no sense." His voice sharpens.

Neshad's patience thins. "KNOLL is unreachable except in extreme emergencies. If we try to contact him now, we risk exposing him."

Bram clenches his jaw. "Raya is taking the risk." He looks over at her, but she is unreadable.

Neshad presses on. "Once the window opens, she will have three days to make contact. KNOLL has provided detailed instructions on the when, where, and contingencies. We will need time to train Raya on these and position her for travel."

Sam asks, "So, we have a few days to decide?"

Don rubs his temple, already feeling the weight of the decision. "Probably less."

Raya straightens in her chair, pushing her hair behind her ear. "Then we'd better get moving."

Neshad signals to Don, who dims the lights. The projector

flickers on, bathing the table in a cold glow.

"What I'm about to share is classified at the highest level," Neshad says, his tone carrying a weight that silences the room. "You've all signed your oaths. You know the consequences of speaking about this outside of this room. But I want to reiterate—this is dangerous knowledge."

No one speaks.

The screen displays the document. It takes a few minutes for everyone to read it and process the implications.

*****TOP-SECRET*****
CONFIDENTIAL

DATE: NOVEMBER 1994
OPERATION: SEMYA

PSYCHOLOGICAL REPORT ON THE MANIPULATION OF БЕТА ASSETS

TESTING REGIME MUST ACTIVATE SOONEST PRACTICAL DATE
SUBJECT/ HANDLER SOURCING TOP PRIORITY

FIRST CRISIS:
- ♦ Required traumatic event significant enough to break natural defenses.
- ♦ Immediate imprinting is imperative; the Controller

must allocate time and
resources to the Asset.

♦ Primary requirement – push
the asset beyond normal
mental and physical limits to
reduce resistance.

♦ Critical objective – instill
fundamental ideas, worldview,
and subjugate loyalty. Use
ancillary resources to promote
where possible.

SECOND CRISIS:

♦ Cathartic instance is expected;
Asset will dissident – a natural
reaction.

♦ The Controller will maintain
the relationship at all costs
without losing the dominant
position. Second imprinting.

♦ Controller is now in a position
to orchestrate and manipulate
further.
INFLUENCE ON DECISION MAKING

♦ Establish dominance through
gradual steps.

♦ Position the asset within
government structures or other

roles with influence over large groups (establish reflexive control)

IF CONTROL IS LOST – INITIATE THIRD CRISIS

- ◆ Reestablish handler's preeminence.
  PRIMARY RISKS:
- ◆ Controller loss, establishing new Controller problematic
- ◆ Outside events- substantial unexpected disruptions
- ◆ Program discovery
- ◆ Recommend termination if a high risk is established
- ◆ Primary response to prevent analytical anomalies and skewed data

LONG-TERM CYCLE. MULTIPLE SUBJECTS MUST BE INITIATED.

RAPID ITITERIVE TESTING REQUIRED.

MODEL ANALYSIS: 73% PROBABILITY OF SUCCESS.

The room falls deathly still as they scan the contents. The words are clinical. Cold.

Neshad continues. "It came to us a few months ago from

KNOLL. It may provide a framework for our discussions."

Don thinks it's *the Doctrine of Patience*

Sam asks, "What's 'БЕТА'?"

"In the Cyrillic alphabet, it means beta."

"Like a test subject?"

Neshad answers, "Yes, in this context, that would make sense."

Raya's breath catches. The room tilts. "It's a roadmap of my life."

Don zeroes in. "Tell us."

Her voice is tight, controlled. "Don't you see, each crisis? Starting with the attack in Sunningham. Masha was there and ready. She was my protector, my controller."

Bram is stunned. "That means my father's murder was part of a plan to indoctrinate you..." He now knew why it happened. Why his family had been torn apart.

Raya reaches over and hugs him. "I am so sorry, Bram. It must have been the start, remember, Masha posed as Hilde. She set the whole thing up so she could be my hero. What a bitch."

Sam's brow furrows. "Masha was Hilde?"

Don pushes on. "What about the second crisis? When did that happen?"

"She pushed me so hard when I was young, right after the attack. Training every day, learning languages—it was relentless. I was at my breaking point. Then we had a huge fight. I remember she made sure we reconciled."

Neshad notes. "She reinforced the bond."

Don knows the answer but asks anyway. They all need to

know. "And when you did not follow her plan, when she thought she was losing you."

"A third crisis. She killed my dad. But I didn't turn to her. I turned to Bram. Masha was nowhere to be found. That makes no sense. She should have pressed her advantage."

"I'll put that on the list of questions for KNOLL," suggests Sam.

Jynx chimes in, "This is a right mad tale altogether... but let me add another twist. Masha—she's Anna Lomouri."

"What?" asks Raya.

Bram's throat bobs. "Didn't I tell you that in London?"

"No. You didn't. I would have remembered that."

"Sorry, I thought I told you everything." Bram is flushed.

Raya settles, having overreacted. "I am just losing my mind over all this."

Jynx picks up the story. "One of me lads ran some high-end facial recognition. Dug up an old photo in old Russian newspaper archives. Got it saved right here on me phone. Anna Lomouri, standin' right next to a fella called Evgeni Antonov. Workin' on somethin' called Case 42."

"What year is this?" asked Don.

"1974." Jynx pulls up the image on his phone and hands it to Raya.

She freezes. The color drains from her face. She stands abruptly, the chair scraping against the floor. "Wait."

Raya sprints to her room, rummaging through her bag, her hands shaking as she pulls out a small, worn photo. The one she found in her father's desk dated 1994. The picture of her mother, Oksana.

She returns, holding it up next to Jynx's screen. The room falls silent.

Jynx exhales. "Holy fuckin' Jaysus."

Sam's voice is barely a whisper. "They could be sisters."

They were truly down the rabbit hole.

Jynx leans back, rubbing his temples. "I need a drink. Neshad, tell me you've got a drop of somethin' decent in this place?"

A strained chuckle breaks the tension, but only slightly.

After a moment, Don clears his throat. "Let's push a little further before we call it a night."

As they settle back in, Sam mutters to Jynx, "Masha is Hilde is Anna. This is insane."

He nods. "That one's swappin' names like cards in a bleedin' deck. Bet she's got more aliases than feckin' socks in her drawer. She must be wonderin' who the hell she is half the time... prob'ly introduces herself twice at parties!"

"Do you think she is Raya's mother?" Sam asks Don.

Don shakes his head. "No, the dates are all wrong. Masha can't be Raya's mother."

Hearing the exchange, Raya bristles. "My mother's dead. My father told me the story before he died. He told me everything." Pointedly looking at Don as if he were Fred.

Raya relays the story of her exodus from Russia. How they coerced her father into being a sometimes CIA asset and mule.

Jynx quips, "They had ya marked from the start, set up like a proper asset, all wired and ready to go. A grim feckin' business, this."

Neshad stays detached. They have a job to do. "What are

we missing?"

"Why does KNOLL want to meet Raya?" asks Bram.

Silence. No one has an answer.

Neshad folds his arms. "Who else is in play?"

Sam frowns. "What about Evgeni Antonov?"

Neshad nods. "Until a few months ago, he ran the SVR. Then he was ousted and replaced by Ivan Kirillov."

"Why was he in the photo with Masha? Is that what we are calling her?" asks Sam.

"Yes, let's call her Masha to keep things simple," suggests Don.

"He worked his way up. Back when that picture was taken, he served as a Russian State Prosecutor."

"Could Evgeni be KNOLL?" asks Sam.

Neshad's voice hardens. "No. And don't speculate on his identity—it's too dangerous."

Don jumps in. "What is CASE 42?"

Jynx shrugs. "We didn't turn up much—court records, sealed tighter than a nun's knickers."

Neshad adds, "I can put analysts on it, but that kind of digging leaves fingerprints. Do you think it matters?"

Jynx arches a brow. "You're the one said anythin' could matter, didn't ya?"

Neshad nods slowly. "Fair. I'll see what I can find."

Bram, still leaning back in his chair, arms crossed, suddenly sits up straighter. "What about Kirillov? What's his story?"

Neshad hesitates. "If Masha was working for Evgeni, odds are she's working for Kirillov now."

Jynx leans forward, catching the flicker of something unspoken. "And?"

"Kirillov is a wild card," Neshad finally says. "We don't know much about him."

Jynx narrows his eyes. "Ah, come on now—what are ya holdin' back?"

Neshad exhales, rubbing a hand over his face. He promised to share everything. No more games. "We've been working to discredit Kirillov."

"How?"

Neshad tells the story of the two thugs he renditioned. How they killed Dmitri Beridze.

Bram's ears perk up, hearing the backstory for the first time.

Jynx puts it together. "So, you've been slippin' whispers down back channels, chippin' away at his foundation. Why?"

"First, it's what we do. We weaken our adversaries. Second, we are hoping it helps give KNOLL some breathing room."

Bram is intrigued. "Why did they kill Dmitri Beridze?"

Neshad has had enough. "That doesn't concern us. Dmitri was an agitator, a writer. His death isn't part of this. We are getting too far afield. We need to figure out SEMYA, what it is, and why did it start?"

Everyone agrees. They have been following too many leads, chasing too many threads. It is getting late, and everyone is tired. They need time to process. They disperse.

But Raya's instincts kick in. Her senses prickle—something's off. A flicker of doubt coils in her chest.

As they all head to their rooms, Bram hesitates, uncertain. Raya had been curt with him—*was she angry*? His feelings for her run deep, but they haven't crossed that final threshold.

Being at her father's house had been too somber—too heavy with grief. But now, sharing a room, the weight of unspoken tension and anticipation lingers between them.

Raya catches his expression, reading the uncertainty in his eyes. She knows she can be difficult, but Bram has been steady, unwavering—the anchor she never knew she needed. Her feelings are just as strong. And she realizes she'll have to be the one to close the space between them.

Wordlessly, she takes his hand and leads him toward the room. He glances around. No one pays them any mind. Why would they? Yet he searches for some kind of approval, a habit he hadn't realized was so ingrained.

Inside, she turns to him, her voice a whisper. "No talking."

She takes the lead. It's slow, deliberate—a quiet dance of touch and breath, of unhurried movements and unspoken understanding. They aren't rushing toward an end; they're finding meaning in each step, in every glance, in the warmth of skin against skin.

If she's going to Russia—if danger lies ahead—she refuses to go with regrets.

They both need rest, but neither will get much sleep. The night stretches on, filled with soft caresses, long embraces, and the comfort that lingers in the space between hushed giggles.

For the first time, Raya and Bram are truly together.

CHAPTER FORTY-SIX

KIRILLOV SEETHES. THE REPRIMAND STILL burns—a slow, festering wound to his pride. He paces his office, eyes skimming the names on his reports, though he isn't truly reading them. He is obsessed—*who is betraying him?* Who is whispering his secrets?

He wants a full-scale purge, an investigation that leaves no stone unturned. But he must be careful. He cannot alert the mole, cannot draw the attention of the Chief of Staff. He needs a trusted advisor—someone who will tell him the truth, root out dissension, and serve as his eyes and ears.

But Kirillov has no such man.

His inner circle comprises cronies, sycophants, and cowards—men as ambitious as he is, men who despise him but fear him more. They serve him out of self-preservation, not loyalty. He controls them through intimidation and paranoia. But now, with suspicion clouding the air, he can no longer tell friend from enemy.

Like all tyrants, Kirillov would be shocked to learn that everyone hates him.

His hands tremble as he grips the phone. He slams it down—the sound cracking like a gunshot in the empty room. Then, with a snarl, he hurls it across the office, smashing it against the massive screen on the wall. The monitor shatters, jagged glass raining onto the carpet.

Outside, in the halls, no one moves. The staff hears the destruction, hears the fury seeping from his office like poisonous gas. But no one dares to check on him. No one wants to be the next target of his wrath.

Kirillov collapses into his chair, chest heaving, and glares at the latest report from KODIAK. He is a man alone. Masha is still missing.

Bram has disappeared. Raya has vanished. If he knew they were in Israel, sharing a bed, he would have had a coronary.

He feels the walls closing in.

With a wordless scream, he snatches the heavy glass paperweight from his desk and hurls it at the door. It splinters against the wood, leaving a deep crack—a scar to memorialize his frustration.

Word spreads fast. From secretary to secretary, from hallway whispers to conference rooms, the message is passed—Kirillov is on the warpath. No one knows why. Some speculate it's a woman who rejected him. Others wonder if he lost a fortune gambling. A few joke, in hushed tones, that perhaps he is simply impotent.

They laugh because it keeps the fear at bay.

Kirillov summons his most trusted department heads and

senior officers. These are the men he wants to trust—hopes he can trust. As they enter the room, he studies them, searching for guilt, for fear, for weakness. He convinces himself he will spot the traitor by their reaction alone. He is delusional.

When he speaks, he fumbles with the delivery. He announces. "There is a spy in our midst."

The room stirs. His officers tense, expecting a hunt for a Western infiltrator. They scramble into action, shouting over one another—they will track all communications, reexamine security clearances, interrogate foreign contacts.

"No." Kirillov's voice is cold, the single word slicing through the room.

They freeze.

He leans forward, voice lower, more poisonous. "The spy is one of us—reporting to the Kremlin."

The reaction is instantaneous: a ripple of confusion, of unease. Then inside, they all laugh—this is Russia. What does he expect? Outwardly, they nod gravely. They feign concern, promising to act swiftly. But they will do nothing.

These men know when to act—and when to hide. If Kirillov is on the way out, aligning with him is suicide. When the next man comes into power, they must not be seen as Kirillov's allies.

Still, the paranoia spreads. Rumors twist. A Western spy? A Kremlin mole? Both?

Suddenly, everyone is afraid. Not of actual espionage, but of the investigations, the interrogations, the scrutiny. They have all been through it before. They know how it ends. Conversations in the office grow stilted. Laughter disappears.

No one trusts anyone.

The whispers reach Yuri—the butler, the bureaucrat, the quiet man in the Directorate of Support. A man Kirillov has never noticed.

But that will not last. Yuri knows how these things go. His department may be a low priority, but eventually everyone will be scrutinized. His heart pounds as he considers the implications.

If Kirillov is looking for a mole, it's only a matter of time before they find something—anything—to justify an execution. Panic grips him. *What if they already suspect him?*

But then, reason prevails. If they knew, he would already be in a cell in Lubyanka. *No—they are blindly searching*, casting a wide net, hoping someone gets caught. He cannot be that someone.

Yuri forces himself to think. Raya is coming soon. Signaling now to stop the meeting would carry its own risk—the timing could not be worse. He must rely on his planning.

He breathes deeply, forcing calm. He mentally reviews his precautions. He has covered his tracks. He has manipulated the system flawlessly. Raya's biometrics have been altered; she will not trigger facial recognition using a false passport.

She is safe. He is not. Yuri knows he will be watched. Everyone will be watched. He must find a way to meet Raya without exposing himself.

But first, he must give Kirillov what he wants. There is one loose end—Anton Popov. The young technician that caught him in the computer room. He is a liability.

Yuri has already laid the groundwork. He has used Anton's

credentials to send messages to a known enemy contact. He has uploaded classified files to an external server—using Anton's login. He has created false transaction records suggesting bribes and payments for espionage. The breach, when discovered, will lead straight to Anton.

His guilt will be undeniable. But Yuri knows the hard truth: Anton must die before he is interrogated. The evidence must speak for itself. Kirillov will have his spy, and Yuri will retain his freedom.

Yuri hates it—but it must be done. He will invite the young man to lunch, set the trap. He needs to move fast. Wiping the sweat from his hands, he straightens his tie and walks out the door.

CHAPTER FORTY-SEVEN

Secure base outside Haifa, Israel 2019

RAYA WAKES WITH CERTAINTY—SHE is going to Russia. The pull toward the truth is too strong to ignore. Locked in her arms, Bram breathes steadily, raw and full of potential. She sees in him the unwavering support she needs, the steadiness she has never had. He is right for her. But loving her will cost him— worry, pain, uncertainty. She wonders whether she has the right to put him through it.

Bram nestles closer, feigning sleep. He knows she is awake—knows she is thinking. His awareness sharpens. He has loved Raya since the moment they met—of that, he is sure. He wants to be her protector, her shield. But doubt creeps in. She isn't waiting to be saved; she is ready to fight for herself. *Is he truly what she needs?*

Across the hall, Sam wakes with a grin. She likes this— being part of something, feeling included. It's a damn soap opera, and she is here for it. At first, she wasn't sure about any of this, but now? She's in. She hopes Don feels the same.

Stretching, she smirks, thinking of Raya and Bram sneaking off like schoolkids. Maybe it's time she found herself a little romance.

Jynx sits alone in his room, awake for hours. Sleep slips further from him with each passing year. He sees this for what it is—a continuation of the same old game: spying, influencing, manipulating. Power feeds itself unchecked, consuming those in its way. These men at the top—they always need a counterforce. If only he could get a damn signal on his phone, he might be able to create some options.

Neshad sees things with perfect clarity: stop the enemy. The mission is all that matters. More important than any individual. More important than Raya. If necessary, she is expendable. They need answers—*how deep does this go?* How much exposure do they face?

Don lies awake, guilt settling deep in his chest. He brought Raya into this, guided her, tried to prepare her. But soon, she will make her own choices. He knows he has been a proxy for Fred, a tool in someone else's game. But now he is free, having resigned from his position. *No—he still has orders.* The question lingers: how much is he willing to risk to remove those constraints?

◆◆◆

By late morning, they gather to untangle the information from the night before. Nothing has changed, yet everything feels different. Theories and conjectures filled their heads overnight, each of them grasping at pieces of the truth. Now, they will work to fit those pieces together.

Sam leans forward, eager to press on. "What do we think is

actually happening here?"

Jynx answers first. "Simple enough, ain't it? The SVR's after craftin' a way to rope 'em in without 'em even knowin'—twistin' their lives 'til they're bound mind and soul to some handler."

"Then, over time, they steer them into positions of power," Don adds. "Compromise them later, leverage the relationship when it matters."

Bram shakes his head, disgusted. "An ultimate betrayal of trust. Cold, calculated, and callous."

Don focuses. "They must have chosen Raya as the BETA for a reason. She seems like one of the first test cases."

Sam considers. "Maybe it was access. Maybe it was convenience—her father was an American, her mother died."

Raya nods. "I was convenient."

Jynx remains unconvinced. "Wouldn't it be makin' far more sense to chase after the sons and daughters of the high an' mighty—big money, powerful sorts, the kind with doors swingin' wide? Gettin' their claws in early, give 'em a bit of hardship, a bit of care... shape 'em into somethin' formidable."

Neshad offers a counterpoint. "That may be the long-term plan, but they needed to move fast. Learn as they go."

Don follows the thread. "What do powerful parents lack? Time. Their careers come first. Expectations are high, but a genuine connection with their kids... often low priority."

Jynx nods. "Findin' the right moment to slip in a master manipulator? Jaysus, that'd be a right killer of a move."

"To scale it," Don continues, "they'd need to refine the model first."

Sam sees the logic. "So, fail early. Find the flaws. Adjust."

Neshad pulls it all together. "An iterative approach. The first subjects were staggered—early prototypes. Each one refined the process. By the time the real targets came into play, they knew it would work and how to perfect it."

A heavy silence settles. They all nod, the pieces falling into place.

Neshad scans their faces. "Are we all agreed? Now is the time for disagreement."

Before anyone can speak, an aide enters, handing Neshad a note. His eyes flick across the message. He looks up.

"Fred is coming. He'll be here in the morning. Says he has new information to share."

◆◆◆

By late lunch, Don and Neshad huddle, deciding it is time to push forward with mission prep.

Don calls everyone back to the table. "When Fred arrives tomorrow morning, we need to be ready. Whatever this new intel is, we're running out of time."

Raya leans in, eager. "Let's go over the infiltration plan."

Neshad nods. "We can make the final call tomorrow, but let's not waste time. You'll have three days to make contact—three locations, same time each day."

Raya sharpens. "What locations?"

Neshad pulls up a map on the projection screen, highlighting different sites. "Alexander Garden, west of the Kremlin. The Pushkin State Museum of Fine Arts. And Arbat Street—a tourist stretch with souvenir stalls, street artists, and cafés."

The team studies the screen as the locations light up.

"You'll stay at Hostel Postel," Neshad continues. "A rundown tourist spot just north of one end of Arbat Street. Fits your cover."

"Which is?" Raya asks.

"A Turkish student from Bomonti University in Istanbul. You're studying Russian, hoping to be a translator. You came to Moscow to deepen your understanding of the culture."

Raya straightens. "I can pull that off."

"These three locations and the hostel form a kind of circuit. Each day, you'll follow a strict route—one location after another at a prescribed time."

Raya nods, committing the details to memory.

"You'll first fly to Istanbul under your current passport for an OIR engagement. From there, you leave everything behind—new hairstyle, new clothes, fresh credit cards, travel litter, and baggage."

She meets his gaze, absorbing every step.

"You'll receive a new passport, complete with realistic entry and exit stamps. Your new name is Reyyan Rendas. We try to keep it close to your real name. Common Turkish. You will leave Istanbul and fly to Moscow."

"And Russian biometrics?" Raya presses.

"KNOLL assures us their system won't pick you up. He's altered it somehow."

Bram exhales, shaking his head. "Hell of a risk."

Raya stays focused. "How do I make contact?"

"You'll wear a red scarf. The contact will wear green. Standard call and response: 'What a pretty scarf.'— 'It was a gift from a friend.' Followed by, 'Is he a handsome man?'— 'I don't remember.'"

Don nods. "Textbook tradecraft."

Neshad doesn't sugarcoat the stakes. "The cold approach is your most dangerous moment. If KNOLL is compromised, we'll have no warning. You have to stick to your legend."

Raya knows from training—legends only hold for so long. "Will you be watching me?"

Neshad hesitates. "That's where it gets tricky. We have watchers, but if we track you too closely, we risk exposing you."

Don's warning echoes in Raya's mind—we are all known.

"What's the exit plan?" she asks.

"You leave the same way you came in. Best-case scenario, no one notices."

Bram scoffs. "And if it's not that simple?"

Neshad levels him with a look. "Then we enact countermeasures. If things go south, Raya heads straight for the embassy and claims status."

"That's a shit contingency," Bram snaps.

Raya smiles at his protectiveness.

Sam asks Don, "Can we help?"

"Fred was clear. Exigencies fall to the Israelis. I don't think more assets will help."

Jynx leans in, voice low. "If ye'd just let me get a signal, I'd sort somethin' out, so I would."

Neshad shuts him down instantly. "Not happening."

Raya ignores Neshad, turning to Jynx. "How?"

"I've got people in my pocket these eejits haven't the faintest clue about. Fellas that owe me, and fellas that owe them—a whole chain of favors waitin' to be cashed in."

She raises an eyebrow at Neshad. "Seems reasonable."

Neshad remains unmoved.

Jynx pushes. "The lads I deal with, they've ways of gettin' Raya out if it all goes arseways. With all the coin you're burnin', Neshad, ye should have a proper plan instead of crossin' yer fingers and hopin' for the best."

"We have exfil plans," Neshad counters. "But we won't trigger them unless it's critical—imminent loss of life."

Raya's voice drops. "And how will you know? I'll be on my own until you figure it out."

She catches Jynx's eye. They'll talk later. He might have another way.

The afternoon drags as Neshad struggles to keep them on task, refining details of the plan. But the team is distracted.

Wondering how this will end. Worried about the news Fred will bring in the morning. Questioning whether the mission is worth the danger.

◆◆◆

After dinner, they unwind. Raya sits on the couch beside Bram, silent, her thoughts unraveling in tangled threads, pulling her in different directions.

She thinks of her father—his choices, the weight he carried, the secrets he kept for so long. She thinks of Masha, her hatred coiled like a slow-burning ember. *Will I ever see her again?*

That will have to wait. The mission comes first.

She thinks of Oraz and Jeren, the couple desperate to escape Romania—their fear, their impossible choices. They didn't hesitate. *Did they ever doubt they'd make it?* She thinks of KNOLL, the mystery that won't let go. *Who is he? Why does he want her?* She thinks of spies—of their usefulness, until they're not.

Then, a memory surfaces, sharp and unexpected: Mr. Kahn's voice from so long ago. What matters most? The question steadies her, grounds her. She knows now she must rely on herself, carve her own path. If freedom is what matters most, then it begins with independence—her choices, her way forward.

She turns to Bram, smiling, grateful, knowing how lucky she is to have him—the only person she truly trusts.

She sees Jynx approaching. She knows what she needs, and she's going to make it happen.

No more bullshit. Her ass is on the line. Raya is about to take charge.

CHAPTER FORTY-EIGHT

HELSINKI, FINLAND
2019

The trip across the Atlantic had been brutal—fifteen days trapped in a cramped, airless berth, hiding from the crew. The first mate smuggled Masha aboard for a steep price. She knew escape might be necessary and was ready for it. Still, nothing could have prepared her for the suffocating isolation, the unrelenting stench of salt and diesel, or the gnawing hunger that clawed at her stomach when food was scarce.

There was no time to plan her departure properly. She acted on instinct, grabbing only the essentials from her apartment, destroying anything that could link her to her past. Every piece of sentimentality—gone. She stuffed the sum total of her life into a knapsack, shedding everything else like a snake slipping free of its old skin. She would travel light.

The ship was called the Heldige Syv. Her Finnish was good enough to know it meant Lucky Seven. She laughed bitterly when she first heard the name. In craps, rolling a seven could mean a lucky win—but the odds always favored the house. The house usually won. Would luck be on her side this time? She would need some luck.

Locked below deck with nothing but her thoughts, time stretched endlessly. She counted the seconds, listened to the waves slap against the hull, and let the creaks and groans of the ship lull her into uneasy sleep. The first mate brought food when he could, but sometimes only once a day—stale bread, dried fish, an apple if she was lucky. Her body, still battered from her fall, was wasting away. She barely noticed. Hunger was a distant concern. She didn't care. This could easily turn into a one-way mission.

She knew instantly that the murder of Phil was a mistake. Killing him would not bring Raya closer—only drive them apart. Raya would not be manipulated with vengeance. If anything, the murder would widen the gulf between them. And yet it was done. She could not undo it. There was only one thing left—answers. And there was only one place to find them.

Moscow.

When the vessel arrives in Helsinki and moves into port, she slips off the ship. Under the cover of night, Masha moves with careful precision—like a shadow, unseen, unheard. The air is biting, carrying with it the sharp scent of seaweed and distant woodsmoke. Her contacts in the city are relics of her past life—smugglers and thieves, people who owe her favors or will make a deal for the right price. They will get her across the Gulf of Finland into Estonia, the first leg of her long, treacherous journey.

From there, she will hitch rides with long-haul truckers heading south across the country. She has money—American dollars, which speak louder than words in the right hands—and, most importantly, she can protect herself from the bandits who prey on the unsuspecting.

Her plan is to follow the Tallinn–Tartu–Võru–Luhamaa route, turning southeast toward the Kordula border checkpoint. That will be the most difficult part. Masha will need to slip into Russia, navigating through the thick, endless forests.

She lacks the proper gear for a cold-weather crossing and knows she will need rest to recover. She'll find a grimy roadside inn near the Pskov Oblast and plan her next leg. There are always truckers willing to take a few extra dollars. She hopes to take the E95 south and then follow the M-9 highway east straight into Moscow. On a good day, the trip takes fifteen hours by car. She gives herself three days.

This is not her first time moving unseen, and maybe not her last. But there is a weight to this journey she hasn't felt before— a pull in her chest, a whisper in the back of her mind. Nineteen days. That's how long it will take her to reach Moscow after Phil's death.

Masha has always prided herself on control, on knowing more than the rest. But now the world moves without her. She doesn't know where Raya is, how she has suffered, or what forces are already in motion beyond her reach. And yet none of it changes her course. She has a mission—one of her own making.

It will be an arduous journey. She will be smart, and if everything holds, she will slip into Moscow undetected. She has people she needs to speak with, and materials she must obtain. She needs resolution.

Fate—or something darker—has set the pieces in motion. If her luck holds, she will soon have her answers.

If her luck holds.

CHAPTER FORTY-NINE

SECURE BASE OUTSIDE HAIFA, ISRAEL 2019

Sam is up early, drawn by anticipation. She steps outside to find Jynx already nursing a coffee and a cigarette, his gaze distant. She can feel the tension in the air—the expectation of Fred's arrival, the next pieces of the puzzle clicking into place.

"I guess our part of the deal is almost done," she says, watching him.

Jynx looks up, smirking. "Ah, sure, I wouldn't be bettin' on it just yet, lass. Plenty of ways this could still go arseways."

Sam thinks back to the night before. "Seemed like you wanted to help Raya. Neshad wasn't budging."

"Aye, that I did. Raya asked for me help, plain and simple," he admits.

She studies him. "So, what's next? I saw you and Raya talking late."

Jynx blows out, watching the smoke curl into the cool morning air. "We'll hear what Fred has to say, but I'd wager Raya's already made up her own mind. Wouldn't be shocked if there be sparks flyin' before the day's out."

When Fred arrives, the team gathers. The room buzzes with impatience, anticipation, and unspoken grievances. Before he shares his news, he wants an update.

"So, what do we get out of this? What's the upside?"

Don keeps it concise. "We only know KNOLL wants to meet Raya, but we don't know why."

Fred's eyes narrow. He looks at Neshad. "And you still trust KNOLL?"

Neshad responds, "We do. He's always been reliable."

Fred considers this. "And the downside?"

Don doesn't hold back. "Raya ends up in Lubyanka, a pawn in some future prisoner swap. The Russians love collecting leverage." The air feels tighter. After two days of being holed up, the tension runs high. Raya is still seething at Fred—his manipulations, his use of her father. She doesn't bother hiding her anger.

Fred's tone darkens as he finally provides his ominous update. "CIA sources report a mole hunt in the SVR. Kirillov is tearing through his own ranks."

Neshad's expression hardens. "I thought we were running this operation."

Fred doesn't flinch. "We have assets. They report to us. Not as high up as KNOLL, but they see things. Would you rather I kept you in the dark?"

Neshad exhales sharply. "No. You're right. It's just... delicate."

"And don't forget, I have veto power. Raya is still my asset."

Neshad's jaw tightens. "Are you pulling her?"

Raya makes her play. "What if I say I'm not going? I'm sick of your games, Fred. Yours too, Neshad. You don't give a damn about me—you just want your damn intel."

Jynx looks on, proud of the way she is playing it. They ignore her—chalking her outburst up to the jitters. Fred and Neshad turn away, whispering between themselves like Raya isn't in the room. Raya clenches her fists, her fury rising.

Bram's voice cut through. "She said she's not going."

Silence.

Sam, testing her role as mediator, leaned forward. "Raya, what do you want?"

Raya stands her ground. "I want my own support. I want people I trust. And I sure as hell don't trust these two." She points at Fred and Neshad. "Jynx gets his phone. He's my failsafe. Bram makes the call. If things go south, they get the final say."

Fred rubs his chin. "You ask for a lot."

Raya's voice is cold. "It's my ass on the line."

Don shakes his head. "They're untrained. No field experience."

"I trust them. That's what matters." She glances at Bram and smiles.

Fred fires back. "Fine. Then you don't go. I was already leaning that way."

Sam smiles. The fireworks are better than she expected.

But Neshad remains unconvinced and unwilling to let it go. He turns to Jynx. "What would you need?"

Jynx smirks. "A proper signal, that's what I need. And a bit of time. I can set things up, keep it quiet. Too many eyes on this, and we might as well be handin' the Russians a feckin' roadmap."

Neshad looks at Fred. "You are the one who wanted to be insulated."

Raya presses on. "If I go—and I mean if—I still need your help with flights, passports. But I need the freedom to trust my instincts without worrying about who has my back."

Don adds. "It has to be clean. In, out. No distractions. We need to work as a team."

Fred loosens a bit, then relents. "What's the objective?"

The team all speak at once.

Neshad suggests, "We need to know exactly what the Russians are planning."

Jynx wants to know, "What's changin'? Why's KNOLL flappin' his gums now?"

"And who is KNOLL?" wonders Bram

Sam asks, "Why Raya?"

Raya adds, almost to herself, "Why didn't Masha press me after she killed my dad?"

Fred cuts through the noise. "Fucking mission creep. One objective—what is SEMYA, and how do we stop it?"

Then he turned to Raya. He sees it now—he realizes she has tested him, and he's underestimated her. This wasn't about operational control. It was about independent power. And she'd just taken hers back. "Are you ready?" he asks.

Raya met his gaze, unflinching. "I'm ready."

Fred nods. "Then you leave tonight."

He turns to Neshad. "I need to get back to Washington. Give Jynx access to his fucking phone."

PART VIII

THE WEIGHT OF SECRETS
2019

"Truth is the daughter of time."
-Aullus Gellius (Roman historian)

CHAPTER FIFTY

MOSCOW, RUSSIA
2019

As the plane descends toward Sheremetyevo International Airport, Raya forces herself to breathe evenly, gripping the armrest as though it might anchor her thoughts. The past thirty-six hours run through her mind in sharp flashes—departure, documents, the moment of no return.

She reminds herself that there is nothing to worry about. She is visiting a foreign country. Her passport is genuine, meticulously crafted down to the last detail. She has drilled her legend—an international student from Turkey on a research holiday—into her memory. It will stand up to scrutiny. If KNOLL has done his part, authorities will not recognize her face, *shouldn't be able to recognize her face*. But uncertainty gnaws at the edge of her composure.

She presses her fingers to her temple. No use dwelling on that now. She is about to meet a man she has never seen before, for reasons no one fully understands. But first, she must pass through immigration—a test she cannot afford to fail.

She practices the meditation exercises she learned a decade earlier from her neighbor, Mr. Tanaka. Anxiety lurks at the edges, a whisper of doubt curling around her thoughts. She does not let it take hold.

Her thoughts turn to Bram. Their parting was brief, but its power still lingers. Between them lies an abiding trust. Words spoken: stay safe. Words unspoken: of love. She feels his absence as she folds the memory away. For now, she must focus.

Her journey began in Istanbul, in a Mossad-run safe house—a plain, unassuming building in a nondescript neighborhood. Upon arrival, the Mossad stripped her of her old life. Every personal item was taken and locked away, as if erasing her past would help her slip into the future unseen.

They gave her new clothes—cheap, practical, designed not to draw attention. A few changes of sweaters and jeans, layers she could wear in rotation without standing out. The colors were muted, nothing bright. Nothing memorable, except a brightly colored red scarf. Her old bag was taken away, replaced with a worn canvas satchel that had seen better days but still held together. It smelled faintly of dust.

They confiscated her phone immediately. In its place, she received an older-model iPhone, slightly scuffed, already loaded with pre-set contacts—names she didn't recognize, numbers with no context. They could track her, but she wasn't to call any of them. That wasn't the point. Instead, they instructed her on how to communicate.

She would use a simple method of sending texts to a

"friend"—basic updates to indicate she was safe. Casual check-ins, mundane notes, nothing that would raise suspicion. Mentioning the weather to signal change. Feeling a bit off. Might be something I ate. Translation: the heat's rising, situation unstable. Telling her friend she was sick would mean it was getting hot, and she needed to get out.

They also instructed her to take photos—tourist shots. Buildings, statues, her meals, the occasional selfie. It helped maintain her cover, but there was another purpose. The team could analyze the background, look for patterns, see who else appeared in the frame. She would be their eyes, without ever knowing what they were seeing.

For half a day, she walked the campus of Bomonti University, immersing herself in its rhythm—the hum of Turkish student life. She memorized details: professor names, course schedules, the best cheap eateries students favored. She learned which bus routes they took, which cafés they frequented. Every detail could matter.

She listened to conversations, picking up nuances, correcting the small inconsistencies in her story. There was too little time for such an undertaking. She stayed up late into the night, reviewing the details again and again.

She would sleep on the plane.

Entering Russia is uneventful. The immigration officer is brisk, his questioning mechanical.

She slides over her passport and visa, calm, composed.

"Reason for visit?"

"Tourism."

"Length of stay?"

"A few days."

He gives her passport only the briefest glance before stamping it with a thwack. Her cover holds. His scrutiny reserved for visitors from Western nations. "Enjoy your stay."

Still, Raya feels the weight of unseen eyes pressing down on her. It is impossible to know if she is being watched. Paranoia is a survival skill, but she cannot let it consume her. She forces herself to walk at an unhurried pace, to blend in.

She takes the train from the airport into the heart of Moscow, gripping the rail in the crowded carriage. Scanning the surrounding faces, searching for familiarity, for suspicion. But she knows it's futile—if she is being watched, she will never see them. She sends a text: she has landed.

After a transfer, she boards the metro to Arbatskaya station, a few blocks from her lodging. Raya moves through the streets with purpose, feigning confidence. She listens to the voices around her, the clipped efficiency of Muscovites moving through their day. She thinks *I don't belong here.*

The Hostel Postel sits on a narrow street, wedged between a pawn shop and a shuttered café. The neon sign flickers, half-burnt out. She snaps a photo. Postel means "bed" in Russian— how original. She almost laughs as she approaches the entrance.

Inside, the air is thick with the scent of old wood and cleaning chemicals. A large, greasy-looking man with thinning hair and a calculating gaze works the front desk. The collar of his shirt is unbuttoned, revealing a thick gold chain. He eyes her as she approaches.

"I help you?" he asks, tone indifferent but watchful.

"I have a reservation."

"Name?"

She almost says Raya but remembers her cover. "Reyyan Rendas... from Turkey."

He flips through a battered ledger, tapping a page. "Common room. Is for men and women—this is normal."

Raya hesitates just enough to seem uncertain. "With men? I don't think so. I want a room with only women."

The man's lips curl in a slow grin. "Maybe... I find you private room, yes?" he suggests, leaning slightly closer, voice thick with implication.

A prickle of unease runs down Raya's spine. Absolutely not. Safety is in numbers. She raises her voice slightly. "No, thank you. A female-only room."

From behind a tattered curtain, a woman's voice snaps, "Boris, give her women's room. Don't be creepy with customers all the time."

Boris scowls, muttering under his breath, but tosses her a key.

The dormitory is sparse—bunk beds lined against the walls, with a single overhead light casting shadows over the chipped tile floor. Empty for now.

Boris lingers in the doorway. "Others will return soon," he says. "You settle in now. We open at five, yes? Out by ten in morning. You take things with you—we clean."

Raya nods, saying nothing. She hopes this is the last she will see of him. Everything about Boris sets her on edge.

She shuts the door and sits on a bed. One step down, many

more to go. It has only been twenty days since the death of her father.

The circuit begins tomorrow.

The next day, Raya begins the circuit, visiting the sites on the preplanned schedule. She packs everything carefully into her backpack, double-checking zippers, compartments, and seams. She leaves nothing behind—not even a stray receipt or an old tissue. Boris will not get a glimpse of who she is or what she carries.

She slings the bag over her shoulder and zips her jacket up to her chin. It's cold this morning—biting, breath visible in the air—but forecasts say it will warm over the weekend. She wraps a bright red scarf around her neck, the only splash of color she allows herself. A student, after all. A visitor. Someone easily forgotten.

She heads northeast from the hostel toward the southern entrance of Alexander Garden. The park runs along the western edge of the Kremlin, a cultivated stretch of green amidst the hard urban sprawl. Today it is covered in a light blanket of frost, trees bare of leaves. One of the first public parks in Moscow, she remembers reading—a place designed to be walked.

As she enters, the manicured precision of the park strikes her: regimented trees, carefully maintained paths, flower beds asleep under a veil of snow. It's beautiful, but there's an austerity to it, like everything in this city. Grand, but never warm.

She walks northward, letting her pace slow with the scenery. After a quarter mile, the landscape changes—fountains frozen mid-cascade, grottos turned to icy alcoves,

402

and stone bridges forming archways over silent pools. She passes the Romanov Obelisk and feels the quiet weight of history pressing in. She turns her phone and takes a selfie.

This is the perfect place for a clandestine meeting—pedestrian traffic, natural bottlenecks, cover from sightlines. Peddlers hawk roasted nuts, small souvenirs, cheap art. People move but rarely linger. Controlled chaos.

Near the Tomb of the Unknown Soldier, at the park's northern tip, Raya glances at her watch. She scans faces casually, careful not to linger, but alert to expressions, body language, anything familiar. Nothing. No flicker of recognition, no quiet nod, no brush of a hand signaling contact. Just foreign tourists with selfie sticks and an honor guard performing its hourly ritual. Maybe this wasn't the place. Maybe not today.

She exhales slowly, turning south to retrace her steps. Her breath clouds the air. The silk scarf, gentle on her neck. Her boots crunch lightly on the salted concrete. Raya looks again at her watch—it has been an hour. She needs to stay on schedule.

Raya exits the park and crosses the busy intersection, picking up Ulitsa Volkhonka. The avenue is wide, its sidewalk thick with the rhythm of daily Moscow—street sweepers, women in fur coats, clusters of students laughing too loudly, old men staring into the middle distance. No one looks at her twice.

Ahead, the gated drive of the Pushkin State Museum of Fine Arts rises in clean white stone. Its façade is imposing, almost intimidating, as if daring her to step inside. She hesitates, then climbs the steps. Before entering, she turns and snaps a photo of the pedestrians below. If she is being followed, maybe the team in Israel will pick it up.

Inside, warmth greets her in waves, accompanied by the hush of footsteps and whispered conversation. At the information desk, a man greets her, handing over a brochure.

"Can I help you?" he asks.

She takes the paper, scanning it. Pre-revolutionary architecture. Greek Acropolis-inspired. The largest museum of European art in Moscow.

"It's enormous," she murmurs, more to herself than to him.

"Yes," he says with a smile. "In the main building alone, there are works by Rubens, Van Dyck, Rembrandt..."

Raya's mind drifts as he continues. Ancient Egyptian relics. Classical statuary. A dozen lifetimes of culture, and she has an hour. She thanks him absently and finds a bench in a quiet corner to think.

This place is too big. Too complex. If KNOLL wanted to find her here, he would have to know exactly where to look. She can't move through every building. It isn't sustainable. Best to keep to the main halls and rotate her presence—first floor today, second tomorrow. Let the pattern emerge naturally. If contact is meant to happen, it will.

She spends an hour looking at the art, waiting for a contact that does not arrive, then departs. Leaving the museum, she resumes her route. She feels watched. Not by a person, but by the city itself—a heavy presence pressing down on her bones. Watching for cracks. Judging her stride.

Are Jynx's watchers out here? Fred's? Neshad's? The thought snakes through her mind. Are watchers watching other watchers? She suppresses the spiral before it starts. That way lies madness.

Raya heads northwest, crisscrossing through side streets until she reaches the intersection of Kaloshin Lane and Arbat Street. Tourists, artists, souvenir stands, the scent of coffee and fried dough in the air—it's almost cheerful. A breath of color in a city that wears gray like armor. She decides to take another photo.

She slows her pace, buys a warm snack from a street vendor, and sips sweet tea from a paper cup. Raya allows herself a moment to blend, to feel like part of the crowd. She checks her watch. It's been two hours. She decides to pick up some dinner to eat back in her room. Then she heads toward the hostel, steps measured, head down.

When she approaches, she sees Boris at the window, watching her. The look he gives is unreadable—blank, but somehow loaded. A flicker of something dark. Her stomach twists.

Did I do something wrong? Did I break cover? She tries to shake the thought, but her pulse is rising. Doubt is a poison; she knows that. Mistakes follow panic. Her training taught her to push through, to stay present, but right now that training feels distant. Thin.

If I made a mistake, I've only missed a meeting. There's always tomorrow.

She inhales through her nose, holds the breath, then exhales slowly.

I wish Bram was with me. He always makes me feel safe.

Her fingers unclench. The key is staying on script. Stick to the circuit. Keep her head. Like any tourist, she snaps a photo of the hostel. Maybe the team in Israel will ID Boris.

She forces herself to smile and enters the building.

CHAPTER FIFTY-ONE

MOSCOW, RUSSIA
2019

ON THE SAME DAY RAYA completes her first circuit, Yuri is still at his desk. He never planned to initiate contact today—maybe tomorrow. There is work to be done. Threads to tighten.

He monitors the city from behind layers of encrypted access, skimming surveillance logs and reviewing field activity reports. If Raya is being watched, he'll know. His access gives him eyes inside the system—encrypted channels, field briefings, surveillance tagging logs. Nothing so far. No whispers of a shadow op trailing a foreign national matching Raya's description.

But he has watchers of his own—unofficial, unnoticed. They are not sophisticated, but they are invisible. If someone is following Raya, they'll feel it before the cameras do. So far, no one has. That gives Yuri room to breathe.

Which means it is time to focus on the next task. Anton Popov. The young computer tech who had interrupted him as he altered the system a few months earlier.

Yuri has learned to compartmentalize. He has to. But as the years pile on, the walls grow thinner. The cost, heavier. He reminds himself he's survived this long for a reason—because he knows how to make the hard calls. For the greater good, he tells himself. Always for the greater good.

He feels the loss. He regrets the necessity. But he is still capable of ruthlessness. That is what this work demands. It doesn't shape the best of men—only the ones willing to live in a moral shadow. He wishes it were otherwise.

It is unfortunate that Anton will die. Yuri likes the boy. That makes it worse. Bright, idealistic. Precisely the type who makes the perfect scapegoat. When the time comes, Yuri will report that Anton confessed duplicity. He will be vague, unsure of what he meant.

Suicide is optimal. Easy to presume guilt. Jump off a building. Step in front of a train. A drug overdose. All are available to Yuri, all within his bag of tricks. When they find Anton dead, they will investigate and find the evidence Yuri has laid. All eyes will fall upon him, deflecting Kirillov. Ingratiating Yuri further, securing his safety.

Near the top floor of Building One, the cafeteria glows with bright, artificial light. It's quiet, sterile. Beyond the floor-to-ceiling windows lies the forest. There's a balcony—old railing, steep drop. Anton arrives on time, eager, polite. He doesn't ask why someone like Yuri wants to spend time with him. He doesn't question his luck.

Yuri observes him carefully, weighing his options. Maybe today is the day.

He doesn't get the chance to decide.

An aide from Kirillov's office walks straight to their table. "Kirillov wants to see you."

Yuri blinks. "When?"

"Now."

He smiles at Anton, careful to mask his tension. "We'll finish this later."

Anton nods, confused, but doesn't ask questions.

Just a pawn, Yuri thinks. He doesn't even know it. Like us all.

The aide leads him to the elevator. Silence. As they ascend to the top floor, Yuri's mind races. *Has something leaked? Has he finally been exposed?*

In the office, Kirillov sits behind his monolithic desk, half-man, half-statue. "Sit."

Yuri sits.

"Are we friends?" Kirillov asks.

Yuri doesn't blink. "Of course. I've always respected you."

"I want to be your friend."

That catches Yuri off guard. He tilts his head, trying to read the game.

Kirillov slides a photo across the desk. Grainy, black-and-white. Surveillance footage—gas station, time-stamped. A woman in motion. Coat flapping. Eyes turned just enough for recognition.

Yuri freezes. He knows that face. Anna, now Masha.

"Why is she coming to Moscow?" Kirillov asks, his voice sharp.

Yuri blinks. "You don't know?"

"That's what I asked you."

"We haven't spoken in years."

"You're her husband."

"Yes. According to the State. We haven't been together for nearly two decades."

Kirillov studies him. The room feels like a trap slowly closing. "This photo was taken yesterday. Off the Novorizhskoye Highway."

Yuri leans back slightly. The M-9. A smuggler's route. Monitored. Dangerous. She knows better—or maybe she wants to be seen.

"You're surprised," Kirillov says.

"I didn't know."

"You didn't help her?"

"No," Yuri replies firmly.

Kirillov leans forward. "If you see her, or hear from her, you'll report it."

Yuri nods. "Of course."

He is dismissed.

As he walks back to his office, Yuri doesn't feel relief. He feels the walls closing in. Kirillov is unraveling. The man is dangerous, unpredictable, and worse—paranoid.

Yuri doesn't sit. He paces. SEMYA had always been a bad idea—he'd known that from the beginning. But Evgeni was so sure. His conviction was infectious, blinding. And for Anna—once she became invested, it was over. He didn't have the strength to object. Not then.

He had hoped it would collapse on its own—a natural failure. Instead, it persisted, and now it seems to be evolving. Yuri set his plans in motion when Evgeni was summarily replaced. He accelerated them after he read the internal reports about the botched murder of Phil—Raya's father. Now, his mission is clear.

To accomplish it, he needs to meet Raya. He needs to ensure Anna does not interfere. He needs to mitigate Kirillov's mole hunt. He needs to compartmentalize.

He presses his palms against his desk, staring at the cold surface. *Focus*. The answers are there. He just has to find them.

Think.

He takes a deep breath. The plan is already in motion. He can't stop it now, but he can control it. He needs to stay two steps ahead.

First priority: meet with Raya. I still have time. Move it to day three. That will give me room to maneuver.

Think. Focus.

Could Anna know Raya is in the country? She wouldn't come without a reason. She must want something—and whatever it is, it could be enough to bring down everything Yuri hopes to achieve.

He stops pacing. *Think*.

I need to find Anna. No—she will find me. Quietly. Invisibly.

She has always been adept at blending in, at moving through shadows. It's her skill, her weapon. Years of working undercover. And if she's here, she won't waste time.

Focus.

Yuri needs to be careful. But if Anna is drawing Kirillov's attention—maybe that buys him time. Maybe it gives him space to breathe. To move. To finish what he started. He mentally lowers Anton on his priority list.

Again, he paces. *Think.*

The meeting with Kirillov does not fool Yuri. He is not a man to make requests. Kirillov will have plans for him.

He will be watching me.

Yuri runs a hand through his hair, frustration mounting. The air in his office feels thick. He should have anticipated this. He should have known his past with Anna would never stay buried.

Ghosts always find a way to resurface.

CHAPTER FIFTY-TWO

SECURE BASE OUTSIDE HAIFA, ISRAEL 2019

TEDIUM AND NERVOUSNESS ARE A terrible combination for the human mind. Both are rampant at the base of operations in Israel.

Jynx commandeers a bunker on the lower levels, setting up a command center with screens and feeds. A quiet space for the conversations he needs to have—it's perfect for thinking, watching, worrying.

Neshad offers support: limited satellite coverage, access to intel briefings, news trickling in minute by minute. Still, there's nothing to do but wait.

Don offers suggestions, keeping his distance from the screens, falling back on tradecraft from missions long past.

Bram huddles with Jynx, restless—unsettled by the stillness. He's Raya's protector, watching her tiny yellow signal flicker across the map like a firefly. All day they watch, powerless to intervene, unable to act.

Bram mutters, "Why hasn't KNOLL made a move?"

Jynx flicks his lighter open, then closed. Click. Clack. "Ah, relax, will ya? He's watchin' her, makin' sure she's not draggin' heat behind her."

Bram feels his skin prickle. He's been watching Raya for two days—her pictures, her path. He dissects every photo, searching for clues, shadows, and unexpected faces.

He lost his dad. He lost his mum. He won't lose Raya. Bram feels his reactions slipping, the control he once prided himself on, unraveling. But he doesn't care. In his mind, he has one mission—to fight for Raya.

Bram pushes on Jynx. "Are your people even doing anything?"

"You'd wanna settle yourself now—show a bit of respect. I'll let that slide just this once," Jynx says slowly, firmly.

Bram is not ready to back down. "Why aren't we getting regular updates?"

"You've been watchin' too many bleedin' films. I don't have operatives, lad—I've got favors. Good ones, earned the hard way. You oughta know that. If it goes sideways, they'll be there. But trailin' after her like shadows in broad daylight? That's no use to anyone, is it?"

The tension simmers, building. Sam watches it unfold—quiet, observant, caught in the middle. She places a hand on Bram's shoulder, offering support.

Bram knows he's overreacting. He can't seem to control it. He needs to pull it together. He relents, if only a little. "Waiting sucks."

Neshad adds, "KNOLL will take his time. He's never acted impulsively."

414

As the second day ends, Raya has not made contact and returns to Hostel Postel. Sam tries to play her role, hoping to bring the team together. "Tomorrow will be the day."

"Should be," Don adds, knowing every mission can end without warning. "You have to trust the asset."

Bram stares at Don. "I don't live in your world. She's not an asset. She's a person. It's our job to protect her."

Jynx chides, "Everyone, just keep your wits about ya. With luck, we'll have some answers soon enough."

Sam has seen enough. She stands, straightening her clothes. "We need a break."

Bram looks up. "There's nowhere to go, nothing else to do."

"How about this? I'll make dinner," Sam says. "Something real. There's got to be a market nearby."

"You're not leaving the compound," Neshad replies.

"I'm not going rogue, Neshad. I want to buy fresh fruit and grill some meat."

Don raises an eyebrow. "Could be good for morale."

Neshad hesitates, calculating. Then: "We'll go together. But no stops. No talking to anyone. Understand?"

Sam nods. "Do we have a grill?"

"I'll find one," Neshad says, half-smiling. "Might need to borrow it from the mechanics."

Sam beams. She feels like she's contributing.

They exit the base and travel a few miles west through farms, olive groves, and past crumbling stone walls. Sam marvels at the rugged nature of the people and the landscape. Near a highway intersection, they finally reach a shopping district.

The market is a warehouse—a far cry from the American-style grocery she hoped for—but it's a treasure trove of flavors and smells. She picks through fruits, selects pre-marinated meats.

"We need wine?" Sam imagines something communal. Family style. Simple.

"We should get back," Neshad replies.

Sam is undeterred. After securing a few bottles of red table wine, they load up the jeep. The journey back is quiet, tense.

It takes longer than expected. They're racing the sunset. Sam glances at the sky as it shifts into deep violet. The air smells dry, like the coming night.

"It is getting dark," Neshad observes.

Sam can see the lights of the base ahead. They're almost at the gate when the shrill, rising wail of sirens slices through the silence.

Neshad freezes, scanning the sky. "Missiles."

Sam's stomach drops. "What do we do?"

"Shelter." He hits the gas, and they speed toward the gate. "Hang on!"

Spotlights sweep the perimeter. Guards scramble, shouting in Hebrew. They gain entry before the base goes into lockdown. Racing toward their billet, they weave past men and women scrambling to their stations.

Neshad slams on the brakes, the jeep fishtailing to a stop. "Run!"

They abandon the groceries—the meat, the wine, the bread.

Inside the bunker, Bram, Jynx, and Don hear the distant explosions, feel the rumble beneath their feet as Iron Dome intercepts fire.

Boom.

The ground trembles.

Thud-thud-thud.

Debris rains down.

Doors burst open. Sam and Neshad stumble inside, breathless.

Bram and Jynx rush to their aid, ensuring they are safe.

"What the hell happened?" Don barks.

Neshad is already on the phone, getting an update. He listens, nods grimly, relaying the information to the group as he hears it.

"Hezbollah fired five rockets. Targeting this base and just south of Haifa. Interceptors caught all five. Debris is landing nearby."

No one speaks. The grill will stay cold. There will be no barbecue tonight.

They sit in the bunker, wide-eyed and wired, adrenaline replacing hunger. Only one day remains.

Sam thinks: Nowhere is safe.

CHAPTER FIFTY-THREE

RAYA IS SHACKLED TO A chair in a cold, damp cell. She doesn't know how she got here, into this prison. A tall, gaunt man enters the room. His uniform immaculate, his eyes flat.

"Who's your contact?"

I've been here before.

He slaps her hard across the face. "What's the location?"

Suddenly she is gripped by fear—imagining herself locked away. Nobody able to help. Fred has forsaken her, Neshad doesn't care, and Jynx's efforts don't matter. She longs to see Bram one last time. *Spies are useful until they are not.*

He pushes her head down, pressure grinding into her spine. "Don't fuck with me."

She is losing her mind.

Raya wakes with a gasp. Someone is banging on the door. Boris.

He opens it, his burly frame filling the space. "You are late. You know the rules. Take your things. Out by ten."

She has overslept. She looks around. Alone.

Watching him walk away, shaking his head, Raya feels relief. For this, she is grateful.

It is Sunday, the third day. She has just enough time to pull her things together and start the circuit. Her flight leaves tomorrow. She could change it, but why bother? She doesn't know what happens next.

Raya heads east a few blocks to the southern end of Alexander Garden. She feels eyes upon her. If it's going to happen, it will be today. She's still shaken by the dream. Is her subconscious warning her? Is it time to send the text—that she is sick, that she needs to be pulled out?

Don's voice echoes: Every agent needs to feel the op. Feel the street. Find your intuition, or you won't last long.

She checks her instincts. Unsure, but she presses on. The sun is high, the clouds have finally cleared. Vendors hawk trinkets, coffee, street food. The park is alive.

She walks the length of it, constantly scanning. Passes the Tomb of the Unknown Soldier for the third time. Her mind drifts back to the dream. Would she be lost here? Arrested? Left unknown to the world? Only Bram grieving the loss. Turning south, needing to make up time, she sees a flash of green at the edge of her vision. Just another hawker, offering a pamphlet. A young girl, hustling a few extra dollars for her family.

As Raya moves past, the girl approaches.

Neshad's warning rings in her ears: The cold approach is your most dangerous moment. If KNOLL is compromised, we'll have no warning. You have to stick to your legend.

"What a pretty scarf."

"It was a gift from a friend."

"Is he a handsome man?"

"I don't remember."

Word perfect. Raya has met her contact.

The girl hands over a pamphlet. "You are very pretty. But better if you go to spa… would be even prettier."

Raya frowns. This makes no sense.

She looks at the pamphlet. Salon Krasoty Elit—The Elite Beauty Salon. Seeing Raya's hesitation, the girl insists: "You should go there. Today. Now. I think you like it, da?"

The knowing look in her eyes urges Raya to agree.

"Yes. I think that is a good idea," Raya replies.

The girl's expression shifts from trepidation to relief. She runs off.

I wish I felt that sense of relief, Raya thinks.

She studies the address. Lenivka Street. She knows it—she's passed it several times en route to the Pushkin Museum.

She sets off, resisting the urge to look behind her. Committed now. Eyes up, pace steady, head clear.

After a brisk walk, she reaches the Salon Krasoty Elit. A basic storefront beneath several floors of apartments that wrap around the block. The far end fronts the glimmering Moskva River.

The street is sparse, just off the main pedestrian corridor. She knows any watchers will be concealed. The building is a warren of places to hide. She snaps a photo and sends it via text. At least Bram will know where she is.

Inside, it looks ordinary. Women having their hair styled. Blow dryers humming. The air thick with floral shampoo,

420

acetone, and something sterile underneath.

Unsure of her next move, Raya acts naturally. She walks to the desk, handing over the pamphlet. "Someone gave me this. The woman suggested you might have an opening?"

Without looking up, the receptionist says, "Nyet. We are full."

Raya remains undeterred. She is here for a reason. "I see. Are you sure?"

The woman finally looks at her—and sees the red scarf. Her eyes flicker. "...Maybe we have opening. If you are patient."

Raya nods. No other option.

"There is lounge in back. You wait there."

She moves through the salon toward the rear door. She doesn't want to lose the safety of a public place, but she has no choice. She is beyond running.

She opens the door and steps into the waiting area—soft lighting, faux leather couches, a humming coffee machine. Disarmingly normal. She exhales, steadying herself. Relieved.

Then the door clicks shut behind her. She turns—and freezes.

Boris.

His hulking frame fills the doorway. He smiles.

She nearly screams. Her hand grips her phone. No signal. Panic coils in her chest. She's trapped.

She tightens her grip on the phone like a weapon, mind racing through exits, plans, anything. But Boris raises both hands, palms out, a pleading look in his eyes.

"Please," he says softly. "...You come for meeting? I am here to help."

CHAPTER FIFTY-FOUR

THERE IS NO REST FOR the team. Sirens wailed throughout the night, shaking walls and nerves alike. The sky still smells of smoke. Everyone is trying to recover from the emotional toll. Raya in Russia. Missiles in the sky. The weight of uncertainty is heavy on them all.

Today must be the day.

Neshad is called out to provide emergency support, but the remaining four—Don, Sam, Bram, and Jynx—have somehow grown closer. The tensions of the previous day forgotten—for now. The shared experience of death does that. There is no space between them, only the work.

They gather around Jynx in the dim bunker, the only light coming from the wall of monitors. A dull hum of equipment fills the silence as they watch Raya's encrypted signal on the map.

Neshad returns as the first ripple of concern hits.

Bram is the first to see it, the change in pattern. "She's starting late. What happened?"

Sam offers, "Maybe she overslept?"

The room goes quiet—then they all laugh at how ridiculous that sounds. A welcome break in the tension.

"Raya? Oversleep?" Don shakes his head.

They huddle closer, watching her tracker begin the circuit.

Don tries to sound calm. "Look, she's a little off schedule, not much."

Sam asks, "Will it matter?"

"Unlikely," Neshad replies. "The windows are wide enough. A few minutes on either side shouldn't matter."

They follow as she moves through Alexander Garden, along its paths, heading north. Spending time at the Tomb of the Unknown Soldier.

They watch as she turns south and stops.

Bram leans forward. "She's lingering. She's off."

Don concedes, "She's past her expected departure time, but not by much. Give her a minute."

Bram works to control his worry. "And if she's in trouble?"

"In the middle of a park? In daylight?" Neshad counters. "She's got her phone. If it goes sideways, we'll know."

They watch as Raya returns to the routine, heading south as expected. They all exhale in relief.

It doesn't last long.

Jynx sits up. "Her route's changing. She's not heading to the museum... she's turning down Lenivka."

"What the hell is she doing?" Don mutters.

Jynx reports, "There's a text comin' through now."

A new image flashes on the central screen—a storefront. Cyrillic signage. Salon Krasoty Elit.

Bram squints. "What is that? Is that a signal?"

Sam tries to lighten the moment. "Odd time to get her hair done." She immediately regretted it.

Bram gives her a cool look.

Don wants to know, "What is she doing?"

No one answers. They all know—this is off script.

Jynx finally offers, "She's holdin' back a bit. Standin' there like she's makin' up her mind."

They watch the tiny yellow dot move across the map toward the entrance. After a few minutes, the signal goes dark. It disappears.

Bram pushes back in his chair. "She's gone dark. We've lost her!"

"She's not gone," Neshad says, voice like gravel, calm and immovable.

Bram paces, breath tight in his throat. "We don't know what that place is. We don't know who's inside."

Sam tries to calm him. "We knew she would make contact at some point. Isn't this part of the process?"

"She sent the photo," Neshad says, quiet but sharp. "That's not panic. That's protocol. She knows we need the location."

Bram knows he's right. He thinks through the possibilities. "It could be the FSB. Do you think it's a trap?"

Jynx speaks up. "Got me walk-by lads in place already— just waitin' on word from 'em now."

They sit in silence, waiting.

"Looks normal enuff," Jynx says cautiously. "Don't smell o' government work—no motors sittin' dark, no hard lads lurkin' about. A lass just stepped out for a blether on the phone, then slipped back inside."

"We don't know yet," Don says. "So, we keep watching. And we trust the agent."

"She didn't call it in," Bram insists.

Don meets his gaze. "She's trained not to—no panicked calls. That wasn't a distress signal, Bram. That was breadcrumb."

Bram's voice softens. "A breadcrumb to what?"

"I'll pull info on the building—floor plan, records," Neshad says. He turns to Bram. "...and we'll start contingencies."

CHAPTER FIFTY-FIVE

RAYA PACES THE ROOM LIKE a caged lion. Her steps are deliberate, not anxious. Every few strides she glances toward the door, measuring distance, timing escape routes. Not panicking yet—alert.

Boris pleads. "Please, you sit now. He come soon."

"Who will be here?"

"You are safe. I move from door, yes?"

Raya nods, but subtly shifts her stance, positioning herself for an escape.

"Is good story, yes? You are visiting salon. Safe."

She sees his point. "If you're going to have a meeting, this is a good setup."

Boris brings her a coffee, but before she can drink it, the rear door opens. Yuri steps in—a silhouette of tailored confidence. Tall, angular, with the posture of a soldier. His suit is dark blue, not flashy but perfectly fitted. His scent—cedar and tobacco. He reminds her of a French diplomat.

He looks at Boris. "You may wait outside. I will call if I need you."

"I watch the street now." Boris exits.

Yuri offers his hand. After a moment, Raya takes it.

"What is this place?"

"It is a useful place for meeting. When the door is closed, it is safe—no electronic surveillance."

"And who are you?"

"Ah, the big question. That's complicated. But I promise to tell you everything."

Raya stares at him.

"First, you should know something. It is important. Anna—Masha, as you know her—did not kill your father."

"Fuck you. She did. I know she did." Raya rises, impulse screaming at her to get away.

Yuri shakes his head. "Are you really going to leave with no answers?"

He's right. She isn't going anywhere. Embarrassed, she sits back down. "Then who did?"

"I am not sure who pulled the trigger, but a man named Ivan Kirillov ordered the hit."

"How would you know?"

"Masha told me," Yuri replies calmly.

Raya's head spins.

"That is why we did not meet yesterday. I was meeting her. She was in this very room."

"What? How is she here? Does she know I'm here?"

"Yes. I told her. She didn't know."

"What does she want?"

"I will explain. I promise. Much has become clear since I spoke with her. We are more aligned now than we ever were before."

Raya asks again. "Who are you?"

"I am Yuri Dadiani. I work for Ivan Kirillov... and I am married to Anna."

It's too much. Raya moves toward the door.

Yuri raises a hand. "Please sit. We'll never finish if you walk out every time I say something that upsets you. Please—be patient."

"I'll stand, if you don't mind."

Yuri exhales. "Hmmm... yes, then we must start at the beginning." He glances at his watch. "It is still early. We have time."

Raya relents and sits.

"When I first met Anna Lomouri, she was the most beautiful girl I had ever seen. We were both working for a man named Evgeni Antonov... a rising star. His rapid success propelled both of our careers."

Raya listens.

"It didn't start that way. She was young... attractive and intelligent. A graduate of the Technical University. A volunteer in the military auxiliary. Her reputation was solid. But she had just come off a difficult assignment... Case 42."

"We found a reference to that. We didn't know what it was," Raya says.

"Then you've done well. You know more than I thought... and probably less."

"What happened?"

"It was 1972. Tbilisi was tense. Factories ran day and night. Streets echoed with boots and whispers. Evgeni was chief prosecutor in the region, only twenty-eight. He convinced Anna to infiltrate a cell of dissidents."

"That was Case 42?"

"Da. Anna was the right person at the right time. They needed someone local. They needed a girl from Georgia."

Raya crosses her arms, jaw tight.

"This group was secretive. The Defense Group, they called themselves. No set program, no defined structure. They published the *Journal of Events*, leaving paper copies on doorsteps, in train stations, on buses. Articles were written under pseudonyms—civil rights violations, judicial abuses, and citizens' resistance."

Raya nods her head slowly, absorbing the story.

"Some members were humanitarians who avoided anything treasonous. Others wanted political struggle, more aggressive action. The government didn't know who they were."

"I bet that didn't go over well," Raya says dryly.

"As you imagine, the commissars weren't happy. The police began investigating. They suspected a woman named Polina Beridze of helping to write and typeset the leaflets. But they had no proof."

"Anna was tasked with infiltrating the group. Eight months undercover in Tbilisi, between the Black Sea and the Caucasus. Hard work even for a trained operative. Anna was your age—or younger."

Raya winces. Subtly, but Yuri notices.

"She befriended Polina. Same age. Polina never saw Anna

429

as a threat. They grew close. Soon Anna was enmeshed in the group, identifying key figures."

"But something happened."

"Yes. She fell in love—with Polina's brother Dmitri. Sensitive, kind. He wanted to expose the crimes but avoid strife. An idealist. She searched for a way to complete her mission without betraying him."

"But she couldn't," Raya says.

"No. There was no way. It ate at her."

"What did she do?"

"In time, Evgeni pushed her. He reminded her of the career advancement waiting for her. She was torn, wracked with guilt. But Evgeni demanded names. Anna must provide the evidence to shut down this group of dissidents."

"It changed her. Didn't it?"

"Yes, her mind altered. In the end, she made the cynical decision—she sacrificed Dmitri. Ensuring her loyalty and future. The first arrests came in January 1973."

"A Faustian bargain. What happened to Dmitri and Polina?"

"They were convicted and sentenced to punitive psychiatry. I don't know Polina's fate. Perhaps she died in prison. Dmitri made it out after ten years, lived in Poland, then England. He was killed a few months ago."

The pieces click for Raya. She remembers Neshad's words: Dmitri doesn't concern us. But she had known.

"They turned her into a monster."

"Just so. And it gets worse. She discovered she was pregnant. Abortions were common in the Soviet Union. But

430

Anna was Georgian Orthodox. To her, abortion was a terrible sin. She couldn't bring herself to do it."

"She's a killer—"

"Yes. But not then. Not yet."

"So, she found you?"

"Yes. I was convenient. It worked. I did love her. I still do."

Raya's eyes narrow. "How?"

"You don't always get to choose. Maybe I had a strong desire to protect her, maybe I needed to be needed. Either way, in time, we drifted. For Anna, everything only made sense if the government was right. She made that choice. I was more liberal."

"So, you moved apart?"

"Yes. I hadn't seen her for a long time before yesterday. She was with you."

"I'm sorry."

"Don't be, please. People change. I have, and so has Anna. She's lived with guilt for a long time—the weight of the choices she made when she was young. She was broken. In need of repair. But now... I think she's found her path. Her chance at redemption."

Raya's voice sharpens. "And you? Is this your path to redemption?"

"I hope so. But to understand, I need to tell you more. This next part... it will interest you greatly." He takes a breath, steadying himself.

Raya nods.

"In October of 1973, Anna had her baby. A beautiful girl. We had been married for months. Even though she was not mine, I thought of her as my daughter."

He looks at Raya carefully, then says, "We named her Oksana."

Raya freezes. "Oksana was my mother's name."

And in a flash, she knows. *Did I know it all along?*

"So, Masha—Anna—is my grandmother. And what does that make you?"

"A step-grandfather, I suppose. I'm sorry. I thought it best to give you the whole picture. To ease you in."

"Well, you were wrong."

They sit in silence, the air between them heavier than before.

A knock at the door. Boris pokes his head in. "There is movement on the street."

With the door ajar, Yuri's phone buzzes. He checks it. His eyes widen.

"We need to move."

He grabs Raya's hand to pull her deeper into the building. She hesitates, then follows. The structure swallows them into a maze of dim hallways as they race for the elevators.

CHAPTER FIFTY-SIX

KIRILLOV HANGS UP THE PHONE. The Chief of Staff wants updates, reports. *They are up my ass.* He feels the loss of control—the tightening leash. He should be at his dacha, enjoying the ski season. Instead, he's here, working on a Sunday, chasing ghosts.

Worse still, there are whispers—the President was seen having lunch with Evgeni Antonov. Only rumors, but disturbing. That man was finished. Done. Buried. But now he's rising again. The capacity for political resurrection in Russia is legendary. Kirillov knows he must show results.

He has two prior failures on his record—one in Germany, one in Australia. In both cases, he pushed for quick results and was repaid with disaster.

In Berlin, control disintegrated after the handler died, and the hastily appointed replacement proved ineffective—unable to maintain the asset's trust or momentum. The operation dissolved into farce.

In Melbourne, the chosen candidate collapsed under pressure, unraveling when an undisclosed drug addiction surfaced—a condition that, under different circumstances, might have been a useful lever, but rendered him completely unreliable.

In both instances, Kirillov acted decisively to contain the fallout. No leaks. No loose ends. Everyone associated with the operations—silenced or eliminated.

He has others in the pipeline. Raya is next on his list. On paper, her circumstances are close to optimal—a promising candidate, primed for exploitation. But Masha—Anna—is complicating everything, threatening to dismantle the careful scaffolding of his plan. *She's fucking it up.*

Drumming his fingers on the desk, he considers his next steps. *Will I need to take active measures again?* Maybe. But first, he needs to buy time, distract the Chief of Staff, locate the mole.

One problem at a time—find Anna. No telling what trouble she'll cook up. He has seen no reports of sightings. *Where the hell is she? Someone must be helping her.*

He calls in an aide. "Where is Yuri?"

"Not responding to calls. Goes right to voicemail," the aide replies.

Kirillov's gut tightens. "Send a team to Yuri's apartment. Search it top to bottom. I want this woman found," he says, sliding the surveillance photo of Anna across the desk.

"If you find her there, arrest them both and bring them to me."

✦✦✦

Raya and Yuri race to the elevators. As they enter, she slings her backpack over her shoulder—everything she owns inside. Yuri presses the button for the fourth floor—the top.

"I have much more to tell you," Yuri says, "but right now, we need to hide you quickly. The man I work for, Kirillov, is looking for me. He'll send people to my apartment."

"What does he want?"

"Anna."

"What about me? Do you think they know I'm here?"

"I don't think so. But we must assume the worst."

Raya nods, reading the tension on his face.

"Kirillov is predictable. If I'm not home, he'll grow suspicious. I need to get you safe first. There's an apartment down the hall from mine. A friend. A woman. I have the key."

Raya lifts an eyebrow. "A friend?"

Yuri doesn't take the bait. "Her name's Natalia. She's not in Moscow right now. You'll be safe there."

"What if they search her place too?"

"It's not known—you should be safe."

The elevator dings. They step out and walk swiftly. Yuri speaks as they move.

"I'll go to my apartment. Let them search. They'll find nothing. Once they're gone, I'll return."

They reach Natalia's door. Inside, the apartment is quiet, dim, faintly perfumed. One bedroom, neat. Feminine.

"Hide your things," Yuri says. "I'll be back soon. They're coming."

As Raya begins to settle in, Yuri hesitates.

"You have friends watching?"

"Yes." Raya wonders what Bram is doing. Wishes he were here.

"Send them a text. Let them know you're safe, but you may need help to get out."

Raya pulls out her phone.

>> *Things have turned worse. I am going to lie down. May need a doctor.*

Yuri leaves. His shoes echo faintly down the hall. But he has miscalculated. The authorities are fast. As he exits the apartment, a soldier rounds the corner.

"There! That's him!"

Yuri doesn't flinch. He walks calmly toward his own door.

"What is this? Who are you?" he says with icy indifference.

"I saw you leaving that apartment," the younger soldier says, suspicion already in his voice.

"I visited a friend," Yuri replies smoothly, attempting to open his own door. "Come, we can discuss."

Inside Natalia's apartment, Raya hears the voices down the hall. Tension coils. She feels exposed.

She acts fast. She throws her bag in the closet, strips off her clothes, and finds an old silk robe. Ruffles the sheets. Smears her makeup. Messes her hair.

Through the door, she hears pounding. Demanding entry.

"Hold on!" she calls, hoarse, annoyed.

Raya opens the door, robe falling slightly open. The young soldier blinks in surprise. "What do you want?"

The older soldier grabs her hair, pulling her face into the light, comparing it to a photo.

Raya screams in Russian. "You're hurting me. What do you

want?"

"It's not her," he mutters, dropping her.

The soldiers exchange glances, then look at Yuri. The implication is clear. They think Raya is a prostitute.

Yuri erupts. "Do you know who I am? You'll pay for this. You think you can just barge in?" He demands their names, rages, performs.

The soldiers don't engage. They have orders from someone scarier than Yuri. They tear through the apartment—tossing cushions, opening drawers—they find nothing.

Disappointed, the older soldier mutters, "Shlyukha," under his breath. He slams the door in Raya's face as they leave.

Yuri keeps up the act—indignant, blustering. Convincing. The scent of scandal, of carelessness, of entitlement—it's all there.

They lead him to his own apartment. Another search. Another dead end. Still no Anna.

Yuri thinks *they'll leave us for now. I hope.*

CHAPTER FIFTY-SEVEN

Secure base outside Haifa, Israel 2019

STILL IN THE BUNKER, JYNX monitors the feeds. The room is quiet except for the low hum of electronics. The team remains on edge, *waiting*.

Neshad and Don huddle in the back, speaking in low tones, heads close. Bram stands, paces, sits, stands again.

Sam needs something to do. Some way to help. "I'm going outside to see if any of the food survived the night."

No one responds. The air is stale, heavy with anxiety.

Sam searches the jeep. The bread and fruit are still edible; the meat she discards. Happy with her small success, she heads back in, hoping to lift the mood.

"Anyone hungry?" she calls.

Before anyone can answer, Jynx leans forward. "Right, so—bit o' stirrin'. Me boys just rang in. Military lorry pulled up. Couple o' uniforms marchin' into the flats."

Bram stiffens. "What can we do?"

Don answers, "The only thing we can—wait."

The tension is palpable. Silence presses in.

"Hold up now—there's a message comin' through," Jynx says.

They all look to the central screen:

>> *Things have turned worse. I am going to lie down. May need a doctor.*

Bram is the first to speak. "Has she been blown?"

Neshad shakes his head. "We don't know. Looks like she's hiding. Riding it out."

Don advises, "We need to be ready. Jynx, pull your team back—give them distance. We can't risk them getting scooped up."

"Already ahead o' ye. Me lads are sharp as flint. Know what they're doin'."

"Let's review options," Don suggests.

Bram offers, "Can we bring her out the same way she went in?"

"You're right—that's one option," Don concedes. "But we could tweak it. Give her a different identity, keep everyone guessing. Change her appearance. Blend her into commercial traffic."

Neshad frowns. "That requires embassy help. A courier for documents. And if they're watching for Raya, they'll watch everyone leaving the embassy."

Sam asks, "What if she got inside the embassy? Would that help?"

"She could shelter there," Neshad says, "but she'd be trapped. Might be able to invoke diplomatic cover in some backwater republic, but not Moscow."

Undeterred, Sam suggests, "I heard once someone was smuggled out in a diplomatic pouch. Built a crate with air pipes."

Neshad snorts. "You've been reading too many stories. Besides, it would take time to build. Too long."

Bram sighs. "Still better than being caught." He hates depending on anyone else for Raya's safety. "What about a private plane, a secluded airstrip?"

Don shakes his head. "That means corrupt controllers. Otherwise, you risk getting shot out of the sky. This isn't the FAA. This is Russia."

Sam, desperate to help, offers: "Okay, then what about a boat? A yacht?"

"Same problem," Don says. "Ports. Coast guard. Unless you can bribe someone—and that takes time."

Jynx grins. "What about a body bag, eh? Knock her out, paint her up, tuck her in a coffin. Say it's a dead aunt—repatriation an' all that."

Sam recoils. "That's awful."

Bram shakes his head in frustration.

"Too complex," Neshad cuts in. "Too many moving parts."

Jynx shrugs. "Ah, Jaysus, I was takin' the piss. You lot are dark. But right enough messin'—what's the real plan, then?"

Looking at Neshad, Jynx knows he has nothing solid. To Neshad, KNOLL is priceless—and Raya expendable. Then his eyes flick to Don and sees the same grim realization.

Bram glares. "Jynx, I thought you had a way. You said you could help. Contacts, bribed guards, something at the border?"

"Ah, bribin' border lads ain't a stroll through the park, now, is it? Only works when they're half asleep and not sniffin' for ghosts."

Bram's voice goes cold. "Then what is your plan?"

"Right oh." Jynx cuts in, hand raised. "I said I have a way—and I do. Just lettin' the daft ideas flutter about first, keepin' the brains warm."

Bram is firm. "What is it?"

"Old school," Jynx says, folding his arms with a grin.

Sam leans in. "How soon?"

"Give me a day. That's all I need. Unless one o' ye's got something faster?"

Bram's voice is clipped. "I'm not sure we have a day. How would it work?"

Jynx shrugs. "We've a special rig—van made for smugglin', snug as you like. Hidden hatch, swap ou' the goods, tuck Raya in proper, nice an' tidy. Won't be a soft ride—rough go of it, mind—but she'll be breathin' on the far side."

"And it'll work?"

"Oh, it'll work, so it will." Jynx says, flashing a grin. "Cross me heart."

Later that night, Bram sits with Jynx—talking. Like a father with a son. Jynx knows Bram needs advice—the kind a parent should give, advice Bram never had the chance to receive.

"Y'know, men sometimes carry a special burden, so they do. But yours, lad—that's a heavier load than most. Lovin' a woman who's thrown herself into danger."

Bram furrows his brow. "I'd rather it be me."

Leaning closer, Jynx says, "There's not a man alive worth

his salt that wouldn't feel the same."

"What do I do?"

"Endure, boy."

Looking down, Bram says softly, "She's trusting me to be there for her."

"Aye, that's right. But you've gotta trust her, ye do. That's how the best loves survive—and grow strong."

Swallowing hard, Bram asks, "How do I do it?"

"Keep your wits about ya. Goin' all mad and shouty won't help a bit. We all want her home safe... that's the truth of it."

Jynx studies him. He sees a boy becoming a man—but not there yet. So, he tells him a tale.

"There was a man, a poet. Long dead. We Irish can't stand him—fuckin' imperialist. But even the worst bastards sometimes spit out a bit o' wisdom."

Bram waits, wondering.

"Name was Rudyard Kipling. Wrote a piece called If—. Bits of it come back when I'm pressed. Starts with, 'If you can keep yer head when all about you are losing theirs,' and ends with, 'you'll be a man, my son!' Can't remember the shite in the middle—but you get me drift."

Keep your head, Bram thinks. The world spinning around him. Powerless to act, everything outside his control. He knows he can't go on like this.

Jynx pokes him in the ribs. "You're jittery, is all. Fear o' losin' what ain't yours to keep—that's not yours to shoulder, y'know lad. Hardest thing's gettin' past your rearing... 'specially when it's loss that marked ya. But that's the trick, see? Stand fast. That's a man's way, innit?"

The words strike deep. Bram may not have Neshad's resources or Fred's confidence, but he has his own path. More than that, he has something they don't: Raya's faith.

Jynx is right. I can't help her if I'm acting panicky. I need to trust Raya the way she's trusting me.

With half a smile, Jynx squints at him. "You're wound tighter'n a drum, Bram. But you're not alone, hear? This work'll chew up the soft-hearted. So, hold steady, aye? For Raya's sake—keep that head o' yours cool and sharp."

CHAPTER FIFTY-EIGHT

MOSCOW, RUSSIA
2019

YURI SITS ALONE IN HIS apartment after the men leave. Shaken, he can only imagine how Raya must be feeling. But he must wait. Kirillov is crafty. There's always a chance men were left behind—a quiet pair in the hallway, listening, watching. He can't risk drawing attention to Raya.

But time is running out. Yuri decides to act. He will take a walk. Something normal. Casual. Reconnoiter.

He slips outside and heads down the street, making a slow circuit around the block. His eyes scan for signs—not just for watchers, but also a signal. A mark scratched in chalk on the back of a street sign. Anna's confirmation that plans are still in motion.

There's a pel'meni shop nearby. He stops in for dumplings. Comfort food. Something they both need. Next door, a liquor store. He buys a bottle of Stolichnaya. The conversation with Raya hadn't gone the way he'd hoped. They'll need the vodka.

The day is drawing to a close. The usual Sunday crowd of

tourists has thinned. Muscovites clear the streets, retreating indoors before Monday's grind. As he nears his building, Yuri sees a group of men loitering near the entrance. His chest tightens. Could they be watchers?

He studies them—shabby coats, worn boots, the weary slump of men with nowhere better to be. Older. Rough. Not Kirillov's type. They look up as he passes, uninterested.

Yuri catches the eye of one of the men. A nod. A moment of recognition. These are not Kirillov's men; they're watching Raya.

Still, Yuri keeps his steps carefully. He doesn't breathe easy until he's back inside.

Yuri knocks gently so as not to startle Raya. When she answers, he can see the distress still etched on her face. She clings to him like a lifeline for a moment. And then it ends. Raya collects herself and sits, regaining her strength. The moment has passed.

While she waited, Raya ruminated—on her choices, the risk she was taking, the gnawing fear. She thought of Bram, of their connection, the reason to persevere, to get home. She had nearly signaled the team in Israel, her fingers hovering over the phone again and again. But in the end, she didn't. If she is going to get answers, she knows she has to stay.

Yuri starts with praise. "You did very well under stressful circumstances. You should be proud."

Her phone pings. She pulls it up and reads aloud.

"I got a text."

>> *boring, audible, rejected, noon*

"What is that—code?"

Raya shows him the what3words app, entering the first three words as she explains.

"This app divides the world into three-meter squares. Every unique combination of three words corresponds to a location. The words are also the confirmation code. The last word is the time—noon tomorrow."

On her screen, Yuri sees the location.

"I know this place. A mile and a half from here, next to a cemetery." He smiles at the irony of the location. "We still have much to discuss. Text your friends. Get them off the street."

She complies and sends:

>> *Feeling better. I need to be alone now. See you tomorrow.*

"Do you think I still need an elaborate escape plan? Things seem to have settled."

"It is better to be prepared," Yuri replies. "Tonight... should be eventful."

"What do you mean?"

Instead of answering, he looks at his watch.

"I need answers," Raya says, firmer now.

"Please eat." He gestures to the food.

She realizes she hasn't eaten all day. Hunger churns in her stomach. The food is delicious.

He pours two short glasses of vodka, neat. Holding one out to Raya, he toasts, "To our health!"

She takes it, downs it in one motion.

Yuri continues his story. "Anna became a trusted infiltrator. Very skilled. Evgeni used her often to root out corruption. She was his favorite. Her success ensured his. And mine, in a way."

"And you?"

"I was the bureaucrat. Background noise. But Anna raised my status."

"You weren't bothered?"

"No. I never felt the need to lead. It suited Anna."

Raya recognizes that version of Anna.

"While Anna thrived professionally, privately she was angry—haunted by regret. She believed that if she'd been stronger, she could have changed everything. She lived in duality. Ashamed of the girl she once was. Unraveling inside. She needed something solid to cling to. The work became that. And Oksana... Oksana became her second chance."

"What did she do?"

"She wanted the best for her daughter. Not just as a mother, but as someone trying to rewrite her own past. Oksana became a way for Anna to fix things. But in the process, she never truly became the mother she needed to be. She grew cold. Distant."

"That sounds like Masha."

"It affected our marriage," Yuri admits softly. "We grew apart. But the loyalty remains. I still love her. I wish she didn't carry so many demons."

Raya holds out her glass. "Pour me another."

He nods and refills it.

"All that time, I grew very close to Oksana," Yuri says. "She was my daughter in every way that mattered. While Anna was off on missions, it was just the two of us. The house felt warm.

When Anna returned, the tension came with her."

Raya stares into the past she never had. Time she should have had with her mother—time stolen by fate.

"Anna pushed Oksana in everything—academics, looks, social circles. There was constant friction. Always fighting. And then another assignment would come, and Anna would vanish for months. Things would settle again. It felt almost normal."

Raya thinks of her own time alone when her father traveled.

"Anna wanted more for Oksana. But Oksana... she was a free spirit. Maybe like you. She didn't know what she wanted yet. That terrified Anna. And eventually, it boiled over."

Yuri's voice tightens. "She pushed Oksana to join the security services. Said it was her duty. She even leaned on Evgeni—asked him to open a door for Oksana, anything. Evgeni remained unconvinced."

"But Anna was persistent."

"Yes. Evgeni, ever the cynic, finally agreed to a test. To see if Oksana could recruit a man at a party. A horrible assignment for a young girl, so unprepared. He thought Anna would reject it; after all, it was her daughter. Instead, she was thrilled."

Raya winces.

"Anna prepped Oksana for weeks. Cover stories, roleplay, tactics. Oksana played along, but her heart wasn't in it."

"She wanted me to intervene. But I was scared. Afraid of blowing my cover. Afraid of what it might cost Israel. I told myself the mission came first. That I had no choice. I made myself a case for cowardice. Just like Anna."

The words hang in the air.

"It strained our special relationship," Yuri says quietly.

"It's a regret I'll carry to the grave. I hope to make amends. To find some kind of redemption."

"Is that why you brought me here?" Raya asks. "For your redemption?"

"Maybe redemption's too strong," Yuri admits. "Maybe I just want to do one small thing right."

He shifts the conversation. "What do you think SEMYA is?"

Raya blinks, the realization hitting her. "It means family. Or seed. A program to recruit kids... sowing the future, turning them into spies."

"Not merely spies. SEMYA wasn't simply recruiting. It was designed to bring them into something stronger than their existing family. A new one built on dependency. A new kind of bond."

Her voice is quiet. "When did it start?" But she already knows.

"The early 1990s," Yuri says. "The empire was collapsing. Men who'd grown up in the mythology of Soviet greatness were watching it unravel. The USSR dissolved. The KGB fractured into the FSB and SVR. Prestige meant nothing. Power was slipping through their fingers."

He continues, "They were scared. But they were also strategic. They knew the tide would turn back someday—and they wanted to be ready. SEMYA was a long game. Twenty, thirty years ahead. A framework to build something that could survive and adapt."

Raya nods slowly, picturing the secretive architects of the future.

"You saw the documents I sent. These men were brilliant—

but locked in a Cold War mindset. Information was still their currency. So, they began there. But even they knew the world was changing."

"The program needed to be flexible," Yuri says. "A skeleton to be shaped over time. They didn't know which tactics would work. So, they experimented."

"How?"

"Various operations designed to 'create circumstances' for infiltration at a high level, tied to loyalty to a key figure in their life. They didn't know what would succeed. So, they launched trial balloons. Start broad, iterate, refine."

Raya shakes her head. "I still don't understand."

"Launch a hundred rockets. Most will miss. Send a few early, see what works—you learn, refine. Over time, you increase accuracy. You build patterns, profiles. You learn which levers to pull, which traumas to exploit. What makes someone loyal?"

"They targeted various countries, looking for soft targets sectors—Foreign Relations, Commerce, Energy, and Treasury. Public servants. They avoided security services—too exposed, too risky. They needed pathfinders. It would take years before SEMYA could run effectively. But they needed to learn early. They needed volunteers."

Only now does Raya begin to grasp the full scope—the depth of the manipulation.

"But now I think it's evolving," Yuri says. "Changing."

"To what?" Raya asks. "What is it becoming?"

"I'm not sure," Yuri admits. "But I think we'll find out. Tonight."

Suddenly, his phone rings. Both of them jump.

Yuri frowns. Caller ID: his office.

He answers cautiously. "Hello...?"

A nervous voice replies, "Ah—this is Anton. Anton Popov."

Yuri's eyes narrow. "Yes, Anton. How can I help you?"

"I work late tonight. And... you are always kind to me. You help when no one else does."

"Yes."

"I know I should not call. But... something is wrong. Kirillov—he filed request. He is searching."

"I know," Yuri says. "An older woman. Anna."

"No, not her. Younger woman. Dark hair. Name is Raya."

Yuri goes still. "Do they have a photo?"

"Yes. From soldier, I think. Did... did someone come to see you? I don't understand. Everything is strange now."

Yuri's heart sinks. Of course. They'd taken her picture while searching. How could he have missed that?

"Yes, Anton. It is confusing."

"I just... I thought you should know. They gave order. They come to arrest you."

"And you called to warn me?"

"You won't tell, yes? That I called?"

"No, Anton. Thank you. I won't tell anyone." Yuri's mind races. This boy... perhaps more useful than I thought.

He turns to Raya. "Time to go." But she's already packed. Ready. Without another word, they rush for the door and down the hallway. Yuri has one last hiding place. If they can make it.

CHAPTER FIFTY-NINE

MOSCOW, RUSSIA
2019

THEY RACE DOWN THE HALL, turning left and right. At the end, Yuri unlocks a small utility closet with a key and checks over his shoulder.

"Quickly now—inside." He pushes Raya through and shuts the door behind them.

"A little cozy, don't you think?" she mutters.

He quietly pushes aside mops and other materials leaning against a ladder bolted to the wall. "Climb. There's a trapdoor at the top. Push it open."

Raya ascends as quietly as she can. Behind her, Yuri follows, pulling the mops back in front of the ladder to conceal their escape.

At the top, Raya struggles with the weight. She grits her teeth, braces her shoulder against the hatch and heaves. Metal groans, then a sharp thunk. The trapdoor flies open, smacking back against the frame.

They both freeze. Hearts pounding. Breath held.

Silence. No shouts. No footsteps. No alarms.

Yuri gives a small nod. They continue to climb through.

The space is dark, circular, with dust hanging in beams of light from narrow windows. It takes Raya a moment to realize she's inside a cupola, a decorative turret. Narrow windows line the dome, offering a view across the Moskva River to the Kremlin.

Slowly, Yuri eases the hatch closed and bolts it, trying to avoid making any more noise. Now they are both trapped.

He opens a crate in the corner, pulling out folded blankets. "We'll be here for a while. No insulation, it will be cold—use these."

"What is this place?"

"A kind of insurance policy. Just in case."

"What happened?"

"Kirillov knows you're in the country. He'll be looking for you... and for me. We stay hidden for now."

Raya spreads the blankets, making a place to sit. They settle beside each other against the wall.

"Did you bring the vodka?" he asks.

She pulls the bottle from her pack.

"We'll sleep here. They'll search, but I don't think they'll go door to door. It should be safe."

Raya shrugs. It's out of her hands now.

"Before we go further, memorize a number," Yuri says.

"What number?"

"Eleven digits. You can't write it down, but you must remember." He recites it, quizzing her until she repeats it without hesitation.

"What does it mean?"

"Patience. I'll tell you. But let me finish my story."

Raya nods.

"Anna was furious that Oksana failed the test. But Evgeni wasn't as mad as she feared. In truth, he was relieved—he had no confidence in her. For him, it worked out."

"You must understand—Anna was deep in SEMYA's planning by then. Her role and prestige had grown. After Oksana's failure, she felt vulnerable."

Yuri's voice hardens. "Some people react badly to fear—especially fear of disappointing others. Anna is one of them. She built her self-worth on approval. When Oksana became pregnant after a night of frivolity, Anna was livid. When Oksana fell in love with Phil, Anna was enraged—furious at her daughter's sacrifice for love."

"She loved him?" Raya asks.

"She did. After what she'd seen between Anna and me, she would never have married Phil unless she truly loved him."

"For Anna, it was treason. Her breaking point came when you were named after Mikhail Gorbachev's wife, Raisa. She disowned her daughter. For me, it was unbearable—abandoning Oksana again, all for the mission. I miss her terribly."

Raya's voice is low. "Do you think Anna killed Oksana?"

"No, I cannot believe that. She died of a blood hemorrhage. Anna would not have been able... there is no way a mother would kill her daughter... no matter how mad she was."

Raya isn't so sure.

"When Oksana died, I was broken. But Anna stood firm.

She wanted to raise you herself—fix her mistakes with Oksana. Phil wanted to take you. I thought it best. Anna was not a good mother. You would be better off with your father. I was losing that fight."

"Something must have changed?"

Raya sees Yuri look at his watch. It is late. She thinks *he's waiting* for something.

"Evgeni had another idea. He suggested we let you go—a sacrifice to SEMYA, for the greater purpose. Anna relented. For her, it was a way to regain status."

Raya is incensed. "I was disposable."

"A harsh truth. But yes. At the time, Anna was broken."

"And you did nothing."

"I told myself the program would collapse. I was glad you were safe with your father. I was furious I'd failed Oksana, but she was gone. I told myself I had no choice. Yes—I failed you."

Raya glares. "What changed?"

"When Evgeni ran things, I knew the plan. I was informed. I tried to push Mossad to act. Sent clues. Nothing happened. Nothing changed."

"Then?"

"Then Kirillov took over. Everything shifted. He's aggressive. We always moved slowly, deliberately—but when two other BETAs failed, Kirillov had every participant eliminated. They cut off my access. I no longer knew what he planned next."

Yuri meets her eyes.

"You were afraid I might be next?"

"When Phil was killed, I knew it was a mistake. I knew

455

Oksana, and I knew you must be just as independent. There was no way it would work—it would never bring you closer to Anna. Yes, I worried for you. I did not know what Kirillov intended. My guilt grew heavy. I decided it was time—I had to tell you everything. It was the only way."

He hands Raya the vodka bottle. She takes a swig, then passes it back.

"What's next?" she asks.

"Tell me the number again."

Raya rattles off the eleven-digit code without hesitation.

"Are you going to tell me what it's for?"

"Yes, of course." He leans forward, ready to explain.

But his phone rings.

He feels Raya's eyes on him as he fumbles to answer. "Hello... yes... she is here... yes... we're safe."

He hesitates, then adds, "Hold on. I'll put you on speaker."

CHAPTER SIXTY

MOSCOW, RUSSIA
2019

IVAN KIRILLOV LIVES ON THE top floor of a luxury apartment complex along Sofiyskaya Embankment. There are several bedrooms and multiple bathrooms. An office with tall windows and a small balcony offers incredible views—it is his refuge, his fortress.

He returns home unsatisfied. Frustrated. No solutions to his problems. Yuri is missing. Anna is still at large. And now, Raya—hidden somewhere in Moscow.

He wishes he'd thought ahead, arranged a diversion—a woman, something to bleed off the anxiety. But tomorrow, they will be found. He pours himself a drink and considers his next move. How to move the program forward, how to secure his rightful place.

From his apartment, he sees the high Kremlin walls across the Moskva River. To the right, the onion domes of St. Basil's Cathedral—built by Ivan the Terrible to celebrate his victories. Kirillov hopes for many such victories himself. Legend has it that Ivan blinded the architect. Kirillov finds inspiration in the ruthlessness of his namesake.

If he leans left, less than a mile away, he can glimpse Yuri's austere apartment block. A man about to learn Ivan is not as gracious as his historic namesake.

As Kirillov settles at his desk, he catches a whiff of perfume. It's unfamiliar. Something is wrong. His mind wavers. He tries to collect himself—*what was I thinking?* His thoughts falter. The city lights outside ripple like water, colors smearing, dissolving.

Then a voice—his mother's. "You look tired, Ivan. What is the matter with you?"

No. She's dead. *What is happening?* He shakes his head, trying to clear his mind.

A hand slaps the desk. Thwack. "I said, what is the matter with you?"

He looks up. Sees a face. *Who is this person? Who dares disturb him?*

"You don't recognize me?" asks the woman.

A young woman. Attractive figure. Dressed in designer clothes. A pencil dress—chic and stylish. She carries a large zebra-print bag with a designer label. On her head, a wide-brimmed hat hides her features.

He blinks. Looks closer. No—she's not young. She's old. Her features obscured behind a mask of makeup. And then he recognizes her.

Anna. Masha.

"How did you get in here?"

She shrugs. "I was trained well. I've been sneaking in and

out of places for a long time. You know this."

Kirillov tries to rise. His legs weaken. He slumps back. His arms are wrenched behind him. Zip ties bite his wrists, locking him to the frame.

"What did you do to me?"

"A small dose of scopolamine. Just enough to keep you under control—docile. I need your compliance."

"The devil's breath..." His mind reels. *She must have drugged the liquor.* "How did you know what I would drink?"

Anna scoffs. "I dosed every bottle. Use your brain."

"You'll get no answers."

"We'll see."

She sets the zebra-striped bag onto the desk with a thud. From the top, she removes a syringe. Preps a shot. "Another dose to ensure I get what I want."

"You are a failure," he slurs.

"No, Ivan. You are. You're flailing. Everyone can see you trying to stay afloat. You can't breathe in these deep waters."

"How dare you? You use drugs, torture."

"I use the tools I was taught."

He slumps further.

"You have choices, Ivan. All bad. Some better than others."

"What do you mean?"

She pats the bag. "You're sitting beside nine pounds of C4. It was the most I could get. Enough to vaporize this apartment."

His eyes widen.

Then she offers him a carrot, a trap dressed as mercy. "You could escape. Relocate. I have contacts. Tell me everything, and you'll be safe."

"I won't tell you anything." He thinks *she lies*.

"Focus, Ivan. Choices. You're already cracking."

"I'll kill you. There's too much evidence. You'll be caught."

"Maybe. You've never struggled, Ivan, known genuine pain. But I've lived harder than you ever will. I'm sixty-five. My life's been spent. I will have my answers."

She leaves him stewing, the drug working deeper. Once he starts talking, momentum will be everything.

Anna walks down the hall and slips into the far bathroom, leaning against the wall. Exhaustion gnaws at her. So many regrets. So many lost chances. She steels herself. She knows what must come next.

It's time to make the call.

"Yuri... do you have Raya? Are you ready?"

She listens to Yuri as he responds.

"Tell her I am sorry—sorry for everything. No, I don't want to speak with her. I've done enough damage. I'll put you on speaker so you can hear everything. Put your phone on mute."

In the cupola, Yuri complies.

Anna's voice returns, sharp and low.

"Now listen carefully. This is where the truth begins."

Yuri glances at Raya. He sees the surprise in her eyes—and the doubt.

When she returns to Ivan's office, Anna quietly sets the phone on the desk and slaps him hard across the face. His head jerks, his eyes flutter. It's time to get answers.

She begins with something simple. "Why did you kill

Dmitri?"

"I told you... in Dubai. He wanted to kill you." Ivan strains to hold the lie, his pupils twitching. The drugs are taking their toll.

"That's bullshit." She sees he is struggling with his answers.

He laughs—short, jagged, manic.

"Ha! You figured me out. He wanted to find you. We intercepted messages—between him and his sister. Maybe he still loved you. Maybe they both did."

Anna freezes. "Polina is alive?"

Ivan smirks. "Ah, yes. You're sentimental. Weak." He bursts into laughter again. "She's immaterial."

"But you killed Dmitri?"

"I didn't want you distracted." He shrugs. "I wanted to impress the President."

Rage coils inside Anna—rage at Ivan, rage at herself. Dmitri—his love, his loyalty. After everything, he still tried to find her. Still loved her. They both did. A crack opens inside her. A new purpose hardens. Ivan will not leave this room alive.

But she must stay focused. "Why did you have Phil Rogers killed? Why didn't you let me finish my mission?"

"You were... moving... slow. You were... soft." Ivan's words slur.

In the cupola, Yuri exhales sharply. Raya gasps.

"That explains nothing. SEMYA had a plan—"

"I needed it... faster."

"Why? SEMYA required patience." But then she knows. Ivan must have made promises.

He's fading, eyes heavy. She needs him awake, alert.

Anna pulls a syringe from her bag—Ritalin, an amphetamine. A dangerous cocktail. She plunges it home.

The effect is immediate. Ivan surges back, pupils blown, grin wide. "You old fool. You know nothing." He leans back, riding the high. "I'm ahead of my time. I brought the methods of corporations, of hedge funds. I modernized espionage."

"You're a businessman, not a spy. What makes you think you're smarter?"

"I convinced the President." He beams, drunk on his own brilliance. The drug works. He's opening up.

"How?"

"Asymmetric. It's not about information—it's about influence. He loved it."

"Explain it to me." Anna glances at the phone, wondering, thinking of Yuri and Raya listening.

Ivan shifts tone. He's no longer in his office—he's back in his lectures, talking to hedge fund managers, pitching to ministers, convincing the President. He is on stage. His voice carries the rhythm of a salesman.

"It's simple. You already have the parts. They're just not integrated."

Anna watches as his energy swells. This is the moment he's been waiting for. He wants to brag.

"You waste too much time on traditional intel gathering. You have the scientists, the technicians—but there are other sources."

She plays along, feeding the spark. "Yes, but we also have more senior assets."

"Politicians. Union heads. Appointees. We compromise their kids, their wives, their businesses. But they can only do so much. Western governments are too distributed. Decentralization is their weakness."

"So, it's political."

"No! Party doesn't matter. Chaos matters. Disruption does."

Anna's pulse quickens. He's truth-telling now.

"Don't we already run influence operations?"

"Of course. Bots. Trolls. Fake groups online. It works. Social media is a blunt tool, but effective. It will only get better with machine learning, with generative AI. Society is becoming hyper-vulnerable. Nobody knows what's real anymore."

"But that's still not enough?"

"It helps. It amplifies. But that's external."

He leans in, searching for approval. When Anna gives none, he barrels on.

"The real value is inside. Quiet hands. In quiet places. Pressing gently."

"Go on."

"Think. What are we missing?"

Anna blinks. She's not sure. She shrugs, playing student to the professor.

"The West thinks decentralization is strength. It's not. It's a crack."

He shifts in his chair. Chest forward, shoulders back, he lifts his chin slightly. He is eager now, proud.

"SEMYA was designed for individual infiltration. Small scale. But what we need—what I sold to the President—is an army of administrators. Bureaucrats. Obedient middle managers. People who don't ask why—they just tip the scale."

Anna sees it. *Damn. The audacity.* In its way, brilliant.

"You want to place assets in mid-level roles. Faster."

"Yes! That's the gap. SEMYA has been too slow. We must switch from a basic asset program to a fully integrated influence operation."

"And that is what you sold to the President."

"If I can prove it works, we scale deployment." *And ensure my future.*

"But we don't operate in that space. The cost would be enormous."

"Nobody does. That's the point. It's a failure of imagination. But you can bet the Chinese are thinking about it. The Indians too. Maybe even the Americans—unless we beat them to it."

His eyes gleam with conviction. Madness or genius—hard to tell. "SEMYA gives us the edge. We already have trained assets—we just need to deploy them differently. It's an investment, but if it works—"

"It won't work."

Ivan reels, surprised by the rebuke. "Why?"

Anna breathes in. "Because it isn't spycraft. It's systems engineering. Weaponized bureaucracy. Too big. Too exposed. It will collapse under its own weight."

"How would you know?"

"Experience. You've applied business principles to a field you don't understand. Espionage works because it's slow, deliberate, devious. Scale kills it. You are out of your depth."

464

Ivan presses forward, desperate. "Think of it—assets around the world. Matched with compromised politicians, online influencers, military leaders. These cogs, these quiet manipulators, will move the world."

"You forget the most important part of SEMYA. The Doctrine of Patience," Anna says coldly.

He sneers. "Patience. I have no patience. It is for the weak. We must move faster."

She shakes her head. The President is a fool to let this go on. He should know better—he must know better. This is his world, the world of espionage. *What is happening within the Kremlin?* He must be under enormous pressure to bet on a lunatic like Ivan.

"How many?"

"Thousands. At scale."

She nods, grim. She knows it will never work. SEMYA was built to be small and elegant. This—this is reckless. "You plan an insurgency."

Ivan smiles like a CEO unveiling a product.

She comes around behind him and pushes his chair on its castors toward the balcony.

"What are you doing?"

She forces him to face the glass doors, looking out over the city—Moscow sprawling beneath them.

"You are too dangerous."

Panic floods his face. He imagines her pushing him over the edge.

"I can help you. Bring me west. I'll tell them everything."

"You killed Phil Rogers. You killed Dmitri. You threatened

me. My granddaughter."

His head droops. "I did what was required."

"Because you were impatient. Reckless."

"I have money," he pleads. "I can help you. Please."

Anna is unmoved. "You ruined it all, for hubris." She slaps his head. "Beg for your life." She is reveling in the moment. His fear, his pleading. A mania has overcome her.

He sobs. "Yes. Please, give me a chance."

"Yes... of course." She offers, disgusted by him.

She watches hope bloom in his eyes—then crushes it. "No. Never. You are a fool." She torments him.

Despair.

She toys with him, her mania surging. "Maybe I'll let you live... let me think."

Ivan weeps.

Anna picks up the phone and disconnects the line. That part of her life is dead.

She leaves Ivan staring out the large windows. She stalks through his apartment, smashing anything that looks priceless.

Ivan hears her moving through the walls, behind the doors. *What is she doing?* Destroying his possessions. His skin crawls. The drugs in his system coil, making his body feel both weightless and impossibly heavy.

He looks out over the city—the lights of Moscow, the Kremlin walls, a view for a man who believed himself destined to rule.

Then silence. No more smashing. His dread spikes. *Has she left? Could he survive?* If he does, he will kill her slowly.

As Ivan looks at the lights, the drugs are crawling through

his veins, twisting his sense of time, of space. He notices a reflection. A glint. A distortion in the glass catches his eye.

He tries to turn his head, but he can't. With his legs tied, he uses his toes. Slowly swiveling the chair. He strains, inch by inch, twisting his bound body to face it.

The zebra-print bag.

Why did she leave it here? His mind is sluggish, muddled. *What did she say was in the bag?*

It is his last thought.

On the other side of the building, at ground level, Anna slips behind the loading docks. She hikes her dress, scrambles over a fence, and drops lightly to the pavement. Adjusts her appearance.

Calmly, she walks onto Bolotnaya Street and crosses the Malyy Moskvoretskiy Bridge. From her purse, she pulls a phone, opens an app, and taps the switch linked to the detonator.

The blast rips through the top floor. A fireball blooms against the night. Debris rains down. Pedestrians freeze, eyes wide with horror.

Anna doesn't look back. She slips across the road, utterly uninterested.

From there, she takes Pyatnitskaya Street, following it a few blocks to an area lined with pubs and cafés. Blending into the crowd.

A perfect place to disappear.

CHAPTER SIXTY-ONE

IN THE CUPOLA, THE AIR is still. Yuri and Raya sit in stunned silence, backs against the wall. The phone line is dead. Both wanting to act, but for a short time, unable, or unwilling to move. Only the echoes of Anna and Ivan's final exchange linger.

Yuri speaks first. "She does love you... you know."

Raya isn't ready to unpack that. Conflict churning inside her.

Instead, she asks, "Did you understand what they were talking about?"

"Yes. Ivan wants pandemonium. That's what the President craves. But Anna is right—it will never work."

Staring at the ceiling, she murmurs, "And the Doctrine of Patience?"

Yuri's answer is tinged with sorrow. "There are those who believe anything is possible, given time."

"What happens now?"

He stands. "Come. Look out the window."

Together, they climb to the narrow openings overlooking Moscow. Yuri points northeast. "That's where Ivan Kirillov lives."

Raya is surprised. "So close. I had no idea."

Suddenly, a thunderous explosion tears through the night, lighting the skyline in a violent flash. The top floor of an apartment complex facing the river erupts in a storm of flame and shattering glass. A shockwave rattles the windows as debris rains down like burning ash.

Yuri's voice is low, almost reverent. "Anna has eliminated Ivan."

Raya's breath catches. "Do you think... she died too?"

Yuri shakes his head slowly; his eyes fixed on the plume of smoke. "That doesn't sound like Anna. She's a survivor."

"Will it stop SEMYA?"

"No. But it kills Ivan's plan. A setback—but not the end."

"So how do we stop it?"

He ignores the question. "Come, sit. We have time."

Unsure, Raya asks, "Will they come for us?"

"I'm sure they'll be looking."

As he speaks, sirens wail in the distance, racing toward the explosion.

Raya shivers. The roar of the explosion still echoes within her ribs. She thinks of Bram—his steady voice, the warmth in his eyes, the way his presence calms her whenever doubt creeps in. *He must be worried sick.*

"They'll probably think it was terrorists," Yuri muses. "Chechens. Ukrainians."

Raya frowns. "But eventually they'll piece it together.

They'll look for Anna. Then you."

"Yes. Maybe. Depends on how much Ivan told them. He was barely holding his plan together. It won't be easy to untangle."

"Should we move now?"

"No. The streets will be swarming with security. Better to wait until morning, when you can blend into the commuter traffic. People going to work—much easier to disappear."

That night, the city lights shining through the windows dimmed, fading into a soft wash of darkness. Their eyes adjust, shapes sharpening until they can just make out each other's faces. Sitting with their backs against the wall, knees drawn up, the two shadows talk. It feels like a dream—like the world has paused for them alone.

Yuri, like a weary grandfather, coaxes stories from her— childhood memories, her training, her father, her ambitions. His voice is gentle, but beneath it lives the old operator. Learning her contours and contradictions. He studies her, trying to understand her more fully.

When he asks about her father, she hesitates. Then she tells him about Phil—complicated, frustrating Phil. She spent most of her life not really knowing him. He always seemed half somewhere else, distracted by burdens she never understood. She admits she grew up confused. Unsure what to make of him... until the end, when he finally told her the truth. How she wished they'd had more time.

Yuri listens quietly, recognizing every word. He understands Phil's burdens. He understands the loss of time.

And he feels the old ache of wishing he had been a better father to Oksana.

"Tell me about Bram," he asks.

"He's... solid. Resolute. He's been through so much and come out the other side—stronger."

"Like you?" Yuri asks.

Uncomfortable with the thought, she pales, uncertain. "I'm not sure."

He studies her. "Do you love him?"

Raya hesitates, then nods. "I think so. I hope so. We need time. But it feels like what I've always imagined love to be—he gives me what I need most: unconditional support."

"That is rare. Finding that. Don't forget it. Don't diminish it."

"I won't," she promises.

They fall into silence. Raya suddenly feels the ache of Oksana's absence—the mother she never knew, the sacrifice made for love. She wishes she could tell her she's trying to be worthy. Trying to become someone Oksana would recognize as her daughter.

Yuri, lost in his own regrets, thinks of Anton, of choices justified and prices paid. He wonders if any of it matters—or if this, right now, might be enough. Enough to make Oksana proud. Enough to justify staying in Moscow for all these years.

At last, he breaks the quiet. "What do you want?"

Raya blinks, surprised by the question. "What?"

"This is your journey. What do you want?"

"I guess... to get out of this alive."

"You will. But after?"

"I always said I wanted to help people. I thought the CIA

would let me do that. But I hate the maneuvering, the manipulation. Now, I want to be free of the bullshit."

Yuri smiles faintly. "Ah. The illusion of freedom," Yuri says softly. "What you really want is liberty. Liberty of thought. Independence."

She shrugs. "That sounds right."

"Then quit the CIA."

She frowns. "How does that help? I want to stop SEMYA."

"You can't, it will continue to evolve."

The words strike like a blow. Her shoulders sag.

He slips an arm around her. "But you can help some of the candidates—the victims."

Her body stiffens. "Victims?"

Yuri remains calm, almost gentle. "Yes. Like you. Victims of control and coercion. They need help."

Her mind races. *How? Where do I start?* "You know their names?"

"At one time, I could have made a list," he says. "But when Evgeni was ousted, I lost access. A mistake."

Frustration flares. "Yuri, this doesn't help."

"There may be a way."

As Raya is about to push for answers, Yuri continues.

He laments, "I tried to warn them. Sent notices. Nothing changed. Leaders didn't act. But you—you can find them, change them. Fight with new ideas, novel approaches."

She scoffs. "Me?"

He grows serious. "The number. What is it?"

She recites the eleven digits without error.

He nods. "Good. Now, send your friends a message.

Confirm your plans. Then we destroy your phone."

Raya bristles. "I'm not doing that. It's my lifeline."

Yuri answers. "Soon it will be a liability. Once they connect the dots, the FSB will track you."

She relents and texts:

>> *Feeling better. Will meet you for lunch. Will be offline.*

She pulls the SIM card. Yuri crushes it under his boot, then smashes the phone.

"Now tell me how," she says.

Yuri settles back against the wall. He decides it is time to tell Raya the rest.

"During my years with the SVR, I helped build operational fronts—companies, organizations, safe houses. Evgeni used one, hidden in plain sight, to access the right people—and their children. It became the backbone of SEMYA. The company is called Bremen-Sarp GmbH."

The name slices through Raya's memory like a blade. "What are you talking about?"

"It's a roadmap. It won't be easy, but you can start there. Within those communities. You can find other SEMYA candidates."

Raya hesitates. "How many?"

"Dozens."

"But without the CIA, I don't have the resources to untangle it—"

Yuri cuts her off. "You do."

Raya looks up, meeting his eyes in the low light.

"You will go to the Island National Bank," Yuri says. "It's in the Cayman Islands."

She blinks. "The Cayman Islands? Why there?"

"The country has strong banking secrecy laws. Numbered codes and passphrases identify accounts—not names."

She frowns. "And that helps me how?"

"Every operative worth their salt keeps an insurance policy," Yuri says quietly. "A way out if the walls close in. I started siphoning funds from Bremen-Sarp years ago—slowly, subtly. It has not been discovered."

She stares at him, stunned. "You... what?"

"When I began, I never imagined I'd stay this long." He gives a thin, sad smile. "But this is my home. I am a contradiction—traitor and patriot both. I doubt I will ever leave."

Raya's voice is small, disbelieving. "And you're giving it to me?"

"The account number," he says, tapping the side of his head, "is your key... to independence."

Raya whispers, almost to herself, "You made me memorize the account number."

"The process is automated," Yuri explains. "I never access it—it's too dangerous. The funds pass through shell corporations, nominee directors, blind intermediaries. Completely opaque."

She swallows. "And it's enough for me to help the victims?"

"Yes." His eyes soften. "By my estimate, several million will have been deposited just in the past year. I don't know the current total, but it is significant. It's yours. Use it. Build your team. Do not rely on the services—no CIA, no Mossad. Stay

474

independent. Contract, consult. Help the victims. And if you cannot help them…"

He hesitates, then finishes: "…undermine SEMYA's influence. Discredit them."

Her voice trembles. "You're doing this… for me?"

Yuri looks at her. He feels older and younger at once. Full of regret, full of hope. "Yes. For you. But also for Oksana… and for myself. You'll have to decide how to use it—and how to shape your future."

"Won't it be discovered," she asks softly, "now that all hell has broken loose?"

"In time, yes. But it will take many months to untangle. You must be careful. Get the money out quickly. Move it somewhere safer. Crypto, perhaps… or layered trusts. Anything that obscures the trail."

She nods, still unsure.

Before they drift off in the thin hours before dawn, they map out each step she must take—where to go, how to move, what to avoid. They go over every precaution, every contingency, until the plan feels etched into her bones. And through it all, Yuri's voice remains steady, soft but unyielding, the weight of his own history behind it: Be careful about who you trust.

A shaft of light cuts through the cupola. Raya stirs, waking stiff and cold. A new day. A day that will decide if she has a future.

Yuri awakens and says, "It's time. You know the route?"

They review the plan again. Raya replies, "Yes—zigzag northwest across the city. Stay on busy streets."

"Correct. Don't rush. The streets will be filled. The hardest part will be leaving this building."

Raya straps on her backpack.

"Put it high on your shoulders," Yuri instructs.

Her fingers fiddle with the clasps. She adjusts the straps and pulls them taut.

Yuri opens the chest, pulling out a thick, shapeless frock—drab gray-brown, stained and threadbare. He places a tattered wig on her head and ties a kerchief over it.

"When you reach the street, walk slowly, but with purpose. Bent over. Half steps. Like someone who's survived too much to hurry. No one will notice a hunched old babushka."

She adjusts the cowl.

"Remember—it will take you two hours to reach the Service Center for Automobiles."

"The gas station?"

"Yes, but also a repair yard. Truckers stop there before heading west."

It is almost time. Raya doesn't want to lose this man—she's already lost too much. "What will happen to you?"

Yuri shrugs with the resignation of a man who has completed his mission. "Who's to say? I'll go to work. Pretend I know nothing. Maybe I'll be fine. Maybe not."

"You could come with me." She knows, even as she says it, that he won't.

"I'd only put you at risk. Remember—these people are victims. Groomed. Manipulated. They need help, not punishment."

She wants to promise something more, but all she can manage is: "I'll do my best."

Yuri grips her shoulders. "I'm proud of you."

She feels it—his pride radiating like warmth in the cold.

"You would've made your mother proud."

Her voice breaks. "I wish I could tell her I love her."

Yuri hesitates, a shadow crossing his face. "I wasn't going to tell you. I feared it'd be too much."

"What?"

"Just before you reach the station, there's a cemetery. The Presnensky Cemetery."

She meets his gaze, eyes searching his.

"That's where I buried your mother. I loved her so much." He checks his watch. "You'll have time... you can tell her yourself."

Raya fights to control the tears brimming in her eyes. "Will I see you again?"

Yuri gives a faint, bittersweet smile. "If fate allows."

Raya climbs down the ladder—Yuri follows, closing the hatch softly behind them. In the dim hallway, they pause. A last look passes between them. No more words; their goodbyes have already been spoken. Each must walk their own path. Yuri turns back toward his apartment. Raya slips into the back staircase, swallowed by the shadows.

Her spine aches, hunched beneath the weight of her pack and the thick, shapeless frock. At each step, she waits to be discovered. Every step feels like a risk. Every step feels like walking out of one life and into another.

Outside, Moscow stirs awake. Pale gray light filters through a low curtain of clouds. The streets hum with morning traffic, the air smells of exhaust and damp stone. Crowds move with mechanical purpose, and no one spares her a second glance.

In the distance—

Pop, pop, pop.

Three sharp cracks ring out, spaced in quick succession. Gunshots? Her heart stutters. Yuri. But there is no way to know. No way to go back. The sound could have been nothing more than an old Lada backfiring. She forces her legs forward, her gut clenched tight.

She passes vendors opening kiosks for the day, uniformed men smoking on corners, a woman sweeping slush from the steps of a bank. Raya stumbles once, hitting the pavement. Her knee catching against a cracked piece of sidewalk. A passerby reaches to help. She shakes her head, mutters a grunt, waves him away. The disguise holds.

A police officer turns in her direction. Her chest tightens, breath caught. She keeps her eyes lowered, her face neutral. Instinct screams to run. Instead, she recalls Sunningham— inside the security hut—when panic threatened to consume her and her mind went perfectly still. She steadies herself now. Waits. The officer looks past her and loses interest.

Invisible—in plain sight. She has never felt so exposed— and so hidden.

Hours seem to pass before the iron gates of Presnensky Cemetery rise before her—black, weathered, solemn, just as Yuri described. She slows at the threshold, passing through the white marble columns. Behind her, the noise of Moscow dulls to a distant murmur, as if the city itself chooses not to intrude.

Trees crowd the narrow paths, their branches heavy with

age. Shrubs knot between old headstones—some leaning, some half-swallowed by earth. It is an old place. A quiet place.

Her footsteps scuff along the pavement, the only sound guiding her forward. She glances around. No mourners. No caretakers. No curious eyes.

She pulls back her hood, and straightens for the first time in hours, adjusting the straps of her backpack. Her legs tremble as she finally stands upright, moving deeper into the cemetery.

Thirteen rows in. Eight stones down. She counts them in silence, then stops.

She has reached her destination—a simple headstone, worn at the edges but clean of debris.

Oksana Lomouri Rogers
1973 – 1995
Lyubimaya doch'. Nikogda ne zabudu.

Raya is thankful Yuri honored Oksana's marriage to her father, Phil, with his last name. It feels right. The headstone is modest, the lettering slightly faded, etched in Cyrillic: My beloved daughter. I will never forget.

Raya drops to her knees. The words catch in her throat. "I'm sorry," she whispers. "I should've known you. I should've found you sooner." She reaches out, fingertips trembling against the cold stone.

"I... I think I'm becoming someone you could be proud of. I hope. I'll try."

She doesn't know how long she stayed, but her internal clock signals it is time to go. Slowly, she rises, knees stiff, and bows her head one final time.

"Goodbye, Mom. I won't forget you."

The Service Center for Automobiles is exactly as Yuri described—half-gas station, half-repair shop. Cars idle at the pumps, engines humming. Grease-stained mechanics lean by the garage bay, smoking, laughing at something she can't hear.

Raya arrives early, before noon, giving herself time to watch. She pulls the cowl loosely over her head; her disguise isn't what it was, but she hopes it's enough. She shuffles past the fuel pumps and into the side lot, where rows of old vending machines stand sun-bleached and fading, relics of another decade. Leaning against the wall, she keeps her eyes moving, scanning every direction.

A blue tanker rumbles into the far corner of the lot, its engine low and throaty. The driver slows, eyeing her through the window—looking for company. Raya keeps her posture loose, face unreadable. When she doesn't react, he hesitates, then pulls away, circling to the opposite side of the pumps.

Minutes later, a white reefer—refrigerated truck—pulls closer. The driver climbs out, jacket worn thin at the seams. He stops at the vending machine beside her.

"Boring," he says.

Raya lifts her eyes. "Audible."

He finishes the code. "Rejected."

She nods. "You're early."

"Couldn't sleep."

A small smile flickers across her lips. "Me neither."

"Front seat for now," he tells her. "We cross the Ring Road

in one hour. Later, I move you to hidden compartment. Too many eyes here."

"Will I be safe?"

"Sure. I don't mess with Jynx. Plenty water, sleeping bag. Refrigeration hides heat signature. Done this before."

She inclines her head in appreciation. "Can you let him know you picked me up?"

"Da." He nods toward the battered vending machines. "Get snacks if you want. Ride is long. Plenty time to sleep."

CHAPTER SIXTY-TWO

SECURE BASE OUTSIDE HAIFA, ISRAEL 2019

BRAM IS RUNNING—BREATHLESS—THROUGH a maze of crumbling walls. Raya is somewhere ahead, in danger. He must reach her. He can hear her voice calling through the dust.

"Bram... Bram. Follow my voice."

Panic hardens into anger. He slams his fists into the wall. Again. Again. Plaster splits under his knuckles. He'll tear through anything to reach her.

Knock-knock-knock.

What is that sound? What's making that racket? Raya is all that matters. Every wall he breaks leads to another—higher, thicker.

Knock-knock-knock. Louder now.

He jerks awake, heart hammering. Wrapped in his blanket like a shroud, legs tangled, breath ragged. *Another dream.*

A heavy thud rattles the door. "It's Jynx, so it is."

"What do you want?" Bram calls out.

"C'mon out now, lad. You'll be wantin' a look at this."

Bram checks his watch. It's after midnight. He rubs the sweat from his face. Raya is still out there. And he is here—safe, powerless. No. *Time to be the man she needs him to be.*

In the bunker, the team gathers. The light coming from the computer monitors casts an eerie glow. Tension hangs in the air like humidity before a storm.

"How many of ye've used Telegram, eh?" Jynx asks, eyes scanning them.

Don replies, "Encrypted broadcast app. Public newsfeeds. People use it when the truth's getting choked."

Jynx nods. "There's a channel—Russia Arise, they call it. Not one o' them state muppets runnin' it. Clean, encrypted. Folks use it to say the truth—stuff the regime don't want out."

Sam shifts uneasily. "So, what happened?"

"There's been an explosion. Big one. Along the embankment, just 'cross from the Kremlin. Whole thing's a bleedin' muddle. RT's not sayin' nowt, so you know it's proper serious."

Bram's pulse spikes. "Do you think it has anything to do with Raya?"

Jynx's face stays unreadable. "We don't know yet. But if they say terrorism, the whole city'll lock up tighter'n a drum. Changes the game, it does."

Everyone understands the implication. Getting Raya out just got a lot harder.

"Right," Jynx mutters, pulling up the feed. "I'll throw it on the big screen."

All eyes turn to the monitor.

A dramatic explosion occurred along the Sofiyskaya Embankment shortly after midnight. There are reports of multiple fire and rescue vehicles on the scene. Security officials refuse to speculate at this time. Unnamed sources suspect terrorism related to ongoing conflicts, but no group has claimed responsibility. Additional information will be reported as it becomes available.

"Where is Raya now?" Neshad asks.

Jynx points at the map. "She's about half a mile from the blast site. Still in the buildin' northeast corner."

Sam frowns. "She hasn't moved for some time."

No one speaks.

Bram feels the tension coil tighter inside him. He hates this—watching a blinking dot on a screen instead of standing beside her. But he forces himself to stay focused. This has to be all business.

He turns to Jynx, voice steady. "Will this screw up the extraction?"

"Hard one to call, y'know?" Jynx admits. "City could shut down tight... or go mad. Roads closed, blockades everywhere. We'll adjust as we go."

"Should we contact her?" Sam asks.

"She has her phone," Neshad replies. "If something changes, she'll signal."

A sharp ping breaks the silence. Jynx leans forward. "Hold up. Update comin' through."

The feed scrolls across the screen:

Emergency crews continue to fight the blaze, working to secure the site and carry out evacuations. Nearby buildings are no longer believed to be at risk as crews gain containment. Reports indicate a man was found thrown from the building. It is not known if his death is linked to the explosion.

All eyes shift back to the glowing yellow dot on-screen—Raya's signal, still holding steady.

Early reports that Chechen militants may be involved remain unconfirmed. Security across the city has been increased. Police and military can be seen staging in key areas.

Bram stands still, alert. "Jynx, are you getting any other reports from your contacts?"

"It's gone late now, lad. Me sources won't be hearin' a thing till mornin', if that," Jynx replies.

"Neshad, anything on your end?" Don asks.

"Nothing. We're working to get satellite coverage," Neshad says.

The minutes crawl by, then hours. Hours of silence. Then—finally—proof of life. Raya's text appears on the screen:

>> *Feeling better. Will meet you for lunch. Will be offline.*

Sam exhales in relief. "Looks like we're still on schedule."

Bram wants clarity. "What does she mean—going offline?"

"She's going dark," Don explains.

On the monitor, the yellow blinking dot vanishes.

"She did that on purpose, right?" Sam asks.

"No way to tell," Neshad replies.

Bram's voice is low, controlled. "We wait. We trust the agent."

Another headline flashes across the screen—

There are uncorroborated reports that the lone victim has been identified as Ivan Kirillov, believed to be the current head of the SVR. Rumors are that he has fallen out of favor with the President. Officials have not confirmed this and have reiterated that these rumors are the work of political rivals and agitators.

The room freezes.

"If Kirillov's dead..." Don begins.

"...then it's related to Raya," Bram finishes.

"We don't know that." Neshad counters.

Jynx exhales slowly. "If it was her, she'll need to disappear fast."

Don turns. "Jynx, where will your team take Raya?"

"Svetogorsk—that's the crossing," Jynx replies. "She'll slip into Imatra, Finland, on the far side."

Bram is resolute. "Then that's where we need to be."

"We can run things from here," Neshad reminds him.

"We're no good to her sitting still," Don argues. "Bram's right."

Jynx nods. "We know where she's headed, so we do. Let's be movin'. She'll hit the border by midnight, give or take."

Eventually, Neshad relents. "Get some sleep. We pack up tomorrow. She should arrive in Finland around midnight—less than twenty-four hours from now. We'll be there to meet her."

The next day, they move as a unit—quiet, focused. Sam throws together a small care kit for Raya: fresh clothes, toothpaste, and a brush. Basic human things. Familiar things.

As they board the plane, Jynx receives a cryptic text from his contact. The meaning is clear. His man has Raya. They're already on the move.

Jynx glances over at Bram. "She's movin' now. Me man's got her. They're headin' straight for the border."

Bram nods once, face set. Not yet ready to celebrate.

CHAPTER SIXTY-THREE

IMATRA, FINLAND
2019

RAYA'S BACK THROBS AS THE truck barrels down the highway. The hum of the tires is relentless—steady, numbing, blotting out any other sounds.

The driver said the trip would take about twelve hours. Raya checks her watch—it's nearing midnight. Too long in the dark, too long without updates. The plan is to follow the M-11 to the E18, heading northwest toward the Imatra border checkpoint and slipping into Finland. But plans are only words, and she has no way of knowing whether they're still on track. If they're still on schedule, she'll be safe soon. If not...

She forces the thought away. She's trusting a man she didn't know existed until this morning to get her out alive. Once they cross, it's only ten miles to the Immola Aerodrome.

Bang, bang, bang.

She startles. For a split second, she thinks it's gunfire—Moscow still in her bones—but no. It's the driver, signaling.

"Quiet now. We approach the border," he calls, voice

muffled through the layers of insulation.

Raya bangs once in reply. Understood.

The box is cold, airless. She curls deeper into the sleeping bag, hands tucked tight. The only barrier between her and the chill. She needs to pee. The rough road has not been kind—her bladder protests with every bump.

In the dark, she lets her thoughts fill the silence. The solitude had been a gift, meditating alone in this cell, this tomb. Hours to sit and reflect—time well spent. She used it to shape her thoughts, sift through her feelings, and chart her next moves.

At first, her thoughts turn to Bram. She remembers how he looked at her—not just with admiration or want, but with belief. He saw something in her—his gaze steady, unwavering. More unsettling than a gun at her back, it asked something of her. Dared her to be whole. They need time, real time, without handlers, without a mission crashing down around them. Time to see what they really are. Her instincts whisper yes—he's the one. But she wants to be sure. She wants to be worthy of the faith she sees in his eyes. She thinks of her mother—Oksana's restless spirit, her stubborn fire. Her desire to find her own path in the face of overwhelming odds. Independence. Raya draws strength from that refusal to break. The defiant choice to be more than what they made her be. A reminder to trust in herself.

Masha. Complicated, broken, brilliant. Betrayer and protector. Raya carries love and anger in equal measure, twisted into grief she may never untangle.

Yuri's face rises in the dark—tired, haunted, kind. His loyalty to Anna. His sacrifice. The tragic self-awareness. He gave her not just truths, but a path. And she will honor that—his secrets now are hers to keep. She hopes he found redemption.

Others flicker through her mind. Jynx, with his grin and brutal honesty. His scheming mind. There's something there—an uneasy alliance maybe, but one that could serve a higher purpose. She'll keep that door ajar.

Fred and Neshad, each dangerous in their own way. Opportunists. She'll play the game with them, but on her terms. Don—maybe he's someone she can count on. Maybe.

And reliable. Sam. Loyal, eager Sam. Always the helper, always watching. Raya sees a bit of herself in her—young, hungry to belong.

Raya dreams of something else. She is out of the CIA. She is running her own program—an operation designed to assist those like her. Helping. The secrets Yuri handed her—the account number etched into her mind. Bremen-Sarp, the Caymans, the Island National Bank. It all feels unreal. But it's hers now. And she'll decide how to use it.

The truck jerks. Stops. Her chest tightens. This is the crossing. Raya hears the driver's door open, slam shut.

It should take a few minutes, but it feels like an eternity. Muffled voices—angry, sharp—cut through the night. Then a loud bang of a truncheon against the bumper.

"What you are shipping? Show me manifest—seychas."

She can't hear the driver's response.

"We inspect. Unload all goods. Now."

Another response she can't quite make out.

She freezes. Her knees curled to her chest. The need to pee is unbearable now, but worse is the not-knowing. *What if they find her? What if this is it?*

She counts every second. She wants to scream. She waits.

More shouting, the men are further away now. Muffled.

More voices. Arguing. Fading.

Then—mercifully—she hears the driver's door open and slam shut. The engine growls to life. The driver shifts into gear, and the truck begins to move. *But where?*

They lurch forward. Then stop. She feels it in her kidneys.

She hears the hiss of air brakes releasing.

Again, they jerk forward, only to halt once more.

She realizes they're in a line of vehicles. She holds her breath, waiting.

At last, the truck rolls steady. Minutes pass. Then it halts.

Raya hears the driver's seat creak. The panel scrapes back, uncovering her hidden lair. Light floods in. She flinches—bracing for shouts, for force, for hands dragging her out—.

Instead, the driver offers her his hand. Calm. "Welcome to Finland."

She stares at him, dumbfounded. Then, she regains her wits. She climbs through the cab, down the steps, and scurries to the side of the road to relieve herself—finally, blessedly.

When she returns, breath fogging in the cold, she asks, "What happened?"

"Small argument with customs," he says, shrugging. "I told them I carry vaccines. Anthrax, maybe. Said if it thaws, could be active, dangerous. They get nervous... didn't want the risk. Bunch of muppets."

She raises an eyebrow. "Really?"

He smirks. "Not really. They want bribe. Whole thing, it's

theater. I know how it works."

Raya exhales, half a laugh, half a shiver. She nods, too exhausted to smile. Too alive not to.

As Raya climbs into the cab, a sense of relief settles over her like a heavy blanket. She is free—out of Russia.

She turns to the driver. "I don't even know your name."

"Is better this way," he replies simply.

They cover the remaining few miles in silence. No questions. No ceremony. When the truck finally pulls into the empty lot beside a dimly lit hangar at Immola Aerodrome, Raya climbs down.

The air is sharp, breath visible. Snow crunches under her boots as she shoulders her backpack. Raya turns to say "Thank you" to the driver, but before she can, the truck pulls away, its taillights shrinking into the night.

She takes stock. Alone. For the first time since Moscow, she is truly alone. She hugs herself, uncertain. *What now?*

She shakes her head. But then hears her name—

"Raya! RAYA!"

The voice shatters the quiet.

Her head snaps up. Bram is sprinting toward her, his coat flapping, hair wind-whipped, face alive with a joy she's never seen before. Behind him, the rest of the team are following close behind.

But Raya sees only Bram.

PART IX

FREEDOM IS FATE
2019

"Every new beginning comes from some other
beginning's end."
-Seneca

CHAPTER SIXTY-FOUR

LONDON, ENGLAND, UK
2019

AS THE TEAM BOARDS THE jet, the pilot is still haggling with the airport administrator to activate the runway lights. It's late, visibility is poor, and the team is running on fumes.

Inside the cabin, tempers flicker. Neshad and Don are arguing.

"We're not going back to Israel," Don snaps.

"It's secure," Neshad shoots back.

"It's spent. That part of the mission's over."

Jynx and Sam exchange a glance. No words, but the meaning is clear—they want out, too. Somewhere safer. Somewhere that feels like home.

The decision lands: London. Don insists on the American embassy. Since arriving in Finland, he's been different—quiet, clipped. He took a call from Fred and hasn't been the same since. The others can feel his need to reassert control.

Raya ignores it. She slips to the rear with the small kit Sam prepared, grateful for another woman's foresight. In the cramped lavatory, she wipes away two days of cold sweat and diesel fumes, changes into clean clothes, pulls her hair back. In the mirror, she studies her reflection—worn, but unbroken. Still her.

When she steps back into the aisle, Neshad is waiting. He peppers Raya with questions.

Bram intercepts, calm but firm. "She's exhausted. You can wait."

Neshad pushes on, ignoring him.

Bram plants himself between them. "Back off."

The cabin stills. For a moment, it seems like Neshad might test him. Then he exhales, retreating a step.

"Fine. We'll talk in London."

From his seat, Jynx smirks at Sam. "Right, that's that, then, innit?"

Bram gently guides Raya toward the back of the cabin. No one follows. Everyone knows to give them space.

No cheers. No champagne. Just the quiet hum of relief.

She's back. She's safe.

The flight to Heathrow is subdued. Engines drone in the dark. Outside, the sky is black. Inside, every mind turns inward—already wrestling with what comes next.

After a full night's rest, Raya wakes cocooned in crisp white linens. Morning light slips through the sheer blinds, tracing soft patterns across the floor. For the first time in days, she breathes without tension. No sirens. No steel walls. No cold.

Beside her, Bram lies still. She knows he's awake—she can feel it in the steady way he waits for her to stir, unwilling to break her sleep.

"Good morning," he murmurs, voice low and warm. "How do you feel?"

She turns toward him, blinking against the light, and a slow smile spreads across her face. "Amazingly rested."

His answering smile carries a softness she hasn't seen in what feels like forever. He's happy—simply to be here, beside her.

"Bram?"

"Yes?"

"Thank you. For everything."

He frowns, puzzled. "Seems like you did all the hard work."

"Yes," she admits. "But knowing you were there... watching over me... that made all the difference."

Pride and embarrassment tug at him in equal measure. He doesn't know what to say, so he settles on the practical. "It's getting late. We should get ready."

"Let them wait." She pulls him into her arms, savoring the warmth, the safety of his embrace.

A soft knock breaks the moment. Bram sighs, pulling on a robe and crossing to the door.

Sam stands there, smiling knowingly. She steps inside, eyes landing on Raya curled in the bed. "I went to John Lewis this morning. Picked up a suit for you—two, actually. Looks like you've lost some weight."

Bram glances back at Raya. The memory hits them both, and they burst out laughing—the same department store where everything began.

Raya lifts the covers, eyeing herself critically: her hips, her ribs. "You may be right. I'm starving."

Inside the secure conference room, fluorescent lights hum overhead. Raya sits beside Bram, hands folded neatly, a glass of untouched water in front of her. Don and Neshad face her across the table. Jynx leans against the wall, arms crossed. Sam stays quiet, scribbling notes.

Raya recounts her story—the fear, the uncertainty, the twisting streets of Moscow. The youth hostel. The vendor in the park. The discreet handoff to the beauty shop. Her escape through dark hallways and back alleys. Her voice is steady, measured, controlled.

But she withholds the most dangerous truths. She doesn't mention Yuri's true identity. She doesn't breathe Anna's name. She says nothing of her mother's grave—or Bremen-Sarp.

Instead, she offers them the cupola. A hiding place. A site for a clandestine meeting.

"KNOLL is frustrated," she says. "He feels nothing's happening. He brought me in to deliver that message."

"Did he give you his real name?" Neshad asks.

"No. Just said he wanted someone to act."

"Is KNOLL dead?"

"I don't know. After I got out, I thought I heard gunfire. Could've been gangs, soldiers... maybe just construction equipment clanging. I wasn't in a position to investigate."

In her gut, she feels Yuri is alive. And Anna, too. But she buries the thought.

Don leans forward. "Why you, Raya? That's what I can't figure out."

She hesitates, then says, "Turns out he knew my mother. He knew I'd been part of the program. He never gave me a straight answer. Maybe he thought I deserved to know what happened. Maybe he wanted me to understand."

Neshad nods slowly. "Fits the profile. That kind of embed changes you."

Don shifts the subject. "You heard about the explosion?"

"We could see the aftermath from the cupola. KNOLL told me that is where Kirillov lived. Assumed he was killed."

"Any idea why?" Neshad presses.

She shakes her head. "KNOLL hinted at rivalry. Infighting. Maybe he was taken out by a competitor."

Don watches her carefully, unsure.

Neshad isn't buying it, but neither pushes further.

"With Kirillov gone, the program may collapse," Neshad offers.

"KNOLL didn't think so," Raya replies sharply.

Don counters, "He's out. He's lost access."

"Maybe. But maybe that's why he chose me."

The room goes still.

"What do you mean?" Don asks.

"I know what it means to be used. Maybe he thought I'd be motivated to help the kids in the program."

"How?" Neshad asks, skeptical.

"I want to look for them." She looks to Jynx. "You've got some unusual capabilities, tools. Maybe you want in?"

Jynx raises a brow, wondering how he could benefit. "Ah, off on a wild goose chase, are we? Grand so—what's it you're after?"

"Research. Computer help. Analysis. Maybe some of that AI stuff people talk about."

Don frowns. "You know the Agency won't love your freelancing."

Raya crosses her legs and looks at him squarely. "Don't you remember? I quit the Agency."

"You never submitted the paperwork," Don replies.

"Consider this my resignation." She states flatly, "I quit the CIA."

Don expected this. They put her through the wringer. Fred won't be happy.

"What do you want to do now?" Neshad asks.

She looks between the two of them. "You could hire me as a consultant. Let me look. I think I may have some unique insights. Maybe I can find some of them."

"And do what?" Neshad challenges. "If you find them?"

"Try to flip them. If that fails, discredit them. And if that fails..."—she glances at Don— "you and Fred can do what you do. Keeps your hands clean. Let's not pretend only one country is involved."

Don leans back. "Fred loves a good firewall."

"What would you call this operation?" Neshad asks.

Raya shrugs. "No idea. Bram said you bought Surrey Investigative Solutions. That might be a good start, a way to move forward. Maybe I'll take it off your hands."

"That might be expensive," Neshad replies. "Complicated. David might have concerns."

"What's going on with David, anyway?" Raya asks. "Why all the subterfuge?"

Neshad smiles thinly. "David's fine. Crossed paths with a few locals who fancied themselves gangsters. Made some bad judgment calls. Bit of overreach. I'm helping him sort it out."

Raya tilts her head. "If it's sorted, then there's no problem. I've got Phil's estate. I'm sure we can make a deal."

Neshad offers a reluctant, "Maybe." *She's up to something.*

Bram's eyes lift. This part is new. She gives him a look that says: Not now. *I'll explain later.*

In her mind, she checks the box and answers another question. *Keep it moving. Keep them on their heels.*

She pivots to Don. "You could be my liaison to the Agency."

"I'm out," Don says flatly. "Retired. Should've left years ago."

Don looks at Sam. "But there's someone who could."

Sam blinks. "Me?"

"Who else handles Fred better?" Don grins.

Sam chuckles. "He is a bear."

Raya nods. "It could work. Lots to figure out. But I'm leaving. You can talk it out. Let me know what you decide."

She rises. Bram follows.

Don calls after her. "We're not finished."

"I am," Raya says. "I need a vacation. I want to spend time with Bram. We'll regroup when we get back."

Jynx smirks, satisfied.

Without another word, she turns and walks out of the SCIF.

"Raya," Sam calls after her. "We're glad you're back."

Raya hears her but doesn't turn around.

She remembers now. The poem of her youth—a

connection to her father. And to a mother she never knew. The feeling of providence, that her story was written long before she was born.

Nine 'tis tha answer, secret kept—never told, nor e'er wept.

That was for the old Raya. A poem of the past.

She slips her hand into Bram's. Together, they walk down the long embassy corridor, and out into the London streets. It was time for her to write her own story.

EPILOGUE

AS THEY WALK UP THE dusty road in Kingston, Jamaica, Bram slips his hand into Raya's. The neighborhood is alive—residential buildings press against small commercial stalls selling street food, bottled water, and bits of household goods. The sun is high, the heat heavy, the scent of jerk chicken clinging to the air.

Despite the everyday bustle, both of them remain alert, every sense awake.

They approach the Temple Shalom Synagogue—a stark white, two-story building with tall glass windows, sitting quietly, dignified behind a low iron fence. An oasis amid the worn, restless streets.

Stepping through the gates, Raya glances back down the road. Always watchful. She feels Bram's gentle squeeze on her hand as they ascend the steps together. The Rabbi greets them warmly at the door. They are expected. He guides them into a small vestibule, its air still and cool, then disappears into a back room.

Inside, they shrug off their backpacks, grateful to be free of the weight. Even traveling light becomes a burden in the summer heat. When he returns, he carries a sheaf of papers, spreading them across the table with reverence.

"Dis is di history of your family, Bram. Di Vidal name—dat was a well-known family back inna di day, seen?"

Bram bends over the documents, hardly breathing. His search for his past has led him here, to these fragile pages.

"I was real sorry to hear 'bout your grandfather's passing," the Rabbi says gently. "May his memory be for a blessing. We never knew your father personally, but we goin' add his name to di records. And yours as well."

"Thank you," Bram says, quietly.

"Two years ago," the Rabbi continues, "we did celebrate three hundred and fifty years of Jewish presence here in Jamaica. A grand occasion. We took time to gather what we could—put our archives in proper order. Yuh come at a good time."

He points to a line in the papers, ink faded. "Now, your grandfather's parents—dem was Soliman and Honora Vidal. Your great-grandfather, he was in manufacturing and export. The rest of di family, well, some names deh listed without occupation. A few, dem marked as labourers... and some, as slaves."

Bram looks up sharply. "Slaves?"

The Rabbi holds his gaze. "It's a part of our history. A part of yours. Port Royal, yuh see, was once a mighty hub of trade. Not all of it righteous."

Bram swallows, turning back to the list of names— unknown to him, yet pulling at him with the weight of blood and history.

The Rabbi shifts to another page. "I have addresses for some distant relatives. Yuh could check dem out, if yuh like. I believe dem would be glad to meet yuh."

Bram brightens. A reason to return. Family. Not just shadows but living people. People he might care for. It feels like an immense weight is being lifted. He looks at Raya and meets her eyes. Without words, he knows she already understands.

"There 'tis one more ting," the Rabbi adds softly. "Your grandfather's younger sister, Rachel. She passed not long ago. Lived to be seventy-nine."

The words stagger Bram. "I never knew him. I didn't know he had a sister."

Raya places an arm across his shoulders. A gentle squeeze—grounding him.

The Rabbi stands, sensing the weight of the moment. "If yuh have di time, we could take a little walk to di cemetery. Her grave not far... just a mile or so down di road."

They have a flight to catch. Philadelphia. A few hours remain.

Bram is about to decline—thinking that Raya must be getting tired. The heat is relentless. "We should probably get— "

"We would love to," Raya cuts in gently.

Bram smiles. In this moment, he feels like the luckiest man alive.

At the cemetery, the Rabbi guides them to a simple

headstone set in the grass. Bram kneels; the words carved into stone blur through the tears in his eyes.

Rachel Vidal
1937 – 2016

He reaches into his pocket and pulls out a folded note—creased, worn, fragile. Raya watches but doesn't ask. She thinks of her own visit to her mother's grave. Different continent. Same ache.

After a few minutes, Raya sees Bram rise. Head lowered in thought. The walk back is quiet. The Rabbi leaves them at the synagogue gates, and Bram and Raya begin the journey toward the heart of town.

Raya scans the street. Ever watchful. But she doesn't speak—not yet. The silence between them feels full, not empty. The city hums around them, indifferent to their secrets. She checks her watch. They have time.

"Are they still following us?" Bram asks.

She nods. "One across the street, fifty yards back. I saw the reflection of a camera lens. Not sure of the other." She smiles faintly.

Bram mutters, "I hate the watching."

"Let them," she says. "I'm done hiding."

"Who do you think it is?"

She considers. "Probably Fred. Or Neshad."

"KNOLL?" Bram wonders.

"No way." She is sure that Yuri would not put her at risk.

A pause, then Bram asks, "What about Masha?"

Raya shakes her head. "Maybe. I don't know."

Bram stops in the road. He turns, forcing her to face him. "Do you think she's still alive?"

She shakes her head. "I don't know," she answers, voice low.

They walk on. Bram fingers the note in his pocket, then pulls it free. "I wrote this at my lowest point. A promise—to find out who killed my father. To find those responsible... make them pay."

Raya teasingly shoulders into him lightly. "We figured it out, Bram."

But Bram is not ready for her playfulness, his voice stays hard. "She still got away with it. Masha destroyed my family."

Raya doesn't argue. She knows.

"If I find her," Bram says flatly, "it won't end well."

"I don't think we'll ever see her again."

The conflict tears at Bram. Between his hatred of one woman and his love for the other. The words hang between them. He looks at her, torn. "I don't want this to come between us."

"Bram," she says softly, "you do what you need to do. I won't stand in your way."

He is still unsure, hesitates. "But will it change us—if I do something?"

She smiles and keeps walking. "I won't let it."

Bram quickens his pace to catch up. "Do you think she's paid a price?"

Raya thinks long before answering. "I don't know. I'm still figuring out my own feelings. But if you're asking me if she's suffered—I think yes. She has."

They continue walking, quiet stretches again. The road curves. A lizard skitters across their path, gone in a blink.

Raya feels it clearly now. Her relationship with Bram. Her sense of purpose taking shape. They've both survived. And more than that, they've found each other in the wreckage.

She lowers her voice. "I still have more to tell. I want you to know everything."

Bram perks up. "When?"

She scans the street. Old habits die hard. "Not here. Not now."

He runs a hand through his hair. He will be patient. She'll tell him when she's ready.

She leans closer, whispering, "Up for a little island hopping?"

"We've got tickets to—"

"A diversion," she interrupts. "Let our watchers puzzle it out."

A grin creeps across Bram's face. With Raya, even uncertainty feels like adventure. At the main road, they hail the third taxi that passes.

She opens the door, hesitates—then looks at the reflection in the glass, to see who is following. And she sees herself. Older than Moscow. Less worn. Sharper. Still not broken.

"Where to?" the driver asks as Raya climbs in.

She looks at Bram, then turns her gaze forward, out through the windshield. "The airport."

Taking Bram's hand, she gives it a squeeze.

"So..." he asks, still puzzled, "where are we flying?"

Raya's eyes gleam. She can't hold back her smile.

"I hear the Cayman Islands are nice. There's a bank there I'd like to visit."

Acronyms and Abbreviations

BSG – Bremen-Sarp GmbH: A covert front company used to funnel funds and manage SEMYA operations.

CI – Counterintelligence: Operations designed to detect and counter hostile intelligence activity.

CIA – Central Intelligence Agency (USA): U.S. foreign intelligence agency.

DOA – Dead on Arrival.

EU – European Union.

FC – Football Club.

FAA – Federal Aviation Administration (USA): Regulates civil aviation and air traffic.

FBI – Federal Bureau of Investigation (USA): Domestic law enforcement and counterintelligence agency.

FSB – Federalnaya Sluzhba Bezopasnosti: Russia's internal security and counterintelligence service, successor to the KGB.

GB – Great Britain.

KGB – Komitet Gosudarstvennoy Bezopasnosti: Soviet Union's main security and intelligence agency until 1991.

LAN – Local Area Network: In intelligence circles, sometimes used metaphorically for secure, isolated systems.

Mossad – Israel's national intelligence agency: specializes in foreign intelligence, covert operations, and counterterrorism.

MP – Member of Parliament.

NGO – Non-Governmental Organization.

OIR – Orava International Relief: NGO with links to intelligence operations.

RT – Russia Today: State-funded Russian international TV network.

SDR – Surveillance Detection Route: A counter-surveillance method used to detect followers.

SIM – Subscriber Identity Module: Chip in mobile phones used to identify devices on a network.

SCIF – Sensitive Compartmented Information Facility: Secure facility for handling classified material.

SIS – Surrey Investigative Solutions: a private investigations firm run by David Klein.

SVR – Sluzhba Vneshney Razvedki: Russia's foreign intelligence service, successor to the KGB.

UK – United Kingdom.

USSR – Union of Soviet Socialist Republics (1922–1991).

VO$_2$ max – Maximum oxygen uptake during exercise (used metaphorically to describe human endurance).

SEMYA – ("Family" / "Seed" in Russian). Long-term infiltration program launched in the early 1990s to recruit, train, and groom candidates for placement in sensitive positions of influence.

Key Characters

(may contain spoilers)

Antonov, Evgeni: Head of SVR, original leader of SEMYA

Avery, Fred: Head of CIA Counter-Intelligence

Beridze, Polina: Russian dissident (sister of Dmitri Beridze)

Beridze, Dmitri: Russian dissident (brother of Polina Beridze)

Biram, Hevel: Head of Mossad (Director)

Chestnut, Don: CIA Officer

Dadiani, Yuri: Russia operative working for SVR

Dadianova, Oksana: Daughter of Anna Lomouri

Dadianova, Raisa: Baby spirited out of Russia after her mother dies

Gill: Bram Vidal's mother

Gurgen: Politician from the country of Georgia

Hilde: Recruiter for Crisis Actors Ltd.

Jynx: Eccentric Irish Traveler

Kahn, Edward: Neighbor in Sunningham

Kirillov, Ivan: Newly appointed head of SVR

Klein, Adam: Son of David Klein

Klein, David: Owner of a private investigations business (SIS), Surrey Investigative Solutions

KNOLL: Codename for Israeli agent

Lomouri, Anna: Agent working for Evgeni Antonov

Morozova, Mariya (Masha): Guard at Sunningham working for Bremen-Sarp GmbH

Popov, Anton: Computer Tech working at SVR headquarters

Robinson, Victoria: Neighbor in Sunningham

Rogers, Phil: Father of Raya Rogers

Rogers, Raya: Young woman living in Sunningham

Tal, Neshad: Israeli agent working in Europe and the United States of America

Vaughn, Samantha (Sam): CIA Officer working for Fred Avery

Vidal, Bram: Young man living in Maidenhill

Acknowledgements

This story has been brewing in my mind for years.

I've been fortunate to travel the world, but the privilege comes with long stretches of solitude—hours spent alone in airports, on planes, and in anonymous hotel rooms. I filled that time by reading voraciously, exploring writers across every genre. Many I found brilliant. Some... less so. And like many avid readers, I eventually wondered if I could do better.

Those quiet, in-between moments on the road gave me space to reflect, imagine, and slowly piece this story together in my head. But where I began and where I ultimately finished are two very different places.

At the beginning of 2025, a professional chapter of my life drew to a close. The project I'd been working on ended. I suddenly found myself without a job—no meetings, no flights, no purpose beyond what I might invent. Normally, I would have jumped right into finding my next position, but this time was different. My kids were growing up, I was getting older, and I had this book inside me.

When I sat down with my family, they encouraged me to follow my dream. "If not now, when?" they asked. I can't thank my wife, Alysa, and my children, Jack and Leigh, enough for believing in me.

I began by creating an outline and reading books on writing. I wanted to build something new, something that felt fresh, while still drawing on the slow-burn tension of the classic espionage thriller. I've always loved stories that give readers time to think, to wonder how all the pieces and people will eventually collide.

Early on, I found a writers' group at my local library—a diverse mix of voices across genres: young adult, romance, fantasy, and literary fiction. Every two weeks I'd submit a few chapters and get my butt kicked. I'd pour my heart into a section I thought was brilliant, only to be told otherwise. I'd take notes, absorb the feedback, and go home to rewrite. One chapter at a time, the story got better, and so did I.

I owe a debt of gratitude to the *Writers' Roundtable* for their honesty, encouragement, and craft. They are Debi Faix, Audrey Pituk, Jeffrey Frisone, Jeanne McKellar, Andrea Corsi, Andrew Young, Peter McMahon, Jill Cottingham and Jim Owens. And a special thanks to the Gloucester County Library System for giving us the space we need to write, argue, learn and grow.

Family members read early chapters too, offering the earliest—and most needed—support. My parents and father-in-law were among the first to dive into the entire story. Their encouragement was good for the soul, but hard to trust. Love can sometimes soften the critique. But at the beginning, what I needed most was belief. I thank Barbara Hansen, Hugh Hansen and Lance Peterman.

Later, I sought out beta readers—friends and strangers alike—and asked them to be tough. I gave them permission to be brutally honest. It's a lonely process, sitting alone with someone's critique of your work, but without that honesty, there's no improvement. To all of them: thank you. Sandra Weaver, Valerie, Bob Maclay, Colin Monro, Dan O. Wilds,

Deanna J. Nelson, Dennis Streppa, Janie Murray, Joanne P. Johnson, Jude Stahmer, Judy Groeling, Lauren Decker, Mike Rude, Peter Bray, Prabir Sen-Gupta, Robert Dodge, Ron Dedels, Stephen Coyle, Jr. and Steve Purlee.

It took five months to write the first draft and six more months of editing, reshaping, and refining to reach its current form. Many modern thrillers open *in medias res*, but I wanted a more deliberate rhythm—a chance for readers to truly understand the characters. My aim was to build emotional and thematic coherence over time, without sacrificing realism merely to accelerate the pace. I wanted the story to breathe yet still hold the reader firmly—irresistibly—engaged. Whether it succeeds is something only you, the reader, can decide.

I hope you enjoy this novel, and plan to stay with me as this series continues. There is much ahead for these characters, and I plan to release the second novel later this year. If you enjoyed the book, please take a moment to leave a review—each one really helps. Feedback is a gift. You can also join my mailing list via my website for occasional updates on future releases. I promise not to flood your inbox—just to share what's next on this journey.

www.mdhansenbooks.com

Thank again for reading,
M. Drew Hansen
2026

About the Author

M.D. Hansen has built a career working with some of the world's leading multinational corporations, including Baxter Healthcare, Cardinal Health, CSL Behring, IBM, and General Electric. With deep expertise in program management, change management, and commercial operations, he has successfully led multiple global transformation projects.

His professional journey and travels have taken him to more than fifteen countries and forty-five U.S. states, where he has gained firsthand insights into different cultures and perspectives. Living and working alongside clients, customers, and friends in these places has shaped his distinctive worldview.

Beyond business, he has climbed the five highest mountains in New England, spent a summer working security for the Rolling Stones, and was elected three times to the board of education of one of the highest-performing school districts in New Jersey—experiences as memorable and transformative as his global career.

A lifelong sports enthusiast, he is a devoted supporter of Philadelphia's professional teams. He admits to an ongoing struggle with his golf game.

He lives in southern New Jersey with his wife, Alysa, and their two children, Jack and Leigh.